CHRISTINA HENRY

THE GHOST TREE

TITAN BOOKS

The Ghost Tree
Paperback edition ISBN: 9781785659799
Waterstones edition ISBN: 9781789096545
E-book edition ISBN: 9781785659805

Published by Titan Books
A division of Titan Publishing Group Ltd.
144 Southwark Street, London SE1 0UP
www.titanbooks.com

First Titan edition: September 2020
10 9 8 7 6 5 4 3 2 1

© Tina Raffaele 2020. All rights reserved.
Published by arrangement with the Berkley, an imprint of Penguin Publishing Group
a division of Penguin Random House LLC.

A CIP catalogue record for this title is available from the British Library.

Printed and bound in Great Britain by CPI Group Ltd.

For Alexis Nixon,
in October country

PART ONE

THE GIRLS

Lauren glanced down at her feet as she pedaled her bike toward the woods. She wore brand-new turquoise high-tops; they looked sort of like the Chuck Taylors she'd wanted, but they were off-brand from Kmart. They didn't have the Chuck label in the back but they were still pretty cool. She thought so, anyway.

They would have to be cool because her mom had told her repeatedly they couldn't afford the name-brand ones. At least no one else at school had turquoise. They were so bright they practically glowed in the summer sun, but by the time she went back to school in the fall they would be properly beaten up and she wouldn't look like a dork.

By the time she went back to school she would be *almost* fifteen (*the end of November—five months away still*), which meant she would be one of the older kids in the freshman class but still younger than Miranda, whose birthday had been the week before. Miranda never failed to remind her that this meant she would get her driver's license before Lauren did, but Lauren didn't care as long as she was riding to school in a car (even if it was not her own) instead of on her bike.

Lauren knew Mom didn't want her and Miranda meeting in the woods. Especially after last year. Especially after Lauren's dad was found near that old cabin. Mom thought Lauren was macabre for going anywhere near the place where her father was murdered.

But Lauren was about as interested in her mother's opinion as her mother was in Lauren's—that is to say, not at all. Mom never loved Dad as much as Lauren did. Her mom didn't understand that when Lauren was in the woods it meant she was in the place he was last alive.

She and Miranda always met under the ghost tree. They'd done so since they were very small, for so long that Lauren couldn't remember who'd thought of the idea first. One of them would call the other on the telephone and say, "Meet me by the old ghost tree," and they would both go.

In the secret shadows of the woods, they could have adventures. They built forts and ran through streams and climbed trees and made rope swings. They made a secret base near the cabin that was tucked away in the woods. This was long before Lauren's dad was found there, and it had been some time since they used it as a base.

In the last year or so things had changed. Miranda didn't like to get dirty anymore, so she didn't want to swing over the trickling little creek that ran through the forest or roll in the dead leaves. Mostly she wanted to do things Lauren was not interested in, like paint their nails or braid each other's hair or talk about boys that Miranda thought were cute— older boys, always, boys that would not be the least bit interested in little freshman girls.

Despite this they still preferred to meet by the ghost tree. It was their special place.

Lauren raced past the Imperial drive-in on the outskirts of town. They were showing a double feature—*The Goonies* and *Cocoon*. The wide lot was littered with rubbish from the night before—empty popcorn cups, candy wrappers, cigarette butts. Sometimes Lauren helped Mr. Harper, the owner, clean up the lot in exchange for $10 and a free ticket for her and Miranda to that night's show, but she'd already seen *The Goonies* twice and Miranda said *Cocoon* was about old people so they never stayed for the second feature.

The back of the movie screen pressed against the woods that brushed against the town. Smiths Hollow was the name of her town, and Lauren had always liked the name because it reminded her of Sleepy Hollow.

She and her dad used to watch that cartoon every year on Halloween, *Ichabod and Mr. Toad*. Even though Ichabod's name came first in the title, the Sleepy Hollow story was actually second in the film and Lauren liked that better. She liked anticipating the moment when the Headless Horseman would appear on screen, laughing his insane laugh and swinging a giant sword.

When she was little she used to snuggle close into her dad's arm when that part came on and her heart would beat so fast, but there was nothing to worry about really because she was with her daddy. Of course it had been years since it scared her, but every year she snuggled up next to him. He always smelled a little bit of grease and oil, even after a shower, and also of the Old Spice Soap-on-a-Rope that she gave him every year for Father's Day.

Lauren wondered if, when Halloween came, she would be able to turn on the cartoon again and watch it with her little brother, David. He'd been too small to watch it the year before.

Miranda had wanted Lauren to sleep over last Halloween, so they could watch "real" scary movies on her VCR. Lauren's family didn't have a VCR, and Miranda definitely viewed this as a drawback to sleeping over at Lauren's house.

They always trick-or-treated together every year, but after their candy bags were full they went their separate ways. Last year Miranda didn't want to trick-or-treat at all, but Lauren persuaded her to go out so Miranda had thrown together a costume of old clothes at the last second and went as a hobo. She'd complained about how lame and babyish collecting candy was the whole time and then got annoyed when Lauren told her that she had to go home after.

"I thought you were going to watch *Halloween* with me," Miranda said. "It's the perfect night for it!"

Lauren shook her head. "We can do it another night. I have something I have to do with my dad."

"It won't be the same on another night," Miranda said. "I can't believe you dragged me all over town to get a bunch of stupid little candy bars and we're not even going to watch a scary movie now."

"I'll take your candy if you don't want it," Lauren said, holding her bag open.

Miranda's mouth twisted up. "No way. I walked for it, so I'm eating it."

She'd gone home in a huff, but the next time Lauren slept over they did watch *Halloween*. Or rather, Miranda watched it, laughing hysterically every time someone was slaughtered by the killer, and Lauren peered through her fingers and hoped she would be able to sleep without nightmares. She didn't like scary movies. Miranda seemed inured to them.

Anyway, Lauren was glad she'd gone home that night, because it was the last time she'd watch *Ichabod and Mr. Toad* with her dad. Less than a month later he was dead.

He was dead and nobody would talk about it. Nobody would talk about why it happened or how. The police chief told Lauren's mom it must have been some drifter, some sicko who went from town to town. But that didn't make a bit of sense to Lauren. Why would some sicko come to Smiths Hollow just to kill her dad?

And nobody ever told her what her dad was doing out that late at night in the woods, either. Every time Lauren mentioned it her mother's lips would go flat and pull tight at the edges and she would say, "We are not discussing this, Lauren."

Lauren reached the scrubby edge of the woods and pulled the brakes on her bike. It was a ten-speed, a grown-up gift for her last birthday even though she wasn't very tall yet and probably never would be. Miranda told her that girls stopped growing like a year after they got their periods, and Lauren hadn't gotten hers yet so she hoped she wouldn't top out at five foot three.

Miranda had gotten her period almost a year before, but both her parents were tall so Miranda towered over Lauren by about half a foot. She also had long, long legs that always looked good in whatever she wore, and Lauren had to squelch the flare of jealousy that bubbled up whenever she saw Miranda looking so cool and beautiful and grown-up.

Lauren hopped off her bike and wheeled it into the forest, following a path worn by her own feet and Miranda's. The bike bumped over the tree roots and kicked up tiny rocks that bit into Lauren's shins.

Some people didn't like the woods near Smiths Hollow. Well, if Lauren was honest, almost everyone didn't like the woods. She'd heard more than one person say they were "spooky" and "uncanny" and "scary," but Lauren didn't think so.

She liked the trees and their secretive natures, and all the little creatures that scurried into the brush when they heard her approach. And there were lots of places to sit and think and be alone and listen to the wind in the leaves. There were many days when Miranda went home and Lauren stayed in the forest by herself, curled into the notch of a tree while she read a book.

Even Lauren's dad had said that the woods made him uncomfortable.

"I always feel like I'm being spied on whenever I walk near there," he confessed to her one day. They were both at the kitchen sink scrubbing their hands—Lauren's were covered in mud, and her father's had the usual contingent of grease from his work at the garage.

"'I always feel like somebody's watching me,'" Lauren sang as she walked, although she didn't really. If anyone was watching she felt that it was a benign somebody.

She liked that song a lot, although Miranda didn't think much of it. Miranda had listened to Def Leppard's *Pyromania* album nonstop since she discovered it the previous year, and whenever Lauren came over she would put it on. Lauren was pretty sure she could live the rest of her life without ever hearing "Rock of Ages" again.

The ghost tree was about a ten-minute walk from the place where Lauren dismounted her bike. Miranda was already there, arms crossed and leaning against the tree with her eyes closed. Lauren wondered what Miranda was thinking about.

She wore a white sleeveless shirt that buttoned down the front, and Lauren could see her training bra through it. Lauren had started wearing a training bra too even though she really didn't need it yet. By the time she actually needed the trainer Miranda would be wearing women's bras, probably.

The shirt was tucked into her jeans—Jordache, naturally, and their ankles brushed against her white Adidas shoes with the black stripes on the side. Miranda always had name-brand everything, because her parents were both managers at the canned chili factory and they would take her to the next town over to go to the mall for her clothes.

She was also an only child, which meant her parents didn't have to worry about having money for the next kid's stuff. Lauren had heard her mother sighing many times that the trouble with having a girl and then a boy was that you couldn't reuse anything. Not that there had been so much stuff around for reusing by the time David was born—he was ten years younger than Lauren, a "surprise package," as Lauren's dad called him. Lauren's parents had thought their late nights with a colicky baby were long gone.

"What took you so long?" Miranda said, straightening when she heard the rattle of Lauren's bike chain. "And what are you wearing?"

What are you *wearing* was what Lauren wanted to ask, but instead she looked down at her Cubs shirt and cutoff jeans and said, "Clothes for playing in the woods."

Miranda shook her hair, an elaborately teased and sprayed mass that had been wrestled into a high ponytail. "We're not *playing* in the *woods*. What are we, nine? We're going to the Dream Machine."

"Why didn't you just say we were going to the Dream Machine?" Lauren asked.

Lauren didn't really care about arcade games except maybe pinball, and she especially didn't like going to the Dream Machine because lately it meant that she and Miranda would stand around watching boys that Miranda thought were cute.

"Tad asked me to meet him there," Miranda said excitedly, ignoring Lauren's question. "He actually called me today."

So why do I have to go? Lauren thought. If she'd known what Miranda had planned she would have brought a book to read. There was nothing more boring than watching some guy playing Pac-Man. Also, what kind of stupid name was Tad? Lauren wasn't sure she remembered who exactly Tad was, either. It was hard to keep track of which boy was at the top of Miranda's scrolling list of interests.

"And he said he's going to bring some of his friends, so there will be someone for you, too," Miranda finished. She said this last bit like she had gotten a really amazing present for Lauren and couldn't wait to hear how much she loved it.

"Oh," Lauren said.

"Let's go," Miranda said. "Leave your bike here. We can cut through the woods and come out behind Frank's."

Frank's Deli was directly across the street from the Dream Machine. Lauren didn't like coming out of the woods there because there were always rats running around behind Frank's. She always told her mother not to buy lunch meat there because of that.

"Don't be silly, Lauren," Mom would say. "Of course there are rats outside. They're attracted to garbage. That doesn't mean there are rats inside."

"It doesn't mean there aren't, either," Lauren said darkly, and refused to eat so much as a slice of roast beef from Frank's. It meant a lot of peanut butter sandwiches because her mom would almost always go to Frank's unless she went shopping at the big super grocery store in the next town and got deli meat while she was there.

"Which one is Tad again?" Lauren asked as she leaned her bike against the tree. There was no worry that anything would happen to it. No one ever stole anything that belonged to the ghost tree.

Miranda hit Lauren's shoulder with the back of her hand.

"He works at Wagon Wheel, remember? We just went there to see him last week."

Lauren dredged up the memory of a greasy-haired guy throwing two slices of pizza in front of them as they'd sat on the tall chairs at the counter, feet dangling. He'd barely acknowledged Miranda's existence.

"That guy?" Lauren asked.

"He looks just like Matt Dillon in *The Outsiders*," Miranda said with a little sigh.

"No, he doesn't," Lauren said.

Usually she let Miranda's statements pass by without an argument, but she couldn't let that one go. Lauren had the poster with the cast of *The Outsiders* on it hanging on the back of her bedroom door, and she got a good look at Matt Dillon every morning. Tad did not look a thing like him.

"He totally does!" Miranda insisted.

"No way," Lauren said.

"Well, he's going to be a junior and he has a Camaro," Miranda said, as if this settled everything.

When Miranda said things like that, Lauren could feel the strings that had bound them together their whole life unknotting one by one. Lauren really didn't care if he had a Camaro, and the old Miranda wouldn't have either. The old Miranda would have wanted to stay in the woods instead of going to the Dream Machine. But the old Miranda had disappeared in the last year, leaving Lauren to wonder why she still came when Miranda called.

Maybe it's just hard to let your best friend go, even if you have nothing in common anymore, Lauren thought, and sighed a little.

They emerged from the woods behind Frank's Deli. Two rats, a very large one and a little tiny one, abandoned the bread crust they were chewing and ran behind the three large metal garbage cans lined up next to the back door.

"Gross," Miranda said as Lauren flinched and made a little squeaking sound.

They heard the sound of soft laughter. Lauren saw Jake Hanson, the son of one of her neighbors, smoking a cigarette behind the electronics shop next door. He was three or four years older than Lauren, so their paths had rarely crossed since she'd been very small. She remembered that once, when she was maybe seven or eight, he'd shown her how to throw a baseball and had spent a half hour patiently catching her wild pitches.

Miranda went straight for the narrow walkway between Frank's and the electronics shop, ignoring Jake entirely.

Lauren paused, because it really went against the grain for her to pretend someone didn't exist. "Hey, Jake."

He was very tall now, at least a foot taller than Lauren, but his jeans barely hung onto his waist with a belt hooked all the way to the last hole. He had on a black uniform polo with the words *Best Electronics* embroidered on the upper left side.

"Hey, Lauren," he said, blowing smoke out of his nose.

She wondered when his voice had started to sound so grown-up. He didn't really sound like a boy anymore—but then, she supposed that he wasn't. He was probably eighteen years old now, or close to it—old enough to have real stubble on his cheeks and not just the stringy fuzz most high school boys sported.

His blue eyes looked her up and down, assessing. Assessing what, Lauren wasn't sure. She'd always liked his eyes, how his blue eyes contrasted with his dark hair, but now something in the way they looked at her made the blood rise in her cheeks.

"Nice shoes," he said, and she couldn't tell if he meant it or he was making fun of her.

"Lau-*ren*," Miranda called impatiently.

"Better hurry," Jake said conversationally. He dropped the end of his cigarette on the ground and stubbed it out with the sole of his black boots. "See you around, Lauren."

"Yeah," she said, jogging after Miranda. She didn't really know why but she felt flustered, and when she felt flustered she got annoyed.

"What were you doing?" Miranda said.

"Saying hi," Lauren said, even more annoyed now because Miranda had clearly heard the conversation.

"You shouldn't say hi to losers like him," Miranda said.

"He's my neighbor," Lauren said. Her face still felt hot

and she knew from long experience that it would take a while for her cheeks to return to their normal color.

Miranda leaned in close to Lauren, stealing a quick glance over her shoulder to ensure that nobody was nearby and listening.

"He deals drugs," Miranda whispered.

Lauren frowned. "Give me a break. Drugs? In Smiths Hollow? Where would he even get them from?"

"There are drugs even in Smiths Hollow," Miranda said mysteriously.

The only thing Lauren really knew about drugs came from movies where a character would occasionally smoke a joint. Miranda had seen *Scarface*, though Lauren hadn't, and had acted like an authority on all things cocaine-related since then.

They emerged from between the storefronts of the deli and the electronics shop. The Dream Machine was directly across the street. All the windows were open. The sound of loud music combined with the persistent bleep of electronics and the occasional whoop of a player was easily heard over the car engines on Main Street.

Lauren looked both ways so they could cross, but Miranda grabbed her arm and pointed toward the Sweet Shoppe a few doors away.

"I need some Tic Tacs," she said. "I ate a tuna fish sandwich for lunch before Tad called. If I'd known he was going to call I wouldn't have eaten anything. I don't want to look bloated in front of him."

She patted her paper-flat stomach as she said this and glanced at Lauren as if she expected her to say *You're not bloated*.

But Lauren was only half paying attention to Miranda. Going to the Sweet Shoppe meant that they had to cross in front of the large glass windows of Best Electronics. Jake Hanson was back behind the counter, cigarette break over, and was hunched over what looked like a pile of black plastic and wires.

She quickly looked away, first because she didn't want to get caught staring, and second because if he did look up she didn't know if she should wave or pretend not to see him. Her gaze shot out into the road and the passing cars.

A maroon station wagon was coming down Main Street and Lauren pretended to be absorbed in Miranda's face as it went by. The one person Lauren never had any trouble pretending not to see was her mother.

2

"Come on, David," Karen diMucci said, unbuckling her son and gathering him out of the back seat. She'd gotten lucky and found a parking space right in front of Frank's, so she should have been in a better mood. It was always exhausting to walk more than a block or two towing David and the groceries, especially in the June heat. Today she would get to avoid that.

Just like Lauren avoided my eyes as I passed.

She tried not to let the irritation she felt leak into her tone, but David heard the bite and looked up at her in that serious inquiring way that he had.

"Let's get some sandwich stuff," she said, deliberately injecting a hearty note. "And then we'll get some ice cream at the Sweet Shoppe after, okay?"

"Okeh," David said.

Lauren and Miranda would surely be gone from the shop by then, Karen thought. Not that she had to avoid her own daughter. But she knew if she saw Lauren now she would be annoyed and unable to keep herself from saying so, and then Lauren would give her the silent treatment all evening for embarrassing her in public.

Karen placed David on his feet and took his hand. He didn't try to squirm away or run ahead the way most other four-year-olds did. Lauren had been like that—always trying to shake her off, even as a small child.

The air-conditioned cool of the deli was welcome after the stifling heat outside. The weather report in the *Smiths Hollow Observer* had said the temperature would reach the mid-eighties that day, but it already felt much hotter because there was absolutely no wind. The heat just seemed to settle in and stagnate, especially on Main Street. There were no trees to provide shade—the town fathers had decided some time ago that there were quite enough trees in the woods and no need for the town to spend money maintaining plant life along the sidewalks.

Karen got in line. There were three other people in front of her, all people she knew by sight but not well. In a small town like Smiths Hollow you knew almost everyone by sight. She was grateful not to be forced to accept sympathetic looks and awkward small talk from an acquaintance.

Lately she dreaded leaving the house for just this reason—that she might bump into someone she knew from the PTA or who used to have their car fixed at Joe's garage.

People who weren't really close enough to be called friends but who felt compelled to stop and ask how she was doing and rub her shoulder and tell her that they hoped things would get better soon.

Karen always did everything she could to hurry along these encounters, checking her watch, saying she had pressing appointments—anything to make the other person just *go*. She hated the false sympathy, the way the conversations would trail off into sighs.

David waited patiently at her side while they stood in line. *Really, he is the best kid in the world*, Karen thought. He was good-natured and thoughtful and it never bothered him to wait anywhere. He would just stare around with his big brown eyes—the color and shape matching hers so exactly that everyone always exclaimed that he looked "just like his mommy"—and think his own little thoughts.

Then later when they were alone, when she was giving him his lunch or they were driving to the bank or playing in the sandbox in the backyard, he would tell her what he'd been thinking of, and it always amazed her that such deep thoughts emerged from the mind of her four-year-old.

"Mr. Adamcek likes for everyone to see his money," David said one day.

Karen, who'd been balancing her checkbook and trying not to cry at the dwindling size of her checking account, had looked up. David was playing with Play-Doh on the kitchen floor. He had newspapers spread around so he wouldn't get the floor dirty—his idea, not hers. He was that kind of kid.

"How do you know that?" Karen asked.

"He takes a long time to put his change back in his wallet, and sometimes he just stands there at the counter and holds his wallet open while he's talking," David said as he rolled the red Play-Doh into a new shape.

Earlier that day Karen had stopped in at the convenience store on her way home from the library because they were out of milk. She didn't really like buying milk from there because it was usually ten or twenty cents more expensive than the grocery store, but the grocery was out of her way and she didn't feel like driving all the way over there.

It was true that Paul Adamcek had been in line in front of her buying three packs of Marlboros, and now that she thought about it she realized he had been holding his wallet open the whole time so that it was impossible to miss the stack of $20s inside the billfold.

"He's going to get robbed if he keeps doing that," Karen muttered.

"He doesn't think anyone will try," David said. "Mr. Adamcek thinks he's really tough."

Karen wondered how David had inferred this. It was true that Paul thought he was a tough guy, but she wondered what David saw that made him realize it.

His preschool teacher had, at first, thought there was

something wrong with David because he was so often silent. He liked to play with the other children and got along with everyone, but he didn't talk very much. People often made that mistake, that kids who weren't talkative were stupid. David wasn't stupid. He just thought before he spoke, and he spent more time looking and listening than making noise.

"Hello, Karen," Frank said when Karen finally reached the counter. He leaned out a little so he could see David. "And how are you today, young man?"

David waved up to Frank, and Frank winked at him.

"What can I get for you today?"

Karen read off her list. "Half pound of turkey, half pound of American cheese, and a quarter pound of roast beef."

When Joe was alive she'd have ordered three times the amount of everything, because Joe had eaten two sandwiches for lunch every day and he didn't like his sandwiches to be stingy with the meat. But Joe wasn't alive and Lauren wouldn't eat anything from Frank's, so there wasn't any point in ordering a lot when there was nobody there to eat it. She couldn't afford to throw away food.

She looked at the premade salads that Frank had in the cooler while she waited. It would be easy to pick up some potato salad to have with lunch, but it would definitely be cheaper to make it herself, and she did have several potatoes in the pantry.

Frank handed Karen her order along with a Tootsie Pop

for David. He kept the lollipops behind the counter for his "special customers," as he called them.

"Thank you, Mr. Frank," David said as Karen handed him the lollipop.

Karen flashed Frank a grateful smile.

"How's that girl of yours?" Frank asked. There was no one waiting behind Karen.

Karen shrugged. "Oh, you know. A teenage girl."

Frank had three grown daughters of his own, so he did know. "She'll be human again in a few years. Just hang on."

"I'm hanging, all right," Karen said ruefully. "By my fingernails."

Frank laughed and waved at David. "Take care of your mama, okay, David?"

He nodded gravely. "Okeh, Mr. Frank. I will."

Karen and David pushed out into the hot June sunshine. "Ice cream sounds like a really good idea, doesn't it, bud?"

David carefully tucked his lollipop into the pocket of his shorts for later. "We haven't had lunch yet."

"I think we can have a little dessert before lunch today. What do you think?"

He smiled up at her. "If you say so, Mommy."

"I say so," Karen said, tucking the bag of lunch meat under her elbow next to her purse. They would have to get their ice cream and eat it quickly. In this weather the meat would spoil before they got home.

They had gone only a few feet when David stopped dead in the middle of the sidewalk.

"What's the matter?" Karen asked.

David tilted his head to one side and then to the other, like he was listening to something coming from far away.

"Mrs. Schneider," David said. "She's screaming."

"What?" Karen said. She crouched down so she could look into his eyes. They were focused on something but it wasn't Karen. "David, what's going on?"

His eyes seemed to come back from wherever they'd gone. He looked right at Karen.

"I told you," he said. "It's Mrs. Schneider. She won't stop screaming. There's so much blood."

3

Mrs. Schneider had spent the morning peering through the curtains at her across-the-street new neighbors. She didn't know just what the world was coming to when Mexicans could move onto a decent street where decent people lived without so much as a by-your-leave. They played loud music in Spanish and they shouted at each other in Spanish and they always seemed to be cooking something foreign.

If they wanted to eat strange food and speak a strange language, then why hadn't they just stayed in their own country instead of coming here to take jobs away from good American folk? she wondered.

She knew that most of the adults in that house had jobs on the canning line at the chili factory and she didn't think that was right, even though Mrs. Schneider didn't know anyone who'd actually lost a job on account of these creeping Mexican intruders.

It was the principle of the thing, she decided. What if a

real American wanted a job at the chili factory and couldn't get one because of them? And one of them was actually a police officer! She'd seen a man that lived there—she couldn't be bothered to remember all these foreign names—climbing into a Smiths Hollow squad car every morning. How could such a thing even be allowed?

She'd noticed Karen diMucci from down the street talking to one of the women who lived there, and their young children even *played* together. Mrs. Schneider had thought about warning her off but then decided that she'd better not. Karen might take offense. Everyone knew that Mexicans and Italians were practically the same, though Mrs. Schneider had to admit that the Italians made better food.

She wasn't a racist, though. There were lots of black people in Smiths Hollow and Mrs. Schneider didn't have a problem with any of them. They were all good and clean and hardworking—well, except for that Harry Jackson, who could be found in the Arena tavern at all hours of the day and night. Though even that was understandable. He just hadn't been the same since his wife got cancer and passed on, so one had to make allowances.

She looked at the clock and decided it was time to take herself to the deli in town and pick up something for dinner. Since her husband died of congestive heart failure five years earlier Mrs. Schneider hadn't bothered with cooking very much. She'd never enjoyed it, had only cooked for him because he liked home-cooked dinners. Most of the time she ate like a bird, anyway—just a half a sandwich or a cup of soup.

There wasn't any point in driving herself all the way over to the next town to go to the large shiny supermarket, even though her next-door-neighbor Mrs. Walker said the supermarket had better sales. Besides, Mrs. Schneider liked to stand by the counter and chat with Frank and catch up on "all the news," as she put it.

Mrs. Schneider collected her purse, double-checked to make sure the front door was locked (*you really couldn't be too careful with these foreigners in the neighborhood*), and went out through the kitchen to the small back porch.

She noticed the flies first, a black swarm of them, many more than there ought to be even on a hot day like today. Her first thought was that a raccoon or a fox had died in her yard, which would necessitate a call to the town hall to have it removed by Animal Control. Like many yards in Smiths Hollow, Mrs. Schneider's backyard abutted the woods and it wasn't unusual for the occasional critter to wander through.

Her husband had put up high fences on both sides so "the neighbors couldn't spy in"—Mr. Schneider had been a fastidiously private man, unwilling to have one of the neighbors spot him grilling and offer a beer that he might be forced to reciprocate—and sometimes animals got confused by the blocked-in lanes, the house and the detached garage, and the fences that enclosed it.

Then the smell permeated her irritated thoughts about calling for Animal Control—it always took them so long to come out, which she considered absurd in a town the size of Smiths Hollow—and she covered her mouth and nose, gasping. The smell was terrible, beyond terrible, and she wondered for a moment if a deer had died back there.

The cluster of flies hovered over the edge of the grass where it dipped down into a little ditch before the woods began. Mrs. Schneider couldn't see clearly from the porch what the flies were picking at, and she sighed.

She was going to have to investigate, and she didn't really care to get closer to the stink emanating from whatever it was. But if she called Animal Control with just a vague "I think something died in my backyard," that smart-mouth dispatcher Christy Gallagher would tell her that she couldn't dispatch Animal Control if they weren't certain an animal was involved.

"That girl is *fresh*," Mrs. Schneider said to herself, using a word her own mother had always used to describe young and disrespectful sorts.

She pulled a white cotton handkerchief out of her purse, then dabbed a little bit of her Estée Lauder perfume in the cloth before covering her nose and mouth with it.

She was going to place her purse down on the porch for a moment but then decided that she'd better not. Anyone could come in the yard gate while her back was turned and run off with her checkbook and wallet. After all, the neighborhood was not what it used to be.

With her purse tucked safely under her right arm and her left hand holding the perfumed handkerchief to her nose, Mrs. Schneider cautiously approached the black buzzing cloud of flies. Her mind had already leapt ahead to the inconvenience—she would have to put off her trip to Frank's while she waited for Animal Control to get their bottoms in gear—and so she stepped in the blood before she realized it.

She felt the sticky pull on her shoe, lifted it up, and peered at the bloody sole. Her nose wrinkled again in distaste. Had this animal bled to death in her yard? She would have to throw these shoes away, and that was a waste of a perfectly good pair of tennis sneakers.

Her gaze was focused on her feet now, picking around the splashes of blood. Then something she didn't recognize crept into her peripheral vision. Or rather, she did recognize it, but she didn't really want to believe it was what it actually was.

Mrs. Schneider gasped, and raised her eyes, and when she saw what was there—what was everywhere, really—she dropped the handkerchief to her side and screamed and screamed and screamed.

4

Sofia Lopez clipped the top sheet to the line and then pushed the rope along so that she could attach the next one. There was nothing nicer, in her opinion, than bedsheets that had dried outside in the sunshine. She mopped her forehead with the inside of her arm. In this heat the whole load would be dried in no time.

"Mama?" Her older daughter, Valeria, stood at the screen door that led into the kitchen. "Can I have some marshmallows?"

Sofia squinted at Val. The girl was eleven years old and obsessed with chemical reactions, so there was plenty of reason to suspect that Val was not going to eat the marshmallows that she'd just requested. More than likely the final result would involve a sticky mess on the floor of her bedroom or a plume of smoke coming out the window.

"What are you going to do with them?" Sofia asked.

"Um," Val said, the toe of her sock tracing a pattern on the floor. "Just, you know, some experiments."

"Experiments," Sofia said flatly. "Do these experiments involve fire?"

"Um," Val said again.

From inside the house Sofia heard her other daughter, Camila, arguing with her cousin Daniel. They were both eight years old and always seemed to want the same thing at the same time.

"Go and see what the problem is this time," Sofia said, turning back to her sheets.

"The marshmallows . . ." Val said.

"When I'm done you can tell me exactly what you want to do with them and then I will decide," Sofia said.

Val sighed and went to separate her sister and cousin.

Sofia liked to encourage Val's interest in science, but she didn't like worrying that Val was going to burn the house down. She wished there was someplace she could send Val where she could safely perform whatever experiments she liked, preferably under the supervision of someone with a chemistry degree.

But there wasn't anywhere like that in Smiths Hollow. In Chicago, maybe, but they'd moved here from Chicago so everyone could have a better life, and that meant that Valeria could observe chemical reactions outside in a backyard rather than in their cramped two-bedroom apartment in the city.

Despite what the Old Bigot across the street thought, neither Sofia nor her husband Alejandro nor Alejandro's brother Eduardo nor his wife Beatriz had been born in Mexico. They were all U.S. citizens, born and bred, and their parents had immigrated legally.

And I'll never tell her that, either. Let her think what she wants about us.

Alejandro had served for ten years in the Chicago Police Department, while Sofia and Eduardo and Beatriz had all worked at the Nabisco cookie factory on the southwest side. Eduardo and Beatriz and Daniel had lived across the hall from Sofia and Alejandro in the same apartment building in the Blue Island neighborhood, and they'd all taken different shifts so they could care for the children.

But all four of them always felt like they would never get ahead in the city, where rising costs made it difficult to even think about buying a house. Even with all seven of them living in this house in Smiths Hollow, they still had more room than any of them had ever had in Chicago. Just having separate bedrooms for Camila and Valeria had saved Sofia's sanity, which had been on the verge of cracking if she heard one more argument about "her stuff is on my side of the room."

Most of the neighbors were friendly and welcoming, and the Lopez families quickly found their place in their new home. Beatriz and Eduardo got better-paying jobs at the chili factory, and Alejandro had no trouble joining the tiny police force. Most days he was able to come home for lunch and he was never late for dinner because, as he put it, "There's really nothing resembling crime in this town." The dark circles that he'd always had under his eyes in Chicago from working shifts that never ended cleared up. And Sofia was able to stay home with all the children because her income was no longer vital.

There was the Old Bigot across the street, Sofia conceded, as she hung up the last of the sheets. Mrs. Schneider was always peering through her curtains at them like she thought Sofia couldn't see her. Whenever the Old Bigot went to the end of her driveway to get the mail she'd glare at the Lopez house like she thought one of them had stolen her social security check.

When the screaming started Sofia at first thought that Daniel had hit Camila again. Even though he'd been told repeatedly that he wasn't supposed to hit his cousin, their arguments usually seemed to devolve into smacking and punching if an adult wasn't there to supervise them. Camila would hit back, too, but she was a pro at making it seem like Daniel was the only one at fault.

Her younger daughter was a born actress, and the slightest bump, bruise, or whack resulted in waterfalls of tears and the kind of melodramatic accusations that would be better suited to a Joan Crawford film—or rather, that movie *about* Joan Crawford, what was it called? There had been a lot of histrionics in that movie, and Camila seemed to be taking her cue from the same director. Sofia was immune to these performances, but Camila still managed to snow her father, who never believed that his little princess was exaggerating.

Sofia took one step toward the screen door, then stopped. The screaming wasn't coming from inside the house but outside it. Had the kids gone out on the front lawn? Alejandro had left the sprinkler attached to the hose up there so they could play in the water on days like today, but Sofia hadn't heard any of them turn the faucet on the side of the house.

Val came to the back door, eyes round, and Camila and Daniel crowded behind her. "What's that?"

Sofia shook her head. "I thought it was you kids."

As soon as she said it, she realized it was an idiotic thing to say. The noise wasn't anything like the sounds the kids made, short bursts of raucous joy or just as raucous arguing. This scream was a long sustained thing, almost impossible in its breadth and length. How could one person scream for so long and never take a breath?

"Stay here," Sofia said.

Camila immediately tried to push past Val to follow her mother—Camila had a nosy streak a mile wide—but Val snagged her around the waist before she could escape.

"Hey!" Camila said, and kicked her sister in the shin with the heel of her shoe.

"Ow!" Val shouted, dropping Camila to the ground.

Camila collapsed and immediately started howling like her ankle had broken upon landing.

"Enough," Sofia said, slashing her hand through the air. Her mother's tone was firm enough that Camila ceased the fake crying immediately and stared up at her in astonishment. "All of you will stay right here while I see what's happening, and you will not put a toe outside unless you want to lose all your privileges for the rest of the summer."

"Yes, Mama," Val said.

"Yes, Mama," Camila repeated.

"Yes, Aunt Sofia," Daniel added.

"I will be back," she said. "If I'm gone more than fifteen minutes, call Papa at the police station."

Val glanced over her shoulder at the clock, starting the countdown from that moment.

Sofia knew the children would be fine—if anything, the younger two would forget where she'd gone in a few minutes and resume their normal activities.

She went around the left side of the house and down the driveway. The Lopez home didn't have a garage, just an open strip of blacktop that ran alongside the front yard and then the house and stopped once it reached the back porch. Alejandro and Eduardo had already discussed putting up some kind of cover for the cars, even if it was just a canopy roof. The summer heat beating inside the cars made them unbearable.

Sofia stopped when she reached the mailbox at the end of the drive, trying to pinpoint the location of the screams. Their house was in a little cul-de-sac, and sometimes sound echoed strangely through the space.

None of the other neighbors appeared to be home—or if they were, they were singularly incurious about the source of the noise. Sofia was the only person standing out in the street, perspiration beading on her forehead.

"Is that the Old Bigot?" she murmured to herself. She started across the street, the heat making the soles of her sneakers feel sticky.

Halfway there she was sure it was, in fact, Mrs. Schneider. What could have the old woman in such a state? Sofia felt vaguely annoyed that she had to ride to the rescue of a person who held her and her entire family in contempt. She knew that Jesus said to forgive, but it was hard to feel the warmth of Christian love toward the woman.

Still, Sofia knew that she wouldn't leave Mrs. Schneider in such obvious distress, even if part of her would like to do just that. She was fairly certain the Old Bigot wouldn't spit on her if she were on fire.

Once she was standing on Mrs. Schneider's front lawn it was apparent that the screaming was coming from the backyard. The screams hadn't diminished in volume or length, although Sofia thought the old woman's voice was getting hoarse. As she unhooked the gate to the backyard

Sofia felt the first stirrings of alarm. This wasn't just some wild hair of the old lady's. Something was really wrong.

The gate clattered shut behind Sofia. Mrs. Schneider stood on the downslope of her yard, close to the edge of the woods that abutted the neatly trimmed grass. The old woman was ramrod straight, her hands down at her sides. Her purse had fallen at her feet and a white handkerchief fluttered weakly in the grass, like a halfhearted surrender.

"Mrs. Schneider?" Sofia called, approaching her.

Mrs. Schneider stopped screaming then, all of a sudden, like she was a tap that someone had switched off. She spun around, saw Sofia standing there, and then raised one stiff arm toward the bottom of the yard.

"Look!" she shouted. "Look what you've done. This neighborhood used to be safe before your kind came here! Look! Look!"

Sofia felt her temper shoot up into the stratosphere. She had always been quick to anger, something she hated because she felt it just played into people's prejudices about hot-blooded Latinas.

"What are you talking about, you old . . ." Sofia said. She'd been about to say *you old bitch*, because that was exactly what Mrs. Schneider was, a hateful old bitch, but then the smell finally permeated her anger and she staggered. "What on earth?"

She covered her mouth and nose with her hand, but that

just seemed to hold the smell closer and she coughed, gagging a little.

"Do you see? Do you SEE?" Mrs. Schneider said, shaking her head with all the righteous fury of a tent revivalist. "This is what happens when people don't stay in their place! I knew your house was full of thieves and murderers."

Sofia wasn't really listening anymore, because she'd seen the thing that Mrs. Schneider was pointing at, the thing that was choking her with its smell, and the bottom fell out of her stomach.

Blood. There was so much blood, and other things that were barely recognizable but had certainly come from a human. By the looks of it, two humans.

"I need to use your telephone," she said, and her voice sounded like it came from a faraway place. "I have to call Alejandro."

Yes, she needed to call Alejandro, and he would bring the police car and the ambulance and he would know what to do about all this.

Sofia turned her back on the mad old woman and her accusing finger and walked toward the back porch. She felt like she was swimming underwater, like the steps of the porch were miles from where she stood.

"Don't you dare sully my house!" Mrs. Schneider shouted. "Don't you put one of your dirty Mexican feet on the porch my husband built!"

Sofia ignored her. She needed a telephone, and there would be a closer telephone in Mrs. Schneider's house. Besides, she didn't want to call from home. She was going to have to explain why the police needed to come immediately and she'd rather the children not overhear.

She was opening the storm door when Mrs. Schneider charged across the lawn toward her.

"Get away from there!" the old woman shouted. "You get away right now!"

Sofia let go of the storm door and turned to face the livid Mrs. Schneider, who'd come up one of the steps and reached for the hem of Sofia's shorts, as if she were going to pull Sofia off the porch.

Somewhere underneath the shock and the underwater feeling, Sofia's anger still bubbled. She'd come over here to help this screaming woman, and the old bitch was only worried about her house being "sullied."

Sofia slapped the old woman across the face as hard as she possibly could. The impact seemed to echo in the air between them, a seismic reverberation.

"I am going to call the police," she said in a tone that she usually reserved for the children, and then only when they were on the thinnest possible ice. "I am going to use your telephone to do this. You will not shout, scream, or impede me in any way while I do this."

Mrs. Schneider nodded, chastened. Her eyes dropped in

the direction of Sofia's off-brand tennis sneakers.

"The telephone is just inside the door," she said. "I think I'll . . . just wait here."

She turned her back to Sofia and lowered herself slowly to the wooden steps of the porch. She seemed very old to Sofia then, at least ten years older than she'd been a few minutes earlier.

As Sofia entered the house she heard Mrs. Schneider begin to sob.

The phone hung just to the right of the back door as advertised. Sofia lifted the receiver and dialed Alejandro's desk phone instead of 911. She didn't want to talk to a dispatcher. She wanted to talk to her husband. She wanted him to come to her right away.

"Officer Lopez," he said.

"Alejandro," she said, and she was surprised to hear her voice crack. "Alejandro, you have to come. There are girls."

"Sof?" he asked. "What's the matter? Did something happen to Val or Camila?"

"No," she said, taking a deep breath. "It's not our girls. It's somebody else's girls. There are two of them, and someone left them in pieces all over Mrs. Schneider's yard."

5

Lauren saw her mother and brother come out of Frank's deli and walk toward the Sweet Shoppe. She wrinkled her nose a little and turned her head away, even though there was little to no chance of her mother seeing her through the window in the dim interior of the arcade.

She stood next to Miranda, who was standing very close to Tad, the greasy-haired (*and also greasy-faced*, Lauren thought) object of her affection who did not look at all like Matt Dillon.

On the other side of Tad was his friend Billy, who also did not look like Matt Dillon and who seemed to have about as much interest in Lauren as she did in him—that is, none at all.

Tad was very involved with his latest round of Karate Champ and they were all supposed to care just as much as he did. Lauren didn't see why they couldn't all at least go and play their own games as long as they were in the arcade, but

Tad liked to have a cheering section around him.

Billy would shout and clap when Tad got a good hit on his opponent, and he apparently understood that as his role. Maybe cheerleading Tad's skill at the joystick was required if you were permitted to ride in Tad's Camaro. Miranda had pointed at the car out front as they entered the arcade, and the only thing Lauren noticed about it was that Tad hadn't bothered to put it in between the diagonal parking space lines.

She didn't think Miranda was interested in the outcome of the latest match. Her friend did seem to enjoy brushing her breasts against Tad's arm as he played the game, though, and Tad didn't tell her to get off so he must have been enjoying it, too.

What would happen if I just left without saying anything? Lauren wondered. Would Miranda notice right away, or only when she wanted to drag Lauren to the bathroom to touch up her lip gloss and talk about Tad?

She'd just about resolved to do it—slip away without telling Miranda—when the howl of an ambulance siren made everyone crane around their video screens and look out the window. The ambulance flew down Main Street, a notable occurrence by itself in a town with few emergencies, but the fact that it was followed by both of the Smiths Hollow Police Department cars had everyone muttering.

"Whoa, wonder what's happening," Billy said.

"We should follow the police cars," Tad said, and looked

ready to abandon his game and run outside to jump into his car.

Lauren knew that if that happened, Miranda would want to follow, and she decided right then that she wasn't going to go with them. She was not going to get herself trapped in Tad's car and then wind up someplace she really did not want to be, like the mall in the next town or at the Make-Out Field. The way that Miranda was rubbing herself against Tad meant the Make-Out Field was a distinct possibility, and Lauren planned on escaping before anyone expected her to kiss Billy.

"They're long gone, man," Billy said. "We'll never catch them."

"The Camaro could," Tad said belligerently, as if Billy had somehow questioned the masculinity of his car.

"Sure," Billy said. "But if you chase the cops at that speed you'll end up getting a ticket."

Tad's shoulders relaxed. "Yeah. And if I get another ticket the Mother Monster said she's going to take away my car keys."

Miranda trilled a long laugh at this. "Mother Monster. That's a good one."

"She's always ragging me," Tad said, and his voice became high-pitched. "'Clean up your room, cut your hair, work more hours at your job.' Jesus Christ, it's summer. Can't she lay off for five seconds?"

"Yeah," Miranda said. "You already work a lot at Wagon Wheel."

"Not that much," Tad admitted, sliding another quarter into Karate Champ. "I was thinking of applying at someplace in the mall."

Lauren felt a headache coming on. It was brewing behind her eyes and soon it would clobber her there, making her feel nauseated and dizzy as it pounded the back of her eyeballs. She'd been subject to these headaches occasionally as a child, but lately they'd become more frequent. If she didn't get home soon she wouldn't even be able to ride her bike without falling over.

She started to say something to Miranda, who was deeply involved in the discussion of Tad's future employment prospects.

"What?" Miranda asked, flashing Lauren an annoyed glance.

Lauren jerked her thumb at the food counter where some bored teens dispensed popcorn and soda and candy. "I'm going to get a Coke. You want one?"

"No," Miranda said. "You shouldn't drink soda, either. The sugar will rot your teeth."

Lauren knew she'd added this last bit because she was irritated that Lauren interrupted her conversation with Tad, and it was the best insult Miranda could come up with on short notice.

"Okay," Lauren said, not caring about Miranda's attitude. She just needed to get away from the noise and lights of the Dream Machine as quickly as possible.

Lauren drifted in the direction of the food counter, glancing back over her shoulder. Miranda, Tad, and Billy were all absorbed in the game. She changed direction and darted for the front door.

As she stepped into the obscenely bright sunshine she wondered how long it would take for Miranda to notice that Lauren wasn't coming back.

She closed her eyes for a second, because the glare of the sun was especially sharp after the dim interior of the arcade, and light always made her headaches worse. When she opened them again her gaze darted along the diagonal parking spaces across the street. Her mother's station wagon was gone, so she and David had gone home.

It was too bad, because Lauren would have liked a ride from her mom at that moment. She wasn't sure she would be able to ride her bike without puking.

Her father had always worried about these headaches, speculating (quietly, to her mother, when he thought Lauren couldn't hear) that Lauren had some kind of neurological disease.

"They're just migraines, Joe," Mom would say in that scathing tone that she reserved for moments when she considered Dad especially stupid. "Lots of girls get them, especially after their periods. It's hormones."

Her dad would always shuffle around then and mumble that he was just worried. Discussing hormones and training bras and anything else that meant Lauren was becoming a woman made him profoundly uncomfortable.

But Lauren had gotten the headaches even though she was still waiting on her period, so she thought it couldn't just be hormones the way her mother said. Sometimes it felt like there was something else living inside her skull that was trying to break out. She'd never told anybody else this, because she knew it sounded stupid.

Lauren cupped her hands around her eyes like binoculars to shield them from the sun and jogged across the street. The up-and-down motion made the peanut butter sandwich and chips she'd had for lunch rise up in her throat, but she swallowed hard and the feeling went away.

She slipped in between Frank's Deli and Best Electronics even though she didn't want to run into any rats while she was on her own. It was the fastest way back to her bike from there, and the only thing that mattered at the moment was getting to her cool, dark bedroom as soon as possible.

She was so intent on reaching the woods that she didn't even glance at the back door of the electronics shop. She didn't realize Jake Hanson was standing there again until he said, "Hey, Lauren," in his lazy drawling way.

It startled her, and she gave a little clipped-off scream.

Her heart pounded in her chest and she knew there was no help for it now. She stumbled a few feet forward, crouched down, and put her head between her knees.

"Lauren?" Jake asked, and to his credit he didn't sound drawling anymore—confused maybe, or concerned.

She shook her head from side to side, though she didn't know if she was trying to stave off the inevitable vomit or just Jake's approach.

Then it came, and her cheeks burned with humiliation as she puked out her lunch a few feet away from Jake Hanson, wishing all the while that he would just go back inside and leave her alone.

She vaguely heard the sound of the back door closing, and thought, *Good.*

After a few minutes she thought she was done, but then her stomach did that tricky thing where it reminded her that there was still a teaspoon of half-digested food left inside her, and she gagged and coughed and out came the rest.

She stayed where she was, waiting to see if there was anything else. Cold sweat beaded on her temples and pooled in the small of her back and soaked the underarms of her T-shirt. She smelled the baby-powder scent of her deodorant and the sharp tang of bile and the garbage rotting in the cans behind the deli.

"Here," Jake's voice said behind her.

Lauren nearly tipped forward into the pile of her own

puke. She hadn't heard him come out of the store again. A second later she felt one of his hands on her back, and then a plastic cup of water materialized in front of her face.

"Thanks," she said. Her voice sounded croaky, not like her own.

His hand on her back felt huge and hot and she couldn't decide if she liked it or if she wanted him to stop.

The point was moot a second later because he took his hand away and said, "Better?"

She nodded. Her face felt redder than it had ever been, like it was literally on fire. The only thing that would make this worse would be if Miranda suddenly showed up. Lauren glanced fearfully over her shoulder then, as if just the thought of Miranda would summon her.

Miranda wasn't there, but Jake was crouched next to her. He didn't seem to be the least bit bothered by the fact that Lauren had gotten sick in front of him. She hoped he wouldn't tell his friends about it later.

"Can you stand?" he asked.

She nodded again and dug her hands into her thighs as she pushed up. Everything swam before her for a second, including Jake's blue eyes (*they really are very blue*, she thought, *dark blue, like sapphires*) and then the world righted itself. *Now to get away as soon as possible.*

Jake had been really nice, really cool actually about the whole thing, but that didn't mean Lauren wanted to stand there and have a conversation with him while she was pale and shaky and badly needed a toothbrush.

"What happened?" he asked.

"I get, um, headaches," Lauren said. "Really bad ones."

"Migraines," he said, nodding wisely. "My mom gets them, too."

Lauren squinted at him, because the sun was still high and bright and opening her eyes too wide made her head throb. "Well, thanks for the water," she said, flapping her hand at her side nervously.

Why doesn't he go back inside? she wondered. Wasn't he supposed to be working? Why was he just standing there looking at her like she'd just flown in on an alien ship?

"I get off in a half hour," he said. "If you want a ride home instead of walking."

"Oh," Lauren said. "Um, thanks, but I left my bike in the woods. I have to go get it or my mom will freak."

"You spend a lot of time in the woods, don't you?" he asked.

"Yeah," she said, wondering why he was trying to have a conversation with her.

"Brave girl," he said.

She didn't know what to say to this. She knew that her opinion of the woods was not a majority one, but she didn't think a guy like Jake Hanson would be afraid of a few trees. Then again, she'd been shocked to discover that her father hadn't liked the forest, either.

"Thanks again," she said, and turned toward the woods, giving him a little half wave.

"See you around, Lauren," he said softly.

She didn't look back over her shoulder, but she was sure he watched her until she disappeared from sight.

The shade of the trees made her feel better almost immediately, although the headache didn't disappear—just receded a little bit, like a fighter taking two steps back before charging in again with a flurry of punches. Still, she thought she might be able to get to her bike and make it home without fainting, which was the key thing.

Lauren had almost reached the ghost tree and her bike when she felt it—a strange sort of shifting, although the shifting wasn't anything external that she could tell. The trees all stood in their usual places and the wind rustled their branches like always and her feet were firmly planted on the ground and her stomach wasn't even queasy any longer.

But still—there had been *something*. A feeling that made her skin prickle and her left eye twitch and cold sweat pool at the base of her spine.

She shook her head even though it made her headache feel like it was knocking from side to side inside her skull. Those were all things that happened to other people when they walked in the woods that bordered Smiths Hollow. They got spooky feelings and broke out in a sweat and talked about ghosts and devils in whispers. But Lauren never felt these things. The woods had always made her feel safe.

Even when they found her father dead under the trees with his heart torn out, Lauren had never blamed the woods. How could it be the fault of nature if her father had gone out in the middle of the night for some reason that her mother would not discuss?

But she'd felt something just now, something like a . . .

A presence.

But that was beyond stupid. There was no floating presence out here, only Lauren and the trees and the chipmunks scampering into the brush.

And then her head exploded, a pain like she'd never experienced before. She dropped to her knees in the dirt, both hands pressing into her head, wishing for anything that would make it stop.

Just make it stop, she thought, and she heard herself whimpering as she fell forward, grinding her face into the dead leaves and soil, trying to tunnel into the cool ground in hopes that the darkness would close around her like a grave and *make it stop, just make it stop.*

There *was* something inside her brain trying to get out, something with a chainsaw and blood in its teeth, something howling, but the howling wasn't pain—it was the kind of howling that meant laughter, and the laughter wasn't the kind that invited others to laugh but the kind that you ran from while your heart slammed against your ribs and your legs moved of their own volition.

Then she saw them—the girls. But she didn't really see them. It was like she was watching a replay of someone else's memory. There were two girls in the woods, walking together and wearing backpacks. Lauren didn't recognize them—they looked a little older than her, and they were probably not from Smiths Hollow. One of the girls had very short blond hair cut like a boy's, and the other had her brown hair tied up in braids that draped over her chest. Something about the girls—maybe the heaviness of their packs—made Lauren think that they were runaways.

The girls didn't seem to be going anywhere in particular, just ambling along to a place where people wouldn't ask them questions, wouldn't wonder where they were going and what they were doing. They both shared the same expression—a kind of half-worried, half-happy wrinkle in their brows, like they were glad to be doing things on their own terms but not sure yet what those terms would be, or if they would be successful.

Then Lauren was aware of another presence, something that didn't see the girls as girls or even humans. It saw them as meat, beautiful bloody red delicious meat.

No! Lauren cried out. *Run away!*

But the girls didn't hear her, because Lauren wasn't really there and because they weren't worried about a monster eating them up. They were worried about someone finding them and making them go home, home where they had been so unhappy and sometimes afraid, and they weren't going to be afraid anymore.

Lauren knew all of this, knew what the girls were thinking and what the thing was thinking and she knew what would happen next and she didn't want to see, didn't want to know any more. Why couldn't she just imagine that the girls had gone on happy together, that they made a new home for themselves somewhere? Why did she have to see what happened next?

It didn't matter if she closed her eyes because the scene was under her eyelids, imprinted on the inside of her brain. It didn't matter if she covered her ears with her hands because she heard the braid girl scream as her friend was torn in half by claws that were from no animal Lauren had ever seen.

But there was something funny about those claws, too, Lauren thought, part of her sunk in the horror of it all but another part dispassionately noting that there was something out of place. Just for a second she thought she'd seen a human hand underneath the claws.

A person? A person was doing this?

How could a person tear up two girls and then eat bits of them and then deliberately drag the remains to a place where they would be found?

Lauren watched—it felt like she was watching even though it was only a scene pressing on the inside of her brain—as the thing gathered up what was left in a canvas sack. The sack left a trail behind as blood drained from what was left of the girls, the half-happy girls who'd walked in the woods.

The vision—if that was what it was—stopped as abruptly as it had started. Lauren sat up and peered around, half expecting that there would be a monster there, a monster with sharp claws and bloody teeth. But there was nothing and no one—not even, Lauren realized, the remnants of the migraine that had left her feeling so crippled just a short while earlier.

The side of her face felt gritty, and she swiped at it with her hand. It came away covered in dirt. She must have ground her face into the soil, trying to escape the things she saw.

The images were fading quickly now, so fast that it was almost like it hadn't happened at all. All that was left was a hollowed-out feeling and an intense exhaustion that made her want to stay right where she was and take a nap.

"Well, no wonder," she said to herself, forcing her feet and legs to move and stand. She'd gotten sick and had the mother of all headaches and then had what amounted to a waking nightmare where pretty girls got slaughtered by monsters. Of course she wanted to sleep.

Despite the strange thing she'd just seen—imagined?—the woods still seemed to be the same refuge they'd always been for her. The rustling of the leaves and the chirping of birds washed away the last vestiges of the nightmare. That was what she decided it was, after all. Just a nightmare brought on by the headache and nothing to worry about at all.

She found her bike leaning against the ghost tree exactly where she'd left it and grabbed the handlebars, pulling it away from the shade of the tree's branches. It was then that she noticed something on the seat.

The seat was dark blue, so it was hard to tell exactly what it was. She leaned her face closer, then reared back in horror.

There was a handprint on the seat, a handprint that almost looked human, with very long fingers that tapered into sharp points.

But that wasn't what had Lauren dropping her bike and backing away. It was because the print had been stamped in blood, and the blood was still fresh.

6

Alejandro Lopez—he preferred to be called Alex rather than Alejandro, because the Americanized name made white folks feel like he was one of them—stood in Mrs. Schneider's violated backyard, a place he'd never thought he'd be permitted to enter. Not that he'd particularly wanted to— you didn't usually rush over to barbecue with a neighbor who considered you subhuman. Despite the horrible thing he was looking at, he couldn't shake the sense of having successfully breached enemy territory.

Alex's partner, John Miller (*was there any more stolidly American name than John Miller?* Alex wondered) wandered back to Alex's side, having lost his lunchtime meatball sub in the far corner of Mrs. Schneider's well-tended yard.

"What in God's name?" Miller said, shaking his head.

This was the same thing he'd said right before he'd puked,

and Alex still didn't have an answer. Luckily, Miller didn't seem to expect one.

One of the other four officers, Luke Pantaleo, was interviewing Mrs. Schneider in her kitchen. Sofia was there, too, with Luke's partner, Aaron Hendricks. Alex could see his wife through the storm door, calmly explaining what had happened.

He might have been impressed by her cool except that Sofia was always remarkably cool under fire. Later, after the crisis passed, she would rage or cry or break down.

Alex had called the chief of police, Van Christie, as soon as he entered the yard and saw what they were dealing with. He'd held off the EMTs—no point in having them contaminate the crime scene—and directed Luke and Aaron to interview Sofia and Mrs. Schneider (his wife had been sitting next to the weeping old woman on the porch steps, her arm wrapped around Mrs. Schneider's thin shaking shoulders), and then gotten on his police radio to call Van.

Now Miller and Alex stood over the mutilated remains of at least two girls. Alex only thought there were two because there were two heads, but the quantity of blood and viscera strewn around made it seem like there might be more.

He sighed deeply, not just because it was terrible but because he'd thought he'd gotten away from this when they left the city. Alex felt he'd seen enough stab wounds and crack overdoses and bullet-riddled bodies to last a lifetime.

They'd moved to this picturesque little town with its charming main street and friendly neighbors where Alex thought the worst thing he'd have to deal with was teenagers getting drunk and causing a ruckus out at Make-Out Field. Now there was this, and this was reminding him of something he'd rather forget.

Don't think about it, he told himself, but still there was a flash of memory—empty eyes staring up at him from inside a dumpster, black flies circling.

Just like now. Alex thought the flies must be calling their friends in the next county, because it seemed the cloud of swirling, dipping, buzzing insects doubled in size every few seconds.

He wondered who the girls were, and who would have to tell their parents what happened.

But what did happen?

"Is this like the diMucci case?" he asked Miller.

Miller gave him a blank look. "Lauren? What happened to Lauren?"

"Not the daughter," Alex said, giving Miller a look. Why would he assume Alex was talking about Lauren? "The father. He was killed last year, right?"

Alex was talking like he hadn't seen the report, hadn't studied the crime scene photos dozens of times already. When he'd joined the force—such as it was, being composed of four patrolmen and one detective who retired shortly thereafter and one largely ceremonial chief of police—he'd been surprised that such a serious crime hadn't been more thoroughly investigated. But whenever he asked about it the other officers got a strange kind of glazed look in their eyes, like they couldn't quite remember what Alex was talking about—just like Miller was doing now.

"Right," Miller said, and his expression told Alex that he was reaching far back into the vault of memory. "Lauren's dad. Yeah, that was a weird one."

That's an understatement, Alex thought, but he didn't say anything else about the diMucci murder. And anyway, even the photos of Joe diMucci weren't as awful as what was in front of them.

The two heads had been placed next to one another, cheek-to-cheek in a horrible parody of a dancing couple, one girl facing toward the woods and the other facing Mrs. Schneider's house. Alex saw that the skin of each neck was shredded and ragged, like the heads had been torn off rather than cut with a sharp object. One of the girls—the short-haired one—still had a few trailing pieces of vertebra peeking out from underneath. The other girl was missing one of her ears.

All around the heads were organs, most of which were unidentifiable because of similar shredding. How could anyone except maybe a doctor tell if that lump of grayish-red jelly in the grass was a liver or a heart? The only thing that was really clear was that the bits and pieces had quite obviously been *arranged*—the heads in the center, the organs radiating outward like planets circling a sun.

"It can't have happened here," Alex said.

"What can't have happened here?" Miller said.

This time Alex turned toward his partner with an exaggerated double take. "Are you drunk, Miller?"

Miller flushed. "No."

"What could I possibly be talking about then?" Alex said, pointing at the heads and the organs and the rapidly increasing swarm of flies.

"I thought you were still talking about Lauren's dad," Miller said.

Why did everyone always refer to him as Lauren's dad? Alex wondered. No one ever mentioned Joe's other child, David, or called him "Karen's husband." It was always "Joe" (maybe followed by "the mechanic") or "Lauren's dad," as if Joe diMucci's primary context had been in relation to his daughter.

Alex decided to ignore the last thing Miller said and continue his initial thought. "If these girls were killed here, in the old—"

He stopped himself before he said "the Old Bigot," which was the nickname that both he and Sofia used in the house to refer to their less-than-charming neighbor.

"In Mrs. Schneider's yard, there would have been a lot of noise," he continued, but Miller hadn't appeared to notice anything. Miller's gears didn't shift too fast and he seemed to still be stuck in the last one. "Not only would Mrs. Schneider have heard it, but the other neighbors, too."

"Okay," Miller said.

The trouble with having Miller as a partner was that he never took rhetorical bait. Alex's old partner in Chicago, Tyrone Robinson, would already have finished Alex's sentences. He would probably be five steps ahead of Alex, in fact, because Tyrone had a lightning-fast brain that was wasted on a patrolman. Alex expected that as soon as he was eligible Tyrone would be a detective.

"And Mrs. Schneider's yard isn't easy to get into from the street," Alex said. "Besides, someone would notice if a guy dragged two girls back here from the driveway."

"Maybe," Miller said, shrugging. "Around here most of the housewives are watching their soaps this time of the day. They probably wouldn't notice if someone was getting murdered right out in the street."

If Sofia heard him talking about her watching soaps she'd probably shout until Miller's ears were scorched, Alex thought, but again decided it was best to try to keep Miller on one path and not acknowledge side comments. Besides, Alex knew that Mrs. Schneider herself spent most of her day hanging out the front window watching her neighbors for proof of their criminal intent. If anything untoward had happened on her watch she would have dialed 911 immediately.

"Anyway," Alex said. "That means whoever did this came

through the woods. Probably killed the girls in the woods, too."

"How do you figure that?" Miller asked.

Alex refrained from explaining what he'd just basically explained—that, in essence, the woods were the only place nearby without prying eyes. The only other option that he could think of was that whoever had done this had killed the girls in his house, then taken the remains through the woods.

"Why plant them here?" Alex said.

"What?" Miller asked.

"Why leave the girls here?" Alex asked. He wondered if the carnage was getting to Miller. His partner seemed more out of it than usual.

He started acting like this when you mentioned diMucci. He's like a record needle that got stuck.

Alex wondered if Miller knew something about diMucci's murder, something that he was trying to keep Alex from finding out. He was about to follow this line of thought when Van Christie opened the gate and entered the yard.

The chief of police was forty-six, a former Marine, and one of the quietest people Alex had ever met—quiet in the lack-of-noise sense, Alex had told Sofia once, not quiet as in not talkative. The chief made practically no sound when he walked, never slammed a door, never raised his voice. Even his car engine was quiet, and this confounded Alex since the chief's car was the same Chevrolet Caprice Classic as the patrol cars.

Christie stopped at Alex's side and surveyed the backyard. "Jesus."

"That's what I said, Chief," Miller said.

"That's what anyone would say, Miller," Christie said. "I think we're going to need the camera from my vehicle. It's in the trunk."

Miller recognized an order when he heard one and hurried off. All the officers had keys for every fleet car, including the chief's.

"What do we know?" Christie asked, turning his thoughtful blue gaze on Alex.

"Not a whole lot," Alex admitted. He told Christie that the other two officers were interviewing Sofia and Mrs. Schneider. "Although it seems like they're taking a while."

"Probably don't want to come out and see this again," Christie said. "Or Mrs. Schneider's raising a fuss. I can't see Sofia giving them a hard time. Who's watching the kids?"

Alex realized this thought hadn't even occurred to him.

"Want to go check with Sofia?" Christie asked, correctly reading Alex's consternation. "You probably want to get her home as soon as possible, anyway. Tell Pantaleo to stay with Mrs. Schneider, keep her in the house. Hendricks and Miller can return to the station and handle whatever calls come in. You can help me with the photos and blood."

Alex jogged up the porch stairs. Even through the storm door he could hear Mrs. Schneider's shrill voice. He pushed open the door and found Pantaleo and Hendricks standing in front of Mrs. Schneider, looking helpless. All three of them turned toward him. Pantaleo and Hendricks looked unmistakably relieved.

"Where's Sof?" he asked.

"She went home about ten minutes ago," Pantaleo said. "Through the front door."

Alex didn't blame her for not returning to the yard. He didn't even blame her for not saying good-bye. He wouldn't have wanted to see what was left of those two girls again if he didn't have to.

"Chief is here. He says Hendricks and Miller should go back to the station. Pantaleo, you should stay here and support Mrs. Schneider."

Hendricks didn't bust out smiling in front of his partner, but it was a near thing, Alex could tell. Pantaleo looked like someone who'd been condemned to walk the plank.

"If Chief Christie is here, I *demand* to speak with him," Mrs. Schneider said. "I want to know what this town is coming to when such things can not only *occur* but be *inflicted* on innocent bystanders."

Alex thought fast. The chief would not appreciate getting roped in by one of Mrs. Schneider's rants.

"We just have to take some photographs and samples of the crime scene, Mrs. Schneider. The sooner we do that, the sooner your yard can be cleared. I'm sure the chief would be happy to speak to you once that's taken care of," Alex said, and gave her his best service-with-a-sober-smile face, one that expressed friendliness while simultaneously acknowledging the gravity of the situation.

Sofia had once asked him if he practiced it in front of a mirror, and he had to admit that he did. It wasn't the easiest thing in the world, to school your face to a certain expression when you were dealing with stressed-out people, and cops almost always dealt with stressed-out people.

As Alex returned outside he wondered what Sofia had told Val and Camila and Daniel. Probably nothing. He hoped nothing. But one of them was bound to notice three police cars parked across the street.

Miller had delivered not only the camera but the little case that contained evidence-collection equipment. Christie was pulling on latex gloves when Alex joined him. He heard the storm door slam shut behind him and caught a glimpse of Hendricks making a fast exit. A minute later he heard the engine of one of the patrol cars fire up and pull away. Alex put on his own gloves and then pointed to the camera.

Christie nodded. "I'd better take the samples. Although you probably have more experience at this sort of thing than I do."

"Nah," Alex said, taking the camera out of its case. It was a standard thirty-five-millimeter Pentax. Alex wondered if he'd be dropping the crime scene film off at McDowell's Camera for development. The station didn't have a darkroom.

"In Chicago there was a team that came in and took photos and collected evidence. Patrolmen just stood around and kept bystanders away from the scene."

He paused, looking around at the high fences that surrounded Mrs. Schneider's little kingdom. "Why aren't there any here, though?"

"Any what?" Christie asked.

"Bystanders," Alex said. He knew at least a few people were home during the day besides Sofia. He was struck by the intense lack of interest from the neighbors. It was also unusually silent for a summer's day. Shouldn't kids be playing outside, running around under sprinklers, biking around the cul-de-sac? Where were the teenagers blasting Michael Jackson from their boom boxes? He didn't even hear the noise of afternoon television drifting through open windows.

It's almost as if everyone is hiding, he thought. *Trying not to be noticed . . . but by what?*

Christie shrugged. "People mostly mind their own business around here. You haven't been here very long, so you're still thinking like a city cop—eyes everywhere. That's not the case in Smiths Hollow."

"Uh-huh," Alex said. The silence suddenly seemed oppressive, an extra blanket on top of the heat. When he raised the camera to his face he felt the sweat on his upper cheekbone sticking under the eyepiece.

He photographed the whole scene from several angles so Christie could start gathering his samples, then got down to do a close-up of the girls' heads. He lifted the camera to his face, adjusting the focus on the girl with the long braids.

The girl looked straight into the camera, opened her mouth, and whispered, "Help me."

Alex jerked back, dropping the camera in the grass.

Christie glanced over at him. "Problem, Lopez?"

Alex shook his head, then picked up the camera again. Christie bent his head over his work. Alex's hands were shaking—not enough that Christie would notice, he hoped. Of course Alex hadn't seen what he thought he'd just seen. It was just the heat and the silence and the terrible strangeness of these murders getting to him.

He refocused on the girl's face, holding his breath.

Nothing happened.

Of course nothing happened, you idiot. It's just your imagination.

Alex had to go around to the other side of the circle to photograph the second girl's face because they'd been placed cheek-to-cheek. He noticed Christie scooping some of the viscera into a plastic bag and suppressed a little shudder.

Yeah, it's getting to you, he thought. He took a deep breath in and exhaled through his nose, an old trick to stop from throwing up at grisly crime scenes. There was no nausea at the moment—he just wanted his nerves to settle. Several flies dive-bombed his head, and he batted them away with an impatient hand.

Alex dropped to his knees and then his stomach and then set the camera against his face again. The short-haired blonde stared off into the distance.

He focused the lens, his finger hovering over the shutter, and her blue eyes jerked toward him and her mouth moved. "We aren't the only ones."

He'd been braced for something like this, he realized, despite his self-assurances that it was all in his head. Very carefully, he lowered the camera to the grass. He felt his heart slamming against his ribs, pushing into the ground beneath him.

Christie did not seem to have noticed anything this time around. For one wild moment Alex wondered if Christie also could hear the girls talking but was pretending not to.

But that was more ridiculous than dead girls speaking. Even the eminently steady Van Christie would react if voices emanated from his crime scene.

One more time, Alex thought, and lifted the camera to his face again.

He was prepared when the short-haired girl stared into the lens and said, "Find them. All the other girls, girls like us. Find them."

He depressed the shutter release, so Christie wouldn't think he was just staring into space, and waited a moment more. There weren't any more messages. The dead girls had said everything they were going to say.

Find them. All the other girls, girls like us.

Alex stood up, casually dusted off his pants, and put the lens back on the camera. The elaborate movements were a disguise, a deliberate trick to slow his racing pulse and his equally racing thoughts. "Never seen anything like this before."

Christie grunted. "Nobody has."

"Well, there was that case you had here last year—Joe diMucci?" Alex said.

Christie looked up at Alex, and his eyes clouded over for a minute, like he was reaching far back into his memory for a man called Joe diMucci.

Same as Miller, Alex thought. *You'd think they would remember a man who'd been found with his heart torn out more clearly.*

"Right," Christie finally said. "Lauren's dad."

There it was again. Not Karen's husband but Lauren's dad.

"Wasn't that like this?" Alex said. "I know it was before my time, but . . ."

"Nah, that was totally different," Christie said, placing the last of the samples carefully inside the case. "That was a drifter."

"A drifter," Alex said. "A drifter who just happened to kill a man and cut his heart out?"

"Must have been," Christie said. "It couldn't have been

anyone from Smiths Hollow. We don't have those kinds of people here."

His tone indicated that the subject was closed. Alex was astounded that the chief of police could so completely disregard a similar crime to the current one in a town with almost no crime. He was about to ask how Christie had come to that conclusion when he decided against it. Better not to show how interested he was. He could poke around on his own later.

"Well, I'm going to have to call the funeral home to collect the remains," Christie said.

"Dean Reynolds isn't a coroner," Alex said automatically, though of course Christie knew this.

The chief nodded. "He'll take what's left of them and keep them in cold storage until the state medical examiner can get here. In the meantime you head back to the station and see if there are any reports of missing girls from the surrounding area. These girls don't look familiar to me. I don't think they go to the high school."

"If they aren't from Smiths Hollow then they probably came here in a car. When I'm finished with the phone calls I'll take a drive around and see if there are any abandoned vehicles near the woods."

"Good idea," Christie said. "The sooner we can identify these girls, the better."

Alex thought he detected another message underneath

Christie's words. *The sooner we identify them, the sooner we can close the case and pretend this never happened.*

He wondered why he was so sure Christie was thinking that, or why the chief of police seemed strangely disinterested.

Find them. All the other girls, girls like us.

Alex thought that maybe after he'd completed his assignments he might just spend some time looking through the old case files.

All the other girls.

What other girls? Alex wondered.

7

Lauren hadn't wanted to ride her bike after finding the bloody handprint on the seat, but she finally conceded that it would take longer to walk it home. Plus, if she walked it and someone else came along the road they might notice the blood.

She didn't have a tissue or anything to wipe it off, so she grabbed a handful of dirt and scrubbed it over the seat until the print was distorted. This left her hands both dirty and bloody, but she scrubbed them on her cutoffs as best she could and thought that it just looked like mud.

Her mother would no doubt complain about the stains on her shorts, but then her mother complained about every little thing Lauren did, so what else was new?

She sat carefully on the bike seat and tried not to think about what was on her hands and under the back pockets of her shorts. It was harder to put away the vision—for that was what it was—of the girls being slaughtered.

Slaughtered by a monster, Lauren thought. *But a monster with human hands.*

It didn't really make sense, what she'd seen. And she would be inclined to dismiss it altogether if it weren't for the handprint.

The handprint muddled things even more, because it wasn't quite human, either.

That's it. Keep thinking about the handprint, because if you think about the handprint you don't have to think about the girls.

Lauren didn't want to think about the girls. The headache was mostly gone but there was a lingering feeling behind her eyes, almost like a bruise.

There was more traffic on the road than earlier. Lauren had gone out right after lunch to meet Miranda, and she suspected that most people were still indoors eating their midday meal at that time. Now they were out running their afternoon errands, picking up library books and groceries, taking their kids to baseball practice. More than one car horn sounded as it went by and Lauren always waved, even if she didn't recognize the person behind the wheel. It was important to act normal, to act like she was just on her way home from an outing with Miranda.

Thinking of her friend made Lauren glad that Miranda wasn't with her when she entered the woods. Miranda would have been grossed out by Lauren's puking, freaked out by Lauren's headache and subsequent rolling on the ground, and completely hysterical about the handprint on Lauren's bike. So it was probably a good thing that Lauren had slipped out of the Dream Machine on her own.

And if Miranda was angry with Lauren and didn't call for a while . . . well, Lauren was okay with that. She hadn't seen the fascination of Tad, and didn't want to spend more of her precious summer afternoons watching him show off at the arcade.

What if Miranda never calls, though? What if she's so mad she doesn't talk to you again?

That, Lauren thought, would probably make her sad, because Miranda had been her friend for a long time. But then she realized that this was unlikely to happen. Once Miranda moved on from Tad she would want someone to talk to again, and of course she would call old reliable Lauren.

But she wouldn't sit around waiting for Miranda, she decided. She would do her own thing.

What is your own thing? a little voice in the back of her head whispered. *Everything you do, everything you've ever done, has been with Miranda.*

"I'll find a thing," Lauren said.

She turned onto her own street, which ended in a cul-de-sac farther down. Lauren's house was the third one on the right, and as she skidded to a stop in her driveway she saw a Smiths Hollow police cruiser approaching the intersection.

She waved at Officer Miller and Officer Hendricks, who

was driving. Lauren liked Officer Hendricks, who was young and had a nice smile and brown eyes with laugh lines around them. If he saw her on the road riding her bike he would always slow the cruiser and roll down the window and ask how she was doing.

Lauren thought that maybe Officer Hendricks really cared that her dad was dead and was investigating on his own and that whenever he asked how she was it was like he was sending her a secret signal, to let her know not to give up and that he was going to fix everything and catch her dad's murderer.

But this time Officer Hendricks didn't stop and roll down the window. He didn't even seem to notice that Lauren was there, even though she was standing in the sun. The car went by Lauren much faster than it normally would on a residential street, and Lauren suddenly remembered the cruisers screaming down Main Street earlier.

She peered down toward the cul-de-sac. The other cruiser and the chief's car were parked at Mrs. Schneider's house, across from the Lopez place. Lauren didn't like Mrs. Schneider—she always yelled at Lauren and the other kids who played stickball or soccer in the street because they made an "unearthly noise."

Maybe something happened to her. Good. At least it's not anyone I like.

She wheeled the bike around to the back of the house. At first she thought she'd just rinse off the seat with the hose but then decided this would draw attention to the very thing she didn't want anyone to remark upon. Lauren leaned the bike against the siding and climbed the back porch steps.

Like a lot of the houses in the neighborhood, the back porch opened into the kitchen. Her brother David sat at the round white kitchen table with a He-Man coloring book and an old cigar box stuffed with crayons—some new, but most of them old and broken with partially peeled labels.

David was carefully filling in Skeletor's costume with a bright blue. He wasn't like other kids his age, who considered the lines obstacles to their true artistic vision. He always stayed inside the lines, shading every character just so.

"Where's Mom?" Lauren asked as she pulled open the screen door and crossed to the sink.

"Cleaning the upstairs bathroom," David said. "She said you're not going to get your allowance this week if you forget again."

Lauren had meant to clean it after lunch. She really had. But then Miranda called and she forgot all about it.

"If she had just waited for me to come home I would have cleaned it," Lauren said, irritated.

It was like her mom did these things just to make her feel stupid, or like she was looking for an excuse to yell at her daughter.

Lauren opened the cabinet under the sink and took out a yellow plastic bucket, a big blue sponge, and the dish detergent. The bottle was nearly finished, but she was only going to use a little bit.

She squirted some detergent in the bucket and then ran the hot water on top of it.

"Whatcha doing?" David asked.

"Going to give my bike a car wash," Lauren said, shutting off the water and taking the bucket out of the sink.

"I want to help," he said, closing his coloring book and jumping off the chair.

"Better check that it's okay with Mom," Lauren said, thinking fast. If David went upstairs she could scrub off the seat without him seeing the blood and dirt encrusted there. "You might get wet."

"Okeh," he said.

She smiled as he ran down the hall to the stairs. He was pretty articulate for a little kid, but he always said "Okeh" instead of "Okay," and had since he started talking.

David stood at the bottom of the stairs and yelled up. "Mom!"

He wasn't allowed to climb the stairs without Lauren or Mom around, and since Mom probably wouldn't hear him the first time Lauren figured she had a few minutes. She hurried outside with the bucket, ignoring the few slops of water that splashed over the side and onto the kitchen floor. She would mop them up when she was done, but for now she needed to get that seat clean.

A few minutes later David pushed the screen door open and let it slam shut behind him, another habit that drove their mother crazy.

"Mom says I can help," he said.

Lauren had already scrubbed the seat and started on the body of the bike. "What are you going to use, your fingers?"

David frowned. "I don't have a sponge."

"Go and see if there's an extra one under the cabinet," Lauren said. She was pretty sure she'd seen one there—a bright pink one still wrapped in store plastic.

"Okeh," David said, and went back inside.

Lauren examined the bike seat in the dappled sun-and-shadow cast by the oak tree in their backyard. The seat was still wet, so she couldn't be one hundred percent certain, but she was pretty sure all the blood was gone. She scrubbed at it one more time with the soapy sponge just to make sure.

Then she heard a squeak, like the rubber sole of a sneaker slipping, and then a crash followed by a cry from David.

The water. She dropped the sponge in the bucket.

David was sitting up, rubbing the back of his head, when Lauren threw open the back door. He wasn't generally a crying child, but a few tears had gathered in the corners of his eyes, so he must have bumped his head pretty hard.

"Hey, bud, are you okay?" Lauren said, kneeling on the floor and gathering him up. She sat back on her haunches and put him in her lap.

"Bunked my head," he said.

"Bumped," Lauren said, smiling. "Or bonked, but not both at the same time. Can I check it?"

He nodded, swiping the tears from his face. There were no fresh ones, so Lauren figured he was probably fine. She carefully touched the back of his skull. There was a tiny little bump there, barely noticeable.

"Want some ice for it?" she asked.

David wrinkled his nose, like he was thinking about it. Then he shook his head.

"It's just a little bunk," he said.

"Bump," she said, and kissed his cheek. "How about a Popsicle?"

"We don't have any," David said. He usually knew better than Lauren did what was in the house, because he went shopping with their mom.

"I'll get you one when the ice cream truck comes around later," Lauren said. "With my money, okay? Because it was my fault you fell down."

"Okeh," David said. "But the ice cream truck might not come today."

"Why not?" Lauren asked. "He comes every day once school is out."

There were a lot of kids on their street, and the cul-de-sac was a safe place for him to park and deal with the packs of children that mobbed the truck the second they heard the opening bars of "The Entertainer."

"He might not come today because of the dead girls," David said.

Two girls walking, hand in hand.

"What girls, David?" Lauren said. She tried very hard to keep her voice calm and even. How could David know about the girls she'd seen in her vision?

"The dead girls in Mrs. Schneider's backyard," he said matter-of-factly. He looked up at Lauren's face. "There was a lot of blood. Did you see them, Lauren?"

"David, did you—"

Just then Karen materialized in the doorway—or at least, it seemed that way to Lauren. Their stairs were really squeaky so normally everyone could hear everybody else going up and down the stairs. It was impossible to sneak downstairs in the middle of the night for a snack without her mother finding out. Lauren was so shocked by David's words that she hadn't heard Mom at all.

Karen looked sweaty and irritated. "What happened?"

"I slipped and bunked my head," David said.

Karen's eagle eye immediately located the drops of water on the floor. "Did you slip on the water?"

"Yes, and it's my fault, I dripped it on the floor," Lauren said. "I'll clean it up now."

Lauren put David on his feet and gave him a little wink and mouthed, *Popsicles later.*

"You should have cleaned it up in the first place," Karen said. "How can you be so irresponsible, Lauren? He could have been seriously hurt. He could have gotten a concussion."

"Mom, he's not going to get a concussion from slipping on the kitchen floor," Lauren said, rolling her eyes. She reached for the roll of paper towels and Karen slapped her hand away.

"Use a kitchen towel, not a paper towel. What do you think we are, made of money?" Karen said. She spotted the wrapped sponge that had flown out of David's hand when he slipped. "And don't use that sponge on your dirty bike. It's brand-new. Use an old one."

"That one was for me, Mommy," David said. "So I could help."

"Did your sister tell you to get it?" Karen asked.

David looked uncertainly from Lauren, who'd grabbed an old kitchen towel to wipe the floor, to Karen. Lauren could tell he didn't want to get his sister in trouble.

"Yes," Lauren said, kneeling down to mop up the water. It was always like this with her mom—nag, nag, nag, complain, complain, complain. Whatever Lauren did it was the wrong thing, even when she tried to do the right thing.

"Lauren, I keep trying to explain to you that we can't afford to waste what we buy, and you're going to use up a brand-new sponge on your bike and then it will have to go in the trash after that."

"Okay, I won't," Lauren said. She was trying really hard

not to yell back at her mom, who seemed like she wanted to pick a fight.

If Lauren yelled, then she would get punished—grounded, or lose her television privileges or that week's allowance, or whatever else Karen thought was fair at the moment (though it never was fair—the punishment never seemed to fit the crime, in Lauren's opinion). She hung the towel on the rack near the sink so that it would dry.

"Don't hang that there, it's dirty from the floor," Karen said. "Put it in the laundry room with the other dirty towels."

"Okay," Lauren said. She started for the laundry room, which was just off the kitchen.

"What happened to your shorts?" Karen said. "They're covered in mud."

"I know," Lauren said, rolling her eyes when she was sure Karen couldn't see her. "My bike got muddy, too, which is why I was cleaning it."

"You should have taken your shorts off first and put them in to soak. Those stains might not come out now."

"Don't you think I should finish washing the bike first?" Lauren said. "I'll probably get dirt on me from that and I don't want to mess up a clean pair of shorts."

"Don't use that tone with me, young lady," Karen said.

Mom always said that when Lauren was right but she didn't want to admit it. Lauren tossed the towel in the pile stacked in front of the washing machine and returned to the kitchen.

"Did you put the towels in the washer?" Karen asked.

Lauren stopped. "No. You didn't tell me to."

"Do I really have to tell you to help out? Oh, yes, I forgot. I do. I just finished doing your daily chore upstairs."

Lauren opened her mouth, then snapped it shut.

I am not going to argue, I am not going to argue, I am not going to argue.

"I'm going to go and finish washing my bike," she said, and went outside.

Her mom probably wouldn't follow her and continue to harangue, because she was always worried about what the neighbors would think. Lauren could have told her that the neighbors could hear her shouting anyway, especially with the windows open. And all the windows were open, because they only had two air conditioners and Mom said they couldn't afford the extra cost on the electric bill. Mom flipped out whenever Lauren left the window fan in her room on if she wasn't actually in there.

"Don't waste a lot of water rinsing it off," Karen called after her. "Our water bill is high enough—"

"—as it is," Lauren finished, but under her breath so Karen couldn't hear.

"No, David, you stay here," Karen said. "I want to look at the back of your head."

David's response drifted out through the screen door. "But, Mommy, I want to help Lauren."

"You both don't need to get dirty," Karen said. "I have enough laundry to do."

Lauren crouched down by the bike, soaping the tires. Had Mom been like this before Dad died? Sometimes, Lauren admitted, although it had mostly been directed at Dad. She remembered Mom complaining about Dad's greasy coveralls and the way he left dirty coffee cups in the sink and used towels on the floor of the bathroom.

And yeah, Lauren thought, *it wasn't very nice of him to do that.*

It was thoughtless, but Lauren had never assumed there was any malice behind it. Her dad had just been forgetful, easily distracted. Mom always acted like he did it on purpose just to piss her off.

A trickle of sweat ran down her spine, and suddenly she remembered what had happened before the woods and the vision and the blood. She'd thrown up behind Frank's Deli, and Jake Hanson had brought her a cup of water.

And put his hand on her back. She could almost feel it there still, like the touch of a ghost.

She felt her face flush. What was she doing thinking about Jake Hanson? He'd been nice to her for a minute, that was all. It wasn't anything special. Besides, he was too old for her. Like, way too old. He wouldn't think a skinny kid like her was cool.

For half a second she thought about calling Miranda, asking

her what she thought. Then she remembered how dismissive Miranda had been, even though Jake was both older and more attractive than Tad. Jake, at least, wasn't so wrapped up in his stupid self that he didn't notice other people.

And he'd touched her, and been kind to her. She wondered if he would be the same if they met again.

8

Miranda had already decided that she was going to lose her virginity with Tad. It was such a weird way of thinking of it, she thought—*losing* her virginity. Like she was going to accidentally leave it somewhere.

She'd heard a lot of girls her age say they were "saving" it for "someone special," but Miranda saw her hymen as a burden that she wanted to be rid of as soon as possible.

Everyone knew that older guys only dated girls who put out, and Miranda was not going to waste her time with some loser freshman. She wanted a junior or a senior, somebody with a car who could take her places that weren't in Smiths Hollow.

After the Dream Machine, Tad and Billy had decided to head over to the pizzeria where they both worked, because they could get discounted slices even when they weren't on shift.

"You want to come?" Tad asked.

"Whatever," Miranda said. No point in making it seem too obvious that she wanted to stay with him for the rest of the day. If she played her cards right she could just slide along with him until dark. She wasn't going to give it up to him today, but she definitely wanted to get him thinking dirty thoughts about her, and that meant a trip to Make-Out Field in his Camaro.

Her parents never noticed if she came home late, and if they did, she could just say she was with Lauren. They never checked to see if she was lying.

The only hiccup in this plan was Billy. Lauren's job had been to take care of Billy, but she'd snuck off at some point during the day. Not that Lauren was super-hot—especially in her kiddie clothes, like she had on today, but her presence would have deterred the Third Wheel situation.

Now Miranda was stuck, tagging along after two older boys, when what she really wanted was for Billy to realize that he wasn't needed and to go home. Billy was the one who was the Third Wheel.

When they got to the pizzeria, Tad asked her what she wanted. "It's half price for me. Employee discount."

Miranda was really hungry and the pizza smelled so good, but she didn't want him to think she was a pig so she said, "I'm not hungry. I'll take a Coke, though."

The sugar and the bubbles in the Coke would make her feel full, and she wouldn't think about how good the pizza looked. She'd read in *Seventeen* about the pitfalls of eating in front of boys. Tad would not think of her as sexy if he spent twenty minutes watching her stuff her face with junk food.

He shrugged and ordered two pepperoni slices for himself and two Cokes. When the slices came Miranda actually felt her mouth water. She didn't even know that was a real thing that could happen. She thought it was only something authors said in books.

Tad slid into a booth and Miranda slid in next to him because Billy was still ordering his food and this was her best chance.

She didn't sit too close to him at first, because he seemed serious about his food and she didn't want to get in his way. Guys got cranky if they were hungry. Even her dad, who almost never raised his voice for anything, was crabby if dinner was late to the table. And Miranda did not want Tad to be cranky with her. She wanted him to be in a very good mood.

"Hey, what happened to your friend?" Tad asked through a mouthful of pizza.

"She had to go home," Miranda said, shrugging. She was going to blister Lauren's ears tomorrow on the phone for wandering off without saying anything.

"Too bad," Tad said. "She was kinda cute, although she seems young."

"She's six months younger than me," Miranda said, wriggling in her seat a little so her breasts would bounce and jiggle. "But she's still a little immature."

Tad's eyes had locked onto the motion of her chest like she was a hypnotist with a swinging watch. "Yeah, you look a lot older."

Miranda gave him a slow smile and wriggled a little closer so her right breast brushed against his left arm. "Want to share a bite of that pizza with me?"

Tad lifted the slice, seemingly mesmerized. She took a tiny mouse bite off the end, nothing that would make her masticate like a cow. The explosion of salt and fat on her tongue almost made her moan aloud and she felt her stomach rumble, but she ruthlessly pushed aside her hunger. If she got up for food now she might lose him.

Miranda carefully chewed the little piece of pizza, darting her tongue out to lick her lips. Tad followed the motion, exhaling a little breath, and she knew he had a boner because he shifted in his seat like he was trying to get comfortable. Then she picked up her Coke and wrapped her mouth around the straw in the kind of manner that would only suggest one thought.

She didn't really care if she had to give him a blow job or not. She really liked the idea of riding to school in Tad's Camaro, maybe passing Lauren pedaling along on her lame ten-speed.

Well, Miranda had given Lauren a chance to get in on the action. Billy didn't have a Camaro, but he did have his own car and he could have driven Lauren to school in it if she'd played along.

Miranda was on the verge of upping the stakes—she thought she could get away with feeling Tad's crotch under the table; there was no way he would miss the message then and it might even hurry things along—when Billy slid into the seat across the booth from them.

Tad immediately sat up straight, ignoring Miranda. She put her Coke back on the table with more force than she meant to. Guys didn't like girls who acted pouty, but fortunately Tad didn't seem to have noticed.

"Hey, guess what R.J. just told me?" He didn't wait for Tad or Miranda to ask but continued on in a rush of words. "Some old lady on Maple Street found two dead bodies in her backyard today! I bet that was why those cops were speeding by earlier. Man, we totally should have followed them. We might have seen the bodies."

"Damn," Tad said, pounding his fist on the table. "That would have been awesome."

"What old lady?" Miranda asked.

Billy looked at her like the furniture had spoken. He obviously hadn't noticed her sitting in the booth at all, which was ridiculous because he'd been standing right there when Tad asked her to come along with them.

He shrugged. "I don't know. Some old lady. Why do you care?"

"My friend lives on Maple Street," Miranda said. "If I knew which house you were talking about, we might be able to go over and look."

"Nothing left to see now," Billy said. "R.J. told me they took out the bodies in an Igloo cooler, so they must have been totally mutilated."

"Like a serial killer chopped them up or something?" Tad asked. "Cool."

Miranda could see her planned evening slipping away. Tad was no longer thinking about Miranda's breasts or Miranda's mouth. He was thinking about the dead bodies.

"Did R.J. say who was chopped up?" Miranda asked.

Billy stuffed half a slice of pizza in his mouth and chewed. "Some girls. Nobody knew who they were."

"Maybe they're from Silver Lake?" Miranda asked. Silver Lake was the next town over, where they had a mall and an actual air-conditioned movie theater with four screens instead of nothing but a lame drive-in.

The thought of the movie theater gave Miranda an idea. "Hey, you want to go to a movie?"

"Nothing playing here except that kiddie movie and the one about the old people," Tad said.

"Not here," Miranda said. "Silver Lake. I think *Rambo* is still there."

"I saw it already," Billy said.

"I haven't," Tad said. "I had to work the night you and Owen and R.J. went."

The memory seemed to annoy him. *Good*, Miranda thought. *Maybe he'll get pissed enough about it to leave Billy behind.*

She scooted closer to Tad and pressed against the side of his body, reminding him of her earlier promise. "I haven't seen it yet, either."

Tad put his arm around her, and it thrilled her because she knew that she'd won. Billy frowned at them as she snuggled in close.

"Yeah, babe. Let's go to the movies," Tad said as her hand slid across his lap.

9

Richard Touhy III was the mayor of Smiths Hollow, like his father Richard before him and *his* father Richard before *him*. In fact, Richard Touhy III could trace an unbroken line of mayors named Touhy all the way back to the first mayor of Smiths Hollow, a man appointed by the Chicago baron who'd either saved the town from ruin or built it from the ground up, depending on who you talked to.

At the moment he very much wished that his father and his father before him had worked at the canned chili factory like everyone else in town. It would be a blessing to worry about nothing more complicated than the mortgage and his union dues and whether his wife was boffing the postman.

He was pretty certain, as a matter of fact, that his wife, Crystal, was boffing someone while he sat in his office every day from nine to five and shook hands with concerned citizens and discussed such stimulating topics as filling potholes and building a community center out at the place the local teens called Make-Out Field.

While Richard had these illuminating conversations Crystal was getting boned by someone, maybe more than one someone, and he knew this because she was always freshly showered when he came home. She claimed it was because she always did her Jane Fonda workout tape in the afternoon, but Richard was pretty sure her workouts didn't involve leg lifts—at least, not Jane Fonda's kind of leg lifts. Aerobics didn't make you glow, and Crystal always had this radiant-lit-from-within look that told Richard more clearly than any love note that his wife was getting it from someone else.

With some effort, Touhy redirected his attention to the phone that he held at his ear. Van Christie's calm voice was at the other end, speaking terrible words about terrible things in a tone that implied his heart rate hadn't yet been raised above sixty-five beats per minute.

Why is the man always so calm? Touhy wondered. He'd never even seen Van Christie's forehead wrinkle in worry.

There was a sudden silence, and Touhy realized it was his turn to talk. "So what are you doing to identify the girls?"

"Nobody seems to think they're local—that is, from Smiths Hollow. We've flagged the departments in the surrounding towns, asking if anybody has reported two girls missing. Lopez seems to think that they came here in a car, so he's out looking for abandoned vehicles."

"If they came from Silver Lake they could have come on bicycles," Touhy pointed out. "It's not that far away."

"If we don't find any abandoned vehicles we'll start looking into other possibilities," Christie said. Touhy could almost hear the other man's shrug.

It was easy for Christie to shrug. Christie wasn't the one responsible for the entire town's well-being.

"I think it's important to keep this out of the public eye as much as possible," Touhy said. "We don't want people to think it's not safe for their girls to be out, especially with the fair coming to town."

The appearance of the traveling fair was something that Touhy had been coordinating for the last three months.

First he'd had to find a suitable place in town for the fair to set up. The huge open field of prairie grass that the high school kids called Make-Out Field had been selected for this. This pleased many of the parents who thought that Touhy wasn't doing enough to deter their children from the sins of the flesh. Touhy didn't bother explaining that teenagers would just find another place to pursue those sins. He imagined that a lot of local girls were going to find their dates' hands up their shirts while they were on top of the Ferris wheel once the traveling fair arrived.

The grass was going to be cleared today, as close to the fair's arrival as possible. Prairie grass would shoot up in the presence of even a little rain, so it was important that the field not get cleared too soon.

Then Touhy had convinced the five members of the town council to agree to allow the fair to set up in the first place. Many of them were concerned that the fair would encourage crime, from public drunkenness to pickpocketing to prostitution.

Touhy had soothed them down with promises that the fair would bring folks from neighboring towns to spend their money, and that meant spending their money not just on midway rides and cotton candy but also on local businesses. Even if that didn't happen, the town was going to make a profit from renting the field. Free money, he'd told them, for an otherwise fallow and useless stretch of land. It was incredible, the way the promise of cash made all those worries disappear.

"I think everything will be cleared up by the time the fair comes around," Christie said.

"I hope so," Touhy said, and the underlying message was *It had better be.*

He rang off with Christie, who promised to keep him updated, and scrubbed his face with both hands.

It was a problem that the dead girls came from out of town. It was a problem because it wasn't supposed to happen. Girls from Smiths Hollow, yes, but not out-of-town girls. And certainly not anyone male. When Joe diMucci was found in the woods last winter, Touhy had worried.

He'd worried because it wasn't Joe that was supposed to be under that tree. It was supposed to be his daughter, Lauren.

Touhy had spent a couple of anxious months after that, wondering if the card house that comprised the town's foundation was going to collapse. He monitored the financial health of the chili factory—the primary employer of Smiths Hollow—like he was monitoring his own blood pressure. He kept a watchful eye on Main Street for *Going Out of Business* signs.

If Touhy was lucky, the thought of these two dead girls would pass out of the town's collective memory, just like the memory of the other girls always did.

It was only Richard Touhy III, and his father before him, and his father before *him*, and so on down the family tree, who remembered. That was the burden of the mayor, the keeper of the Secret, the one who made certain it was enforced.

Well, there was one other person who seemed to know the Secret, but she never told anyone and she couldn't do anything about it anyway.

Ten years earlier Touhy had seen the film *Jaws* at the drive-in with Crystal. This was before she took up her afternoon escapades (*but maybe they weren't really escapades, maybe she was just doing her aerobics tape like she said she was*) and seemed to still enjoy spending time with him. He'd certainly enjoyed the way she snuggled closer every time the maniac shark ate up another clueless swimmer.

But the thing that really struck him in that movie was the mayor. Everyone in town acted like the mayor was just heartless, letting people go swimming when there was a giant shark gobbling up anyone that strayed into its path. But Touhy understood that character. The mayor of Amity was just trying to make sure his people survived. He wasn't heartless. He was thinking about the greater good, and the greater good meant a few swimmers might end up digesting in a monster's belly for the sake of the rest of the town.

Touhy had taken the mayor's job from his father just two years prior to that night at the drive-in, and the deaths of two girls since he took office had been weighing heavily on him.

Once he saw that film he realized that he should shed some of that burden. After all, it wasn't as if *he* were the one killing those girls. And he'd certainly put a stop to it if he thought such a thing *could* be done.

If he didn't perform his duty, everyone in town might be killed.

Touhy shuddered, imagining every man, woman, and child in Smiths Hollow massacred. He could almost see the scene—baffled FBI agents (because of course the FBI would be called in) entering house after house, only to find the occupants dead—no survivors of the most mysterious mass murder in American history.

That was *not* how Touhy wanted the general public to think of Smiths Hollow. He wanted his town to be a shining beacon of success and productivity in a region mostly known for failure. He wanted other municipalities to gaze at his town with jealousy and aspiration.

There had been the failure with the mall—Touhy could admit that; it had been shortsighted of him to let Silver Lake outbid him with better tax breaks. He'd been thinking of Main Street, about protecting the businesses there that would otherwise face competition from large national chains. He still thought he'd done right in that respect, but the construction of the mall had brought jobs and growth to Silver Lake that were unprecedented. If he'd been more forward-thinking he might have been able to save Main Street *and* get the mall.

And of course, the addition of the mall would have meant more residents. More residents meant more girls.

This was, Touhy knew, a very hard way to look at it, but it was still true. Once someone moved to Smiths Hollow, they never left. Or rather, they might try to leave—go away to college or the military, live for a few years in Chicago or some other city—but they always returned.

Which meant there was always blood to feed the beast.

If he thought about it, Touhy was really doing a public service.

Anyway, after a while people forgot about the girls—even their families. The memory of the mutilated body found under the tree would fade away, to be replaced by a conviction that their daughter had died in a car accident or some such thing. Or the memory of their child would fade away altogether, as if she had never existed.

Touhy wondered if this was how it had always been—if the memory of the girls' deaths would fade and morph into something else—or if there had been a time when the people of the town had known, too. Maybe the knowledge had dwindled only to the line of Touhy as time passed.

But then there had been Joe diMucci. It was supposed to be Lauren—Touhy had drawn the name from the lottery as he did every year—and he had fully expected to hear the report of her death the next day. When he heard that Joe had been found under the tree, his heart removed from his chest, he'd panicked.

Would nobody be safe? And after that, would it also mean that the factory would close, that businesses would collapse, that the town would come to ruin?

None of those tragedies had occurred, and after a while Touhy decided they were safe. He still didn't understand how Joe had ended up in the woods instead of Lauren, though.

He drew the name, and that seemed to be enough—usually. The next day the remains would be found and Touhy could pretend it wasn't going to happen for another year, like the way people thought of their annual dental cleaning. Out of sight, out of mind—at least until that circled date appeared at the turn of the calendar.

But now there were these girls, these mystery girls. Their names hadn't been drawn from a lot. They weren't from Smiths Hollow. They weren't supposed to die in the woods. Which meant that if complete ruin hadn't arrived before this, it only meant that it was keeping its own time.

Not on my watch, Touhy thought. If he had to sacrifice every girl in town to maintain the status quo, he would do it.

There were always more girls.

Touhy glanced at this watch. Perhaps no one would notice if he slipped out for a little coffee break.

Maybe he would go home and have a sandwich with his loving wife. He had a sudden, powerful need to know just who Crystal was doing aerobics with every afternoon.

10

Karen watched Lauren scrubbing the glass dish that had held the baked chicken legs they'd eaten for dinner. She felt the criticism rise up in her throat—Lauren wasn't cleaning the corners very well, and if you didn't get that off, there was buildup—but she swallowed it down again. Lauren was barely speaking to her as it was, after Karen's outburst that afternoon.

The thing was, Karen *knew* when she was being ridiculous. She knew that half of what she said to Lauren was just nitpicking, that Lauren was basically a good kid and that every time Karen gave her a hard time for no particular reason, she was driving her daughter further and further away.

But she would see Lauren doing something that was just a little bit off, or thoughtless—like leaving the water on the floor earlier—and rage would fly up, totally unconnected to the severity (or lack thereof) of the crime. And even as she was shouting she could see herself from outside her body, see how unreasonable she appeared and how helpless she was to do anything about it.

Karen resolutely turned away from the sink and pulled the tablecloth off the table, taking it outside to shake out the crumbs. She didn't need to pick another fight with Lauren—and she could be honest enough with herself to admit that it *was* picking a fight. She'd been feeling uneasy ever since Sofia Lopez called and told her that she'd found Mrs. Schneider screaming her head off in her backyard because two girls had been mutilated and left there.

All day long Karen had been trying to forget that . . . well, she didn't know what it was that had happened to David on the sidewalk. A trance? It had seemed, at the moment that it happened, like he was sleepwalking or having some kind of waking nightmare. And when it was over he had smiled up at her and said, "Ice cream?"

Karen hadn't known what to do. If David didn't remember what he'd said, there was no reason to remind him—why would she remind a four-year-old that he'd just been speaking in tongues about blood? So she bought him a strawberry ice cream cone and a vanilla one for herself but hadn't tasted a bite of it.

Then Sofia called and told her what happened on the block earlier in the day and Karen froze in shock, unable to respond. Not because of the girls, though that was shocking enough. But because David had known, and David should not have known.

"Karen? Are you still there?" Sofia asked.

"Yeah," Karen said. "I'm still here. I was just stunned."

"If you saw it you would have been even more stunned. I don't know how I didn't lose my breakfast all over the Old Bigot's grass. Karen, it was hideous."

Karen didn't ask for details. She didn't really want to know any and besides, Sofia probably didn't want the kids to hear the gory details.

I bet David would know if I asked him, Karen thought as she carried the tablecloth back inside. Not that she would ask him.

Lauren had finished washing the dishes and escaped the kitchen while Karen was outside woolgathering. She'd left everything to air-dry in the rack instead of toweling it off and putting it away, and Karen gritted her teeth before she shouted her daughter's name.

She could hear the music blasting from Lauren's room upstairs, anyway—Lauren was unlikely to hear her mother screaming while Prince's "When Doves Cry" was turned all the way up. Karen had heard the song more times than she cared to count since *Purple Rain* was released, and she was ready for Lauren to move on to a new obsession.

Karen made a half pot of decaf coffee—she couldn't

handle caffeine at night anymore. She couldn't even have a can of Tab after three p.m. or else she'd be staring at the ceiling, listening to the house settle while everyone else slept.

And I might be up tonight anyway, because I think my child had some kind of psychic vision. Though that's absurd.

How else, though, could David have known about the bodies and Mrs. Schneider? It had to be a psychic experience.

She shook her head. Just thinking the words "psychic experience" made her feel like an idiot. Psychic kids were something from a Stephen King book, like that one that got made into a movie with Drew Barrymore last year. Karen tried to remember what it was called—something about fire? The little girl could start fire with her mind? But David wasn't like that. That was the kind of thing that only happened in fiction.

For half a second she wished that Joe were there, so she could talk to somebody about it. Somebody who wouldn't tell everyone in the neighborhood.

Then she remembered that Joe had been useless at talking, would have dismissed her fears.

She also remembered that the reason why Joe wasn't there was that he'd gone out to meet his lover and gotten killed instead.

He'd thought Karen didn't know about the other woman, but she had. She was about twenty times smarter than him to begin with, and he hadn't tried very hard to hide what he was doing. He stopped coming home for lunch, asking Karen to pack something for him or saying he'd eat out instead. There were sudden work emergencies that kept him late at night—people who just had to have their car fixed by the next day. And whenever she asked him about these emergencies his eyes would slide away and he'd say she didn't know the person who brought the car into the shop.

She didn't mind, in a certain sense. Once Joe started getting sex elsewhere he stopped badgering her for it. It had been a long time since she'd wanted to have sex with him. Most of the time she just went along with it so he would leave her alone and she could go to sleep.

Every time she looked at him she'd think of all the little things that he did—leaving his shit around for her to clean up, ignoring her when she was talking, or worse, talking over her and dismissing whatever she was concerned about. It was hard to feel romantically interested in someone who thought it was stupid when she got annoyed that he left a dirty glass in the sink.

And okay, she could admit to some degree that it was stupid. It was just a little thing. But little things added up. They could just have easily added up in the other direction, but Joe wasn't interested in changing. Maybe if she felt less like he was just another child she had to pick up after, they might have worked things out. They'd never had a chance to find out.

If Joe had lived she might have become a divorcée instead of a widow.

This, of course, was the real reason why Lauren and Karen were always fighting. It wasn't because Lauren was a teenage girl and her hormones were peaking and making her nuts—at least, that was only part of it.

The other part of it was that Karen was relieved Joe was dead, and Lauren could never forgive her for that. It wasn't anything Karen had said or done specifically. Lauren had managed to ferret it out on her own, even though Karen denied the accusation.

The only thing Karen *could* do was deny it, because you don't tell your daughter that you are glad her father is dead.

David was in the living room playing with Silly Putty. He liked to take the color comics page of the Sunday paper, spread Silly Putty all over his favorite panels, and then press it into the paper until the panel was transferred. Then he would show her the picture he'd impressed into the clay before rolling it up again and starting over with a different picture.

He was sprawled on the floor with the paper spread out before him so he could view all his choices at a glance. The plastic egg that the Silly Putty was stored in was on the coffee table, both halves neatly clipped together. David was the opposite of Lauren—he never left his things lying around for someone else to trip on or clean up.

Karen would have liked to take credit for this, but she

knew it was just in his nature—just like it was in Lauren's nature to leave her dirty socks on the floor wherever she happened to take them off. Like Joe.

Karen sat on the couch with a cup of coffee and watched her second child, and wondered.

"Look at this, Mommy!" David said, holding up a piece of putty with a panel from *Prince Valiant* pressed into it.

"Very good, sweetheart," Karen said, but she didn't really see it. All she saw was David, standing on the sidewalk, his eyes blank and far away and then coming back to look straight at Karen.

"It's Mrs. Schneider. She won't stop screaming. There's so much blood."

11

Miranda toyed with the French fries Tad had left on the table and swallowed the tears that she felt building in her throat. She was not going to cry in a public place, especially not with those bitches looking over at her every few minutes.

She didn't understand what had gone wrong. Tad ditched Billy at the pizza place, just like Miranda hoped, and when they got in the Camaro he'd kissed her and even did a quick grope of her breasts before grinning and starting the engine.

When they arrived at the mall they'd discovered that the next showing of *Rambo* wasn't for an hour, so they decided to walk around for a while. Tad had put his hand in the back pocket of Miranda's jeans while they did so and she did not object, letting him squeeze her ass whenever the impulse occurred to him. She could see his boner pushing at the front of his jeans and figured he wouldn't be able to keep his hands off her during the movie.

Then Tad had decided he was hungry again, so they went to the food court. He wanted French fries so he went to McDonald's, and Miranda decided that she needed something in her stomach before she passed out. The smells coming from the food court were making her insides twist up. She still didn't want to eat like a piggy in front of him, though, so she went to Orange Julius and got a drink and hoped the fruit would help her feel full.

Tad was already sitting at the table eating one of two Big Macs when she joined him. There was a large pile of fries and ketchup dumped onto the paper liner of the tray.

"Have a fry," he said.

"I'm good," she said, holding up her drink.

"Girls never eat, huh?" Tad said, shoving three fries in his mouth at once. "Guess that's how you keep your figure."

He looked her up and down and she leaned forward and put her elbows on the table, squeezing her breasts up with her arms. Tad nodded approvingly.

"You're pretty hot, babe," he said.

It was the second time he'd called her that, and Miranda had an odd feeling that it was because he'd forgotten her name. But that was ridiculous. They had talked on the phone, hadn't they?

"So you liked the first *Rambo* movie?" she asked.

"Yeah, Sylvester Stallone is awesome. His arms are huge in this one—did you see the poster? I wonder how much he lifts."

Miranda didn't bother pointing out that the poster he referred to was actually a painting. Besides, she'd seen other Stallone movies and knew his arms were pretty big.

Tad curled his own skinny bicep. "I got a set of free weights for my birthday. I'm going to get massive before the school year starts."

"Do you play sports?" Miranda asked, thinking he wanted to try out for football or something. Why else would he want to build big muscles?

"Nah, sports are for jocks," Tad said. "I just want to be big so that everyone will know they can't mess with me."

She didn't think really huge guys were attractive, but the important thing was what Tad liked, not her. Every article she'd read about catching a boyfriend had mentioned being interested and attentive—to ask questions that kept him talking and not spend too much time talking about herself.

And Miranda had done everything *exactly* right. She'd avoided eating in front of him. She kept the conversation on him and let him dictate where they went and what they did. She'd let him feel her up.

All of Miranda's plans were falling into place. Her virginity would be gone in three weeks, tops. Of course she wouldn't let him bang her on the first date. She had to string him along.

On the first day of freshman year she'd be riding shotgun in Tad's Camaro and Lauren would be sweaty from riding her bike to school like a little kid.

Then those three bitches had sat down across the food court from them. Miranda had noticed them buying food at the McDonald's a few rows behind Tad's seat. She'd noticed because all three wore tight jeans and tight neon-colored tank tops, although each one had a different color. They looked like they just came out of a Life Savers roll, Miranda thought.

Every one had teased bangs and a scarf in her hair like Madonna, and their wrists were covered in plastic bracelets.

Miranda noticed that their breasts were barely contained by the tank tops, and she thought maybe her plan of wearing the button-down shirt had been too subtle. Her thought was that Tad would look at it and want to unbutton the buttons, but maybe she should have put the merchandise on display, as it were. Possibly she could slip into the bathroom before the movie and unbutton the top two buttons.

Then one of the neon Life Saver bitches had caught sight of them and waved and called, "Hey, Tad!" and she was pretty far away across the food court, so everyone turned to look and saw her boobs practically hanging out of her pink top.

Including Tad, who waved and jumped up to go talk to them without saying a word to Miranda.

Now it had been at least ten minutes since Tad went over there, and Miranda wondered when he would come back. He'd sat down at the table with the other three girls and seemed mesmerized by the jiggling of the pink girl's chest. If he didn't come back soon they would miss the movie and all of Miranda's plans would be for nothing.

She dabbed one of the French fries in ketchup and put it in her mouth without thinking. Then another, and another, until she realized half the container had gone into her little piggy belly.

At least Tad didn't see me, she thought, hastily wiping her lips and fingers with a napkin.

She sighed and checked her watch. Maybe she should just call her mom and ask her to come and pick her up. No, she decided, reconsidering. Janice (Miranda always called her "Janice" in her mind, though she didn't quite have the guts to do so to her face) would be on her second or third highball by now, and she'd probably wipe out in a flaming explosion between their house and the mall.

And Dad would give her a lecture about the evil that boys do, not knowing that Miranda knew all about that evil and wanted it inflicted on her as soon as possible.

"Hey, you look like you lost your best friend," a male voice said, and then He slid into the seat across from Miranda.

She looked up in surprise. "What are you doing here?"

He held up a bag from the Gap. "New pants. Speaking of best friends, where's Lauren?"

Of course He would ask about Lauren. Miranda shrugged. "At home, I guess. I came here with . . . someone else."

She was unable to keep her eyes from sliding left, in the

direction of Tad and the Neon Bitches.

"Ah," He said, following her gaze. "You can do better than him, a pretty girl like you."

Miranda sat up straighter. She'd never noticed before how He had such nice eyes. And he was older than Tad—an actual *adult*.

"Tell you what—let me give you a ride home," He said. "Maybe he'll show up tomorrow with flowers if you leave him here."

Miranda smiled. A ride home. Twenty minutes in the car to convince Him that she was just as grown-up as He was. It shouldn't be too hard. He'd already said she was pretty.

12

THURSDAY

Lauren didn't expect to hear from Miranda the next day at all. She assumed her friend would be so irritated at Lauren for ditching her at the Dream Machine that Miranda wouldn't call for at least a week. So she was surprised when the phone rang right after breakfast and Miranda's voice said, "Meet me by the old ghost tree."

"I can't," Lauren said, which was true. "Mom went shopping in Silver Lake and I'm watching David."

"Lame." Miranda huffed out an annoyed breath. "After lunch?"

"Probably," Lauren said, although she didn't particularly want to meet Miranda. She had no desire to get dragged off to the arcade again. "She should be back by then. Listen, we're not going to the Dream Machine, are we?"

"God, no," Miranda said. "Why would we hang out in a place like that with a bunch of kids?"

Lauren frowned at the phone. "But yesterday . . ."

"Yesterday I realized there's no reason for me to waste my time on a child like Tad," Miranda said loftily.

But you're a child, Lauren thought, though she didn't say so. Fifteen wasn't very grown-up, and Lauren could admit that to herself even if she would die before saying such a thing to her mother.

"I'll meet you at one," Miranda said, and hung up.

Lauren put the phone back in the cradle and stared at it, like Miranda could see her glaring. "What if I don't want to go?"

The only possible explanation for Miranda's sudden disdain of the Dream Machine was that Things Had Not Worked Out with Tad. Which meant Miranda had shifted her attention elsewhere. Which meant that she wanted Lauren to listen to rapturous descriptions of the virtues of Miranda's new target, and Lauren didn't want to.

She reached for the phone. "I'll call her back and tell her I don't want to go."

But her hand stopped before she even picked up the receiver. If she called Miranda back and said she didn't want to meet, then Miranda would want to know why, and if Lauren said why they'd probably get into a fight and Lauren had a feeling that any fight they had would mean the end of Miranda and Lauren. No more meeting at the ghost tree, no more best friends forever.

Though best friends forever doesn't seem very likely anymore, does it?

Lauren had thought—and she was a little ashamed of this—that they would just sort of drift away from each other when the school year started. There would be more kids to meet in high school, because Smiths Hollow was large enough to have three elementary schools (two public ones and a private Catholic school, though not many kids went there) and all those schools fed into the high school.

Miranda would have her own interests, which seemed to involve older boys and cars, and Lauren would have her own interests, and they would both float into their respective streams with no hurt feelings.

Telling Miranda she didn't want to meet up—that would lead to actual conflict. And Lauren didn't know if she wanted actual conflict. It made her a little ashamed, to realize she was such a coward that she couldn't even stand up for herself to a girl she'd known since she was small.

But then that was part of what bothered Lauren about Miranda lately, anyway—that she made plans and assumed Lauren would go along with them, that she didn't listen to Lauren's (admittedly feeble) protests. If Lauren actually tried to assert herself, Miranda would melt into the ground.

Like the Wicked Witch of the West in the old movie.

She could see Miranda being swallowed up, her fancy Jordache jeans and cheerleader-high ponytail disappearing while her voice feebly croaked, "I'm melting, I'm melting."

Swallowed up by darkness, Lauren thought, and then wondered where the thought had come from. She shivered, because it was full of malice, and she didn't think that malice was her own.

There's someone out in the woods.

In her woods, the woods that had always welcomed and comforted her. Someone had left a bloody handprint on her bike. Someone had killed two girls and left their pieces in Mrs. Schneider's backyard.

There was a lot of blood.

That was what David had said. Lauren was certain that their mom wouldn't have allowed David to investigate, and she'd scrupulously avoided talking about the incident in front of him. Mom had only mentioned it to Lauren in an undertone after dinner, adding, "I don't know any details, Lauren. I just know that the kids in the neighborhood will talk and I wanted you to be aware of the situation."

That "situation" had been the reason why Officer Hendricks drove by their house in the squad car yesterday, and probably even why he hadn't noticed Lauren standing in the driveway.

There would have been nothing left of those girls but bits, and that would make anybody freak out.

She had been trying hard not to freak out herself,

because the very fact that the dead girls existed somewhere outside the vision she had yesterday was something she was trying hard not to acknowledge. Did it mean she was psychic or something?

And what had she really seen? A monster? Or a man?

The memory had faded almost immediately after, leaving something like a weak afterimage, but it sort of looked like both. Like a man with a monster inside him, and monster claws. Or maybe it was a monster with a man inside him, and human hands.

All she knew for sure was that she couldn't talk to anybody about it. Miranda would scoff—if she let Lauren get a word in edgewise, that was—and her mother would probably make an appointment with a psychiatrist (all the while complaining about the extra expense).

"Except David knew about it," Lauren said.

"I knew about it?" David asked.

Lauren jumped and spun around, clutching her chest melodramatically. "Jeez, are you trying to give me a heart attack?"

David stood in the kitchen doorway holding his G.I. Joe figure. "Only old people have heart attacks."

"Nuh-uh. Anybody can have a heart attack. Except little kids like you," she amended. She didn't want David to start worrying about having a heart attack.

"What did I know about?" he asked.

Lauren stared at him blankly for a second, and then she remembered. "Oh. That."

She didn't know if she ought to talk about it with David. Mom might get annoyed, especially since she'd made such a point of not discussing it until David had gone to bed the night before.

Well, Mom was always annoyed with her anyway.

"How did you know about the girls who were killed in Mrs. Schneider's backyard?"

David's head tilted to one side, and his eyes seemed to go to a faraway place. "They weren't killed there. They were killed in the woods and put in the yard later."

"Yes, but how do you know that?" Lauren felt her heart beating faster, realized her hands were shaking.

David shrugged. "I heard it."

"You heard it?" *Surely he hadn't heard the actual murder take place, heard the girls screaming.* Mom never let David go into the woods. "Not for real."

He tapped the side of his head with his G.I. Joe figure. "No. In here."

Lauren remembered falling to the ground in the woods, rolling in the dirt and clutching her head. She remembered the pain of her vision, the terror of it, and gave David a horrified stare.

"You heard the girls dying?"

He pressed his mouth flat, like he was considering this.

"Uh-uh. Just Mrs. Schneider screaming and then I kind of knew why she was doing that, because of the blood."

Thank the lord for small favors, Lauren thought. It was something her mom always said, and it had never made much sense to her until that moment. She wouldn't have wished that vision on her worst enemy, much less on her little brother.

But why had he heard it in the first place? Why had she had a vision? Was there something wrong with them—with both of them?

"Did you tell Mom?" Lauren asked.

David nodded. "Yeah."

"And what happened?"

"She bought me ice cream."

"Did she say anything about it?"

"About what?" He fiddled with the G.I. Joe figure, clearly losing interest in the conversation.

"About the girls," Lauren said patiently.

David shook his head. "No, she just asked me what kind of ice cream I wanted."

Typical, Lauren thought. Their mom probably didn't want to think that anything was weird or wrong with David, so she would just pretend it didn't exist.

If Lauren's vision had occurred in her mother's vicinity, then Lauren would have gotten yelled at for rolling on the floor and making a fuss. And there definitely would not have been ice cream.

"Can we play checkers?" David asked.

"Sure, bud," Lauren said, but she wasn't thinking about board games. She was thinking about the girls in the woods.

Lauren went to the hall closet to take out the checkerboard, David trailing behind her like a pull-along toy. She had to stand on a stepladder to reach the shelf with the games on it. David waited patiently for her to hand the checkers set down to him.

"Want to play Candy Land, too?" she asked. It was easier if he decided while she was already standing on the stepladder.

"Okeh," David said. "He said they were sweet like candy."

Lauren had the second game pulled out partway from the pile, but David's words startled her so much that she yanked it too hard and it fell to the floor. The box burst open and cards and gingerbread men scattered all over the bottom of the closet.

"Lau-ren," David said, kneeling to pick up the pieces.

"David," Lauren said, climbing down and crouching next to him. She put her fingers under his chin so he would look up at her. "Who said that?"

"The monster that ate the girls," David said, calmly stacking the cards back inside the box. "He said they were sweet."

"I thought you didn't see what happened to them," Lauren said.

"I didn't," David said. "I just heard that, at the end."

"At the end? End of what?" Had David actually seen the

massacre and just not wanted to tell her so?

His eyes got that faraway look that meant he was thinking hard, or trying to remember. "At the end of the screaming."

She shouldn't be pushing him on this, she realized. If David's brain was trying to protect him by letting him forget the details, then she should let it. Lauren ruffled his hair, which was brown and straight and thick, and he jerked his head away.

"Don't," he said. It always annoyed him when she did that.

She did it again and he ran out of the closet and into the hall. "Can't catch me!" he shouted.

"Oh, yes I can!" she said, running after him, but very slowly so he could get away.

You should let him forget, she thought. *Even if you can't.*

David's laughter trailed behind him. Lauren pinned a smile to her face, but she couldn't stop thinking about what David had said.

He said they were sweet like candy.

Like candy.

The monster.

13

Alex Lopez sat at his desk and forced himself to think of the girls. Specifically, the girls' heads talking to him.

Because it was a very strange thing. He found that if he didn't think of that exact moment, didn't hear their voices and see their mouths moving, his brain would slide away from the memory of the crime scene.

Like it was trying to forget that it ever happened.

Like something was trying to make Alex forget it ever happened.

And when he mentioned the fruitless search that he'd done yesterday for the girls' car to Van Christie, it had taken the chief a minute to remember what Alex was even talking about.

"Oh, right," Christie said. "The mayor wants us to keep this as quiet as we can. He's worried about the summer fair."

"Of course he is," Alex said, but low enough that Christie didn't seem to notice.

Alex liked a lot of things about Smiths Hollow, but Mayor Touhy was not one of them. Most politicians had two faces, but Touhy's second face was made of sharkskin.

He decided to write down everything he remembered about the girls in the small notebook he carried in his pocket. He wasn't a detective, so he didn't carry it to make notes about cases. Mostly he used it to jot down things Sofia wanted him to pick up on the way home.

Alex tore out the pages in the front that had things like *Elmer's glue (Val school project)* and *napkins* and *don't forget oil change* written on them.

The notebook suddenly seemed full of possibility, all those blank pages waiting for his thoughts.

On the first page he wrote *THE GIRLS*, directly in the middle of the page in all caps, like it was a chapter title. As he wrote it he felt the pen wobble and he had to grip it hard to make sure the words actually got written down.

When he finished writing he half expected to see the words fade into the page and disappear. A bead of sweat trickled over his cheek and he wiped it away with his wrist.

Miller was sitting at his desk across from Alex. His feet were up and he was reading an issue of *Time* from the previous month with Madonna on the cover. Alex fully expected the cover of this magazine to end up hanging on the wall behind Miller, which was already papered with photographs of the singer torn from countless publications. The area behind Miller's head looked like the inside of a high school kid's locker.

Miller looked up as Alex wiped his face. "What are you doing?"

"Making some notes," Alex said.

"On what?" Miller asked.

"The dead girls," Alex said.

"What dead girls?" Miller asked.

"The ones in Mrs. Schneider's backyard yesterday? Don't you remember? You puked in the yard when you saw what was left of them."

As he said this, the scene from the day before grew sharper in his own memory, like speaking the words made the dead girls real.

"Oh, yeah," Miller said, and then went back to his magazine. He expressed no curiosity or interest in what Alex was doing at all.

There's something wrong here. It was the same as when he asked about Joe diMucci—a sense that the person he was speaking to had no memory of the incident, and that they had to dredge it up from the furthest reaches of their mind.

Even he was struggling to hold on to the details. Were there two girls, or one? Or three? His mouth felt dry. They were slipping away from him, and he couldn't let that happen. There were more girls than those two.

Two, he thought. *That's right. There were two.*

Yes, one with short blond hair and one with long brown braids. And they spoke to him.

They spoke to him and told him that there were more.

He'd been charged by the dead to find them.

He remembered now.

He wrote quickly then, put down everything from the moment he stepped into the yard right up until the girls delivered their message. His hand shook and the back of his uniform shirt grew damp but he wrote it all, all the details, even the ones that would make him sound crazy if he told someone else about them.

Nobody was going to read from this notebook but him, and he wasn't about to insult the memory of those dead girls by pretending that the vision of them speaking hadn't happened.

It was weird that it didn't bother him. Receiving messages from beheaded girls wasn't half as strange as the way everyone but Alex had already forgotten them. It was easier, somehow, to believe in ghosts than in collective memory loss.

There is something wrong with this town, Alex thought. Why hadn't he and Sofia noticed it before they bought the house here?

Alex knew why. Because they were so desperate to get their kids away from the city before something happened to them. Because they were exhausted from the constant hand-to-mouth struggle. Because they saw the house in the cul-de-sac and the smiling neighbors (*okay, all except one—Mrs. Schneider had only scowled at them from the start*) and the big yards and thought that Smiths Hollow was just perfect. And when Alex and his brother and sister-in-law all found jobs so easily it was just the cherry on the sundae. Why wouldn't they move as quickly as possible?

But girls got killed in Smiths Hollow. That was what the dead ones had told him.

Find them. All the other girls, girls like us.

At the bottom of the narrative about the crime scene he wrote, *Find the other girls.*

He didn't want to forget about the other girls.

The act of writing down what happened seemed to fix yesterday's event in his mind. It seemed more solid, less likely to slide away from him. That was good.

He stood and Miller looked up at him like a hopeful puppy. "Time for lunch?"

Alex looked at his watch. "It's only ten thirty."

"But I'm hungry."

"Go to the vending machine and get something then."

"Nah, I want French fries."

Miller went back to his magazine, perfectly content to wait until Alex was ready to get lunch with him rather than find something for himself in the meantime.

Alex didn't tell Miller where he was going, and Miller

wasn't interested since it was clear that he wasn't going to McDonald's. Miller wouldn't care if Alex was going into the basement, which was a good thing, because Alex had a feeling that he wasn't supposed to go down there.

All case files from previous years, whether active or not, were kept organized by month and year in file cabinets in the basement. Christie had given Alex the strong impression during Alex's interview that most cases in Smiths Hollow were minor crimes with an obvious perpetrator. He never mentioned that there might be multiple cases of slaughtered girls.

Alex shook off the feeling that he was doing something wrong. He was a police officer; there had been two bizarre and gruesome murders the day before. It only made sense to go back through the case files for similar crimes.

He didn't have a ton of experience (*okay, no experience, you were just a patrolman*) investigating murders, but he'd hung around enough detectives to know that most murderers didn't start right off with a big killing like the one yesterday. There were usually smaller crimes first, indications of future terrors.

And if Christie found Alex in the basement digging around in the file cabinets, that was exactly what Alex was going to tell the chief.

He was not going to say that the dead girls had told him to find the other dead ones.

That was between him and the girls.

The file cabinets were coated in a thick layer of dust.

Nobody ever comes down here for any reason, Alex thought. Once the calendar year was over, the files were deposited in the next empty drawer and never thought of again.

But why?

Alex held that in place in his mind. *Why?*

Find the girls. Then maybe you'll find out why.

Find the girls.

He opened the newest filing cabinet, the one with all the files from the previous year, and started digging.

14

Lauren and David's grandmother called just after their mom got home from her shopping expedition. Lauren put four cans of store-brand green beans on the floor (she was transporting them to the pantry) and picked up the phone.

"Hello, Lauren?" Their grandmother didn't sound like a frail, fluffy old lady. She had the kind of commanding voice that made everyone in the vicinity stand at attention and obey whether they meant to or not. She never bossed Lauren around, but Lauren bet it wasn't easy for her mom growing up.

"Hi, Nana," she said.

Her mom looked up from the paper bag she was unloading and gestured for the phone.

"Do you want to talk to Mom?"

"No, not right now," Nana said. "Lauren, do you think you could come and visit me this afternoon? You could just pedal over on your bicycle."

"Sure," Lauren said, though she was surprised by the request. What could Nana want to talk to her about?

"One o'clock or so?" Nana said. "You can eat your lunch first."

"Okay," Lauren said.

"Very good," Nana said, and hung up. Nana wasn't much of a small-talker.

"Why didn't you give me the phone?" Mom asked, her mouth twisting.

Here it comes, Lauren thought with an inner eye roll. Her mom hadn't had an opportunity to dig into her all morning.

"Nana said she didn't want to talk to you right now, but she wants me to come over and see her after lunch."

"Why just you?" Mom asked.

"I don't know." Lauren picked up the cans of beans and headed for the pantry, hoping to avoid an argument. It wasn't her fault if Nana didn't want to talk to her own daughter.

"You should have given me the phone anyway," Mom said, following Lauren and standing in the doorway of the pantry as Lauren stacked the beans on the shelf next to a box of Minute Rice. "No, don't put them there. Put them next to the other vegetables so I can keep track of what we have and what we don't have."

Lauren moved the green beans next to the cans of carrots and Veg-All mixed vegetables. She could tell that her mom was looking for something else to find fault about but couldn't, so she went back to complaining about Nana.

"What if I needed you to watch David this afternoon?" Mom said. "She never thinks of anybody but herself."

"I would have told her that," Lauren said.

"Told her what? That she's selfish? I hope you wouldn't be so rude."

"No," Lauren said. "If I needed to stay with David I would have told her. And she would have said to come another time."

She's not unreasonable, Lauren thought. *Not like you.*

Mom pressed her lips together and said, "Put those boxes of spaghetti away, please."

Which was her way of saying that she wanted to complain about something else but couldn't think of anything and so settled for telling Lauren what to do.

After lunch Lauren got on her bike and headed for Nana's house. Mom and David were playing Snap at the kitchen table when she left. Mom didn't have to let David win, either, because he had surprisingly fast reflexes for a little kid.

Nana lived in a big old house at the top of the only hill in Smiths Hollow. It was the oldest house in the town, Nana told her once. Lauren liked it because she could see almost all of Smiths Hollow from there.

The ghost tree looked like it was waving to her from the woods when she stood on Nana's porch, like it was watching the house for a secret signal.

Damn, Lauren thought, suddenly remembering Miranda's phone call. *I was supposed to meet Miranda after lunch.*

Nana's house was the opposite direction from the woods, but Lauren had a couple of quarters in her pocket and knew there was a pay phone at the gas station between her house and Nana's. If she was lucky Miranda would still be at home.

She rode into the parking lot and skidded to a halt in front of the pay phone attached to the side of the convenience store building. Several people were filling up their cars, and all four parking spaces in front of the building were full. One of the parking spaces had a Camaro in it.

Lauren peeked inside the store from where she stood and saw the back of Tad's greasy head. He and Billy were standing in front of a display of potato chips.

She turned her back on the front door, hoping that she could finish her call before they came out—or if they did come out, maybe they wouldn't notice her.

She dropped the coin in the slot and dialed Miranda's number.

The phone at the other end rang once, twice, three times.

"Come on, come on," Lauren muttered.

"'Lo?"

It was Miranda's mom. She sounded like she was speaking from the bottom of a fish tank.

Or the bottom of a bottle, Lauren thought.

"Mrs. Kowalczyk? It's Lauren."

"Lauren?" The way she said it was like she was trying to place Lauren's face in her mind, even though Lauren had practically lived at her house since she was small.

"Yes, is Miranda there?"

"She was going to meet you, I thought?"

"Yes, but I've had a call from my grandmother and I have to go there now, so I was hoping Miranda hadn't left yet."

"Oh," Mrs. Kowalczyk said. "No, she's gone."

Shit, Lauren thought. Miranda was going to be really pissed at her.

"Can you tell her when she gets home that I'm sorry and I'll call her later?" She thought this message was easy enough not to get too garbled when Mrs. Kowalczyk passed it on to her daughter.

"Of course?" she said, but with a question mark at the end so Lauren wasn't sure if the message had been simple enough.

Lauren hung up the phone and risked a glance over her shoulder. The Camaro was still there but Tad and Billy hadn't come out yet. She swung her leg over her bicycle, her stomach churning a little.

She'd never ditched Miranda at the ghost tree before. And since Lauren had walked out of the Dream Machine yesterday, that would make two days in a row.

Even Miranda could not be so clueless as to ignore that.

"Hey, Lauren!"

She winced, shoulders hunching. Tad and Billy must have come out of the shop and spotted her. What would she say if they asked why she'd left yesterday?

Who cares what they think, Lauren? You thought they were losers anyway.

But there was a tiny part of her that wanted them to think she was cool, even if she wasn't. Even if she was just a skinny girl in a Purple Rain T-shirt and jean cutoffs and the Kmart version of Chuck Taylors.

"Lauren!"

The voice was nearer now, and she couldn't pretend not to hear. She turned around.

Jake Hanson stood there.

She felt the tension ballooning in her chest deflate, to be replaced by a different kind of tension. Blood rushed to her cheeks. "Oh, Jake. Hi."

"Are you feeling better today?"

His eyes were so blue and seemed so sincerely interested in her that she had to look down. When she did she saw he was wearing black Chuck Taylors today—real ones, not off-brand like hers.

Of course, he has a job, she thought. *He can buy whatever he wants.*

He was staring at her and his expectant smile was starting to fade around the edges. She realized she'd never answered him.

"Um, yeah," she said. "Loads better."

He wore a white T-shirt with a black-and-white photo of a soldier repeated four times on it in a square. On the side it read *THE SMITHS* in big black capital letters.

"What's that? Some kind of ad for the town?" she asked, pointing at his shirt.

He laughed, and his smile seemed really big and white. He had a little dimple in his left cheek that made him look younger.

"Nah, they're a band," he said. "From England."

"Oh," Lauren said.

She didn't know any bands from England except for Duran Duran. A couple of years earlier she'd really been into Duran Duran, had even joined their fan club. Her dad had taken her to the post office to buy a special stamp for the envelope because the fan club was in Birmingham, England.

"What kind of music is it?" Lauren asked, even though she knew she should leave. Nana was waiting for her.

"Hmm," Jake said. "Kind of chirpy and depressing at the same time. Guitars, no synthesizers like all that radio garbage."

Lauren felt her cheeks get even redder. She liked all of that radio garbage, but she could tell that it was not cool to do so.

Well, what do you expect? You're just a dorky kid and he's a college student. Of course he knows more about everything than you do.

"It was, um, nice to see you," she said, not wanting to prolong this awkwardness any longer than necessary. "I have to get to my grandma's house."

"Oh," he said, and he seemed kind of disappointed, although maybe that was her imagination. "Well, I'll see you around, Lauren."

"Yup, see you around," she said, and rode away as fast as she could.

When she got to the stop sign at the corner she gave a quick sideways peek back over her shoulder and found him staring after her. He had a strange look on his face, one she couldn't define. Lauren hurriedly turned her head forward again so he wouldn't catch her looking.

Why did he seem to be everywhere all of a sudden? Lauren hadn't thought about Jake Hanson in years, and now she'd seen him twice in two days.

"Stop worrying about Jake Hanson," she told herself as she coasted toward the bottom of Nana's hill. "The important thing is that you didn't have to talk to Tad."

Once the road began to climb she stood up on the pedals rather than change gears. The lower gears always made her feel like a hamster on a wheel, like she was going to slide backward if she didn't keep her legs pumping.

Lauren heard a car coming up the hill behind her. For a brief and panicked second she thought it might be Jake Hanson following her. *What should I do if it is him? Should I wave? Should I pretend I didn't see him? I don't even know what kind of car he drives.*

She kept pedaling, because the best thing was just to pretend that the car wasn't there. It was unlikely to be Jake Hanson, although she didn't know who might be driving this way.

There was no other house on the hill, only Nana's. It stood alone like a watchtower, and even though there was plenty of space to build more homes, nobody had.

The car pulled even with her. She could see the hood just out of the corner of her eye—a wide, black sedan.

A male voice called, "Hey, Lauren."

Lauren was trying so hard to pretend the car wasn't there that the sound of her name made her jerk the bike handles suddenly to the right. She lost her balance and tipped over in a heap, her elbow scraping the edge of the road where it met a shallow ditch that ran along the side.

"Shit," she said. She felt her face filling with blood, knew she would be bright red when she stood up—not to mention covered in gravel and generally disheveled.

The car came to a halt and as she untangled herself from her bike Lauren noticed it was a Smiths Hollow police car.

Please don't let it be Officer Hendricks, she thought, but of course the voice that had called her through the window had been his and a moment later he was leaning over her, his eyes concerned, offering his hand to help her up.

"I'm so sorry, Lauren, I thought you realized I was there. I just wanted to say hello and see how you were doing."

I did realize you were there, but I was being stupid. And he usually did say hello when he saw her, even if he had to drive out of his way—as he'd clearly done now. She said, "It's okay, I was thinking about something else."

She didn't want to take his hand even though part of her had always wanted this very thing, but in her imagination when this happened she would not be sweaty and embarrassed. Then she decided it was better just to get it over with. His hand was big—he was a very tall man—and it swallowed up her much smaller one. He lifted her with ease.

"Where are you off to? Your grandmother's house?"

Lauren lifted up her right arm to examine the underside. There was a scrape there, not serious enough to warrant a Band-Aid, but it looked raw and angry.

"I have a first-aid kit in the car," Officer Hendricks said. "We should clean that off."

"Oh. Um. I think it's fine," Lauren said. Normally she would want to stay and talk to him forever, but she didn't want to linger while she was in this state. If she was clean and wearing nice clothes that would be different.

Not that he would look at you anyway, you stupid dork. You're almost fifteen but he's like twenty-three or something. He's definitely too old for you.

"The least I can do is help you clean up after causing your

accident," he said, and smiled in that way he had, that way that made his eyes crinkle at the corners.

"Okay," Lauren said. *Gosh, your conversation is just scintillating. You're really going to make him think you're mature for your age.*

She left the bike where it was and followed Officer Hendricks to the passenger side of the car. She wondered where his partner was—he was almost always with Officer Pantaleo.

He took the first-aid kit out of the glove box while she hovered nervously behind him. First she'd run into Jake Hanson and now this happened. She felt off-balance, not like herself.

Get it together, Lauren. Just talk to him like a normal person.

"Let me see that arm," he said, opening the kit and placing it on the roof of the car.

He pulled out a small bottle of iodine and a gauze pad wrapped in paper. Lauren held up her arm obediently as he tore open the gauze pad and poured some iodine on it.

"This will sting," he warned.

"I know," she said, wincing as he gently swabbed the scrape.

"So you're going to your grandmother's house?" he asked.

She realized she'd never answered him earlier. "Yeah, just for a bit. Then I'm going to meet Miranda."

This was a lie. She had no intention of going to meet Miranda afterward, but she didn't want Officer Hendricks to think she was some lame kid who spent her summer afternoons hanging out with her grandma.

Even if Nana is a really cool grandma, she thought with a pang of guilt.

"And what are you two girls up to today? Nothing illegal, I hope?" he asked with a twinkle in his eye.

"No, we're just hanging out in the woods," Lauren said, flushing again. She wouldn't even know where to begin to do something illegal. She knew he was just teasing her, but she didn't have the wherewithal at the moment to play it cool, to banter back.

"The two of you like to hang out at that big tree, don't you? The one that looks like it was struck by lightning?" he asked.

"Yeah, we always have," she said. "Ever since we were little."

He pushed the used gauze back inside the torn packet and then put the trash inside an empty coffee cup in the car. Lauren stood there for a moment, watching him put away the first-aid kit.

"Can I give you a ride the rest of the way?" he offered, turning back to her. "We can put your bike in the trunk."

The thought of sitting in an enclosed car with Officer Hendricks while he smiled at her and made conversation was too much. She raised her hands in a warding-off gesture, backing away.

"Oh, no, no, that's totally fine. It's not that much farther and I don't want you to go out of your way."

"It's no trouble," he said.

"No, it's fine." *Jesus, Lauren, how many times are you going to say "fine"?* "Thank you. Thanks for cleaning my arm."

"If you're sure?"

"I am," she said, giving him a little wave. She hoped that the wave looked confident and friendly.

"See you around, then, Lauren," Officer Hendricks said. He got in his car, made a U-turn, and headed down the hill.

As soon as he was out of sight she felt her shoulders slump. The only way that could have gone any worse was if she'd puked in front of him.

Well, you did that yesterday in front of Jake Hanson and suddenly he seems to think you're the most interesting person in the world.

She shook her head. Jake had only wanted to see if she was okay from yesterday. And Officer Hendricks had only wanted to see how she was doing, the way he always did ever since her dad had died.

Lauren dusted the gravel off her legs and picked up her bike. It was going to be a huge pain to start climbing the hill from here, with no momentum to help. She sighed, swung her leg over the bike, and dug into the pedals again.

Lauren thought her grandmother's home looked like a crumbling castle, a place full of secrets and wonder. The windows were large, like staring eyes, and there was a wraparound porch and even a turret. The guest bedroom was in that little tower, and Lauren always felt the vast permutations of possibility when she stayed there, like the wardrobe might open up and lead her to another world, or maybe a prince would stand outside asking her to let down her hair.

Other kids—including Miranda—thought that it looked like a haunted house. Lauren knew that some of them would dare others to run up and touch the porch, or would climb the hill with the intention of egging the windows on Halloween.

Nana didn't mind the kids looking to prove their courage by touching the building, but every Halloween night Nana sat on her porch all night with a hunting rifle leaning next to her and stared down anyone foolish enough to approach her home with ill intent. She also had a bucket of candy for anyone with enough guts to trick-or-treat from her. Since so few children were brave enough (and so few parents wanted to make the climb) they were usually richly rewarded in the form of handfuls of candy instead of one measly piece.

Nana was waiting for Lauren on the porch, sitting in her rocker reading an Isabel Allende novel. She wore a pair of faded blue jeans and a loose-fitting plaid blouse. Her long white hair was bound in a single braid at the back of her head.

A can of Tab was open on the small wooden table next to her, and Lauren knew she'd probably had a half-dozen cans already. She didn't think a seventy-year-old woman should be drinking so much caffeine and chemicals, but Nana—her real name was Joanne Gehlinger, but she always went by

Jo—did what she wanted no matter what other people said.

Lauren leaned her bike up against the porch and went up the stairs to kiss her grandmother's cheek. Nana and Lauren were about the same height—just a bit over five feet—but Lauren had the advantage over her grandmother at the moment because she was wearing sneakers and Nana was barefoot.

"Hi, Nana," she said.

"You probably thought my call was strange," Nana said, collecting her book and pop and pulling open the screen door.

"A little," Lauren said.

Inside it was cool and dark, because Nana had the shades on the windows pulled down. She didn't have any air conditioners in the house ("the electricity would go haywire if I put them in, I bet"), but keeping the sun out of the rooms during the long summer days went a long way toward keeping the house comfortable.

"Do you want a Yoo-hoo?" Nana asked, and Lauren followed her into the kitchen.

Lauren would rather have a cold Coke, but she knew Nana didn't have any, only cases of diet soda. "Sure."

She could have asked what Nana had called about, but Nana would tell her in her own time and her own way. Lauren was always willing to let her do that, though her mother would have demanded to know as soon as she arrived.

Once Lauren had her drink they went into the living

room. Nana's furniture wasn't preserved in plastic or covered in tapestried roses like so many of the older people Lauren knew. She had a comfortable rust-colored corduroy couch and two big blue armchairs and everywhere there were hand-crocheted blankets and pillows that invited you to curl up and stay awhile.

Nana's bookshelves had actual books on them, not knickknacks, and her walls had real paintings instead of prints and the tables had sculptures. The paintings and sculptures were purchases from art galleries that Nana visited on monthly trips into Chicago.

Lauren considered pretty much everything about Nana to be awesome, and she hoped that when she was old she could be just like her. In the meantime she wished she could come and live with her grandmother instead of staying at her own house.

Although that would mean abandoning David.

Well, things weren't as bad for David, were they? Mom doted on David, never yelled at him about anything. If Lauren left, then Mom would have what she wanted—a perfect child—and Lauren would have what she wanted—a home where she wasn't criticized just for being alive.

Lauren sipped her drink and waited for Nana. Her grandmother seemed uncharacteristically hesitant, especially since she'd basically demanded Lauren drop all her afternoon plans to come over.

Not that my plans were so great, Lauren thought. *More listening to Miranda about some guy.*

Maybe I should just tell Miranda . . .

Tell Miranda what? That they shouldn't be friends anymore? Or if they were going to stay friends, then Lauren wanted to have an actual say in their plans?

It hadn't always been like this. When they were small they were two peas in a pod, and whatever one wanted the other wanted, too. They'd always been in perfect sync until last year.

Then Miranda had gotten her period and gotten breasts in quick succession. After that she only cared about makeup and clothes and boys.

Lauren knew she might care about those things some time in the future, too. It was part of growing up, becoming a woman, all of that. But Lauren wasn't ready to grow up yet, and Miranda was in such a hurry.

"Lauren, do you know the story about the witches?" Nana asked. It was typical Nana, no small talk to ease you into the conversation, no segue from something innocuous.

"You mean the witches who were supposed to live here?" Lauren asked.

"Yes."

Lauren shrugged. "Just that there were three witches and one of them fell in love and because of that she died. She was the youngest one and after that there were no more witches."

"Do you think they were real witches?" Nana asked.

"There's no such thing as real witches," Lauren said, though Nana's piercing stare gave her tone much less conviction than it should have had.

"Yes, there are," Nana said. "And they have real power."

"What, like magic?" Lauren said with a little laugh. "They do spells and fly around on broomsticks?"

Nana ignored this. "I want to tell you a story, Lauren. A real story, a story that my mother told to me. I want you to listen to me, really listen. You don't have to believe, although things will be better for you if do. But listen."

"Okay, Nana," Lauren said, struck by the absolute solemnity of her grandmother's face. Lauren didn't know what any of this was about or why Nana suddenly seemed so serious. "I'll listen."

PART TWO

AMONG THE WITCHES

There was a hill just off the center of town, a lonely and inexplicable hill: a hill that should not be, for it blighted an otherwise perfectly flat and reasonable landscape.

The hill—and the house that sat upon it—watched over the people and buildings below, though it was the kind of gaze that left the back of one's neck prickly and uncomfortable.

Without this hill it was just an ordinary Midwestern burg, a town that appeared almost magically when coal was discovered nearby and the rich barons from Chicago needed men to dig it up.

But the vein ran dry faster than in other parts of Illinois, and many of the men who came to dig went elsewhere to do their work, and the town became nothing but a dirt strip in between empty storefronts. The few people that remained spoke hopefully of one of those barons bringing a factory for folks to work in, and perhaps bringing some folks to fill up the empty space, while he was at it.

On the western side of town, the land was split open, ugly seams dug into the prairie. On the eastern side, a manic tangle of trees bumped insistently up against the geographical edge of civilization. If one walked through these woods, one might find oneself starting at the way the shadows seemed to breathe and curl around a neck, an ear, a wrist. The trees there kept the same time as the hill.

There was one particular tree, too—a lightning-struck tree that arced up toward the sky that carved it, impossibly huge next to its neighbors. A tree with branches that curled like sharp claws looking for skin to scrape.

All the townsfolk (when there had been townsfolk to speak of) had avoided that tree, for it wasn't right that a tree seemed to whisper and stare and reach out when a person passed by.

And all the while, the hill and the house upon it watched.

And all the while, the tree waited for the signal from the hill.

Atop this hill lived three women, and of course these women were witches. "Of course" because what else could they be, as they were three women living together without men's company—always a suspicious action. Men must have lived there once, though no one could remember their names, for these women were grandmother and mother and daughter.

There were always a grandmother and mother and daughter, no matter how much time passed, always three but not always the same three. The daughter never seemed to be a child, though of course she must have been once.

The daughter was a spinster, a word so sharp it bleeds when touched. Spinsters are not bachelors, carefree and elegant. Spinsters are thin at the edges, full of dust and longing.

Or so the townspeople thought, even though somehow there was always another mother, and another daughter.

Spinsters are witches, and old women are witches, and single women are witches because they simply must be. Women without men must be up to no good.

So the house on the hill was the home of witches, from the beginning and until the end. There were always witches there.

But we do not believe such things. We do not really believe in witches, believe in the eye of newt nor the bubbling cauldron. We frighten each other with the tales of women on the hill, spinning dark magic, but in our hearts we know they are only ancient husks rustling in mothballs. They could not really bring harm to us.

We do not believe such things.

Until they do bring harm.

Until we wrong them, and they curse us.

He was a princeling, a dark-eyed son of the town savior—the man with money who brought the longed-for industry to a place choking on scraps of coal dust. When he walked about town all the young girls sighed (and some women who should know better, too—he was that sort of man).

His father had built a factory, a factory where people would put meat shipped from Chicago into cans. Those cans would reboard the train and travel all over the country, and though the work was hard and sometimes dangerous, everyone was grateful for the work in the first place. Anyhow, it was less dangerous than coal.

The arrival of the train and the factory meant the empty town was suddenly full, and more houses were built and more streets were laid and named, although no one ever thought it a good idea to cut down the trees on the eastern edge. No, they would just smooth out the land where the coal used to be and leave those trees alone.

So the hill and the trees kept their time, and watched, and waited.

And the man who'd brought the town back to life built a large house on the north end, a house that almost defied logic, huge and white and towering. Its upper windows glared at the hill but gazed benevolently down upon the creation of its owner—a productive, bustling paradise of workers.

And from the hill, the daughter of three looked down at the dark-eyed princeling as he strolled about with sighs in his wake. She saw him, and she wanted him for her own.

They called her a spinster but she was not so old for all that—just past twenty, and young enough to make a fool of herself over a handsome man.

She had charms aplenty, charms that spent years hidden by the fading dresses passed from mother to daughter, but she spent enough time watching from the windows to know how to make those charms sparkle.

Her mother and grandmother watched too, watched the daughter of three perform the same rituals that they had once performed. This was the way of things, for of course another daughter must come soon so the line would remain unbroken.

And so the daughter of three went out into the world.

When the dark-eyed princeling saw her red hair shining in the sunlight and her charms out on display in a fashionable new dress, he had to have her for his own. She saw his look and knew what it meant and so did all the sighing girls that followed him.

They looked at the daughter's red hair and blue eyes and ample curves and decided all those things were very common and that the only reason the princeling offered her his arm was that she was a witch. Their faces were green and so were their tongues and they whispered behind their hands (as the princeling stared enchanted at the daughter of three) that everyone knew those women at the top of the hill were witches.

But he didn't hear them calling her a witch and he didn't care for their sighs anyway. He'd never wanted anything from this one-train town until he saw the daughter standing on the sidewalk.

He took what he wanted from her, and she got what she wanted from him, and soon enough her belly was rounder than it had ever been before.

The three women at the top of the hill wanted nothing from the princeling except what they'd already gotten—the seed that planted the next daughter. But the princeling's father didn't believe this.

The only interest those three women could have, in his mind, was in dollars and cents. That was all he cared about and so that was what everyone else must care about, too. He had a very fine match arranged for his lustful princeling with another baron's daughter, and he was not about to have his carefully laid plans spoiled by a red-haired tart showing up on his doorstep with a squalling babe and claims of paternity.

That baby, he decided, could never be.

The daughter sat at the window of the house on the hill and sewed clothes for her coming daughter and thought fondly of her time with the dark-eyed princeling but more fondly of the day when her own red-haired child would arrive.

The father of the princeling sat at the desk inside his enormous monstrosity of a house and thought fondly of the day when the threat to him and his own would be gone.

First he tried sending a man to the house on the hill with money. The old crone who answered the door had, the man later told the father, looked upon him like one views a crawling thing in the dirt. She shut the door and never touched the sack that he held out to her in offering.

The father imagined then that he had offered a price too low. Well, that was no matter. He'd half expected this, though he always tried to pay the least amount for what he wanted the most. Of course they would want more to stay quiet.

What he did not know was that the princeling, against all expectation, had fallen in love with the red-haired witch and wanted, above all things, to see his daughter and hold her in his arms. He had no interest in the arranged match and told his father so, and then he went to the house on the hill and told his lover that he wanted to marry her.

This was a thing that had never happened before, for the three were always careful to choose men that would happily abjure their responsibility.

Still, though it was unexpected it was not entirely unwelcome to see the princeling on his knees before the daughter, offering her a silver ring infused with his love. It would not be such a bad thing, they decided, to have a man about the house. They might even learn to live as others did.

So the daughter said yes, and there was more joy than could be imagined in that house on the hill.

But the father of the princeling could not allow such joy. It fit with none of his plans.

And so he planned anew, to make his world right again.

Her name was not Daughter, but Elizabeth, and her lover called her Liz, or Lizzie, or Eliza, but never all of the syllables unless he sighed them out in her mouth in the dark of night.

The princeling's name was Charles, and he was the fourth of his line to be given the mighty name that was attached to many surnames, but he preferred to be called Charlie.

All through the long hot summer Charlie and Liz planned for their life together and their daughter (for of course it was a daughter growing inside Liz's belly—the three only gave birth to girls).

Charlie had an idea that they might build a little house for themselves—not in town, not beneath the scowling face of his father's house, but in the forest. While he respected the mother and grandmother of his Lizzie, he also longed to have his wife for himself. Lizzie, though she had always been content to be with her mother and grandmother, agreed that a snug little nook under the trees was just the thing for them.

So every morning Charlie went out into the woods (though he never walked near the lightning-struck tree—he was a happy man and had no need of ghosts and shadows) and chopped down trees and cut and sanded them and made a little cabin in the woods.

This cabin he made deep in the trees, far from the town and the hill. He wanted no friendly visits from neighbors, nor prying faces that would pass gossip in the general store. He only wanted his wife and his daughter and their circle of love.

You might think that in this living place that the trees would be angry at such use, but Charlie always planted a little seed to replace the ones he took down, and the ones that were cut and sanded could feel the love that he layered into the walls and so they were content too.

His soft princeling's hands grew hard and callused, and his slim princeling's shoulders grew round and strong. His face, so white from years spent lounging in parlors, turned brown under the glare of the sun and soon it seemed that anyone from his old life would not even recognize him.

But his father recognized him. His father would always know him whatever Charlie's disguise, and his father thought that it was a disguise, a whim that he would outgrow. How could his son, *his* son, the son of one of the wealthiest men in the Midwest, want to spend all his life in poverty with the slattern who'd seduced him? It couldn't possibly be, though the evidence of his eyes told otherwise. He would save his child, though, save him from the unhappiness that was the only possible outcome of this match. And then Charlie would marry the girl his father had chosen, and their wealth would double and their standing in society would triple, and all would be as it should be.

By the end of summer Elizabeth was nearing her time and Charlie was nearly finished with their new home, though he had not yet allowed Elizabeth to see it. Every day she watched him walk and whistle into the cover of the forest, carrying his sack of tools and a lunch she packed for him. Every day he would return to the hill with a pleased smile on his face and she would glance at him hopefully and he would say, "Not quite yet."

She knew he only wanted to surprise her, to make it special, but she was burning with curiosity and decided one day that she would follow him into the woods.

Now Elizabeth had rarely left the hill since her belly started to grow. When she did she was always accompanied, by her mother or grandmother who glared away any impertinent questions about her marriage, or by Charlie, who laughed them off with that easy way of his (he had not forgotten what it was like to be a princeling, after all, or how to charm).

This was because they all wanted to protect her—from rude tongues at the least, but the mother and grandmother felt the growing menace from the baron's side of town and wanted to keep their daughter, and her daughter, away from harm.

The grandmother and mother would never have allowed Elizabeth to go out on her own, and so she slipped away while they were busy with other tasks.

We all know what happens when we are too curious, when we stray out of bounds, when we don't stay within our borders. Sometimes, adventure happens and our lives are changed forever, our borders expanded and our horizons stretching far into the distance.

But sometimes, terrible things happen and our lives are destroyed forever, our borders shrunk to the size of the pain in our hearts, our horizons dimmed.

Because, you see, Charlie's father—the baron from Chicago who had Saved the Town, the man who would not be thwarted—had set one of his servants to watch the hill, day and night.

This servant, he was not the sort of servant that you keep in your house and allow to serve coffee to the neighbors. He wasn't even the sort that might black your boots or care for the horses in the stable. He was the sort that you pass money to in the shadows, the sort that you only see when the gleam of his eyes and the gleam of his knife shine out of the darkness.

This servant saw Elizabeth's red hair reflecting the sun and her round figure moving slowly from the hill to the trees. He knew his time had come. He knew what was expected of him.

So Elizabeth followed Charlie, and the man with the knife followed Elizabeth.

The scream that followed seemed to rent the whole world in two. It cleaved through the air, brushed across the treetops and made them shudder. It arrowed through the town, made heads turn and mouths whisper. And it pounded against the windows of the house on the hill and made the mother and the grandmother sink slowly to the ground, arms wrapped around one another.

Charlie heard his Elizabeth scream. He dropped his bag of tools and his carefully packed lunch and ran, ran, ran following the fading gasps of that scream through the woods.

But it was too late, for the man with the knife knew what he was about and what he was being paid for (that sort always do), and he had done his deed and disappeared back into the shadows before Elizabeth's cry faded away.

Charlie found his lover, his wife, the mother of his child thrown upon the ground like garbage and there was blood everywhere, so much blood, blood pooling around her and running into her beautiful red hair and staining the silver ring he'd given her. Her life was gone and so too was the life of the child within her and Charlie fell to his knees and took them in his arms and wept.

The trees all around nodded in sadness and the wind cried with him and the animals of that dark, dark forest bent their heads.

The creature that lurked in the shadows under the lightning-struck tree heard the signal from the hill. It was awake now, and hungry, and knew its time had come.

Charlie picked up the blood-soaked thing that used to be Elizabeth and carried her through the woods, and through the town toward the house on the hill.

When he passed the townspeople, some of them cried out at the sight of him and others tucked their mouths behind their hands and whispered that they knew it would come to this; that Kind of Woman could only come to this end.

The women chittered and chattered and said that

Elizabeth was probably meeting men in the woods while her poor devoted husband had been off building a cottage for her and when he found out he stabbed her to death.

It never occurred to them, not to any of them, that Charlie's father—the great baron from Chicago, the man who saved the town—had set a wolf upon his son's wife.

The mother and the grandmother were standing at the door, dry-eyed and sober, when Charlie reached the top of the hill. Very gently, oh so gently, they took their daughter and the daughter inside her from the man who'd loved them both.

"We'll take care of her now," they said.

The mother kissed him on his left cheek, and the grandmother kissed him on his right cheek. He nodded to them and they all knew that this was the last time they would see one another, for Charlie had work to do now.

He turned away from the house on the hill and started toward the huge frowning edifice that hid his father. His heart beat very steadily and his feet followed its cadence as he deliberately marched through the main street letting everyone there see him and the blood on his clothes.

The town constable tried to approach Charlie (he was the constable, after all, and people with blood-soaked clothing were of interest to those who would uphold the law), but Charlie only stared at the constable until that worthy lawman sputtered and backed away and suddenly remembered he had to be elsewhere at that very moment.

Charlie marched up the steps of his father's house and knocked on the door with his bloodied hands. The door was answered by his father's butler, and the butler's eyes widened in surprise as he took in the young master's appearance.

"Bring me to my father," Charlie said.

The butler bowed his head and wondered how the young master had gotten into such a state, but it wasn't really his place to speculate, so he followed his orders and brought Charlie to the breakfast room.

His father was reading the daily papers from Chicago (carried specially for him on the train every day) and eating toast. Of course word had already reached him of the terrible tragedy in the woods, but it was not for Charlie to know that, so when he looked up from his coffee it was with an expression of mild puzzlement.

"Charles? This is a surprise. You look a mess. Why don't you wash up and we'll have breakfast together."

He said these things because he expected his child to listen and to obey, because he thought now that the slattern was dead Charlie would return to him. He didn't see the look in Charlie's eyes, didn't realize that he'd lost his child forever that day. But he didn't live long enough to regret it.

The servants in the kitchen heard the sound of a struggle, of breaking china, and then a brief, angry cry. When the maid and the footman rushed in they found the master on his back on the table with a butter knife embedded in his throat. The young master stood calmly before him and when they stared at him he said, "Take everyone in the building and get out of the house."

It never occurred to them not to follow his orders. There was a strange resolve about him, something that shimmered on the air, and they didn't want any part of it.

A half hour after all the servants filed out of the largest house in town they saw the smoke billowing from the windows. A moment later the young master came out on the porch and stood before the door with a rifle in his hands.

The fire brigade was called and they rushed to the house, but when they tried to climb the steps Charlie raised the rifle and told them to keep off. When they protested that they didn't want other buildings to catch fire he told them to do what they must for those other ones but to leave his father's house alone.

When the conflagration was at its highest and the whole town had come out to watch the spectacle of the baron's house burning to the ground, Charlie calmly walked inside and was never seen again.

As for the mother and the grandmother, well, the town had long called them witches.

So witches they would be.

There had always been the knowledge of witch-lore in their past. Only witches would have settled on such a lonely hill near the lightning-struck tree, for people with no magic chose to stay out of its direct line of sight.

But that had been long ago, the stirring and the spells, the witchcraft and the magic. That was the work of their grandmother's grandmother and her daughter and *her* daughter. The practice had mostly faded out since then, with the exception of a few household spells to help plants grow or to make the dust fly out the window instead of settling on the floor.

The magic hadn't faded even if the practice had. The spark was in their veins, and their grief and anger fed it. The memories of all the spells of their foremothers waited on their tongues.

They knew how to raise the Dark Thing that slept in the woods beneath the lightning-struck tree, the Thing that watched for the signal from the hill. It was hungry, so hungry, and it was waiting.

It had been waiting for so long.

The spell needed blood to make the charm stick, for nothing was as powerful as blood magic. But blood they had aplenty, from their own veins and from the body of Elizabeth. There were other things that were needed, too—herbs from the garden, and spiders torn from their webs, and symbols drawn on the floor and the walls, and the silver from the ring Elizabeth wore.

They laid the remains of their daughter and their daughter's daughter in the center of the big room where they had once laughed with her. Then the grandmother and the mother joined hands and began to chant.

The townspeople were still gathered in the center of town, watching the baron's house burning to the ground and the baron's son with it. When the witches began their chant all eyes turned toward the hill, for the spell carried across the air and into the woods.

The Dark Thing that lived there opened its eyes.

The people of the town huddled close to one another, for there was a chill in the air that pierced flesh and bone and fixed its clawed hands around their hearts.

The voices on the hill rose and fell, and the people of the town waited for the blade of the axe that loomed over them.

The mother and the grandmother were furious in their grief, and so they laid the curse upon all the town and all the descendants of those who lived there.

That all were complicit was the witches' most fervent belief, for the people had wanted the baron and his money and it was nothing to them if he killed their daughter.

If money was what they wanted, then money they would have. The town would always be prosperous, and everyone would always have what they needed.

But every year they would lose a daughter, just as the witches had.

No family would be exempt, and no family could leave. They and their bloodlines were now tied inextricably to this land and this woods. If they tried to leave, they would find themselves returning, though they would not know why.

And to make sure the charm was firm, the witches blessed all the women of the town (and their daughters, and their daughter's daughters, and so on until the end of time) with fertility. There would always be daughters for the sacrifice.

But the mother and the grandmother, they were too old to have more daughters, and after their daughter was gone their line was ended.

But the curse would go on and on even after the witches were gone, even when the house on the hill became an empty haunted place for a time, before another woman brave enough to live there arrived.

The children of the town forever after would huddle in sight of its blank staring windows and dare one another to touch the front door, and then they would all run back down the hill screaming.

Still, it didn't quite look like a curse. You see, the town did prosper, that town with the house on the hill. All around them other towns withered and died, their industry drying up and moving to other places, other countries, but this town never faltered.

They never faltered even though every year a girl went missing, and later that girl was found dead.

Those girls were always found in the woods, and what happened to them cannot be spoken.

And nobody would speak of it, though everyone had a

sense there was Something Wrong, something seething beneath the surface of their picturesque little town. Everyone pretended things were just fine, and all the neighbors made casseroles for the families that lost their daughters, and they waited for their turn.

Then one year, a man was found in the woods, near the pretty cabin that had been empty for as long as anyone could remember. This man had his heart torn out, and no one could say what had done it, or why or how, and nobody wanted to say anyway.

Nobody talked about witches, or a curse, or the girls that went missing or the Dark Thing that slouched through the dry-leaved forest and seemed to seep out of the soil into the very air. No one spoke of those things.

But after the man died, things went wrong.

He was the wrong sacrifice.

And the Dark Thing that waited for its yearly blood and bread found it was no longer bound by the rules of the curse. It could slither along in the forest, or slither its way into the body of a man if it wanted. It was so much easier to move among the sheep if it was disguised as one of them.

It was free now, free to choose its own meal at its own time, and to eat more than one a year. It could feast now. It wanted to feast.

The sacrifice had been wrong, so it went looking for the right one.

PART THREE

STRANDS

1

It was a good story, and it was well told. But when Nana got to the end bit, the bit about the man being found in the woods, Lauren felt like her grandmother had struck her. How could Nana use Lauren's father's death in this story, like it was just a dramatic plot point? How could she so callously throw that out there without any regard for Lauren's feelings?

Lauren had been buying it all up until the end. The story of the witch and the man who loved her had struck the perfect tragic note, like an old-fashioned legend. And the notion of a creepy presence in the forest didn't even seem that farfetched. She liked the idea of a local story that explained so many of the funny things about Smiths Hollow, even if it wasn't really true.

Of course it couldn't be true. It was just a story. Even if Nana had decided to add her father's murder into it.

Maybe she thought it would help me? Like there would be

an explanation even if there wasn't a real explanation.

Yes, that must be it. Although Lauren considered the method a little thoughtless, and telling a story like that to explain her father's horrific murder seemed more like the kind of thing you'd do with a younger kid.

A kid you wanted to terrify.

And the thing of it was . . . Nana seemed to think she was telling a *true* story. There was something in her manner, in the intent way she stared at Lauren. And a true story meant that she believed all that stuff about the girls.

But the idea that one girl was getting killed every year was ridiculous. Everyone would know about it. There would be communal outrage.

"It's impossible," Lauren said.

"What is?"

"That." Lauren waved her hand around in Nana's general direction, her gesture encompassing the whole story. "There's no way any of it's real."

"Why can't it be real?" Nana asked. She seemed genuinely interested in Lauren's answer.

"Because we would know," Lauren said. "And I don't know any girls who've been killed in the woods. Mom would never have let me near the ghost tree if girls were getting killed there all the time."

She remembered then her vision in the woods the day before, the pain that had split her skull, the bloodied handprint on her bike seat. And the dead girls in Mrs. Schneider's backyard.

But that was something that just happened. It hasn't been going on for years and years. And everybody knows about it—everyone on the street, everyone in the town. It's not some kind of weird secret.

"But you do know girls who have been killed there," Nana said gently. "Jennifer Walton. She was in your first-grade class. Callie Bryzinski. She was in your sixth-grade class. Holly Becker. Your third-grade class. Terri Zimmerman. She lived four houses away from you. Paula Lisowski. She was your babysitter for two years."

"What are you—no," Lauren said. "No, I would *know* if they were all murdered. It would be in the newspapers. And on the TV. Reporters would come from Chicago. And everyone would be talking about it. None of those things ever happened. Not ever. Jennifer Walton's family moved to North Carolina."

"*After* their daughter died, and they moved back three years ago because you can't leave Smiths Hollow, even if you've already made a sacrifice."

Lauren shook her head. "And Paula Lisowski went to college. She was a really good artist. She wanted to go to NYU."

"She died before she graduated high school."

"Stop saying that!" Lauren shouted. "Stop telling me things that I know aren't true. This stupid story has gone far enough."

Lauren stood up, feeling flushed and unreasonably angry. Why was her nana acting this way? Was she trying to scare Lauren for some mysterious reason of her own? "And anyway, if everyone forgets about the stupid curse, how do *you* know about it?"

"Because we are a branch of the same tree that made those witches, long ago."

"Now I really know you're making it up," Lauren said, and hot tears sprang to her eyes. Why was her own precious nana doing this? "Are you trying to make fun of me? Do you think I'm dumb or something?"

Nana looked stricken. "No, Lauren, I never—"

"You just said that there were only three of them, that there were always three. One grandmother, one mother, one daughter. And since in your story all of them died, including the daughter's baby, we couldn't be related to them. So your story is just a lot of bullshit." Lauren clapped her hand over her mouth. She only ever swore to herself, or maybe when she was around Miranda, but never in the presence of an adult.

"That's right," Nana said calmly, ignoring Lauren's curse. "I did say that. What I didn't say was that when the first three witches, the very first of them all, settled here, the oldest woman had a sister that did not come to live with them. She and her descendants stayed in their little town, pretending that they were not full of magic. But when the last three died, one of those descendants came here. And that woman was my great-grandmother."

"That's very convenient," Lauren said. "The sudden appearance of a magical sibling and her children, so that the line doesn't die out at the end of your story."

"You can believe or not," Nana said. "I told you that at the beginning."

"I don't," Lauren said, stalking toward the door. "I'm going home."

"I thought you would be different than your mother," Nana said.

No words could have arrested Lauren's movement quicker. She wasn't like Mom—nitpicking, closed-minded, always miserable.

"I *am* different from her," she said. "I am nothing like her *at all*."

"Then tell me about your visions," Nana said.

"How did you—?" Lauren almost asked, but then decided she would admit to nothing. And making that decision hurt, because Nana had always been a trusted confidante. She'd always felt she could tell her grandmother anything. But if Nana was going to act like this, then that weird vision Lauren had was none of her business. "What does that have to do with your story, and these supposed murdered girls?"

Nana huffed out an impatient breath. "If you are the descendant of a witch—and you are, whatever you might think at the moment—then you are the right age to start showing manifestations of that power. It usually begins in adolescence."

Then why does David know everything that's happening? Lauren thought. David wasn't even in grade school yet. Lauren really hadn't had time to let what happened yesterday sink in, and now Nana was telling her that she was a witch, or something like one.

Magic wasn't real. Yes, something strange had happened to both her and David, but it didn't mean they could cast spells or whatever. And Lauren definitely didn't believe in curses.

"Even if I did believe we had some kind of magical bloodline—and I don't, just saying it out loud is ridiculous—you still can't prove that it has anything to do with a bunch of dead girls. Because there are no dead girls. Nobody would live here anymore if that were happening."

"I told you in the story—nobody can leave Smiths Hollow. They can go for a little while, but they always find themselves returning. Because that, too, is part of the curse. The monster must have meat to feed on, and those three witches made certain it would have it. And there *are* dead girls. Many, many girls. One every year, and the only one who remembers them is me. Well, me and one other."

"Why only you?" Lauren asked, finding another logical flaw in Nana's story. "Why not Mom, or me? We're all related."

"Your mother is too mundane," Nana said, her voice hard. "If she ever had any magic to speak of, she's suppressed it so thoroughly it will never come out again. She closes her eyes and pretends that what she doesn't want to see isn't there. So of course she would ignore the girls, the way she ignores everything that doesn't suit her. And as for you . . . well, once you know what's happening you'll find it easy to remember. Too easy."

Nana sighed, and it was a sigh filled with more grief than Lauren could comprehend. She almost went to her grandmother then and put her arms around her. She almost said *Let's forget all of this* and *I love you, Nana*.

But then Nana said the unforgivable thing.

"There wasn't a girl last year, though. There was supposed to be. But your father went in your place."

2

Miranda walked around the ghost tree for about the billionth time, checked her watch, and found that it was only thirty seconds after the last time she checked. Where was Lauren? She was never this late.

Maybe her mom was still out.

But if so, then why hadn't Lauren called before one? They'd set a time. They'd agreed.

And Miranda was going to burst open if she didn't tell *somebody* about Him. Of course, she couldn't tell Lauren His real name, because He was *technically* an adult and if anybody found out about Him and Miranda then He could get in a lot of trouble because she was jailbait.

Not that anything had happened last night. But Miranda *knew* something was going to happen, could just *tell* from the way He watched her and the way He had touched her shoulder before she climbed out of His car, telling her to be careful. She could feel Him watching her all the way up the path to her front door.

And He was *so* much better looking than Tad, and nicer, too. Miranda knew He would never abandon her in a mall food court for some slut in a neon tank top.

She looked at her watch again. One thirty. How much longer should she wait? She was starting to get really pissed off. Lauren had just walked out of the Dream Machine yesterday without saying a word and left Miranda looking stupid in front of Tad and Billy. Not that Tad and Billy mattered at all now, but it was the principle of the thing. You don't just go off and leave your best friend without saying a word.

Well, maybe I should keep Tad as a backup. Because He isn't going to drive me to school in His car, and I do not want to spend the next year taking the dorky school bus. We'll have to keep our relationship a secret, so I can pretend to be Tad's girlfriend at the same time.

Miranda was sure He would understand. It was the kind of thing that happened in grown-up relationships all the time—a public lover and a secret one.

"You don't even have a relationship yet," she said to herself. "Don't get ahead of yourself."

But they were going to have a relationship. He was going to be the one who took Miranda's troublesome virginity. She knew. She *knew*.

And I'm sure He's a better kisser than Tad, anyway. Tad

had attached himself to her face like an octopus sucker, and she'd just kept telling herself it was all in service of the Camaro. But He was probably a very good kisser. He wouldn't be rough.

There was a rustle in the woods behind her. *Finally*.

"Lauren, what took you so—oh. It's you. What are you doing here?"

It wasn't a very welcoming thing to say to Him. But she hadn't expected to see Him there, in the place where only she and Lauren went. And besides, she wasn't wearing good clothes or lip gloss or anything. She self-consciously smoothed down the hem of her shorts, which had gotten wrinkled. Her armpits were sweaty from pacing around, too, and she bet her hair was frizzy from the heat.

"I heard you and Lauren like to come here," He said. "I was hoping to find you."

Miranda felt a swell of happiness. She'd been right. He wanted her. But then something He'd said snagged on her pride.

"You wanted to find me *and* Lauren?" she asked suspiciously.

That would make more sense, since He knew Lauren first. But it wasn't really what Miranda wanted to hear, especially after He asked about Lauren first thing the night before. She'd almost let herself forget that. He only came to see her because of Lauren. Boring Lauren who still dressed like a little kid and was stuck at home with her brother because her mommy said so.

"Well," He said, giving a shrug that made Him look like a guilty little boy. "I was hoping that you would be alone. And here you are."

Yes. Here I am. She knew that He wasn't really interested in Lauren. Who would be when Miranda was around?

She took a couple of steps toward Him, then stopped. What if Lauren came along just at that moment and ruined everything? There was still a chance she could show up. They had to get away from here before that happened.

Take me away, she thought. *Take me somewhere we can be alone.*

He had stopped about ten or so feet from the ghost tree, leaning against one of the many oaks that surrounded it. His posture told Miranda that He wasn't in a hurry to go anywhere in particular. His eyes moved from her bare ankles and up her legs, over her torso and finally to her face. She stared right back at Him and He smiled.

"Want to walk with me, Miranda?" He asked.

"Yes," she said, and let Him take her hand and lead her into the woods.

3

Alex hadn't wanted to draw attention to what he was doing, so he'd made a mental note to not get caught up in the search and spend so much time in the basement that someone would notice. He'd spent an hour getting dusty as he searched through the files from the year prior, looking for any cases that were similar to the still-unidentified girls in Mrs. Schneider's backyard.

This was both easier and harder than expected. Easier because violent crimes were very rare in Smiths Hollow, so he could tell at a glance if the file was worth further investigation.

It was harder because he had to wade through an ocean of minor break-ins, juvenile shoplifting, and complaints about neighbors having noisy parties. He noticed that Mrs. Schneider featured prominently in a number of these and made a mental note to ask Sofia if she wanted to throw a potluck picnic for the block on the Fourth of July. Let the

Old Bigot complain about the noise when everyone in their neighborhood was outside enjoying themselves while she sat in her living room and choked on her own bile.

Alex knew that he should probably show some compassion for her, given the circumstances of the previous day, but somehow he just couldn't dredge it up for a person like her.

By eleven thirty he'd found no violent crime from 1984 except that of Joe diMucci. He thought there were plenty of similarities—the removal of body parts for one, though the girls had been beheaded and dismembered, and diMucci had his heart removed.

He was fairly certain that the type of wound was similar, but he'd have to compare the photos of diMucci's body to the ones he'd taken of the girls yesterday to be sure.

Some kind of escalation, maybe? Alex thought, and then laughed at himself a little bit. That was something from an FBI novel about serial killers he'd read once. He had about as much experience profiling as he did investigating murders—none at all. But nobody else seemed interested in the dead girls.

Alex thought that under normal circumstances some kind of outside investigator would be called in to help them—detectives from Chicago, maybe, or yes, the FBI. They were a tiny town with a tiny police force that spent most of its time breaking up Friday night fights at the local watering hole. Two mutilated bodies should justify some kind of assistance.

But Christie didn't seem to be inclined to do that, and

Mayor Touhy wasn't interested in bad press that might put his precious summer fair in jeopardy.

How is he going to feel if some killer uses his fair as a hunting ground? Pretty damned stupid.

Alex went to find Miller for lunch, because he knew if he didn't, Miller would come looking for him and he didn't want to answer any questions about what he was doing in the basement. He had an odd feeling that all the files might suddenly disappear, or the department building might be torched in the night. He'd be more willing to dismiss these thoughts as paranoia if he hadn't struggled just to write down *THE GIRLS* in his notebook.

They drove out to Sam's Dairy Bar, because Miller decided he desperately needed a chocolate shake to go with the French fries he craved.

Sam's was a pretty typical roadside shack place with burgers and hot dogs and fries plus shakes and soft serve. Sofia didn't like Alex eating a lot of junk food ("I don't care if you're still fit, that much grease isn't good for anybody"), so he limited his fast food to once a week and brown-bagged Sofia's chicken salad on whole-wheat sandwiches the rest of the time.

"Three chili dogs, one large fry, one chocolate shake," Miller said to the skinny teenager working behind the counter. He took out his wallet. "What do you want, Alex?"

"Chicago dog and a Coke."

"No fries?" Miller couldn't imagine a day passing without eating fries.

"I would have said fries if I wanted fries," Alex said.

He scanned the parking lot while he waited for Miller to finish the transaction. It was the usual summer midday crowd—families with young kids eating ice cream cones, groups of teenagers splitting fries and sundaes. The small radio just inside the front window was playing "Everything She Wants"—a song Alex had heard too many times in the last couple of months, ever since his normally sensible and science-obsessed Val had fallen in love with Wham's lead singer, George Michael. The air was redolent with the scent of frying oil.

He recognized almost everyone by sight if not by name, which just went to show how small Smiths Hollow really was. Alex and his family had only moved in a couple of months before but at least half the people who caught his eye waved and said, "Hi, Officer Lopez!"

There was one notable exception, though. A solitary white man eating a cheeseburger at one of the picnic tables. Alex didn't recognize him, and something about the man made the back of his neck prickle.

It wasn't that the man looked suspicious. Or that he looked like a serial killer. It was more that he Didn't Belong. Alex could practically see the sign above the man's head that marked him as an outsider.

And it wasn't "outsider" as in "from Silver Lake." The man wasn't from anywhere near Smiths Hollow. His clothes were too expensive and so was his haircut. His shoes were too shiny. And he watched the lunch crowd at Sam's Dairy Bar with a faint expression of contempt in his eyes, like he'd bought a ticket to a particularly amusing zoo.

Miller walked toward Alex, carrying a tray loaded with food. They grabbed an empty picnic table. Alex made sure to position himself so he could keep an eye on the stranger.

Alex noted that there were two cardboard trays of French fries. "I said I didn't want fries."

Miller shook his head and pushed the second tray at Alex. "Gotta have fries, man."

Alex wondered sometimes what the inside of Miller's brain looked like. *Madonna, French fries, Pabst Blue Ribbon, and the Cubs*, he thought, answering his own question. How did somebody like that become a police officer?

"What are you looking at?" Miller asked. He took a bite of his chili dog that made half of it disappear.

"There's a guy over there that I don't recognize," Alex said, absently picking at the fries that Miller had pushed in front of him.

"Even I don't recognize everyone and I've lived here my whole life," Miller said. "Who are you talking about?"

"There's a guy sitting by himself under the tree," Alex said. "No, don't turn around."

"What do you think this is? A spy movie?" Miller said, ignoring Alex and twisting around on his seat. He squinted at the figure under the tree. The stranger was now carefully wiping his hands with a handful of the tiny white napkins that were standard issue at roadside shacks and diners across America. "That rich-looking guy?"

"Yes," Alex said, rolling his eyes. "Why don't you just announce it to everybody?"

Miller turned back and shoved the rest of the first hot dog in his mouth. "Probably from Chicago," he said, talking through a mouthful of chili.

Alex winced. "For chrissakes, don't talk with your mouth full. My kids have better table manners than you."

"What's the big deal about that guy?" Miller asked. "I bet he's driving through on his way to somewhere more interesting."

Alex shrugged. "Something about him."

Miller grinned at him. "Well, if he's that suspicious you can go over and ask him what he's doing. You *are* a duly sworn officer of the law, Alex."

"Maybe," Alex said, picking up his hot dog. He'd eaten half the fries without really noticing what he was doing.

He didn't exactly stare at the stranger, but he didn't really let him out of his sight, either. Miller ate the rest of his lunch with the kind of focused concentration normally associated with scientists trying to find a cure for cancer.

They were just about done when the stranger finished up

his own lunch and tossed the trash in a nearby garbage can. Alex thought about hurrying Miller along so they could follow the man and then decided he was being absurd. Didn't he have enough extracurricular projects at the moment?

He did, however, note that the man climbed into a red 1984 Pontiac Fiero with a Chicago city sticker. Alex would definitely notice that car if he saw it again. Very few people in Smiths Hollow drove recent-model cars, and that city sticker made it stand out.

The man put his car in reverse and backed onto the county road without a second glance at the crowd. But Alex was certain the stranger had noticed him watching all the same.

4

George Riley had noticed the cop—some people sitting near Riley had called him "Officer Lopez"—giving him the evil eye at the dump where he'd stopped for a burger. How could he not notice? It was Riley's job to notice such things. A good journalist noticed everything. You never knew what might be important.

Riley wondered what a Hispanic cop was doing in white-bread Smiths Hollow. The census data indicated that less than five percent of the town's population was not white and/or descended from Irish, German, or Polish immigrants. It was not unlike most of Chicago in that respect. Riley had learned to speak Polish early in his career because there were still parts of the city that had more Polish than English speakers.

The Hispanic cop had assessed Riley, drawn conclusions, and made a mental note to keep track of this stranger in town. Riley had seen it all on his face. That face wasn't stupid, though, for all that he probably wasn't very good at poker. He made a mental note of his own to investigate Lopez's background. It might come in handy.

His partner, now—he'd looked like a big dumb piece of meat, typical high-school-football type gone to seed with brains to match. The kind who would punch first and ask questions later. He'd been far more interested in his chili dogs than a stranger in town.

That was what Riley wanted. A police force more interested in local goings-on than in him. Because there was a story here in Smiths Hollow, and he was going to be the one who made it national. And once that happened Riley was going places—to New York or L.A., to a national news beat. No more Chicago crime reporting, no more sordid stories of drug deaths and gang wars.

Riley had called his buddy Paul Nowak—a fellow graduate of Northwestern's prestigious school of journalism who'd decided to return to his small-town roots in Smiths Hollow—the night before for their weekly chat. Nowak had been the only person Riley could tolerate at Northwestern. The program had been stuffed with earnest-eyed students looking to Change the World with their reporting. Everyone wanted to be the next Woodward and Bernstein, taking down corrupt institutions and winning prizes and getting book deals.

Riley, on the other hand, wanted to be a star. He had no intention of staying in newspaper reporting. He wanted Dan Rather's job, and the *Tribune* was just a stepping-stone to get there.

His friend Nowak was a laid-back, just-the-facts type. He didn't have any burning ambitions but he was a very good writer—better than the local rag deserved, actually—and his easygoing manner often fooled people into telling him more than they intended.

Riley had never understood why Nowak had returned to the tiny burg that birthed him rather than parlay his degree into a job at the *Tribune* or the *Sun-Times*.

But Nowak told him that he liked Smiths Hollow and there was nothing wrong with the local paper. Nowak was now the editor (by default, since the previous editor had retired) and claimed that running the *Smiths Hollow Observer* was better than any staff reporter job in the city.

"I make my own hours, buddy," Nowak had told him once. "And as long as I cover all the high school sports and the town council meetings, everyone is happy. I don't have to build a network of sources or have secret meetings in parking garages in the middle of the night."

Of course, real estate in Smiths Hollow was a lot cheaper than in Chicago, so Nowak's piddly salary went further than Riley's did. And Riley had an affection for things he couldn't really afford—Italian-leather shoes, for example, and the flashy new Fiero he was driving into Smiths Hollow proper. If he thought too hard about his Mastercard bill, that burger he ate would probably come right back up.

He turned on the local top forty station and David Lee Roth blasted out of the speakers, singing "Just a Gigolo." Riley didn't really care what music was on as long as there was noise. Noise helped him think, which was reason number 108 why he could never live in a quiet little town like Smiths Hollow.

Of course, Smiths Hollow wasn't quite as quiet as advertised.

During their conversation the previous night Nowak had casually mentioned that two murdered girls had been found in the yard of some old biddy.

"Who are they?" Riley asked.

"Nobody seems to know," Nowak said, his tone the verbal equivalent of a shrug. "They aren't from Smiths Hollow. The chief asked me to put their photos in tomorrow's edition. Maybe someone will recognize them."

"That's a pretty big story for you, huh? Two murders in that town must be worthy of a headline."

"Oh, no," Nowak said. "Christie wants me to keep it quiet until we find the girls' families, no details. So it's going on page three."

Riley's ears pricked up. "That doesn't seem right. Since when does the town chief of police dictate what goes in your paper?"

"I don't mind," Nowak said.

"You should. Whatever happened to freedom of the press?"

"Don't pretend that you care about the Bill of Rights," Nowak said, laughing.

Riley scowled into the phone. "I care about the Bill of Rights. And anyway, you should put those girls' pictures on the front page if the police actually want them to be identified. Tons of people skip right to the sports section."

"I don't know if I want to put them on the front page anyway," Nowak said, his tone suddenly sober. "They did their best to clean them up and the pictures will be in black-and-white, but you can still tell the heads aren't attached to their bodies . . . especially if you know."

"They were *beheaded*?" Riley asked. "Talk about burying the lede, Paul. So . . . do they think it's a serial killer or something? Are they going to call the FBI?"

Riley had read Thomas Harris's *Red Dragon* the year before and since then had done some research on FBI profiling. He had a sudden and exciting vision of being the first reporter to get in on an emerging serial killer story. That would raise his profile, all right. He could be like Jimmy Breslin with Son of Sam.

The idea that Nowak might want to report on the story himself never entered Riley's mind. Nowak was buckling under small-town pressure already. He'd never give two beheaded girls the proper consideration they deserved.

"I don't think they're going to call the FBI," Nowak said.

"Like I said, they're trying to keep things quiet out of respect for the girls' families."

More like trying to keep things quiet so their total incompetence won't be noticed, Riley thought, but he didn't say it.

"Maybe I'll take a drive down there tomorrow," Riley said. "I don't have anything special going on here for a few days, and I have personal time coming."

"Well, I'll be glad to see you. But don't think you can come down here and turn this into some big splashy story. The chief and the mayor won't be happy with me if that happens."

"Don't worry. I wouldn't do that to you," Riley said, lying through his teeth.

Nowak lived in one of the little developments that branched off the main street of town. He'd given Riley detailed turn-by-turn directions, but he wasn't expecting his old college friend until after four p.m. Plenty of time for Riley to poke around the village, maybe have a drink at the bar. Plenty of time to listen to what people were saying about the murdered girls in their midst. The whole town was probably buzzing.

He parked the Fiero in one of the diagonal parking spaces on Main Street, where it drew admiring glances from a small crowd of teenage boys who'd just emerged from the arcade.

There was a bar a few doors down from the arcade that he'd noticed as he parked. He locked his car and strolled in that direction. A neon Budweiser sign shone in the window and the sign over the wooden door proclaimed its identity as *Tiny Lounge*.

There wasn't very much loungelike inside, Riley noted. It had Typical Bar written all over it—dingy green flooring, dingy leather booths, a handful of regulars sitting at the long wooden bar determinedly sucking down beers delivered in frosted mugs.

A few heads turned toward him, their gazes mildly interested in the newcomer, but they quickly returned to their beers once they realized they didn't know who he was. Riley grabbed a seat at the end of the bar, two seats away from a wrinkled white guy who looked old as dirt. There were about four gray hairs left on top of his head and they all stood straight up like baby duck fuzz. Despite the early summer heat he was wearing a red plaid flannel shirt and jeans with worn work boots.

The bartender, a guy who looked like he was in his early thirties (and also lifted weights if the size of his arms was any indication), lifted his chin in Riley's direction. Riley interpreted this as a request for an order.

"Old Style," he said.

The bartender nodded, drew the beer off the tap, and put it in front of Riley with a little cocktail napkin. "Buck fifty."

Riley handed him two dollars. "Keep the change."

He nodded and turned away.

Riley had hoped that there would be some conversation going and he'd be able to slide into it unobtrusively. He didn't think leading with *Hey, what do you think about those murdered girls?* would garner a good result.

But if they were already talking about politics or the Cubs or the White Sox (which was a lot like talking about politics) then he could casually join in and quietly mention the tragedy at some point when the crowd warmed up to him.

Frankly, he was surprised that they weren't already talking about it. Those dead girls had to be the biggest thing to happen in this town since the chili factory opened. Not only was there no discussion of the murder, nobody was discussing *anything*. The radio wasn't on and the TV that hung over the bar was switched off. Not one of the patrons spoke to another.

Riley nursed his beer for a bit, waiting for his chance, but it never came. Two of the six patrons drained off their beers and left without even acknowledging the bartender, who stood with his arms crossed watching all of them like they were misbehaving students.

After twenty or so minutes Riley decided he couldn't take the oppressive atmosphere any longer. He finished his beer, placed the glass on the cocktail napkin, and walked out, letting the door slam shut behind him.

That was the least convivial bar I have ever been in, he thought as he blinked at the abrupt change from the dank gloom of Tiny Lounge to the blistering sunshine outside.

On Main Street all the little residents of Smiths Hollow went about their business—buying lunch meat at the deli, picking up nails and bolts at the hardware store, wiping ice cream and snot off the faces of their screaming children. Much to Riley's disappointment they were all acting completely normal—not a whiff of fear, suspicion, or scandal anywhere.

You'd think nobody was murdered here at all, Riley thought.

He walked in the direction of the arcade, thinking vaguely that the town's teenagers would be talking about it. Kids loved it when anything horrible happened. As he did, one of the Smiths Hollow patrol cars rolled by.

In the passenger seat was the Hispanic cop Riley had seen earlier. The man didn't even bother trying to disguise his interest as the car rolled by. He stared right at Riley in a way that made Riley feel squirmy inside, like he was a child caught doing something wrong.

He shook his head from side to side, trying to dispel the feeling. Riley had just as much right to be in this lame little town as anyone else did. He changed his mind about going into the arcade. There was nobody more pathetically obvious than an adult in a room full of kids playing video games. They wouldn't want to talk to him, and anyway, that cop might decide Riley was trying to pick up underage girls or something. No, he'd have to think of something else.

At the opposite end of Main Street there was a three-story brick building that had that generic town-administration look. Riley bet that was where the mayor's office was located. And the mayor hadn't wanted anyone to know about the dead girls. He was trying to keep it quiet, and to Riley's mind that was suspicious behavior.

He stopped at his car and grabbed his notebook and the Philips portable cassette recorder that he kept in there. In a pinch he could take shorthand notes but he hated doing it and anyway, the presence of a tape recording every word made it less likely that he would be rudely refused by the mayor. Politicians hated to be caught on tape saying anything that might alienate a voter.

The brick building was home of—among other public services—the town courthouse, the municipal water authority, and yes, the mayor's office. Several people were going in and out of the building—some with the officious paper-carrying look of people heading to meetings, others with the midday pinched mouth and eyes that meant they were finally escaping for their lunch break. The lobby was cramped for such a large building—just a tiny entranceway with two elevators off to one side and a bored-looking security guard opposite. The guard told Riley to sign into a large notebook, not bothering to check the signature or the destination. Riley took the elevator to the third floor.

The mayor's office was the third glass door on the right and indicated with no fanfare. White block letters read **MAYOR RICHARD TOUHY**, and behind the glass was an empty desk where a secretary ought to be. Riley knew this because there was a large official-looking appointment ledger on one side of the desk and a typewriter on the other.

Out to lunch, Riley thought. *Convenient.*

Beyond the secretary's domain was an open door. Through that door Riley saw a spindly-looking man with thinning brown hair talking on the telephone. Whatever he was hearing wasn't making him happy, because his thin face twisted with annoyance.

Good, Riley thought. He'd catch the man off-balance and without a guard dog to prevent him from entering the mayor's inner sanctum.

He pushed the door open and pressed the record button on the tape recorder. Riley didn't want to miss a thing.

5

The mayor wasn't completely certain how the man had weaseled his way into the office. Wasn't Harry supposed to check who was coming into the building and who they were going to see? What was the point of security if they weren't going to try at all? He made a mental note to speak to Louie Reynolds, the head of security for the building, about it later. The mayor of Smiths Hollow was supposed to be accessible to the residents of the town, but not that accessible.

Rebecca had just stepped out to get a sandwich for both of them, and in the intervening fifteen minutes this stranger had knocked on his door, interrupting an unproductive conversation with Van Christie regarding the still-unidentified girls.

Touhy noticed the cassette recorder immediately, its bright red button engaged in the "on" position, before he really took a good look at Riley's face. Anyone carrying a tape recorder was trouble, in Touhy's opinion. His clothes seemed to indicate that he might be a banker or a developer, but the tape recorder said otherwise.

The man was dressed in shiny Italian leather shoes, a pair of good-quality gray flannel trousers, and a crisp blue button-down shirt that, despite its clearly elevated price tag, showed that the stranger was sweating. Touhy didn't attribute this to any kind of tension, however. It was hot enough outside to fry the proverbial egg on the sidewalk.

When the stranger entered the room, a waft of cologne preceded him. Touhy disliked men who wore cologne, though he knew it wasn't that unusual these days. In his opinion men shouldn't wear anything that smelled stronger than their Old Spice aftershave.

"Mm-hmm," he said into the phone, not wanting to indicate to the stranger who was at the other end of the line. "Listen, can I give you a call back? Someone's just arrived in my office."

Christie, accustomed to sudden interruptions at the mayor's end, had given a noncommittal grunt and hung up. Touhy carefully placed the phone on the receiver and stood, buttoning his jacket.

"May I help you?" he asked, his tone striking just the right balance between friendliness and certainty that the stranger was in the wrong place.

"George Riley," the man said, holding the recorder in his

left hand and sticking out his right hand for Touhy to shake, which he did automatically. "I'm a reporter from Chicago and I was wondering if I could get a quote from you regarding the murdered girls."

Touhy blinked, although the expression on his face didn't move a fraction of an inch—the result of long practice at taking questions meant to catch him off-guard.

Cracks, he thought. Nobody outside Smiths Hollow was supposed to know about the girls. And no girls born outside Smiths Hollow were supposed to be sacrificed. First there had been the two mystery girls—girls not from here, and not taken at the time they were supposed to be taken—and now there was this nosy newspaperman with his flashy clothes and too-white smile asking about them.

There were cracks in the molding that surrounded the town. Something had gone wrong when Joe diMucci died instead of Lauren.

What next? Touhy thought, and felt a momentary surge of panic that the chili factory would close down. If the monster was running free, if the outside world found out what was happening in his town, then the terms of the curse might fall apart. Yes, that would mean fewer murdered girls (*though it might mean more*). But it would also mean the community might face the same economic ruin as all the other towns around his, and that was unacceptable.

All these thoughts came and went in an instant, never

visible to the intruder who'd disrupted his day. He made a show of checking his watch. "Why don't you sit down, Mr. Riley? I have about ten minutes before another meeting, but I'm happy to answer a few of your questions in the meantime."

A faint expression of surprise passed over Riley's face, and Touhy thought he'd expected hostility. That wasn't Touhy's way. The best course of action was always to seem like you were giving a person what they wanted even if you really weren't.

They settled into their respective chairs. Riley placed the recorder on the edge of Touhy's desk.

"You don't mind if I record this, do you? Your quotes will be more accurate than if I try to interpret my shorthand."

Of course I mind, you son of a bitch, Touhy thought. But all he said was, "Not a problem."

"Now, regarding these girls . . . who are they?"

"We haven't yet been able to identify them," Touhy said smoothly. "We believe they came from out of town, and we are contacting other police departments in the area to see if there have been any reports of missing persons."

"And can you give any details on what exactly happened to them? I heard a rumor that they had been beheaded."

Where did you hear that? Touhy wondered just who had been blabbing to this man. It couldn't have been Christie or anyone on his staff. Although . . . maybe Lopez. He was from Chicago, just like Riley. And he was a recent addition to Smiths Hollow, so maybe the curse hadn't fully taken effect yet. Yes, perhaps he should have a personal word with Lopez. Quietly. No need to get Christie involved.

Riley watched him expectantly, and Touhy realized he hadn't responded.

"The investigation is ongoing. I'm sure you understand that we can't release any details at this time that might compromise finding justice for these poor girls."

"I understand," Riley said, a little smile playing across his face.

Touhy rather thought that he did.

"How about a description? My paper has a much longer reach than the Smiths Hollow local—no offense, Mayor—and anyone looking for these two would be more likely to read about it if I wrote about them."

"I'm afraid I don't have a list of their physical characteristics on hand," Touhy said. "Perhaps you would like to phone Chief Christie? I can give you his telephone number. Now, if you'll excuse me, I do have other commitments today."

Touhy would call Christie to warn him as soon as Riley left, but he wasn't worried about the chief giving away any information. Christie wasn't the talkative type. Besides, the curse was working on him—Touhy could tell. Christie had trouble focusing on the conversation whenever the girls came up. If Touhy could just stop Riley from nosing around, then the whole thing would quietly fade away from public consciousness. As it was supposed to.

"Of course. Thank you for your time," Riley said, standing up. Touhy also stood and shook the other man's hand again.

He wasn't just shuffling Riley out before the reporter could ferret out some real information. The fair was supposed to set up today and he wanted to be there when they arrived.

The fair was his baby and he didn't want it to look like some sordid traveling camp. It should be a glorious paradise of clean, wholesome fun for all of the families of Smiths Hollow—and the neighboring communities. The Silver Lake mall would have nothing on Smiths Hollow's fair. Touhy would see to it.

Once folks came into town for the fair they would stop and have dinner at one of the local restaurants, or shop at the boutiques on Main Street. And when they saw how charming Smiths Hollow was they would return again and again with their dollars and Touhy would have fulfilled his mission as mayor—to keep the town financially secure.

If he didn't, then all the blood spilled meant nothing.

Rebecca returned carrying a paper sack with Touhy's deli sandwich. She paused in the open doorway, staring at Riley uncertainly.

"Mayor Touhy?" she asked.

"Mr. Riley was just leaving," Touhy said, taking the paper sack from her. "Thank you, Rebecca. Do you think you could give him the phone number for the police station? I promised it but don't have it handy."

She nodded and stepped out of the way for Riley, who followed her as she went around to her desk.

Touhy closed the door behind him, but very softly. He wouldn't want Riley to think he'd been unwelcome.

6

Miranda opened the back door carefully, not wanting to slam the screen door and let her mother know she was home. Janice was probably out cold on the sofa in any case. If her mother was still awake she'd be on her fourth or fifth drink by now and wrapped up in *Days of Our Lives* or *Ryan's Hope* or whatever it was she watched in the afternoon. So Janice probably wouldn't notice the state of Miranda, but she wasn't taking any chances. Her mother could occasionally be very observant.

Miranda wanted to go upstairs and wash her face and change her clothes before her mother got a good look at her. The seat of her shorts and the back of her shirt were stained with dirt and she was sure her face was flushed. She toed out of her sneakers, left them in a heap on the mat, and ran lightly on bare feet down the carpeted hallway.

There was a double-sized doorway into the living room that opened out to the foot of the stairs and the front foyer, but the back of the sofa also faced that direction. When Miranda risked a look around the doorjamb, she saw the back of Janice's permed head. Her mother was lolling forward slightly, a sure sign that she was dozing.

Janice had been coming home earlier and earlier from work for the past couple of years, so that lately it seemed like she returned home at lunch (liquid, of course) and never went back in for the rest of the day. Her mother and father were both managers at the chili factory, so Miranda assumed her dad covered for her mom.

Either that or Janice's work was so inconsequential she was able to finish it by midday. Miranda didn't really care except that it meant that in the summer Janice was hanging around the house trying to act like a parent. If her mother had been at work as she was supposed to be, then Miranda would have been free to come and go without someone trying to find out where she was going and what she was doing and who she was going with.

Thank God for Lauren, Miranda thought as she climbed the stairs on tiptoe, avoiding all the places where the stairs creaked. She'd been sneaking into the house past her curfew since she was ten and had never been caught. Miranda could always tell her parents she was going out with Lauren and they would never question it.

Thinking of Lauren reminded her that Lauren had never shown up that afternoon.

Or maybe she did, Miranda thought, *but you were gone by then. Off into the forest with Him, and serves Lauren right for ditching you yesterday.*

She hugged her arms around herself, unable to stop grinning. He'd taken her into the woods and while she hadn't lost her virginity it was only a matter of time. He couldn't keep His hands off her. She had never felt so powerful as she had when He put His arms around her. There'd been a look in His eyes, a wild neediness, that was only for her.

"No one can know," He whispered into her mouth. "It's our secret."

And of course she knew it had to be a secret, because she was underage. Not that He was so very old, but it was technically illegal for Him to be with her. Which was a really stupid concept, Miranda thought as she undressed down to her underwear.

If she knew what she was doing, then why would they get in trouble? Who cared what age she was? It wasn't like He was tricking her into having sex—or something close to sex. She wasn't some naïve little dummy from the country.

She examined her breasts in the mirror, pushing them up a little by pressing her upper arms against the outside of her chest. Yeah, her breasts were pretty grown-up-looking. And they weren't all saggy yet like her mother's. If she dressed right she could pass for eighteen, she bet.

Then He could take her out to dinner—not in Smiths Hollow, of course, because a nosy someone would be sure to see and report back to Janice and Bob—but somewhere a few towns over, where they wouldn't bump into anyone. Maybe all the way to Chicago. It was only forty-five minutes on the train.

He'd pressed her into the ground with His body and He'd felt like a man, sort of strong and gentle at the same time—not a flailing octopus like Tad. He'd shown her what to do and how to make Him feel good and when He gasped she knew He wouldn't think of anybody but her. Nobody else could make Him respond like that, Miranda was sure.

She turned sideways in front of the mirror to look at her chest from the side and noticed a purpling bruise at her hip, just beneath the line of her underpants. In her excitement over her conquest she'd forgotten about that thing that happened. It had only been for a second, and she must have imagined that look.

He'd grabbed onto her and squeezed hard enough to make her cry out. She'd opened her eyes and He'd been watching her with a . . . well, she didn't really know how to define it but He'd looked *hungry*. Except it wasn't in a hungry-for-your-body kind of way, but more like He actually wanted to eat her up.

Like He wanted to hurt her.

Don't be silly, Miranda thought. *He apologized. It was an accident. He just got overexcited. And you imagined that look.*

She put on a fresh T-shirt and shorts—Janice would never notice that she'd changed, and even if she did Miranda would just say she'd gotten dirty playing in the woods. Which was true, in a sense. She giggled to herself and then covered her mouth.

Miranda went into the bathroom and washed her face and brushed her teeth. She brushed her hair and then put it up in a fresh ponytail. Then she went into her room, pushed the lock on the door, and pulled out her stash of *Cosmopolitan* magazines from under her bed.

There were always good sex tips in *Cosmo* and even though He would obviously be able to tell that she was a virgin because her virginity would be in the way, she didn't want to seem totally inexperienced. She also had some Jackie Collins novels hidden beneath the mattress and she thought it would be a good idea to go back and review the steamier bits.

Her father, Bob, disapproved of "that garbage," which was why the books were hidden. Miranda thought he was probably just jealous that other people—even if they were fictional characters—were getting laid when he wasn't. She figured that Bob and Janice hadn't had sex since Janice got pregnant.

Two hours later she heard her mother's slow tread at the bottom of the stairs. Miranda knew it would take Janice a few minutes to get to the top, so she had plenty of time to stow her magazines under the bed, tuck *Hollywood Wives* back in between the mattress and box spring, unlock her door, and lie back down on her bed with a harmless copy of *Seventeen*.

She'd just flipped to a fashion layout in the center of the magazine when Janice knocked once and pushed open the door. Her mother gave her a bleary look.

"Have you been home long?"

Miranda glanced at the clock. "A few hours."

That seemed safe. She didn't know when Janice had fallen asleep on the couch.

"Lauren called to say she couldn't make it and that she would call you later. She was sorry you'd left already. Did you wait long?"

Stupid bitch, why did she call the house? What if Janice wants to know what I was doing all that time?

"For a while," Miranda said noncommittally.

"I'm making meat loaf and potatoes for dinner," Janice said.

Oh, boy. Dried-out ground beef and lumpy potatoes and gravy from an envelope. Maybe she should call Tad and tell him to take her out to make up for abandoning her the night before.

"Okay."

Her mother shut the door and Miranda let out the breath she'd been holding. Good thing Janice had no curiosity whatsoever. Or maybe she just had a headache. She'd had that slightly squinty look that meant her head was pounding.

Well, Miranda had gotten out of that without the third degree. But she was going to call Lauren later and tell her to keep her dumb mouth shut in the future.

7

Karen didn't know what had happened between her mother and Lauren that afternoon. She didn't know because neither of them would tell her, despite the fact that Karen had called her mother and demanded to know what had caused her daughter to leave her bike in the backyard instead of putting it away properly and then run upstairs and lock the door of her bedroom.

Karen called her mother and Mom had only said, "It's between me and Lauren," which left Karen with the same wrenched-stomach feeling that she always had when the two of them put their heads together and left her out.

It was ridiculous that she should feel this way, feel like a high school girl who wasn't allowed to join the cool-girls club, but she always had. Karen had never been close to her mother. She'd always felt that Mom held herself away, kept secrets she didn't want to share with her daughter.

But she was happy to share them with Lauren, the blessed grandchild, Karen thought sourly. Even when Mom and Lauren argued, as they were now, she was abandoned on the periphery.

After getting no answers from her mother, she'd gone upstairs to bang on Lauren's door and demand them from her instead. But Lauren had only told her, "It's between me and Nana."

Karen wished she could draw the words from her daughter's throat, force them to emerge purely through the effort of her own will.

No matter how long she stared at the grainy wood of Lauren's bedroom door, her child did not emerge and tell her what was wrong. And it was difficult not to feel that she had failed, that if Lauren loved her better, trusted her more, this would not be. Lauren should have run into her mother's arms if she was weeping, but she'd run past her instead.

It was always that way. Even when Lauren was small she'd choose her father over her mother if she skinned her knee or bumped her head. Lauren had never wanted Karen, would twist away from her if Karen tried to console her or kiss her cheek.

When Karen had David, his behavior had been a miracle. He always wanted to cuddle with her, always wanted to be held by her or walk next to her and hold her hand. He'd spent so much time right next to Karen that Joe had muttered darkly about David being a "mama's boy."

"What's the matter with that?" Karen had demanded. "Why can't he prefer me to you?"

"Don't want him to grow up to be a sissy, that's why," Joe said.

Privately Karen didn't care if David was a "sissy," but all she'd said to Joe was, "He's still a baby," and Joe had subsided.

Part of Joe's irritation had stemmed from the fact that David had steadfastly refused to be interested in the tiny baseball glove and soft rubber baseball that Joe bought him when he was three.

The boy didn't have any interest in trying to catch the ball when it was tossed or chasing it around the yard when he missed it. Joe had watched in increasing frustration as David had been distracted by the bees buzzing in the clover and worms pushing through the surface of the lawn. Nature was not a thing a proper boy should be interested in, in Joe's opinion. The only thing a boy should be doing outdoors was getting dirty playing football or some such thing.

But Lauren had been happy to catch the ball when Joe threw it, and to throw it back hard enough that Joe gave her what he considered to be a great compliment—"You don't throw like a girl."

Lauren's face had glowed when he said that, but Karen had wanted to say, "What's wrong with throwing like a girl? What's wrong with being a girl and liking girl things? Why are we less than you? Why is Lauren better for not behaving like me?"

But she never said those things, because Joe never listened. And even if he had listened, he wouldn't have understood.

Karen left Lauren to her own devices until dinnertime.

"Can you go and tell your sister dinner will be ready in ten minutes?" she asked David. He sat at the kitchen table coloring.

"Okeh," he said, and hopped off the chair. His bare feet tapped along the hallway and up the stairs.

Karen collected his coloring book and crayons and put them on the sideboard so she could set the table. She wiped sweat off her forehead with her forearm as she placed the last fork. She had roasted a chicken with carrots and potatoes even though it was hot and having the oven on made the kitchen unbearable.

But a chicken means leftovers, which means I can get two or three meals for the price of one.

Chicken salad, chicken soup. Or maybe chicken enchiladas? Depends on how much chicken is left, really.

She would never forgive Joe for canceling his life insurance without telling her. Never.

And she would never forgive him for continuing to take the life insurance payment out of their checking account and using it on God knows what. Hotel rooms for the slut he was fucking, probably.

Now she had to make their meager savings stretch until

David could attend kindergarten and she could get at least a part-time job.

Although maybe Sofia would babysit, Karen thought. *But does it make sense to pay out half of your salary to a sitter?*

Whenever she thought about money or the future, her lungs felt tight. Everywhere she looked, the options were limited and terrible.

Lauren hated it when Karen told her she couldn't have the same jeans as Miranda, or the sneakers that would mark her as one of the in-crowd. But Karen couldn't justify the cost when they needed to eat.

And when she told her daughter that, Lauren would give her that look, that hateful look that she saved just for her mother—the one that let Karen know that Lauren thought she was inadequate in every way.

David's little feet tap-tap-tapped down the stairs and down the hall again. He stopped in the doorway.

"Lauren said she's not hungry," David said.

No, we aren't having any of that, Karen thought. She said to David, "Okay, honey, I'll go talk to her."

The chicken was supposed to come out in a few minutes so Karen jogged up the steps and arrived, out of breath, in front of Lauren's door again.

"You will come down to dinner," Karen said.

"I'm not hungry," Lauren said. Flat. Disrespectful.

Karen took a deep breath so she wouldn't start kicking the

door. Sometimes she felt so helpless in the face of her daughter's attitude that she wanted to break everything in sight.

"I am not going to stand here arguing with you through this door. You will come down or you won't get your allowance for the next month."

She turned on her heel and went back downstairs, just in time for the timer to start beeping that the chicken was done.

And when Lauren had dropped her butt into her chair a few minutes later, Karen had congratulated herself for managing the situation so well. Even if Lauren did have an expression on her face that would be more appropriate if the world were ending, or perhaps a member of Duran Duran had died.

But if Lauren pushed her carrots around the circumference of the plate one more time Karen was not going to be held responsible for her behavior. Lauren acted like Karen was trying to force-feed her poison.

David watched his sister with a quizzical expression, although he ate everything with his usual relish. He'd always been a good eater. He hadn't been one of those babies that didn't want to transition from bottle to solid food. Whatever Karen had spooned out of the Gerber jars, David had happily eaten.

He'd always been her happy child. Lauren was a colicky baby, a tantrum-y toddler and a sullen grade schooler. Now she was an angry teenager and Karen half wished she could trade her for a different child.

In fairy tales fairies would take away a human baby and leave a supernatural replacement. Maybe that was what had happened. Maybe Karen's real baby, a happy, smiling Lauren, had been taken away to fairyland and they'd left this forever-dissatisfied girl in her place.

She's your daughter, and you love her.

Yes, she loved her daughter. But it had been a long time since she liked her.

"Do you believe in magic?"

Karen gave a little start. It was like Lauren had seen inside her brain, or heard the traitorous thought that a changeling had been left in her place.

Don't be ridiculous.

Lauren glared at her, like whatever answer she gave would be the wrong one.

Karen gave a half glance at David, worried that Lauren might say something about Santa Claus or the Easter Bunny not being real.

"I think that we don't know or understand everything in the universe," Karen said carefully. "So magic is possible, I suppose."

"Like spells and witches?" The words shot out of Lauren's mouth like live ammunition.

This has something to do with her argument with Mom, Karen thought. She'd have to tread carefully, because if she by word or deed offended Lauren, then any chance of discovering what was troubling her would be gone forever.

"I don't know if there are witches like you see in the movies—"

"How do you know?"

Karen tried again. "Well, there isn't any evidence of—"

"Oh, what the hell do you know?" Lauren shouted, slamming her fork down next to her plate. "Nothing. You know nothing about anything."

"Watch your language!" Karen said. "You don't talk that way in my house."

"And that's all you care about, isn't it? How people act in 'your house' and where they put their stuff in 'your house.' It's not even your house anyway. It was Dad's money that paid for it," Lauren said.

"And that's where *you* know nothing," Karen said through her teeth. "Your father's business would never have come close to paying for a house this size, especially when it bled away money. He was always performing labor for free, or discounting auto parts for people. It was my money, my inheritance from my father that paid for this house."

And it's the only reason we stay here. Because there's no mortgage to pay off and no rent to pay.

Lauren looked slightly chastened at that, but in the way of all teenage girls she decided to disregard the facts that didn't suit her.

"Dad did that because he cared about other people. He

was helping them out. Not like you. I've never seen you so much as help an old lady across the street."

Every word was like a punch to Karen's heart, her lungs, her stomach. Karen volunteered her time at Lauren's school as a lunch monitor, had delivered meals to the elderly, had watched other people's children for free so that they could go to jobs or run errands. There were so many things that she did, but Lauren didn't know about them because she didn't brag about them the way Joe had.

But it didn't matter. She didn't have to justify her behavior or explain herself to a fourteen-year-old girl.

"Go to your room," Karen said, her tone as frosty as a midwinter wind.

"Get out of my room, go back to my room, make up your damned mind," Lauren said, pushing her chair back from the table.

"You have lost your next two months of allowance," Karen said. "Keep talking to me like that and you'll be grounded for the rest of the summer. No more sneaking off to the arcade with boys."

"I wasn't sneaking!" Lauren shouted. "And Miranda was the one who brought those boys."

"I don't want to hear your excuses," Karen said.

"You NEVER LISTEN!" Lauren said. "YOU NEVER EVER LISTEN TO ME! I HATE YOU!"

Well, there it was. Lauren had finally said the thing

she'd been saying without actually saying ever since Joe had died. It wasn't completely unexpected, and Karen knew that lots of teenagers said things they didn't mean in the heat of the moment.

Yes, that was it. It was only the heat of the moment. Lauren was upset about some argument with her grandmother. This wasn't about Karen at all. It couldn't be, because the baby who'd grown to life beneath her heart couldn't be looking at her with eyes that spewed venom a second before her mouth did.

"I WISH YOU DIED INSTEAD OF DAD!"

Karen felt part of her heart fall away then, plummet deep into some bloodied abyss.

This girl who she'd carried inside her body, this child who she'd sung over and dreamed of, this baby who she'd loved more than any other human being alive on the day she'd been born—this child, her only daughter, wished she'd been murdered in her husband's place.

And there was nothing Karen could do as Lauren ran from the room with tears in her eyes. There was nothing she could say because her voice was stopped by the tears clogging her own throat, the ones that she would not let fall.

8

Mrs. Schneider stood at her kitchen window and stared out at the backyard. The police had, of course, cleared away the abomination that had soiled her property the previous day. But somehow every time she looked outside she thought she could still see it there, like an afterimage burned on her eyes.

"Disrespectful," she muttered. "If someone wanted to murder some worthless girls, then they should have left them somewhere else. Not in my yard."

She could only imagine what Mr. Schneider would have said about this. He'd fenced in the yard so they would be protected from this kind of harassment—from any kind of harassment, really. Mr. Schneider had understood that People Would Impose On You if you didn't make it clear that under no circumstances whatsoever were they permitted to borrow your gas grill, let their children cross your property line or even accidentally toss a ball into your patch of grass.

Mr. Schneider had always dealt with lost balls (or Frisbees or whatever else the "noisy little bastards," as he'd called them, had thrown) firmly by putting all such rubbish where it belonged—in the trash can.

This had not endeared him to the parents of the "noisy little bastards" but, as Mr. Schneider so often said, he was not there to make friends. He didn't particularly care if the neighborhood families hated him. Mrs. Schneider supposed it would have been different if they'd been able to have their own children. But God had not seen fit to bless them with their own offspring. So there were no little Schneiders to carry on the family name, and Mr. Schneider made war with the children in the cul-de-sac instead of teaching his own son how to throw a baseball.

"And I would have been able to teach him properly, as well, so it wouldn't end up in someone else's yard," he said.

He was unfazed by the eggs and toilet paper that decorated the front of their house every Halloween.

Unfazed because, as Mrs. Schneider recalled, he sat in the front window and wrote down the names of every one of the little brats who had the audacity to do such a thing and then brought that list to the chief of police. The chief was then forced to talk to the parents of all the rotten apples, which meant they were punished—very often by being forced to return to the scene of the crime and clean up their mess.

"As someone should clean up this mess," she said, for

when she glanced in the yard again she saw those girls' heads, the shiny viscera scattered all around, and the buzzing cloud of flies hovering like a sending from a demon of hell.

But then she blinked and the vision was gone again.

"This never happened before those Mexicans moved into the neighborhood," Mrs. Schneider said.

She felt a tiny flush of guilt at this, because that skinny little mother from across the street had called the police and then put her arm around Mrs. Schneider until they came. That was very neighborly of her—what was her name? Foreign-sounding name.

"Sofia," she said. "Why can't foreigners give their children good solid American names, like Elizabeth or Jennifer?"

The only Sofia Mrs. Schneider knew of was Sophia Loren, and she was definitely a foreigner.

"Italian," she said. "Even if Loren isn't a wop name. Trying to pretend she's something she isn't."

She wondered what Mr. Schneider would have said if someone had tried putting dead bodies in their yard while he was alive.

"He would have called the chief of police," she said. "But I talked to Van Christie already."

Yes, she'd talked to Van Christie while that dirty Mexican policeman stood in her yard. His wife may have come inside her house (the woman had not been invited; she'd just barged her way in), but Mrs. Schneider would not lower her standards so far as to offer coffee to a man who represented everything she hated.

She was sure that the death of those girls had something to do with that family across the street. Never mind if one of them *was* a policeman.

"I should call the mayor," she said.

But she knew Richard Touhy, and his father too, and they were both the same. He wouldn't want to hear about anything that made his town seem less-than-perfect. And on the telephone he could say anything he wanted while rolling his eyes at her.

"Disrespectful," she said.

Yes, Richard Touhy was disrespectful. But he would have to listen to her if she met him in person. He wouldn't be able to do the crossword puzzle instead of taking her concerns seriously.

"This never happened before those Mexicans moved here," she muttered. "They're probably over there sacrificing humans to their ancient gods in the backyard."

She'd heard something about that once—that Mexicans used to sacrifice people to the sun. Was it on a program that Mr. Schneider watched—one of those *National Geographic* specials? She herself had never had any interest in primitive cultures, but he had enjoyed that sort of thing. Yes, human sacrifice. That explained many things.

Only people like that could have done the horrible thing

that had been left in her yard. And the wife, the one who seemed nice enough (although Mrs. Schneider recalled then that the wife had slapped her and that was not acceptable, not at all) had been sent over to make sure Mrs. Schneider didn't talk to anyone about it. And the husband was in the police force so he could cover it all up.

It all made sense now.

And she was going to explain those things to Richard Touhy, whether he wanted to hear them or not.

She should telephone a few other people, as well. She had friends who were also unhappy about the presence of foreigners in the cul-de-sac. If they knew what had happened to her then they would contact Touhy and complain as well. He would be forced to take action if a large group of his constituents approached him about the same issue.

He would have to get rid of those Mexicans.

"Yes," she said, deciding to call Ethel Wagner first. Touhy could keep, for now. "There are going to be some changes around here."

9

Lauren knew she shouldn't have yelled at her mother like that. Mom was the revenging type. She was probably downstairs thinking up every possible thing she could take away from Lauren—her allowance, her telephone privileges, her television time.

No more meetings under the ghost tree. No more riding her bike wherever she wanted to go.

But Lauren had been biting her tongue for days, suppressing her irritation at Mom's constant nagging. When they were sitting there at the table and she asked Mom about magic, Mom had given her that slightly superior look that she always gave when she thought Lauren asked a stupid question.

And it had just been the last straw.

But it wouldn't have happened at all if Mom had just *left her alone* the way she'd asked her to. Lauren wasn't hungry, hadn't wanted to eat at all. Moreover, she hadn't wanted the burden of being expected to sit up straight, shovel food in her mouth, and make meaningless conversation when she was dealing with a personal crisis.

"But nooooo, Mom said I had to come downstairs or I would lose my allowance."

Which was profoundly unfair, because Lauren did a ton of chores around the house and spent a lot of time watching David and she *earned* her allowance. Her mom shouldn't be allowed to take it away just because she didn't like Lauren's attitude. Lauren's attitude shouldn't come into it at all. She'd done the work and she deserved the money.

And she was saving her money so she could buy a real pair of Converse sneakers.

"Not like these stupid cheap ones," she said, picking up the sneakers that she'd thrown near the bedroom door when she came home earlier. She threw one as hard as she could against the wall. It hit her *Purple Rain* poster and the corner of it ripped.

"Goddammit!" Lauren screamed. She threw the other sneaker at her closet door. It made a satisfying thump but the cheap wood had a dent in it.

"Great, something else for Mom to yell at me about," Lauren said, and flopped facedown on her bed.

The comforter was an ancient pink one that she'd had since she was nine or ten. There was an underskirt made up of pink ruffles that went around the box spring and covered the underbed area (*because God knows we can't have anybody seeing what's under the bed*, Lauren thought sourly).

She'd been begging for something more grown-up. What she really wanted was a red plaid quilt she'd seen in a catalog, and plain sheets in red or white or gray. The sheets on the bed at the moment were threadbare and covered in a Raggedy Ann print. And her other sheet sets weren't much better— strawberry patches and daisies and Holly Hobbie prints. Whenever Miranda came over she made fun of them.

Lauren knew that it was unlikely her mother would ever be able to afford the particular quilt she wanted from the catalog. But she'd seen a halfway decent set at Kmart—a plain blue comforter that reversed to gray and a set of blue and gray checked sheets. The price hadn't seemed outrageous to Lauren, but her mother had said no immediately.

Lauren never got anything she wanted.

"If I were really a witch I'd make money appear," she said into the comforter. "I'd buy anything I wanted. I'd take my money to the music store and buy twenty tapes if I wanted. I'd have a new denim jacket and new sneakers and Jordache jeans. No, Sasson. Even Miranda doesn't have Sasson."

And now she was back to the thing that she really didn't want to think about—that bullshit story that her nana had told her about Smiths Hollow and the family of witches. The more she thought about it, the angrier Lauren got.

Why had Nana tried to push that stupid garbage on her?

Did she think Lauren was an idiot?

She rolled over onto her back and spoke to the ceiling. "If there was a stupid curse and a bunch of stupid girls were dying, everybody would know! Does she think I'm dumb? And what was that crap at the end about being magical?"

Magic wasn't real, even if her mom did try to make her feel better by answering so carefully. Lauren could admit, now that she was cooling off, that Mom had been trying not to offend her.

But that doesn't change the fact that she's annoying ninety-nine percent of the time and she never lays off me.

She felt a sudden and profound longing for Miranda—not the new Miranda, not the one who never listened to her—but the old Miranda. Miranda used to keep Lauren's secrets. She used to wrap her arm around Lauren's shoulders when she was sad. She used to care about Lauren as a person, not a prop.

If Miranda had been who she used to be, Lauren would have called her right away after the disaster at Nana's house. She would have whispered, "Meet me by the old ghost tree," and Miranda would have been there.

But not anymore.

And you forgot Miranda today, anyway, so what kind of friend are you? Lauren thought with a guilty little start. She'd never called Miranda back to say why she'd been unable to come today. She wondered if Miranda was mad about it.

Who cares? If she's mad then you won't have to deal with her dragging you around to places you don't want to go anymore.

Lauren sat straight up, climbed off the bed, and went to the window. Her room was in a little nook just below the attic, and the one thing she really liked about it was that there was a built-in bookshelf and window seat beneath an old-fashioned window that pushed out instead of going up and down. She didn't know what kind of window it was called, although maybe she could look it up in the encyclopedia.

Her room looked over the front yard and the street. There was a large oak tree in their yard and just enough of the branches reached out to block the view so that she couldn't see down the street to the right, only what was directly in front of the house and a little bit to the left. The window was open to let the air in and she heard the kids down the street playing in the cul-de-sac. There was the crack of a bat against a ball and a variety of cheers and groans. Lauren wished she could go out there and play with them, but she was too old now.

A movement to the left caught her eye and she saw a little orange Gremlin driving slowly up the street toward the cul-de-sac. She couldn't see the driver but it seemed like the car slowed for a moment in front of her house, but maybe it was her imagination. Lauren strained to see where the car went, but the leaves were too thick and it disappeared out of her sight.

"Nobody who lives here has a car like that," she said. She didn't usually care about stuff like cars, but an orange Gremlin stood out.

She thought about trying to sneak out of the house to see where the car went.

Why do you care so much?

She didn't care, not really. She was just angry and sad and confused and a whole bunch of other things at the same time and she didn't want to think about Nana or what Nana said. She wanted to think about anything else but that.

I am not a witch. Just because I had some weird vision yesterday does not mean I am a witch.

Yes, that vision. It was strange, because it should have stuck in her mind. She'd seen—*well, more like "seen,"* she thought, mentally putting air quotes around the word—two girls get killed, and her own head had felt like it was going to explode. So the incident should have been constantly in her thoughts.

But it wasn't. Instead, it was like she completely forgot it for long periods of time, and when it came back to her it was like a swimmer pushing up from the depths of a very deep pool, gasping for air.

"And there was the blood on my bike seat," she murmured.

She thought she'd acted very strange there. She'd washed off all the blood like she was guilty of something, instead of showing someone. (*Not Mom, she wouldn't have been helpful.*

Before today I would have said Nana. Why didn't I show Nana?)

Was it because she felt guilty? Why should she feel guilty? It wasn't her fault, what that monster had done to those girls.

But maybe it's your family's fault, if Nana isn't lying. Maybe some ancestors of yours cursed this town when they were grieving and furious and wild with those feelings. Maybe they lashed out in anger and because of that, innocent people have died.

Maybe if your vision had come sooner you could have saved them.

The thought made her gasp. *No. It was already over and done before you saw anything. There wasn't anything you could do.*

And what if you did have a vision sooner? How could you fix it? Tell the police that you think someone might be murdered in the woods later?

Officer Hendricks wouldn't smile at her with those kind eyes anymore then. He'd think she was crazy, and so would everybody else. They'd say, "Poor Lauren diMucci. Her dad got killed and it's finally made her nuts."

She thought she might be halfway to the nuthouse already. She was thinking about her vision like it was a real thing, instead of an especially vivid side effect of a particularly bad migraine.

"Which was all it was, because there are no such things as witches and magic powers," she told herself.

Except something happened to David, too.

And there was the blood on her bike seat. The blood in the shape of a man's hand, but with claws.

Doesn't mean it's a monster. It could be a serial killer. Like Freddy Krueger.

Miranda had made her watch *A Nightmare on Elm Street*, and though Lauren spent half the movie peeking through her fingers, she'd seen enough to know the killer wore a glove with razor blades for fingers.

It was a lot more likely that some weirdo was copying the movie than that a monster lived in the tree and it came out at certain times.

So Nana was full of it, like Lauren thought.

Though that still meant a killer was running around somewhere. Possibly wearing a glove with claws on it.

And he touched your bike with that bloody glove, which made the strange handprint.

Then you, like a total dummy, washed off all the evidence.

Why had she done that? She could have taken it to the police station. Even if she couldn't tell them that she thought a murderer touched the seat, they still would have thought it was weird. She bet Officer Hendricks or Officer Lopez would at least have taken some pictures or something.

Instead she brought it home and scrubbed it off so thoroughly that the bike, formerly mud-spattered, appeared brand new.

It had never even occurred to her at the time to do

anything else. She'd panicked. She'd acted like she'd done something wrong.

Why? Stupid, stupid, stupid.

Lauren caught movement out of the corner of her eye and glanced out the window.

Jake Hanson stood at the end of the driveway, looking up at the house.

Lauren jerked away from the window automatically. She didn't want him to see her.

What was he doing there? As far as Lauren knew, he didn't live at home. He was away at college most of the year, and the rest of the time she was pretty sure he had an apartment of his own.

She ran to the light switch by the doorway and turned off the overhead light in her room. Then she returned to the window but stayed back far enough and to the side of the glass that he wouldn't be able to get a good look at her. If he did look up at her window he might think she was just a shadow.

He was staring up at her bedroom window, and something about the way he looked made her think that he knew she was there.

Was he concerned about her because she'd acted so strange earlier? His manner at the gas station had indicated he wanted to talk to her, but she'd rushed away.

And why did he seem so interested in her all of a sudden? Was watching her puke yesterday that attractive?

"Attractiveness does not even come into it," she said. "You're in high school and he's in college, so don't get any weird ideas."

But she did have a weird idea. She had a weird idea that he *was* attracted to her.

Stupid. He's so much older than you are. Why would he want to hang around a kid like you? She hovered in the shadow near the edge of the window. Half her face was pressed against the wall. Her fingers curled around the sharp edge of it. Her palms were damp and she didn't know why.

He smiled then, slowly, a smile that knew all her secrets but promised to keep them.

Everything inside her chest felt all fluttery then, like a moth-jar set near the flame of a candle. She gripped the corner of the wall with slippery fingers.

Then he walked away. He hadn't tried to ring the bell or wave at her in the window or indicate in any way that he wanted to speak to her.

Disappointment crashed over her, washing her body from the top of her head down to her heels. Whatever Jake Hanson was up to, he wasn't interested in her.

If he were, then he would have actually tried to talk to her instead of standing in the driveway staring at the house.

"Stupid," she repeated again. All she did was think stupid things and do stupid things.

She collapsed on the bed again, all the weight of

everything that had happened in the last two days pressing down on her.

The truth was, even though there had been blood on her bike seat and there were clearly two dead girls in Mrs. Schneider's yard, that didn't necessarily mean that the thing she saw was the thing that happened. So maybe there was no vision after all—just a weird coincidence.

"They were carrying backpacks, though," Lauren muttered, covering her eyes with her arm. "What happened to their backpacks?"

She wasn't sure where exactly the murders took place, but if she could find the backpacks, then . . .

Then what?

Then at least she would know for sure that she wasn't completely crazy, that whatever she had seen while in the throes of that migraine was true.

And it would be evidence, evidence that could help the police. It wouldn't matter then that you washed the blood off your bike.

She imagined presenting the girls' backpacks to Officer Hendricks, imagined how he would smile at her and the corners of his eyes would crinkle up.

But how was she going to get out to the woods to explore? If Lauren knew her mother (and she did know her), then she was downstairs plotting to keep Lauren stuck in the house doing chores for the rest of the summer.

You'll just have to sneak out.

But what if you get caught?

It would be worth it if she found the girls' backpacks, or maybe some other kind of evidence that would prove useful.

You would be like a hero. You would be helping find out who killed them. Your picture might even be in the paper.

Miranda would be so jealous if that happened. Lauren thought that might be good for her, actually. Miranda was too used to being the sun around which all the planets of her life revolved.

Her mom couldn't monitor her every second of the day. Sooner or later there would be a chance for Lauren to sneak out. And what was Mom going to do then? Ground her again?

She couldn't chain Lauren to the bed, or lock her in her room. That would be child abuse. All she could do was say, "You're grounded," and if Lauren didn't cooperate then those words were useless.

It was a strange realization, that her mother was not all-powerful. That part of her authority stemmed from Lauren's belief in it and Lauren's compliance.

I don't have to do what she says.

She could refuse to give Lauren her allowance, though. That was definitely true. There wasn't a lot Lauren could do about that unless she was willing to steal money from her mom's wallet.

Her stomach squelched nervously at the thought. No, she didn't think she could do that.

Well, when she was fifteen she would be able to get a job and her mom's piddly allowance wouldn't matter anymore. Even if she had to wash dishes at a restaurant or something. Lauren didn't care as long as she could get out of the house and make her own money.

Lauren rolled onto her belly and saw that the book she'd been reading was across the room on top of her dresser. She wanted to read, but she didn't want to get up and get it. All the frantic bike riding and emotional conflicts of the day were catching up with her. She felt like something was pulling her down, like her body was filling up with molten lead.

You're a witch.

"Okay, Nana. Prove it, then," Lauren said.

She held out her hand in the direction of the book and concentrated hard. Her eyebrows scrunched together. The muscles in her neck strained. Her back teeth ground against each other, but nothing happened. Shouldn't the book just fly into her hand if she had magic powers?

"Of course not. Because there's no such thing as witches. Or Jedi, either," Lauren added.

She didn't think any amount of running or doing handstands would make it possible to move objects with her mind. Nor would a cape and a spellbook. It was all a lot of garbage.

She didn't really feel like getting up to get her book,

though. It was easier just to stay there and look at the ceiling and think about everything in her life that had gone wrong in the last couple of days. The sun shone outside her window, but her eyes drifted closed.

When she woke up the sun was still shining, but she could tell from the angle that it was morning. Her abdomen hurt, a sharp twisting pain between her hips, and there was a thick wet feeling in her underwear. For half a second she thought she'd peed in her pants. Then she realized that she'd gotten her first period.

The second thing she realized was that the book she'd wanted the night before floated in the air next to the bed.

PART FOUR

THE FAIR

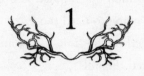

1

FRIDAY

Lauren fully expected her mom to flip out over her behavior the night before, and that might have happened if she hadn't needed her mom's assistance finding the sanitary pads.

Mom had taken one look at Lauren's red face and the clean pair of underwear clutched in her hand and said, "Well, that explains a few things." Then she went into her clothes closet and pulled down a box of Stayfree maxi pads. She handed the box to Lauren. There was a woman walking on a beach in a white dress. Her dark hair blew in the wind and she looked unreasonably happy for a person who presumably had her period, Lauren thought. Across the bottom corner of the box it said *Beltless*.

"Do you need any help?" Mom asked.

"Uh, no. I think I can figure it out," Lauren said.

"Rinse out your underwear and leave it in the bathroom. I'll put something on it to take the stains out after," Mom said.

•

"Okay," Lauren said in a tiny voice.

When she came out of the bathroom Mom was waiting with a bottle of Midol. She handed Lauren two of the pills and said, "You're going to need those."

Lauren returned to the sink, put some water in a paper cup, and swallowed the pills.

When she came out of the bathroom again her mom hugged her.

"I'm sorry about yesterday," she said.

Lauren stopped herself from jerking back in surprise, but only just. She couldn't remember the last time she'd heard Mom say she was sorry.

But since Lauren wanted Mom to stay in a good mood and not decide to enact any punishments for her behavior, Lauren said, "I'm sorry, too."

"If I had known . . ." Mom said, trailing off. "It's hard to keep your emotions steady just before your period."

Lauren had heard this, had seen articles about PMS in some of the magazines that Miranda liked to read. Was that what had happened to her yesterday? Had she freaked out because her hormones were going crazy and she didn't realize it?

No, you really were angry with Nana. And hormones don't explain the floating book, she thought. But that was information she was keeping to herself.

Nobody would ever believe her about the book. Not unless she could duplicate that event, and since she didn't know how it happened in the first place, she didn't know how to do it again.

Her dreams had been strange, half memory and half imagination, dreams of the ghost tree and the girls in the woods and also of a red-haired witch and her grieving lover.

Just before her eyes opened she dreamed of being caught by the ghost tree, of the branches pulling her inside so she was embraced by the rough bark. But there was something else there with her, something that was made of the night, something with teeth that wanted to devour her.

She woke covered in sweat and her body felt like it was made of swollen pain.

As soon as she realized the book was floating next to the bed, she'd uttered a tiny scream and then it dropped to the floor.

Lauren realized her mom was looking at her expectantly, that she'd gotten lost thinking about the book.

"I guess, yeah, I didn't really know what to do with myself yesterday," Lauren said.

"Well, you can lie down if you need to," Mom said. "The first few times seem like they're especially hard."

"Thanks," Lauren said. "I guess I'll see how I feel later. Maybe I'll take a walk or something, get some fresh air."

She threw this out casually, laying the groundwork for some forest exploration. She hadn't forgotten that she wanted to look for the girls' backpacks.

And I'm not bringing Miranda with me, either, she decided.

Miranda would just ask a lot of questions that Lauren didn't want to answer. And if they did find any evidence of the dead girls in the woods, then Miranda would be sure to try to claim any glory for herself.

Like always.

It was somewhat startling to realize this was true and not just random resentfulness. Miranda always did push herself into the spotlight and leave Lauren standing in the wings.

"A walk would be good for you," Mom said. "Do you want to come down and eat something? I could make pancakes."

Lauren didn't really feel like eating pancakes, but her mom gave her such a hopeful look that she agreed. And it was worth it when David cheered as Mom took the griddle out.

Breakfast was a completely argument-free meal, and Lauren couldn't remember the last time that had happened. It was before Dad died but it had to be a long time before, because Mom and Dad had squabbled over every little thing the last few years.

Lauren helped clean up without being asked, and she reflected that it was a much happier house when the air wasn't carrying the remnants of an argument like a malicious fog.

"Wanna play Sorry!, Lauren?" David asked.

She really didn't want to. She wasn't really in the mood for a board game and she was hoping to get out to the woods early, before Miranda called and asked her to go somewhere.

But she was enjoying the rare peace, and she knew that if she said yes her mom would smile in approval and then later when Lauren disappeared for a while Mom wouldn't complain.

Karen went upstairs to sort the laundry and left Lauren and David in the living room. Lauren unfolded the game board on the coffee table.

"What color do you want to be?"

"Red. Are you going to find the girls today?" David asked.

Her hand stilled above the game box, the small bag of red pieces in her hand.

"What . . . what do you mean?" She felt her heart hammering away, startled into frantic action by her baby brother's words.

"You're going to look for where the girls are. Or were." David said it as a statement, not a question.

"How do you know that?"

David shrugged, taking the bag of pieces from Lauren's hand and carefully setting them up in the red home base area.

"I just know," he said.

"Like you just knew about the girls in Mrs. Schneider's yard?"

"She was screaming."

Lauren considered her brother in light of everything Nana had told her yesterday. It seemed to her that David was much more of a witch than she could ever be. There was no reason for a four-year-old boy to know about these things.

And she hadn't breathed a word of what she intended to do that day, even out loud to herself.

"David," Lauren asked as she set up the blue pieces for herself, "can you . . . ?"

She hesitated, because she felt that to say what she was thinking out loud would be like crossing the Rubicon. Her sixth-grade social studies teacher, Mr. Connolly, had used that phrase once and when she asked what he meant, he told her it was a way of saying a step that you couldn't take back.

There are so many things happening that I don't understand, she thought. *And I think that I need to understand.*

David didn't prompt Lauren to continue. If she never asked the rest of her question he wouldn't wonder about it, or pester her. That was just David. He was really a patient little kid.

And is that because of his nature, or because he can read people's minds and so he doesn't have to ask?

"Can we go to the fair this weekend? On Saturday?" he asked.

Lauren, who'd been about to say the thing rolled up under her tongue, felt like she'd been caught wrong-footed.

"Uh. Sure, bud," she said. Maybe she wouldn't ask him after all. Maybe, if he really could read people's minds, it was better not to know for sure. "What do you want to do most, eat cotton candy and funnel cakes or ride the merry-go-round?"

"Cotton candy," David said, almost absently. "I think you

have to be there on that day. He wants you to be there."

Lauren rubbed her arms. She felt cold all over.

"Who wants me to be there?"

David tilted his head to one side, like he was listening to a conversation in the next room. "Dunno. But it's important. He wants you to see something."

"Okay," Lauren said.

This was the perfect opportunity to ask how David knew these things. Who was "he"? Why would "he" want Lauren to see something?

Is David talking about Jake Hanson? And if he was, how come Jake Hanson suddenly seemed to pop up everywhere?

Why was Jake standing outside her window the night before, smiling up like he knew she was there?

"Can I go first?" he asked.

"Go first?" Lauren asked.

"In the game," David said.

She'd forgotten about the game, even though the board and pieces were laid out in front of her. "Sure."

"You have to shuffle the cards," he said patiently.

"Okay," she said, and picked up the deck. She felt somehow the moment was gone, that if she asked David about mind reading now, he would only give her a puzzled look.

I bet Nana would know what to do.

No, I'm not going to see Nana.

She was still angry at her grandmother. And she didn't

need Nana cluttering up her head with stories just now.

"Cards," David said, holding out his little hand.

Lauren put the deck on the table and watched David draw a 6.

"Can't move," he said. "I'm stuck."

Me too, Lauren thought.

Maybe in the woods she would be able to get unstuck. Maybe out there she'd find out what really happened to those girls. But there was no one to talk to in the meantime. No one to help her. It was just Lauren and her migraine-vision and a thin thread of hope that if she knew for sure how those girls died, then she could also figure out if Nana's story was true. If Lauren really was a witch. Or something.

"Your turn," David said.

Lauren drew a one, which meant she could move one of her pawns out of home base.

"Lucky."

"Yeah," Lauren said, looking at her pawn standing all alone on the game track. "Lucky."

2

Alex really was not in the mood for the fair. The captain decided that Alex and Miller would rotate shifts with Hendricks and Pantaleo and that there would be at least one pair patrolling at the fair at all times from open to close—which was from eleven to eight every day, and until ten p.m. on Fridays and Saturdays. The chief tried to soften the blow with the promise of overtime pay ("already authorized by the mayor, who's grateful for our presence"), but Alex didn't care about the money.

He cared about the hours he was going to spend walking in the heat, dealing with out-of-towners who lost their kids in the crowd or got their pockets picked by teenagers. And when he wasn't dealing with petty theft and children distracted by the sight of balloon vendors, he'd be giving directions.

People, Alex had noticed, had a firm belief that a police officer in uniform was better than a compass any day. It wouldn't matter that maps were handed out with the tickets at the gate. Why consult a piece of paper when there was a policeman right there?

But all of these irritations were secondary to the knowledge that as long as the fair was in town he wouldn't be in the station. And if he wasn't in the station then he couldn't search the archives for the other girls.

After his lunch with Miller the day before, they'd gotten stuck dealing with a fender bender on the county road. Once blame had been assigned and the drivers taken away with their cars by AAA, Alex and Miller were called to Pete's Roadhouse, which was about three miles away from the accident on the same county road. A wannabe bike-gang group had gotten embroiled in a fight with a couple of members of a real bike-gang group.

The fight broke up pretty quickly once the uniforms (and more importantly, their sidearms) appeared, but it had still taken Alex and Miller almost two hours to take down all the witness reports and determine just who was going to pay for the bar's damages.

By the time all this was done their shift was over. It would have appeared deeply suspicious for Alex to go digging around in the basement archives, so he'd headed home, frustrated that there was no time for him to work on his search.

He thought that in a regular town—or even back in Chicago—he would have been praised for using his own time to work on an active case. At the very least there would have been indifference—an *it's your time, do what you want* kind of attitude. But he didn't think that would be the case here.

It wasn't anything that had been said outright. Alex just sensed that somehow the department was being steered away from any real investigation of these murders.

But who's doing the steering? The mayor? Or someone else?

He couldn't admit, even to himself, that there was some kind of supernatural force at play. He couldn't admit this even though he'd physically struggled just to take notes on everything he knew so far. He couldn't admit it even though two girls' decapitated heads had spoken to him.

Alex was certain that if anyone knew what he was doing they would find a way to stop him. And he didn't want to be stopped.

He owed it to the dead girls, and he owed it to the living girls of Smiths Hollow. He had two daughters. The thought of Camila or Valeria falling under some madman's knife nearly paralyzed him. And if something happened to one of his children like what happened to those dead girls, then he would want to know. Alex couldn't imagine what was going through their parents' heads, the worry and the waiting.

So he needed to identify them, even though Christie wasn't exactly prioritizing their identification. And he needed to find out if there were other victims.

The third item on his list was to find out who the stranger

was—the one he'd seen at Sam's Dairy Bar, the one whose clothes and car and attitude marked him out as an outsider.

Alex didn't know why he felt this person was linked to the murders, but he did. It wasn't necessarily that the man was the perpetrator—although it wouldn't hurt to rule him out completely. It was, again, a sense—a sense that this person was tied to everything that had happened, or a sense that he would be important to the outcome.

Alejandro Lopez wasn't accustomed to all these vague feelings, these hunches, this lack of firm and solid footing. Smiths Hollow had gone, in the course of a day, from the friendly town that welcomed his family to a shifting, seething mass of quicksand that could pull them under.

It wasn't just the murders, either.

That night Beatriz had told Alex and Sofia at dinner— after the children went outside to play and they were all enjoying a second glass of wine—that there were rumors of job cuts at the chili plant. Alex's sister-in-law tended toward anxiety, and it was all over her face as she told them this.

"I don't think we should get too worried about it, Bea," Ed said comfortably. Alex's brother was not the worrying sort, the complete opposite of his wife. "Pam McLaren— she's on the line next to me—told me that these rumors go around every couple of months, usually right after they've done a lot of hiring. And we were just hired as part of an expansion, so it's just about time."

Bea shook her head, her smooth dark bob swirling around her chin. "This isn't the same. I overheard some of the men at the next table talking at lunch yesterday. They seemed concerned that this time was different. A couple of them were actually talking about moving away if the cuts happened."

"Moving away to where?" Alex asked.

"To Chicago, to work in the Nabisco factory. Wouldn't it be funny if we moved out here only to move back?"

"Not really funny ha-ha," Sofia said, frowning. "And anyway, it doesn't make sense for us—or even those men— to move to Chicago. You know what we were paying in rent only got us a fraction of the space we have now. Do you really think those guys, who've lived in big houses all their lives, are really going to downsize just so they can keep working in a factory? That big mall just went up—there are lots of jobs there."

"But no guarantee that you'll get forty hours, and those hours will be all over the place. And factory jobs have the best benefits," Bea said. "You know that. What will we do if we don't have health insurance?"

Everyone was silent at this, because if Bea and Ed both lost their jobs, then at least one of them would need to find a position with benefits. Though they were both young and healthy now, they wouldn't always be. And accidents could happen at any time.

Alex received health insurance through the police

department, and always had, so even if Sofia had to go back to work she could take a job without worrying about the benefits package. Alex felt a little guilty about this, although he knew he shouldn't. It was his job and he'd earned it. God knew that he'd earned every dime and benefit in Chicago. Though his position in Smiths Hollow had reduced his stress and workload by more than fifty percent, he figured he was still due some psychological rollover from his CPD years.

"Let's not borrow trouble," Sofia said finally, breaking the silence. "There's enough trouble to go around without worrying you'll be fired."

"I think the correct term is 'let go.' It sounds more like they're gently releasing you down the river instead of forcibly removing you from your livelihood, you know?" Ed said.

"I don't think the correct term will matter if we're both jobless," Bea said.

Alex heard the back door slam, then pounding feet thundering along the hallway. Camila and Daniel appeared in the doorway, faces flushed.

"Can we have some Popsicles?" they asked, almost in perfect unison.

"If you help clear the table," Sofia said, rising with an empty plate in her hand.

"Told you," Daniel said. "We should have waited another half hour."

"I don't mind helping out," Camila said primly, although

Alex saw her nose wrinkle. "Anyhow, all we have to do is put the dishes in the dishwasher. It's better than washing them and drying them and putting them away."

"And the faster you do it, the faster the Popsicles will appear," Bea said.

No one brought up the subject again that evening. More interestingly—or strangely—to Alex, no one brought up the murders, either. Not even Sofia, who'd been a witness to the atrocity.

It was almost as if she'd forgotten what happened.

The way that Chief Christie had seemed to forget what happened.

The way Miller, too, had needed reminding that he'd puked his guts out at the crime scene the day before.

Yes, there was something very wrong in Smiths Hollow. And Alex needed to find out what it was before it disappeared from his memory, too.

Before he forgot about the girls who'd called to him in dead voices.

Before whoever—or whatever—cut those girls to pieces did it again.

3

Lauren went out after lunch, leaving her bike at home. She could cut into the woods from the cul-de-sac at the end of the road. Mrs. Schneider, of course, never let anyone through her yard—not even a raccoon—but pretty much everyone else expected the neighborhood kids to use their yards as access points and didn't mind.

She only needed her bike if she was going straight to the ghost tree, and she didn't want to start at the ghost tree today.

Lauren had a small green canvas duffel bag that used to belong to her father slung over her shoulder. She had carefully packed this bag with all the things she thought she would need if she actually came across the crime scene.

It was easier for her to think of it that way, to consider it in a distant and scientific manner. If she didn't, then she might remember that two girls were murdered in the woods she had loved since she was a child and that those two girls had died screaming and terrified.

But you're going to help them. You're going to find evidence that will help identify them and catch their killer.

It was a noble mission that she was embarking on, actually. It wasn't really about proving she'd had a vision.

In the bag she had a pair of leather gloves (also her father's, taken from his dresser while her mother was downstairs making sandwiches for lunch), a flashlight (because sometimes the tree cover made the interior of the forest as dark as twilight), and two large black trash bags (for evidence, if she found it). She also had a sleeve of Fig Newtons, a bottle of water, an extra Stayfree maxi pad, and a packet of tissues. These last two were Just in Case of a Period Emergency, although she really didn't know what that might entail— uncontrollable hemorrhaging? Was such a thing possible? And if it came down to it, would she have the guts to change her pad right there in the middle of the woods where anyone might see her?

Of all the days for my body to finally start catching up to everyone else.

Lauren had prepared her bag of necessities and then dashed outside and hidden it behind a pile of beach chairs stacked on the side of the house. Mom was still acting very sympathetic and Lauren didn't want her asking questions about the bag or getting annoyed that Lauren was going into the woods. She seemed keen on the idea that a little walk would help Lauren feel better, but Lauren didn't think her mom would agree to a long hike.

Up until a couple of years ago (when she discovered Ray Bradbury and Stephen King), Lauren had loved reading the Trixie Belden mysteries and at the moment she felt a lot like Trixie, off investigating a crime.

Don't have my beautiful best friend Honey with me, though.

Miranda used to read those books too, before *she'd* discovered Jackie Collins and Rosemary Rogers. Back then Lauren and Miranda had played Trixie and Honey in the woods, solving innocuous crimes like the theft of the Hostess apple pie and the case of the missing terrier (a worn stuffed toy of Miranda's substituting for an actual barking dog).

If you're going to solve a crime, then think like a crime solver. Don't reminisce about things you used to play with your best friend.

Lauren frowned. There were two things that she knew for sure—that the girls' bodies had ended up in Mrs. Schneider's fortress of a backyard, and that the person (*monster?*) had touched her bike seat with his (*its?*) bloody hand.

The murders had occurred somewhere between the yard and the ghost tree. So she would start from the woods behind Mrs. Schneider's house and hope that she picked up a trail from there.

Lauren walked on the edge of the road—there were no sidewalks in her development—thinking about what she'd seen in the throes of her migraine two days before, and about the floating book, and also about David and his sudden predictions.

Her abdomen felt puffy and twisted at the same time, and she'd put on jeans instead of shorts even though it was hot out. She was afraid—and she knew it was an irrational fear—that her period might leak out of the side of her underpants and then the blood would run down her legs and if she wore shorts then everyone would see.

Her jeans felt tight in the waist and she wished she'd put on sweatpants instead, but her mom didn't think sweatpants were appropriate for anything except school gym class. Some of the girls in Lauren's class had started wearing stirrup leggings to school in the spring, but like so many other trends, her mom had said they couldn't afford it and that Lauren's jeans were fine for schoolwear.

As soon as I get into the woods I'm going to unbutton the top button. It actually felt like her pants were squeezing all of the blood out of her body and it was pouring into the maxi pad that she'd carefully applied to her underwear.

I might actually have to change it in the woods, even if I don't want to.

She was so preoccupied with her bloated, pulsing body— that was how it felt, like her body was an alien thing attached to her head—that she almost missed the bright flash in the corner of her eye.

The orange Gremlin that had cruised slowly by her house

the night before was parked in the Hansons' driveway.

So it's Jake's car, then, she thought. *And he's still in there, visiting his parents. He must have stayed overnight.*

She hurried past the house, suddenly worried that he would see her from a window and come out to talk. Lauren did not want to talk to anyone at the moment.

She thought he would be able to tell that she had her period if he talked to her, that he could divine the knowledge from the way she stood or held her head or some such thing. Of course every girl got their period and Lauren never knew if Miranda had hers unless Miranda actually said so, but still. It was like something intensely private was somehow now happening out in the open just because Lauren had left the house. The last person she wanted to see was Jake.

And the second-to-last person is Miranda. Nope. I'd much rather go on this adventure without her. They'd never gone a whole day without seeing or speaking to each other, at least not that Lauren could recall. But Miranda had never called Lauren the day before, after their missed meeting, and she hadn't called that morning, either.

She must really be angry that I ditched her.

Lauren didn't feel as guilty about this as she supposed she ought to, and that made her feel bad about not feeling guilty.

It could be the beginning, though, of the quiet-drifting-away that she'd secretly hoped would happen. It could mean that Miranda had found someone else to be with, someone who would be more interested in Aqua Net and boys in Camaros.

Lauren cut through the Arakawas' yard—Mr. Arakawa was almost always traveling for business, and Mrs. Arakawa spent most of the day cleaning their house until it gleamed. They had a grown-up son away at Stanford University and they liked to see the kids around the neighborhood now that their nest was empty. They never minded if Lauren or anyone else used their grass as a pathway to the forest.

Mrs. Arakawa was in the front room vacuuming—Lauren could see her through the picture window—and she waved as Lauren went by. Lauren waved back but didn't knock on the door to say hello, the way she sometimes did. If she knocked then Mrs. Arakawa would offer her tea and a snack, but Lauren had a mission and she didn't want to be interrupted.

The Arakawas' backyard was as neat as their house—the patio furniture wiped down every morning and free of spiderwebs and bird droppings, the water hose coiled neatly and hung on the side of the house. The diMucci yard always needed trimming, and there was inevitably a toy or bike or folding chair to trip over.

Lauren disappeared into the cover of the trees, and as always she felt that she was returning to a safe place, a place where she belonged. She didn't understand why she felt this, and why she still felt it despite everything bad that had happened here in the last year—her father's death, the runaway girls.

And if Nana is to be believed, then something terrible happens here every year, though nobody knows about it except her.

And one other, she said. I wonder who that is? I wonder why I didn't think to ask at the time. Who else could possibly know, or why? That is, assuming it's all real to begin with, which I'm not sure I believe anyway.

Lauren made sure she was far enough back into the trees that nobody would be able to see her at a casual glance, but not so far back that she couldn't see the rear yards of the houses that went around the cul-de-sac. From the Arakawa yard Mrs. Schneider's house was three houses to the left. Lauren definitely did not want to get caught by Mrs. Schneider, although the old lady was usually watching out the front window and not the back one. She thought she could get close without Mrs. Schneider seeing her—and anyway, if her feet never touched the grass then she was technically not in the yard.

That might work in a court of law but probably not if Mrs. Schneider catches you. And the old lady was mean as anything. She'd probably scream the neighborhood down if she found Lauren within ten feet of her property.

So Lauren would be careful—so, so careful. All she needed was a little bit of a trail to follow anyway. If there were obvious signs leading away from the Schneider place, then she wouldn't need to go close.

In some parts of the woods the forest floor was mostly

clear around the bases of the tree, enough so that a person could walk freely even where there wasn't an actual path. But here, behind the houses, there were lots of scrubby little bushes, some of which had thorns and a few that were covered in poison ivy leaves.

Lauren was very allergic to poison ivy. Due to her habit of roaming around the woods in shorts, she inevitably ended up with a rash several times each summer and was subjected to the indignity of oatmeal baths and calamine lotion. She was glad for her long pants now despite the heat, but she'd be careful not to rub her bare arms or hands against the leaves.

The sun pushed through the trees, making little patches of light. Lauren heard the Lopez kids (their house was almost directly across the cul-de-sac from Mrs. Schneider) squealing and laughing. *They must be playing in the backyard. I didn't see them out in the front.*

Lauren liked all three kids, but she didn't want to bump into them now. They would be curious about what she was up to. She hoped that they didn't roam in the woods behind their place.

Once she was positioned with Mrs. Schneider's yard in view (and no sign of the old woman), Lauren searched the ground for signs of anyone's passage.

There's got to be footprints.

Or blood.

This thought emerged unbidden from the place in her

brain where she saw the person (*monster?*) putting what was left of the girls in a bag, when she had the vision by the ghost tree. She distinctly recalled that the bag was dripping as he (*it?*) walked away.

If what she saw in her head wasn't a lie, there would be a blood trail leading up to the Schneider yard. And certainly footprints of some kind—there was no way someone could cross through all of the scrub without leaving signs of their passage.

Broken branches, or leaves on the ground. Shoe prints in the dirt.

There wasn't quite enough light to see everything on the ground clearly, but there was too much to use the flashlight. She crouched down, but not too low. She definitely didn't want to crawl through the brush and end up covered in thorn scratches and ivy rash.

She didn't see any obvious signs of passage, which was annoying. Surely someone walking through this rarely crossed area would leave a trail behind them?

Lauren wished she knew exactly where the girls were found in the yard. It would be easier if she could focus on one section rather than try to scan every little thing.

I wonder if Officer Hendricks would tell me.

No, he wouldn't tell her. She was just a kid, and there was no reason for her to ask that question. Besides, what was she going to do—go home and call the police department and then come back to the woods to continue her work?

She was at it for at least a half hour before she found anything useful.

At first she thought she hadn't seen it at all. Her eyes were straining so hard, looking for a sign, and numerous times her overheated imagination interpreted a smashed berry or a bit of mud as a sinister bloodstain.

But this time it *was* a bloodstain. A very clear splash of blood, not bright red anymore but a rusty brown, on one of the thick poison ivy leaves. It was too high to be a random bit of dirt, and there had been no rain in the last couple of days so it wasn't mud.

Lauren put her face as close to the stain as she dared. *Yes, it's definitely blood.*

She thought she could smell a sharp copper remnant underneath the scent of greenery. And there was something about the stain, too, something . . .

Glittery? She scowled. No, that wasn't right. It wasn't like craft glitter or costume glitter or anything like that. But there was something that sparkled inside the bloodstain, or around it. A few small shining particles catching the sunlight.

What could that be? Lauren had definitely paid attention in science class, and Mr. Higgins had never mentioned any quality in blood that would make it sparkle.

"Well, okay, you found some blood so don't worry about the sparkling. Just work backward," she murmured.

She walked a few steps farther into the woods. The scrub began thinning out pretty quickly away from the border.

Probably because it's less sunny here.

Less sun meant less light, and that meant it was harder to see any tracks or stains. But Lauren found a second splash almost immediately. Even in the shadow of the trees she spotted the glittering particles, like a vein of fool's gold inside a matrix of rock.

Weird. Really weird. But helpful.

She stopped searching for blood or tracks and instead scanned everywhere for more of the glittery particles. Once she did that she could see the path ahead of her clearly—one bloodstain followed by another and another, marked out like bread crumbs in the forest.

This isn't the blood, she thought suddenly. *This is me. This is magic.*

(there's no such thing as magic)

Her pace quickened. Whether it was magic or some trick of the light, she'd discovered the trail and she was going to follow it back to its source.

The trail led deep into the woods and soon Lauren realized she was heading in the direction of the old cabin in the woods.

Her footsteps slowed, and then stopped.

What if the killer is living out here? In the cabin? What if he sees you and comes after you?

"Oh, Lauren, you dummy," she moaned.

She hadn't thought this through at all. She'd only been thinking that two murders happened in the forest a few days ago, not that the murderer might be hanging around looking for more victims.

If Miranda had been with her, she would have laughed her head off and told Lauren that in horror movies the killer always came back for more. But Lauren didn't like the kind of horror movies Miranda liked. She didn't mind being scared and she liked things with creepy atmosphere, but she didn't like to see a bunch of girls getting cut up by a madman with a knife. At least that was what it seemed all those movies were about.

And that's what happened here, she thought. *A madman with a knife cut two girls up into little pieces and what are you doing? Running off through the woods right to the place where he did it. You didn't even tell anybody where you were going.*

If this were one of Miranda's movies you'd be the next victim. And you'd deserve it.

But what to do? Should she continue on? If she didn't, would she be able to find the blood trail again?

If she did, would she run into the killer?

The woods, her woods, the place where she'd always felt safe and comforted now seemed to loom over her. The trees had eyes that followed and leaves that reached for her. They were going to smother her, take her into their bark and keep her there forever.

Her heart pounded hard in her chest. Her eyes darted around at every little sound, every flutter of a bird's wing, every rustle of branches with the wind.

The song she'd been singing a couple of days earlier came back to her, suddenly sinister.

"I always feel like somebody's watching me . . ."

Footsteps sounded behind her. *The killer. He came around behind me. He's here.*

She whirled around, saw the silent figure standing just a few feet away from her, and screamed.

4

"Jesus, I think one of my eardrums is bleeding," Jake said, holding his hand to his right ear.

"What are you doing here?" Lauren asked.

Her voice sounded shrill to her own ears. Her hands shook and she'd dropped the duffel bag when she'd spun around. She felt ready to dash away at the slightest provocation, a trembling little rabbit in sight of a fox.

Jake reached back and rubbed the back of his head in a sheepish gesture. He'd gotten his hair cut, Lauren noticed now. It was short in the back and a little longer on top.

Kind of like Matt Dillon in The Outsiders, she thought, and wondered if Miranda would agree.

But Jake's new haircut was not the point. The point was that he was standing there in her woods (*my woods???*) very close to a murder site—because she was close to it now, she felt it deep down in a way that wasn't just a hunch. Her eyes widened. *Is Jake here to hurt me?*

"What are you doing out here?" she repeated, and this time it was sharp, demanding an answer.

"I, uh, followed you," he said.

His eyes were so blue they practically glowed, so full of appeal for understanding. Normally those eyes would make her feel out of sorts—silly and weak at the knees. But she was scared and getting angry now, too, and it didn't matter that he had beautiful eyes.

"You *followed* me? For how long?"

He rubbed the back of his head again, and Lauren wondered if he was missing his ponytail.

"I saw you go into the woods from my parents' house."

"You've been following me for like an *hour* and you never said anything? What are you, some kind of stalker?"

All her fear was gone now, the empty spaces filled in with anger. How *dare* he. How *dare* he follow her and watch her and never say anything until now.

And it wasn't just that Jake had behaved like a creepy jerk. She felt, somehow, that he had intruded on something private. This was her business. She was the one who'd seen those girls in her head, not Jake. This was between Lauren and the monster.

Yes, it is a monster. Whether it's a man or a thing with sharp teeth and claws it's still a monster, and I can call it that.

Jake looked at the ground. She half expected him to start drawing patterns in the dirt with the toe of his sneaker. He gave off the unmistakable impression of a student caught out by the principal.

"I just wanted to talk to you. Every time I see you you're running off somewhere else," he said. His voice was so low she had to lean forward to hear.

"If you wanted to talk to me you could call my house like a normal person," she said, and then she remembered the previous evening. "Why were you standing outside my window last night?"

"You saw me?" he asked. "I thought you were there in the window, but I couldn't be sure. Why didn't you come down and talk to me?"

"Why didn't you knock on the door?" she said.

He nodded at that, like she'd scored a point.

"And anyway, what do you want to talk to me for?"

Jake looked right at her then, like he wanted to make sure she understood what he was going to say next.

"I always liked you, Lauren."

Her heart felt like it stopped and then restarted in her chest, revving like an engine in high gear.

Liked me? He likes me? But that's not right. He's so much older. He's been away at college, with college girls.

"Don't make fun of me," she said flatly, and turned away, picking up her duffel bag.

She started off, barely able to see the blood trail for the tears in her eyes.

Don't waste them on him, Lauren. She swallowed hard and swiped at her eyes.

"Hey, wait," he said, and a second later he grabbed her arm.

She shook him off. "Don't touch me. I never said you could touch me."

He put both hands in the air. "No touching. Hey, listen."

She kept walking.

"Come on, Lauren. Just . . . two minutes. Just give me two minutes. I wasn't making fun of you. Really, I wasn't."

Her sneakers stopped moving even though her brain was saying, *Don't listen to him, he's only going to laugh at you now.*

"Can you turn around? I don't want to talk to your back."

She turned slowly, reluctantly, the push and pull of her conflicting feelings nearly causing her to dart away.

Like a little rabbit in the same clearing as a fox, that's what you thought before. Do you want to be the little rabbit?

No, she didn't want to be a rabbit. She wanted to be a fox—a clever, beautiful fox that would show its teeth if it had to.

"I just wanted to, like, get to know you," Jake said. "Even when we were little I liked hanging around you. But every time we meet, you run away from me like I've got a disease."

"I do not."

"You do. So I thought maybe the timing wasn't right or whatever, because you know that one day you were sick and yeah, I get that you wouldn't want to hang out after that. And yesterday you seemed like you were in a hurry to go somewhere. Last night I thought I would go up to your door and ask you to come out for a walk, but then I didn't know if your mom would think it was weird, and anyway, what if you said no? I couldn't tell myself you were in a rush to go somewhere else then. It would just mean you didn't like me."

He was afraid she would reject him? *What?*

"And then I saw you go by my parents' house a little while ago and thought it was a chance to talk to you. So I followed you out—I was a little ways behind you because I had to put my shoes on—and I saw you go into the woods. When I caught up with you I saw you crawling around behind Mrs. Schneider's house. I didn't know what you were doing but you seemed really . . . intent."

"I was looking for something," she said, because he gave her an expectant glance.

"Well, that much was clear," he said. "And then all of a sudden you took off running like a dog on the scent. It was all I could do to keep up with you."

She didn't know what to say to all of this, or what to feel about it. She'd always felt she was behind everyone else, especially Miranda. While Miranda was thinking about boys and grown-up things Lauren was still a child in the forest, building forts and playing pretend. But now this boy—she supposed he was technically a man, because he was legally an adult—was standing there saying he thought of her as a woman, not as little Lauren from down the block.

He'd stood outside her window, too afraid to come to the door and ask her to come out. And he'd chased her through the woods, all in the hopes that she would talk to him.

Lauren felt the first tugs of adulthood then, a land she'd thought was a far-off country still. She didn't know it was really so close, or that she'd come upon it so fast.

And she felt a deep flush of pleasure that Jake Hanson, who really was good-looking (*unlike Miranda's Tad, and he was older to boot, and that was quite a catty thought, Lauren*), thought enough of her, or the memory of her, that he would pursue her.

Even a fox is chased by dogs, she thought, but then her natural sense asserted itself.

"But . . . why me?" She gestured at him, up and down, and then at herself. "You're so much older than I am."

"Not as old as you think," he said. "I only just turned eighteen three weeks ago. And you're fifteen, right?"

"Not until November," she said automatically, then felt her cheeks heat. Why had she said that? Why had she pointed out that she was even younger than he thought?

"But I thought you were away at college already," she said quickly, to cover up her mistake. "And that you had an apartment and everything."

"I graduated from high school a semester early," he said.

"If I hadn't taken extra courses I would have only graduated two weeks ago. I was staying in the dorms at UIC last spring. And yeah, I got an apartment with a couple of other guys when I came back a few weeks ago but I didn't know them really well. I moved out yesterday and back with my folks."

"Why?"

He wrinkled his nose. "They were both stoners. I didn't realize that when I told them I'd take the third room. Luckily my name wasn't on the lease because I wasn't eighteen yet when I agreed to move in with them. So I just packed up my clothes and came home. My parents don't mind. I think my mom is happy to have a chance to feed me. And the laundry's free."

Somehow as he talked he seemed younger to her, much less the cool and distant older man. They were only three-and-a-bit years apart, after all. And he'd only just *turned* eighteen.

Maybe it isn't so weird that he's attracted to you. You're not that bad-looking.

Just thinking this made her tug self-consciously at her hair, which she'd braided into a single plait down her back so it would be out of her way. *Nothing says* little girl *like braids. Maybe you should get one of those magazines Miranda is always reading. Unless Jake likes the Laura Ingalls look.*

(Jeez, who cares what he thinks about your looks? Weren't you doing something? What happened to Trixie Belden on a mission? What about the dead girls?)

"So anyway," Jake said, and Lauren realized she'd let the silence go on too long, and that she should have said something back, given him some indication that his interest wasn't entirely unwanted.

Because it wasn't entirely unwanted, she realized. She remembered the feeling of his hand on her back, and how gentle he'd been when she got sick.

That must mean he really likes you. If he can watch you puke in the weeds and still run after you, then he must be sincere.

"Anyway," Lauren said, and smiled at him.

He must have seen something in that smile, because he said, very fast with all the words running together, "Anyway I was wondering if you would go to the fair with me tomorrow night?"

"Like a date?" Somehow she'd never considered the possibility of a date. He would walk with her and buy her cotton candy and sit next to her on the Ferris wheel. Maybe he would hold her hand. Maybe he would put his arm around her.

He grinned then. "Yes, like a date."

Tomorrow. Saturday. She saw David's face in her head, heard David's voice.

He wants you to be there. He wants to show you something.

Was Jake the "he" David was talking about? At the time Lauren thought David was making some kind of sinister prediction. But maybe he just caught a glimpse of Jake asking his big sister out on a date.

That's weird, too, though. It's not normal for four-year-old boys to see the future.

"I always liked that about you," Jake said.

She realized she'd gone away somewhere in her head again, and found him watching her with a half smile.

"Liked what?"

"The way you thought so deeply about things. You were like that even when you were tiny. Always serious, and your eyes far away. I wanted to know where you were going. I wanted to know if you would take me there with you."

Were eighteen-year-old boys supposed to speak like this? Were they supposed to see so much?

"I'll go out with you," Lauren said. "But I promised my brother David I'd take him to the fair tomorrow."

Jake sidled a little closer to her then—not close enough to touch, just out of arm's reach. But she felt his presence in the way she hadn't a moment before, felt the inhale and exhale of his breath mixing with hers.

"Well, it's totally up to you—but maybe you could take him in the afternoon and I could meet you later? Or I can go with both of you in the afternoon if you'd rather."

Lauren wrinkled her nose. "You want me to bring my little brother on our date?"

He shrugged. "I don't mind. As long as I'm with you."

As long as I'm with you. Six words that changed everything in an instant. Six words that made her heart sing.

"Okay," she said.

"Okay?" he said. "You'll really go out with me?"

"Yeah," she said. "I'll take David in the afternoon and then I'll come back and meet you."

"Don't you think I should come and pick you up? So your mom knows who you're with?"

"Are you from the planet of perfect boyfriends? Most guys wouldn't care if a girl's mom knew where she was."

"Your mom is my parents' neighbor. And Smiths Hollow is a small town. Don't you think she'll be mad if you go out with me and finds out from somebody else?"

He was right. Lauren knew he was right. And even with their temporary truce it would take only a little explosion to tip them back into the war zone.

But Lauren didn't think her mom would really like the idea of her on a date with someone, either. If Lauren told her mom she was going to meet up with Jake at the fair, though, it would sound a lot more casual.

Because it is casual. It's not a big deal. It's not like you're getting engaged or something. He's just taking you to the fair.

(HE'S TAKING ME TO THE FAIR OH MY GOD)

"I'll tell her I'm meeting you," Lauren said.

Jake gave her a skeptical look.

"I will. Cross my heart and hope to die," Lauren said, and made an X over her chest with her forefinger as she did.

"Okay," he said.

There came an awkward pause then, because they were standing alone in the middle of the woods and neither one of them seemed to know what to do next.

"So . . . what is it you're trying to find out here?" he asked. "Or are you going camping?"

"Camping?"

He gestured to the bag.

"No, it has my, um, gear," Lauren said.

"Gear for what?"

He wasn't being nosy. He wasn't trying to pry into her business. He was just curious, as anyone would be, about her strange behavior.

But it feels like he's being nosy and this is my thing my search it's between me and the killer and Jake doesn't have to get involved.

(He could help you. And you wouldn't be alone out here.)

Yes, it would be nice if she weren't alone. But she wasn't scared. Not even a little bit.

(liar)

It wasn't about fear. Not really. It was about whether Jake was trustworthy.

You agreed to go on a date with him. You have to trust him a little.

Jake watched her, and she sensed both his amusement at her mental tangents and his patience as he waited for her to finish.

"So, you know about those dead girls that were found

a couple of days ago?" she said.

"Dead girls?"

"There were two dead girls in Mrs. Schneider's yard," she said.

It seemed like the memory was struggling up from somewhere deep and buried, like something that happened a long time ago rather than recently. She saw his eyes cloud in confusion, then clear.

"Oh, yeah," he said. "I think my mom mentioned it. What about them?"

"Well," Lauren said, and decided very quickly not to mention anything about her vision or the floating book. She'd only sound like a crazy liar. "I heard that the police didn't know who the girls were. There was a bit in the paper about it, about how they were trying to identify them. They think the girls came from somewhere else."

"So you're . . . what? Trying to find out who they were? By doing what—pretending to be Nancy Drew?"

"Trixie Belden, actually," Lauren said. "I'm following the trail of blood from behind the yard."

"What makes you think you'll find anything other than blood?" he asked.

It wasn't a laughing-at-your-stupidity asking. It sounded like he was genuinely curious.

"I thought maybe they might have dropped something in the woods."

"Like an ID?"

"Yeah," she said, shifting the bag a little on her shoulder. "Like an ID, or a bag, or even a dropped library book."

"And what will you do if you find something?"

"Take it to the police," she said. "So that they can find the girls' parents. Because they would want to know."

He brooded on this for a minute, then said, "Lauren, doesn't it upset you at all to be out here?"

"Why would it upset me?"

"Your dad died here, didn't he?"

"Yeah," she said slowly. "But I've always spent time in the woods. My dad dying is something that doesn't really have anything to do with that."

Jake opened his mouth, then closed it. It looked like he wasn't sure he should say what he was thinking.

"What?" she asked.

"Don't you think that maybe the person who killed your dad might be the same one who killed those girls? They were all cut up, right?"

This hadn't occurred to her, and she didn't know why.

"No. I mean, yes, the girls were all cut up, but I don't think it had anything to do with my dad." There was no way she could explain about her vision. "Listen, do you want to help me search?"

Jake looked at his watch. "I have to go to work at four.

So I can stay out for maybe an hour, then I have to go home and get ready."

She nodded and pointed to a splash of blood on the ground nearby. "See that?"

He squinted. "That little brown mark?"

"Yeah, that's blood," she said.

"How do you know? It could be anything."

"I know," she said. She was not going to explain about magic and sparkling particles, either. "Just trust me, okay? I'm following the trail, so you look around as we walk and see if anything pops out."

"Okay," he said.

It took Lauren a minute to pick up the trail again, and even then part of her brain was preoccupied by Jake's presence. She didn't have a lot of experience (okay, no experience) with boys, but he was a lot more considerate than, say, Tad. Lauren couldn't imagine Tad agreeing to traipse through the woods after Miranda—not unless there was an arcade out there, or some other opportunity for him to show off and have his sycophants cheer for him.

But the old Miranda would have come with me.

She needed to stop thinking that, because it just made her feel sad. Her friend was changing and so was she. It was part of life.

"Are you still friends with anyone you were friends with when you were a little kid?" Lauren asked.

Jake shrugged. "Not really good friends. There are a couple of people that I still kind of talk to from middle school, but mostly we all got interested in different things in high school. It's not like we hate each other or anything. We just kind of lost touch."

"Oh," Lauren said.

The blood trail was becoming more obvious, the splashes of blood easier to see. She thought they must be closing in on the killing site. Her stomach lurched in anticipation.

"You're thinking about Miranda, aren't you?"

"Huh?"

"You and Miranda. You're not as close as you used to be, are you?"

Lauren shrugged. "Not really. We're . . . interested in different things, I guess."

"Yeah, it's pretty obvious what she's interested in," Jake said.

Lauren stopped, giving him a hard stare. "What does that mean?"

He rubbed the back of his head in that sheepish gesture he'd used earlier. "Nothing."

"No, you meant something."

"It's just that she kind of has a reputation already," he said. "The guys I lived with—they're a few years older than you, and they already know about her."

"What, exactly, is it they know?" She heard the ice in her

voice, was half-surprised he didn't frost over just from standing near her.

"She's, well, easy," he said, his eyes going everywhere except her face. "A bunch of people saw her groping Tad in the booth the other night at Wagon Wheel, and it didn't seem like she cared who saw her."

"How come a girl is easy when she wants the same damn thing every boy wants, but nobody talks about the boys?" Lauren said angrily. "How come boys can bang all the girls they can find and they're practically given a trophy for it, but girls are called sluts and everyone talks about them?"

"I didn't mean—"

"Oh, go home, Jake," she said. "I don't even want you here."

Lauren stomped away, her chest swelling with anger.

She didn't want to have sex so soon, but so what if Miranda did? It was her business. And she didn't think Jake was the kind of person who would be an asshole about it, but here he was repeating gossip.

Tears were in her eyes again, and she didn't know what she was crying about anymore. Jake? Miranda? The girls no one seemed to care about? Or was it all just her period and being a teenager and other stupid shit like that?

She wasn't looking where she was going, couldn't see for crying anyhow. Jake's footsteps were behind her again and she sped up. She didn't want to hear his apology right now. She wanted to be alone.

"Lauren, listen, I'm really sorry—"

"Go away!" she shouted.

"No, come on, you've got to hear me out—"

"I don't!"

"You're right, you really are, I never thought about it before . . ."

He stopped, trailing off.

Lauren swiped at her face and glared at him. "What? What did you never think about before?"

He wasn't looking at her. He seemed to have forgotten all about their argument.

"Lauren. Look."

They had stumbled into a clearing without noticing. Lauren sucked in a sharp breath.

There was blood everywhere—*so much blood, how could there be so much blood? Why was it still red and not brown and faded?*—and bits of viscera that the killer hadn't taken with him. Scraps of cloth were scattered like party confetti, and there was one brown moccasin with its sole facing up. It seemed very small and sad without its owner.

Black flies buzzed, bloated and drunk, around the clearing. All around them was the smell of rot and death and the sharp tang of that impossibly fresh blood.

There were two fingers—it looked like an index and middle finger—lying in the dirt right next to each other, like they'd been sliced cleanly away from the hand and dropped in place.

There were three silver rings stacked on the middle finger.

Over here an ear, over there a jagged piece of bone with a few shreds of skin hanging off it. All pieces of the dead girls that the monster hadn't bothered with, or neglected in his haste.

Like a child that didn't clean up his room properly, and left bits of his toys behind.

"We should go," Jake said, a tremor in his voice. "We shouldn't be here. What if the killer comes back?"

Lauren ignored him, turning on the spot, trying hard not to think about the parts scattered everywhere as pieces of human beings. It was easier to think of them as doll parts, as broken toys, because if she really focused on them she would just scream and never stop.

Like Mrs. Schneider had when she found the girls in her yard. David said she did that. She screamed and screamed.

"Lauren, let's leave."

"I can't go yet," she said. "I have to see if—there!"

She pointed across the clearing. Something purple and something blue had been tossed carelessly in a bush.

Lauren picked her way across the clearing, carefully not touching any of the bits scattered on the ground. She heard Jake following behind and glanced back to see him stepping only where she stepped, like they were in a minefield and they were avoiding unexploded ordnance.

When Lauren reached the bush she realized she'd have to

go around it, because she didn't want to open the backpacks in the clearing. In fact, she didn't want to spend any more time in the clearing than absolutely necessary.

A few of the flies circled her head and she batted at them with something like loathing. They were slow-moving and fat and they'd spent the last two days feeding off what was left of those girls. Lauren didn't want them touching her. She didn't want one to land on her hair or her arm, not even for a moment.

Jake followed her as she sidestepped until they were back under the trees. Then she went around to the other side of the bush and discovered a new problem: the bush was both large and filled with thorns.

"I can reach it," Jake said.

He couldn't really—he had to wade a little ways into the bush before he could grab the packs—but he didn't complain about the thorns pricking him.

"Wait," Lauren said, just before he picked them up. She dug around in her bag and pulled out the leather gloves. "Take these. So you don't, like, get your fingerprints on the bags or whatever."

"I feel like a criminal," Jake said as he pulled them on.

"You're protecting the crime scene," she said.

"We could protect it better by finding the nearest police officer and leading them out here. Isn't Officer Hendricks your buddy?" he said, but he grabbed the packs and pulled them out.

"He's not my buddy," she said. "He was nice to me after my dad died, that's all."

She felt strangely embarrassed that Officer Hendricks had even been mentioned. Lauren didn't think Jake, who wanted to take her out on a date, should bring him up. She'd always had a little crush on him—even if she only acknowledged it now, at this very moment. It was like realizing Jake was interested in her made her recognize her own feelings about Officer Hendricks.

He had a nice smile, and nice eyes, and he had always been kind to her. For a long time she'd harbored that secret hope that he was quietly trying to find out what happened, that one day he would arrest the person who killed her father.

But of course he wasn't really doing that . . . and she thought she'd known it all along. She'd only felt helpless and sad, and hoped someone who wasn't helpless could take that feeling away.

And anyway, I'm not helpless. If I can do this—track the murderer's path through the woods—then maybe I can find out what happened to my dad, too.

Because nobody cares. Nobody cares except me.

She wasn't ready to believe that Dad had his heart cut out by a monster that ate the town girls as sacrifices. No, she wasn't ready to believe Nana's story, because there were no other dead girls. There were no other bodies. Everyone would know. There were only these two. Just the ones she'd seen in her head walking through these woods and carrying the backpacks that Jake was trying to pull out of the thorn bush.

Jake winced as he cleared the bush and dropped the packs on the ground. Lauren saw that the thighs of his jeans were covered in thorns.

"My mom is not going to be happy to wash these," Jake said, pulling some of them out with his gloved fingers. "Why didn't the killer take these packs with him? Wasn't he worried about somebody finding these? I thought the police could check all kinds of things now, not just fingerprints. Like they can find hairs and clothing fibers and stuff like that."

"Maybe he didn't care," Lauren said. "Or maybe he didn't think of it. It looks like he was in a . . ."

"Frenzy?" Jake suggested. "I gotta say, I'm glad I didn't have a big lunch, because I don't think my stomach is going to be right for the rest of the day."

Lauren took two black plastic garbage bags out of her duffel. "Can I have the gloves back?"

Jake paused, a large thorn between his thumb and forefinger. "What are you going to do?"

"I'm going to open the bags and see if there's anything useful inside, like an ID. Then I'm going to wrap each bag separately in plastic."

"Why not just leave the searching to the cops?" Jake said. "Seriously, Lauren, I think it's amazing that you found this at all, and that you're being so coolheaded about it, but . . ."

"Why wouldn't I be coolheaded? Because most girls would scream their heads off when they saw what was on the other side of that thorn bush?"

"You said it, not me."

"But you thought it," Lauren said. She sat back on her heels and looked at him expectantly.

"What?"

She held out her hand. "Gloves."

He took them off slowly, as if he were reluctant to let her have them.

Lauren took them and put them on. They were warm inside, and for a second it was like he was holding her hand.

Stop worrying about stupid girly romantic things. You came out here to do something.

She stood the purple backpack up and unzipped it. Inside was a ball of clothing rolled together—a plaid flannel shirt, corduroy pants, a plain white T-shirt, a pair of denim shorts. Underneath that were three squashed Twinkies, a bag of plain potato chips, and a library book. Lauren pulled out the book—a travel guide to California—and glanced inside the front cover.

"Joliet Public Library," Lauren said.

"So at least one of them was from Joliet. I think that's enough, really. Just wrap up the bags and let's get out of here." He looked at his watch. "I really do have to leave soon."

"So go," Lauren said, feeling around the bottom of the pack

for anything else that might prove useful. "I'm fine by myself."

Jake didn't say anything to this. After a minute the silence was awkward so she looked up.

He was staring at her. She couldn't read his expression so she said, "What?"

"Do you really think I'm going to leave you by yourself five feet away from a pile of body parts?"

"Those body parts aren't going to come back to life and strangle me," Lauren said. There was nothing else in the bottom of the bag. She zipped it closed again.

"You know, you're a lot more confident when Miranda isn't around."

She paused in the act of unzipping the second pack. "Yeah. I guess I am."

It wasn't just the lack of Miranda. She felt stronger now, more like the person she was meant to be. She wasn't worried about saying or doing the wrong thing. Maybe it was because she'd decided to take concrete action about the vision. Maybe it was because Jake had already shown her that he was vulnerable to her and she didn't have to fear his ridicule.

Maybe it's because you did magic.

"I'm almost done," she said, by way of apology.

The second bag was much more densely packed than the first one, and much more practically, as well. There were two pairs of pants, six neatly folded squares of underwear, a raincoat, a sweater, three pairs of striped socks that clearly came out of the same package. A small plastic bag contained a bar of soap, a travel-size bottle of shampoo, a yellow toothbrush, and a half-used tube of Colgate. On top of everything was a canister of Planters salted peanuts, a bruised apple, and a sandwich wrapped in waxed paper. Lauren didn't think it was a good idea to unwrap it after it had been sitting in a backpack in the woods for two days.

In the front zip pocket Lauren found a package of tissues, a few maxi pads in a Ziploc bag, and a pink My Melody wallet.

She held the wallet in her hand for a minute, the cheerful rabbit on the exterior making her unaccountably sad. There was a Sanrio store a few towns over and when Lauren was younger sometimes her mom would take her there as a treat so she could buy Hello Kitty stationery and My Melody stickers.

She remembered the way the store smelled, sort of plastic with wood shavings underneath plus a faint sweetness, like cotton candy lingering in the air.

Lauren zipped the wallet open. Inside were twenty-two dollars in small bills, a few coins, and a Joliet Junior College student ID for Rebecca Posner. The girl with the long brown braids grinned out at Lauren from the photo.

Help me.

Lauren blinked, because she thought she'd just seen the girl's face morph from smiling to scared, thought maybe Rebecca's mouth had moved.

She moved the ID a little closer to her face.

"What are you looking at?" Jake asked.

Help us.

Lauren nearly dropped the plastic rectangle then, as Rebecca's face transformed into a screaming jack-o'-lantern, her eyes rounded and terrified and her mouth open.

"What are you looking at?" Jake repeated. "Is there something wrong with that picture? Do you know her?"

Lauren glanced up at Jake and when she looked back the photo had returned to normal.

"No. It's nothing. I thought I saw something—"

"Like what?"

"Nothing," she said. If she told him that the ID picture had changed, he would think she was either spooked or crazy.

She loaded each pack into one of the black plastic garbage bags, wrapping each one carefully. The packs were too bulky to fit inside her small duffel, so she handed one wrapped bag to Jake and she took the other.

"Are we going now?" Jake asked.

"Yes," she said.

"Thank Christ," he muttered.

Lauren didn't answer, because she wasn't thinking about Jake or their date or even what the police would say when she brought them the girls' backpacks.

She was thinking of that face grinning up at her from the photo, the face of the happy girl whose last word was a scream.

5

The last person Miranda expected to see in that part of the woods was Lauren. She hid behind an old oak wide enough to keep her body out of sight and peeked around the edge. Lauren and Jake Hanson were walking back in the direction of Lauren's neighborhood, carrying large plastic bags. Were they out here picking up trash?

Miranda snorted to herself. *Real romantic, Lauren. Why don't you take him down to the pharmacy and ride the mechanical pony for a dime while you're at it?*

But the sight of them together, and this deep in the woods, annoyed her. She and Lauren almost always stayed near the ghost tree, and she hadn't imagined that Lauren would even enter the forest without her. She was such a little mouse. Miranda thought that without her friend, Lauren would sit at home and play board games with her weird little brother until she was desperate. And when she was desperate she would call Miranda and beg her to go out somewhere cool in Tad's Camaro.

Miranda had very deliberately not called Lauren, waiting instead to see if her so-called best friend would call her after standing Miranda up the day before.

Tad had called to apologize for losing her at the mall. Those were his words, "losing her." As if he hadn't deliberately walked away to flirt with those sluts in neon tank tops. Miranda had played it cool, but not too cool. She still wanted him to drive her to school in the fall. No way was she taking the bus or getting sweaty riding a bike. And at the end of the conversation he offered to take her out to the fair the next day, so Miranda knew he was still hot to get into her pants.

I might even let him, she thought. *But there's no hurry now.*

But Lauren hadn't called, not even to say that she was sorry.

And even worse—she was in the woods with Jake Hanson, of all people. What was he doing with Lauren? Miranda knew that they weren't up to what *she'd* been up to most of the morning. *He* had met her in the woods again and taken her into the old cabin. There was a proper love nest set up in there now, with pillows and blankets and cloth to cover the one small window.

He'd told her that it was vitally important that no one know about them, so Miranda told Janice she was off to meet Lauren again. She didn't think this would backfire since Lauren couldn't be bothered to be friends anymore.

Really, Miranda thought, getting angrier the more she thought about it. *I've done so much for her. I tried to set her up with Billy so she could double-date with me and Tad and she walked out without a word. I've tried over and over to give her hair and makeup tips so she doesn't look like such a gawky little kid, but she never takes them. And then when I ask her to meet me she ditches me and then never even tells me she's sorry.*

Miranda was angry about all of these things, but she was extra-angry that Lauren was walking around the woods with Jake Hanson.

How could he possibly be interested in her? He's a man and she's a little girl.

Not Miranda, though. Miranda was a woman now.

She hugged herself with her arms. Finally, *finally*, her virginity was gone. And she'd lost it not to an octopus-handed teenager but a *man*. A grown-up man who'd done things to her she hadn't imagined were possible, no matter how many Jackie Collins novels she'd read.

And in the darkness of the cabin she hadn't seen that look in His eyes, the one that had given her pause the day before. The one that made her think He wanted to eat her up.

Don't be silly, Miranda. It was just your imagination.

Though there had been a moment—one moment—when it seemed like His teeth bit down a little harder than necessary. There was a sore spot on the inside of her right thigh that was sure to bruise. But that was just a little rough play, nothing to worry about.

It wasn't because He was a monster who wanted to hurt her.

He left her very early, by ten a.m., but Miranda had stayed in the cabin for a few more hours. She'd brought a small pack with a lunch and some magazines, and she felt absolutely decadent lying on the blankets naked while she flipped through her *Mademoiselle* and *Cosmopolitan*.

Around midafternoon she decided Janice would be drunk enough for her to sneak home. She was better prepared this time to encounter her mother even if Janice wasn't passed out. There was a brush and hair spray and deodorant in Miranda's bag, and Janice would never know that she had spent the morning writhing underneath her lover instead of building forts or whatever other kiddie thing Lauren liked to do in the woods.

Jake and Lauren disappeared into the trees, the sound of their murmured voices growing quieter. Miranda was glad they were gone, because she didn't want to run into them.

I wish I could tell Lauren what happened, though.

Miranda didn't have to tell her friend who she'd been with all morning. Lauren would just be shocked—and probably furious, too.

But Miranda and Lauren had always shared their secrets and their milestones, and this was something Miranda had always thought she would tell her best friend.

Maybe we're not best friends anymore. The thought made

her feel like there was an empty place inside, a hole where Lauren used to be.

She wanted to run after Lauren then, to grab her hand, to ask her to ditch Jake and go with Miranda to the old ghost tree.

Meet me by the old ghost tree, she thought, wondering if she thought hard enough that Lauren could hear her.

Lauren would never hear one particular thought, because Miranda would barely admit it to herself. It was just a tiny whisper, barely a brush of wind from somewhere in the back of her mind.

I don't want to be alone. Please don't leave me alone.

6

Alex found his opportunity to sneak down to the archives late in the afternoon. Hendricks and Pantaleo were out patrolling. Christie was in a meeting with the mayor about the security preparations for the fair. About two hours after lunch Miller fell asleep in his chair, his head lolling forward onto his chest. Miller had his legs up on his desk at the time. Alex wondered if he would stay in that position or if the rolling wheels of Miller's chair would slowly creep away until his feet crashed to the ground.

Would he wake up if that happened? Possibly not.

Once Alex and Miller had been out on the county road with the speed gun and Miller had conked out in the passenger seat. When an out-of-towner in a yellow Mustang went by doing a cool eighty-five miles per hour Alex had flipped on the lights and sirens and pulled out behind him. Miller slept right through the sirens and the rapid acceleration of their squad car. He snored through Alex getting out to ticket the driver and all the way back to the pullout where they'd started. In fact, Miller didn't open his eyes until they were parked again and Alex turned the engine off. After this incident Alex found himself worrying that if Miller's house was on fire he would sleep right through the sound of the smoke alarm.

Alex thought that if Miller rolled right out of the chair and ended up on the floor, it wouldn't even break the rhythm of his snores.

Though it was tempting to stay and wait for the outcome, Alex thought it better to try to get some time in searching the records before all his time was taken up patrolling the fair.

It doesn't make sense for us to do it, really. The town should hire private security.

He double-checked to make sure the front door was locked—all the officers had keys. He didn't want someone to sneak in and slit Miller's throat.

Such a thought would have been laughable just three days earlier. The most dangerous thing that Alex would have considered was someone coming in and dumping a milkshake on Miller's head as a prank.

But someone had cut those girls up into little pieces. And someone had killed Joe diMucci and taken his heart out of his chest. And nobody talked about these things. Nobody seemed to even remember that they happened.

Alex started in on the files from 1983, the year prior to Joe diMucci's death. The 1984 search had yielded nothing until he came across Joe's file under the *November* tab. It was the same for 1983—nothing until November.

A seventeen-year-old girl named Jessica Gilbert had gone missing on November 12 of that year. The girl was an honors student, the secretary of the student council, a violin player, and the captain of her volleyball team. She had no boyfriend and only two close friends, the same ones she'd had since grade school. In other words, she was a high achiever who never even broke her parents' curfew and therefore was unlikely to be a runaway. The girl was last seen wearing a red plaid flannel nightgown climbing the stairs to her own bedroom after kissing her parents good night.

The next morning her mother was surprised Jessica wasn't out of bed and downstairs eating breakfast early, as it was a school day and Jessica usually had to meet with the student council on Monday morning before classes began.

When Mrs. Gilbert went upstairs to check on her daughter she found the bed unmade and Jessica nowhere to be seen. She went through every room in the house but her daughter was not there. The front door was locked with a deadbolt and a chain latch, and both of those had been secured when her husband went out that morning to get the newspaper—she'd heard him slide the chain latch open as she stood in the kitchen making coffee. The back door had also been locked, although that had a simple knob lock. But Mrs. Gilbert was certain Jessica hadn't gone out that way because her daughter didn't have a back door key, only one for the front. And the two keys for that door were on her own and her husband's key rings.

When Van Christie asked Mrs. Gilbert what she thought had happened to her daughter, she seemed completely at a loss. She didn't think Jessica would have been able to climb out of her bedroom window—there was no tree limb to grab, or thicket of bushes below to jump into. In fact, there was nothing outside Jessica's window except smooth yellow siding.

Jessica had gone up to her bedroom the night before, carrying a thick library book under her arm. And sometime between the ten o'clock news and sunrise the next morning the girl had disappeared from her home without a trace. Her shoes weren't missing, nor her wallet. There was no indication that she'd left the house of her own volition.

There wasn't any sign of a struggle, either, or a broken window or picked lock. Jessica was simply gone.

Despite the extraordinary circumstances and the fact that Jessica was a minor, Van Christie had not called for a search. In fact, his notes in the file indicated that he thought the girl had run off with someone and would be home soon.

Alex grew angrier and angrier as he read the file. Christie's behavior had been almost criminally incompetent. He hadn't undertaken a search. He hadn't notified the police departments of nearby towns to be on the lookout for the girl. Christie hadn't done anything, as far as Alex could tell, except go to the Gilberts' house and take a statement.

He'd just waited until a couple of teenagers looking for a quiet place to grope each other had stumbled upon Jessica Gilbert's remains out in the woods. Then Christie took the photos, notified the family, and filed everything away.

The entire incident barely caused a ripple in the quiet waters of Smiths Hollow. Alex bet that if he checked the newspaper records of the time he would find no front-page story, either.

Just like now. Two girls were found brutally murdered and as far as Alex could tell most of the townspeople didn't even know it had happened. Although he didn't condone sensational journalism, there at least ought to have been a warning for the sake of public safety. Should parents let their kids go about unsupervised with this kind of killer on the loose?

The crime scene photos were shockingly familiar. The girl had been dismembered and beheaded, and the remains arranged in a strange pattern on the ground. It could have been the same set of photos that Alex had taken a few days earlier.

"When Christie arrived at the crime scene the other day he acted like he'd never seen such a thing before," Alex murmured.

He looked at the date Jessica Gilbert went missing. November 12, 1983. Something twanged in his memory.

Alex pulled out the file on Joe diMucci. Joe had left his house on November 12, 1984, and his body was found the next morning.

Some kind of anniversary? Alex went back to the cabinets and drew out all the files for November 1982. There were only five of them. Smiths Hollow really didn't have much crime to speak of.

But the crime that it did have was more horrifying than he'd ever imagined.

The third report in the pile was about a girl named Sarah Villaire. Sixteen years old and—reading between the lines—nothing but trouble. She'd been arrested for shoplifting, vandalism, drunk and disorderly—even soliciting (apparently she'd attempted to trade sexual favors for the purchase of alcohol). She lived with her divorced mother; her father's legal residence was in Indiana.

The report that Christie took from Sarah's mother was disturbingly similar to the one about Jessica. The mother—listed as Miss Tanya Mazur—had seen her daughter go to bed on November 12, 1982 around eleven p.m. Miss Mazur stayed up for some time after, watching a film that Sarah wasn't interested in. The mother and daughter lived in a small, one-level cottage with four rooms and a bathroom.

Miss Mazur was, by her own admission, nervous about the possibility of a break-in since they were two women living on their own. Before she went to bed herself she walked around the house checking the windows and both the front and back doors. Each door had a slide bolt lock as well as a keyhole lock in the knob. All of these were secure.

Sarah had snuck out of the house after dark before, but Miss Mazur had checked her daughter around one a.m. and Sarah was sleeping soundly.

The next morning Sarah's mother woke around seven a.m. Both the front and back door were still locked and bolted when she got up. She made a habit of checking these because an unbolted door meant Sarah had gone out in the night.

Miss Mazur cooked breakfast and then went to her daughter's room to wake her. She found the bed empty. Sarah's bedroom had one window, which was easy to climb through, but it was locked from the inside.

"It was like she just disappeared into thin air," Miss Mazur was quoted as saying.

Christie had done no follow-up on this case, either. There had been no interviews with her friends or neighbors, no search for a missing minor, no public call for witnesses or assistance. Just the bare facts of the disappearance were taken into the report with the later addition of the discovery of the girl's remains.

In the woods. In the same place that Jessica Gilbert's were found a year later, and Joe diMucci's were found a year after that.

And all three of them had gone missing on the same day.

Alex realized his heart was beating hard in his chest, like he'd been out running laps. Just what had he stumbled onto here, exactly?

It was fairly obvious that there was some kind of cover-up. It was even clearer that the mayor was involved somehow, as Christie seemed to take his marching orders from Touhy's office. Christie was always the only officer listed on the reports.

Was Touhy a murderer, and Christie was covering for him?

Or were Touhy and Christie hiding the murders for some other reason?

Why, though? Why would anyone keep this from the community? Why would they actively prevent the murderer from being caught?

Because that was definitely what happened. Christie didn't even bother with the pretense of an investigation. A person went missing. They were found dead. The case was filed away and forgotten. Wash, rinse, repeat.

It was easier to search now that he had clearer parameters. Alex pulled out all the November files from the last five years, and every year he found the same thing.

Marilynne Simmons. Went missing November 12, 1981. Found dead November 18.

Veronica Hawthorne. Missing November 12, 1980. Found dead on Thanksgiving day.

Bernice Charpentier. Missing November 12, 1979. Found dead two days later.

Every year a girl went missing on November 12. Every year her body was found in pieces in the exact same place in the woods.

Every year.

Every year and nobody ever spoke of it.

Every year a girl was brutally murdered and Smiths Hollow went about its business as if nothing happened at all.

Except for last year. Last year there hadn't been a girl. It had been a man—Joe diMucci. But there had still been a dead body.

Was there no outcry because people didn't know? Or—and this was much, much worse—because they *did* know but somehow accepted it as a part of life here?

Alex rubbed his eyes. *You're getting tired. The whole town isn't part of a vast conspiracy to . . .*

His thought trailed off. To what? To sacrifice one girl a year? Was the town full of Satanists or something?

"This isn't some weird horror movie, Alejandro," he told himself.

But there is something weird going on.

He heard the sound of boots on the floor upstairs—a heavy tread, probably Miller freshly awake from his nap and heading to the bathroom to piss out the giant pop he'd had with lunch.

Alex didn't want Miller to know what he was doing. Either Miller was as clueless as he seemed (which was very likely—Alex thought it would be hard work to pretend to be that simple) or he was part of Christie's cover-up. Either way, Alex didn't want Christie to find out.

He hurriedly put away all the irrelevant files and collected the ones of dead and missing girls that he'd found. Then he dashed up the stairs to the hallway and peeked right. The bathroom door at the far end was closed. He felt absurd sneaking around, like he was a child trying not to get caught by his parents.

Alex moved down the hall toward the main room of the station. He had to pass Christie's office, but the door was closed and there wasn't any sound of movement inside.

There was no air conditioning, so the windows in the front room were open—not that it made a bit of difference, really, as the whole station was like a sweltering oven. Alex heard the *whoosh* of cars passing by outside on the road, and the unmistakable buzz-call of a red-winged blackbird. The air was still and heavy and he was pretty certain there was no one in the building except him and Miller.

He dashed to his desk, stuffed the files in his backpack, put the pack back inside the bottom drawer, and tried to look busy. It wasn't that difficult, since he needed to organize all the statements from the roadhouse incident into a coherent report—writing reports was not Miller's strong suit so he generally left that to Alex.

Why is Miller even here? Alex thought, although it didn't

come from a place of malice. He liked Miller fine. He just didn't seem that interested in being a police officer.

Alex supposed it wasn't easy finding qualified people in a town this small—it was one of the reasons why Van Christie had been so eager to hire him.

The door to the bathroom banged open. Miller reminded Alex of his kids, the way every door needed to be thrown against the wall with all the force they could muster.

"Where were you?" Miller asked as he settled back into his sleeping position on the other side of the desk.

"Just went out for some air," Alex lied. "It's stuffy as hell in here. Are you taking another nap?"

"Fair duty starts tomorrow," Miller said, closing his eyes again. "Gotta sleep while I can."

Alex didn't mind if Miller took another snooze. It meant he'd leave Alex alone to think. He had a lot to think about.

If all the other deaths had happened on November 12, then why had those two girls been killed this week? Why were the bodies found in a residential yard instead of in the woods? Was there a copycat killer?

That was an even bigger nightmare—the idea that there might be two of these guys running around.

Whether there was one or two killers it was pretty clear that Christie was treating these two murders the same way he'd treated all of them.

He was going to pretend they hadn't happened, and

everyone in Smiths Hollow would continue knowing nothing.

Or pretending nothing happened.

Alex wasn't a detective. He didn't have any training. But he was going to expose Touhy and Christie, expose the murders that had been happening under everyone's nose.

Yeah, you're going to righteously demand justice, Sheriff Lopez, he thought. *But just how are you going to do that?*

7

Lauren and Jake emerged from the woods the same way that Lauren had gone in—through the Arakawas' yard. Mrs. Arakawa's white Mazda 626 wasn't in the driveway and Lauren was glad. She didn't want to answer any questions right now about what they'd found in the woods, or why she'd gone in alone but returned with Jake.

From the Arakawa house there was a fairly commanding view of the cul-de-sac and the houses on the street beyond. Lauren saw Jake's bright orange Gremlin in his driveway six houses away from the cul-de-sac. A few houses past that was Lauren's home.

There was a police car parked in front of her house, and she saw her mother standing by the mailbox talking to Officer Hendricks.

Her first thought was *Great, I can hand these bags over to him right now.*

Her second thought was *Then Mom will know what I was doing and she'll get pissed.*

"Listen, can we put these in your car for right now?" Lauren asked. "I know Officer Hendricks is right there, but I don't want my mom to know what I was doing."

"Sure," Jake said.

His answer seemed automatic, so she looked at him and saw that he hadn't noticed the police car or her mother at all. He was looking at a red Pontiac Fiero parked in front of Mrs. Schneider's house.

"Whose car is that?" Jake asked.

"I dunno," she said. "I don't usually notice cars."

"Yeah, but who would visit her? She's like the actual living embodiment of the Wicked Witch of the West."

Lauren shrugged. "Even the witch had flying monkeys who liked her."

"They were her servants," Jake said. "Like her slaves. They didn't like her. They had to do what she said. Anyway, you don't think a flying monkey drove up to Mrs. Schneider's house, do you?"

Lauren giggled, then covered her mouth with her hand.

"Why do you do that?"

"What?"

"Cover your mouth. You have a nice smile."

For the hundredth time that day she felt her face heat. Why did every stupid thing he said make her blush?

"I just—well, I giggled and it sounded silly and I wanted to stop."

"Or you could just let yourself laugh. You're allowed to, you know?"

It was funny, because when he said that she realized she hadn't really allowed herself to laugh, or to be happy at all, since her father died. She'd spent the better part of a year angry—angry at her mother for not loving her father enough, angry at the police for not doing anything to catch his murderer, angry at Miranda for changing, angry at herself for staying the same. There was a kind of relief in the realization, a feeling of lightness that she hadn't known in a very long time.

"You're right," she said. "I am allowed to laugh."

"But who is at her house?" Jake asked, indicating the car again.

"I don't know why you care so much," Lauren said.

"Nobody around here has a car like that. I would have noticed. And it's not brand-new, so it's not something that was just bought. I don't know. I just have a bad feeling."

"Anyway," Lauren said, steering him to their side of the street. Maybe if they stayed close to the houses her mom and Officer Hendricks wouldn't see her. From what she could see they were very deep in conversation.

Lauren felt an odd little burst of jealousy at that, the idea that her mom could engage Officer Hendricks (whom she'd only just acknowledged as an unattainable crush and thought she'd dismissed from her thoughts forever) in such a way that he wouldn't notice anyone else on the street.

And this feeling was immediately followed by one so full of nastiness that she wished she could wipe it from her brain.

What's she doing flirting when her husband hasn't even been dead for a year?

Lauren didn't even know for sure that her mom *was* flirting. There was a quality in her stance, something about the tilt of her head that made Lauren think that there was flirting going on. Or maybe it was because Officer Hendricks and Mom were standing a little too close together.

For all you know they're standing close together because they're talking about a breakthrough in Dad's murder case and they don't want anybody else to hear.

Lauren didn't think that was the reason, really. She didn't think that at all.

It looked like they were flirting.

Why do you care?

(Because he's not supposed to—)

He can flirt with whoever he wants. You're not going out with him.

(Well she's not supposed to—)

You know that Mom and Dad weren't happy. Don't you think she has a right to be happy?

(No)

Lauren knew then that she *did* think that. She didn't think her mother had a right to happiness now that her father was dead. All she thought her mother was allowed to do was be miserable until she died, too.

And then she knew just how unfair she'd been to her mother. *I'll be better*, she promised herself. *I really will.*

As they passed by the Lopez house, Lauren noticed Sofia weeding the front flower beds and stopped.

"What now?" Jake asked. To his credit, he didn't sound as exasperated as he probably felt.

"I don't want my mom to see the bags, or know what I was doing. I'm going to give them to Sofia so that when Officer Lopez comes home he can look at them and then take them to the police station. You keep going, though. You have to go to work."

And I don't really want my mom to know that you were with me, either.

"Okay," he said, handing her the other black plastic garbage bag. "I'll call you later, all right?"

"Oh. Um. Yes," she said. Of course he was going to call her on the phone. He wanted to go out with her. There wasn't going to be radio silence until Saturday night.

He waved and turned away, and she stood there for a moment with a bag clutched in each fist and a strange feeling in her heart.

She ought to be able to enjoy this, this first-boy and first-date thing. She ought to be allowed to feel uncomplicated and giddy. She didn't feel that way, though. She felt like she was doing something wrong, that she was being pulled in a direction she shouldn't go.

Lauren knew it was because of the girls, and Nana's story, and the fact that she might be a . . .

(witch, witch, you're a witch)

"Lauren, is something wrong?"

Sofia Lopez stood a few feet away, wearing green gardening gloves, cut-off denim shorts, a tank top, and a large quantity of garden dirt. Music drifted from a small transistor radio near the flower beds.

"Mrs. Lopez," Lauren said, and took a deep breath. "I need a big favor from you."

8

Sofia Lopez stared at the two plastic-wrapped packages that Lauren diMucci had left on her dining room table. She didn't want to touch them, felt vaguely that they were like grenades with their pins pulled partway out.

She couldn't leave the bags on the table. If Lauren was right—and she'd certainly believed she was right, Sofia could see that—then these bags were valuable evidence. If they weren't moved, one of the children was sure to find them and grow curious about what was inside. It was fortunate that all three of them were off playing elsewhere when Lauren arrived.

They'd been in the backyard earlier but as the other children of the neighborhood drifted out to play, the lot of them had migrated to another yard, one that had a tree house. Daniel and Camila had run inside only long enough to collect a large quantity of snacks for the prolonged stay in this arboreal paradise. Val had decided then that she'd had enough of her sister and cousin for one day and taken her bike out to a friend's house on the other side of town.

Sofia knew she really should move the bags before the children came home. To the hall closet, perhaps, or to her bedroom upstairs.

Sofia shook her head. She didn't want to take them upstairs. These things were tainted by death and if she brought the bags into her bedroom then the miasma would seep into everything. Death would stalk their dreams, hers and Alejandro's, and they wouldn't be able to cleanse the room of its stench.

"You're being fanciful," she told herself firmly.

She was not a superstitious woman. She was a good Catholic and she knew very well that death did not cling to objects and that if her dreams were troubled she could always pray to the Virgin Mary.

And yet she still didn't want to touch them.

Maybe it was because she'd seen what the murderer had done to those girls. Maybe it was because Mrs. Schneider had screamed like that, screamed like an alarm that couldn't turn off.

Maybe it was because for the last few days Alejandro had looked haunted, the way he had when they lived in Chicago and he saw death every day.

She didn't want to touch them.

They weren't her responsibility. She felt a surge of

resentment. Why had the diMucci girl given these horrible dirty things to her? Sofia had seen Officer Hendricks just down the street talking to her mother. Lauren could have walked straight to her own house and handed them directly to a police officer.

She explained why. She didn't want her mother getting upset at what she was doing in the woods.

Sofia supposed she could understand that. Lauren always looked pinched and worried, to Sofia's mind, even when she was supposedly having fun. Her smile never went all the way to her eyes. It didn't take a psychologist to realize that her father's death had upset her and Karen.

But Sofia didn't want these things, the possessions of two girls who'd been hacked into pieces, in her dining room.

So she called Alejandro, and told him in no uncertain terms that he needed to come and collect them right away.

9

Riley sipped the weak tea that Mrs. Schneider had served in overly fussy china cups. The tea barely washed away the bad taste in his mouth.

The woman had been deeply suspicious when he called asking for an interview.

"What do you want an interview for? I don't need my name in some Chicago paper. The Smiths Hollow local is good enough for me."

"Well, Paul Nowak is a friend of mine from school," Riley said easily. "And he gave me a call because he's very concerned about the parents of these girls. You see, they're having trouble identifying them because they don't seem to be from the town."

"What does that have to do with me?"

"I'm going to do a write-up for my paper and you're a key witness. I'd very much like your opinion on who could have done this and why," Riley said.

She was silent for a moment, then said, "Come to my house at two p.m. That Touhy won't do anything about the problem unless he's got some *pressure*. I can see that now."

She gave him her address so rapidly that he'd barely gotten a pencil into his hand to write it down before she hung up the phone.

At the time he'd been well pleased that she wanted to apply pressure to Touhy. From the moment Nowak told him about the incident he felt the mayor wasn't handling the situation properly. Someone in this town was killing kids, and the impression he'd gotten from both Nowak and the mayor himself was that he wanted the whole thing swept under the carpet. It was important that people knew what was happening.

In the name of public safety, of course. Not because this story is potentially huge and you want to be the one to break it.

But almost from the moment Riley sat down in Mrs. Schneider's lace-doilied living room he'd been subjected to an almost never-ending stream of bile about the Hispanic family that lived across the street.

"And one of them is even a *police officer*, if you can believe that. How convenient for them. They sacrifice these girls in some kind of pagan ritual and their handy police officer is there to destroy the evidence and point the finger elsewhere."

Mrs. Schneider took a breath and Riley saw this as an opportunity to get a word in edgeways.

"Leaving aside the issue of whether this family is guilty, why do you think the bodies were left in your yard in particular?"

"Because *they* hate me," Mrs. Schneider said with an imperious jerk of her chin. "They wanted me to feel terrified in my own home. I haven't felt easy since they arrived, and they know that I'm the only one on this block who sees them for what they really are. I'm not the only one in town, though. A group of us are putting together a petition to have these people arrested."

Riley was startled that the woman would go this far. He didn't think anything would come of it, because petitions by crazy old ladies weren't going to result in arrests for a major crime, but still. The vein of her hatred was deep and committed.

"So they put the bodies in my yard because they want me to leave. They know I'm the only one who is brave enough to identify them. And all the other bodies were in the woods, so this is obviously an intimidation tactic."

Riley sat up straight and put the teacup down on the table. "What other bodies?"

Mrs. Schneider's eyes clouded over and her mouth twisted in confusion. "Other bodies?"

"You just said that there were other bodies. In the woods."

"I did?" Her hands fluttered in her lap, searching for something that wasn't there.

"Yes." For a moment he'd thought that there really was a huge story here—bigger even than a couple of dead girls. But as Mrs. Schneider stared into the distance he thought it more likely that this was just another part of her fantasies.

Sure, a cache of bodies in the woods, all killed by those Dangerous Mexicans.

He wondered if Alejandro Lopez would speak to him. Police officers usually didn't talk to reporters unless it was cleared by their department, and in Chicago he was more likely to encounter a press liaison than a beat cop. Riley didn't think there was a press liaison in this one-horse town, though. Hell, he'd been able to walk right into the mayor's office without an appointment.

"Yes," Mrs. Schneider said. Her voice was dreamy, far away. "The bodies. All those girls. One girl every year, just like clockwork. When I was a young girl I thought I might be one of them. My number never came up in the lottery, I suppose. Not that it's the kind of lottery you want to win, you know. I was happy to lose, and I'm sure my parents were glad, too, if they thought of it. It's funny how people usually don't, you know. Everyone knows, but they don't know they do. Even if it's their girl that's been taken. But it's not the right *time*, you know. That's what has been troubling me. It's not the right time for it to happen."

"One girl a year?" Was this something she'd read in a book, or seen on TV? Even Richard Touhy couldn't hide the death of one girl a year. Just how deep did this woman's twisted fantasies go?

Maybe she's senile. I don't know why I even bothered coming here.

He put his teacup carefully into the saucer. She didn't seem to notice. Her mind was somewhere far away.

"One girl every year. Yes. My Janey was one of them, in 1959. They told me that she was hit by a car, one of those boys drag racing with other boys, but it wasn't true. She was out in the woods, just like all the others. There wasn't enough left of her to fit in a mason jar, you know. Except for her head. He always leaves the heads behind. Mr. Schneider never really was right again after Janey died. All the joy went out of him.

"I had her late, so late we thought we would never be blessed. I was almost thirty-five when she was born. Full of spit and fire, she was. She had red curls all over her head. Beautiful thick red curls that shone in the sun."

Riley didn't say anything, because he felt that to speak would be to break whatever spell Mrs. Schneider was under.

"And Mr. Schneider loved her so much. Oh, she was his sun and moon and stars. Nothing was too good for our little Janey. Jane Katherine Schneider, that was her name, but we always called her Janey. I never saw a girl that could do figures so fast. You could put any two numbers in front of her and she would be able to solve them before you could blink. My Janey.

"It was very strange, you know. We always thought it was very strange that she went missing, because we saw her go upstairs to bed that night. It was very chilly, I remember, because she was wearing her flannel nightgown instead of her lawn one, and she asked me for an extra blanket for her bed.

"Mr. Schneider locked the house up tight—he always did, he was nervous about those hoodlums with their greasy hair and their whaddyacall-ems . . . flick-knives?" She made a gesture with her hand like a switchblade opening. "And Janey was safe and sound in her bedroom, which was in the attic. The attic had a little window but not one that you could climb out of and anyway, there was no way down unless you put a rope through there. We didn't find a rope or sheets tied together or anything. That window was shut up tight because it was cold outside.

"When Janey wasn't in her room the next morning, Mr. Schneider just about went crazy. He called the police and every neighbor on the block. We didn't have so many neighbors then, and no single mothers or Mexicans or black folk, either. He ran up and down the street calling her name. He asked the police chief—it was Van Christie's father back then, Noel Christie—if there could be a search, but Christie wouldn't do it. Said the town didn't have enough resources. Ridiculous! As if everyone in Smiths Hollow wouldn't have turned out to find our girl. Every person we knew was asking how they could help. They would all have come out for a search party, but Christie said no. He always said no.

"Nobody knew how she got out of this house and into the woods, but three days later there she was just the same, all cut into pieces like the rest of them. Like those girls in my yard."

There were tears now, making rivulets in the thick powder she had applied to her face. Riley didn't know what to do or say to all of this, which was a first. How did you ask a follow-up question after a story like that?

"I'm very sorry for your loss," he said, stumbling over the words.

He knew instantly that he shouldn't have spoken. The foggy look in her eyes cleared.

"What loss?" she snapped.

"The loss of your daughter?" He couldn't help the querulous ending. Her abrupt change of mood had him confused and defensive.

"I don't have a daughter," she said, brows pulling together in a tight knot. "I never did."

"But you said—"

"I don't know what kind of game you are playing, Mr. Riley, but I assure you it's entirely offensive. My husband and I longed for children all our lives and were unable to have them. Do not try to tell me that I had a daughter when I know very well I did not."

Riley decided he'd had enough of this. The woman was— if not flat-out batshit crazy—definitely senile. He stood up. "Thank you very much for your time, Mrs. Schneider."

She blinked, seemingly startled by his abrupt change of mood. Then she returned to her normal imperious manner.

"I hope you will include everything I've told you in your article, Mr. Riley. Those Mexicans are a menace and the public should be aware of that."

Riley nodded—he had no intention of printing the old woman's racist screed—and hurried out of there before she either started up ranting again or drifted off into another weird trance.

Once he was on her front stoop he sucked in a deep breath. Even though Mrs. Schneider's living room was air-conditioned and it was hot as hell outside, the air still felt fresher than in her house.

Behind him he heard the sound of the old woman laboriously relocking the four locks on her front door. *If there were ever a fire in this house she'd probably die of smoke inhalation before she managed to get the door open.*

He walked slowly down the driveway toward his parked car, thinking about all the things the old woman had said. He felt a trickle of sweat run down his back. It was damned hot out—really too hot for mid-June, and it hadn't rained much. All the lawns in view already had grass turning brown around the edges, or dried patches. They were end-of-August lawns and it was only the beginning of summer.

Just as Riley reached his Fiero, a Smiths Hollow squad car pulled up in front of the house across the street. Alejandro Lopez climbed out of the car, giving him that sideways cop glance, the one that let you know they knew you were there and they were watching.

Riley made a sudden decision and crossed the street. Lopez stopped, his hands on his belt, his impassive cop's eyes waiting. Lopez was about five-eight or five-nine, same as Riley, so when they stood across from each other they were eye-to-eye. Lopez wasn't wearing the hat that came with his dark blue uniform. Riley saw it on the passenger seat of the squad car.

The police officer had black hair that was long on top and short on the sides. The top was combed back. His eyes were very dark, so dark Riley couldn't see the pupils. They were eyes that gave nothing away.

"Officer Lopez?"

Lopez nodded.

"George Riley." Riley held out his hand and Lopez shook it. There wasn't any of that false machismo in the handshake either, and Riley knew immediately that Lopez didn't feel he had anything to prove to a stranger.

"Listen," Riley said, lowering his voice to a confidential tone. "I was just across the street interviewing Mrs. Schneider—"

"Interviewing her for what?" Lopez asked.

"Oh, I'm a reporter from Chicago," Riley said, then hurried on before Lopez decided to walk away. "Don't worry, I'm not here looking for an interview from you. Although I wouldn't mind if you gave a statement."

He tried his usual self-deprecating smile, the one that usually put people at ease, but Lopez didn't look like he relaxed a single muscle. If anything he was more wary than before.

Because he's part of the conspiracy to keep the news about the girls away from the public?

"So what do you want, Mr. Riley, if not an interview?" Lopez asked.

"I wanted to warn you about that old lady. She seems to think you and your family killed those girls that were found in her yard a couple of days ago," Riley said.

"Thanks, Mr. Riley, but we're already aware that Mrs. Schneider doesn't want us here," Lopez said. He started to turn away.

"She also told me a strange story about one girl being killed in this town every year. Said that her own daughter Jane was one of them, back in 1959."

Lopez turned back slowly. Riley had hoped to startle him into a reaction, but this man was no fool.

"You just moved here from Chicago, didn't you?" Riley said. "So you couldn't possibly know anything about this business."

"What business would that be?"

"This business about a girl dying every year. Sounds like some kind of old wives' tale, doesn't it? A yearly sacrifice."

A sacrifice for what, though? Riley thought. Why on earth would girls go missing and die once a year, every year, for more than thirty years? It couldn't be one person doing it. And why would anyone stay here if it was true? If Riley lived here and had a daughter he'd have her out of this place. No, the old woman's story was just that—a story. A strange and haunting story, to be sure, and she certainly seemed like she believed it when she told it. But her belief didn't make it true. She also believed her neighbors were part of a Central American death cult.

But there was something about it that nibbled at the back of his mind. Somewhere in there was the ring of truth.

"I don't think you should take what Mrs. Schneider says very seriously, Mr. Riley. Does Chief Christie know you're out here interviewing a witness?"

"I'm not required to ask permission of the town, Officer Lopez," Riley said. "We do have freedom of the press in this country."

He didn't say *What are you hiding?* although the impulse to do so was very strong.

"I didn't say we didn't," Lopez said easily. "I just know that Mrs. Schneider was in a lot of distress after the . . . event. And Christie would want to know that you're speaking with her. This case is still open."

"Sure you don't want to go on the record?" Riley asked, pulling out his notebook. He knew what the answer would be.

"I think you ought to speak with Chief Christie," Lopez said. "Thanks for the warning about Mrs. Schneider."

He walked away then, leaving Riley dismissed. It didn't bother him, though. Maybe he should talk with Christie, at that. It would be irresponsible to publish a story without getting a quote from the chief of police.

And maybe he would check the town records while he was at it. It would be a simple thing to verify if the Schneiders ever had a child named Jane, and if and when she died. It was possible that Mrs. Schneider had given birth but the child had been disowned for some reason. That made more sense than a death, actually.

If your child died young—suddenly, tragically—your house would be like a shrine to that child, or at least that was the way Riley figured it. But there were no photos of this child anywhere, no sign that she ever existed.

But what if something terrible happened to your child, and you just wanted to forget?

Speculation was useless. Facts were verifiable. He'd have a look at the town records.

A woman came out of the house to Lopez—his wife, Riley assumed—and as she did a white Chevrolet Chevette entered the cul-de-sac and then pulled into the Lopez driveway.

"Beatriz?" Mrs. Lopez said as a second woman climbed out of the car, crying. "What's the matter?"

"I lost my job at the factory!" Bea said.

"What?" Mrs. Lopez said, hurrying to the crying woman. Officer Lopez was a step behind her. "What happened?"

Riley hadn't moved a muscle and he wasn't about to start now. He had no idea if this woman's job loss was in any way relevant to his story but his basic philosophy was "no information is bad information."

"I wasn't the only one. Two hundred people were laid off today," Bea said as Mrs. Lopez put her arm around Bea's shoulders.

Two hundred people from a factory. She must be talking about the chili canning factory. That place employed most of the town. Layoffs like that would be a huge blow to the local economy.

Alejandro Lopez looked at him then, and the look clearly communicated that Riley shouldn't be standing at the end of the Lopez driveway watching the family drama like a television program.

Riley held up his hands in surrender and walked back to his car. He saw Mrs. Schneider's front curtains twitch. He wondered if the old woman had already forgotten the tale she'd told him.

For that matter, she might have forgotten his identity entirely.

He climbed into his car and headed toward the *Observer* office. Pete would point him in the direction of the town records.

He'd find out if Mrs. Schneider ever had a daughter in the first place.

And then he'd go and see Chief Christie, and see what he was hiding.

10

Alex stood on the lawn and waited for Riley to drive away. He wanted to make sure the man was gone before following Sofia and Bea into the house.

Alex heard Bea's sobs coming from the kitchen. He saw the black plastic garbage bags that Sofia had called him about on the dining room table.

He desperately wanted to know what was in those bags. He also wanted to talk to Lauren diMucci about where she found them. Sofia hadn't been able to give him a great deal of information. She only told him that Lauren had found some things that belonged to the two dead girls in the woods, and that Lauren didn't want her mother to know what she'd been doing so she asked Sofia to take them.

But Alex knew he couldn't go through the bags while his sister-in-law was in the kitchen crying. First because Alex and Sofia and Ed and Bea had come to this town together, and they were a family. If Bea lost her job it affected all of them.

And second because if he didn't make at least a token effort to soothe Bea, then Sofia would make sure he heard what an insensitive clod he was later.

He couldn't stop himself from opening the bags, though. The pull of his curiosity was too strong.

Inside each bag was a backpack. Lauren must have searched the bags herself if she knew for certain that the packs belonged to the dead girls. That meant her prints would need to be eliminated from the evidence, and she'd have to come to the station.

Alex didn't want to handle the bags himself without plastic gloves. The smart thing to do, in normal circumstances, would be to take the bags back to the station and search them there, preferably while the chief was watching. But these were not normal circumstances. He was certain that if he brought evidence related to the girls' murder back to the police station, it would disappear into a black hole. The reports he'd spent the afternoon reading were proof of that. Whether by his own will or some external direction, Christie was not going to do anything about the murders.

She also told me a strange story about one girl being killed in this town every year. Said that her own daughter Jane was one of them, back in 1959.

Could those murders really go back that far? Just what in the hell was going on in Smiths Hollow if it was true?

Well, he could check the files as soon as he got back to the station. He knew the name of Mrs. Schneider's supposed daughter and the year of her supposed death. He hadn't even known the old woman ever had a daughter.

It wasn't as if they were friendly neighbors.

He knew Sofia kept some gloves under the kitchen sink for cleaning, which meant he'd have to go into the lioness's den if he wanted to search the bags here at home.

He carefully reclosed each bag and folded the excess plastic underneath each backpack. The kettle whistled in the kitchen, which meant Sofia was making some restorative tea for her sister-in-law.

"Ed's job is still safe for the moment," Bea said as Alex walked into the kitchen. "My supervisor understood that we both couldn't be jobless. But I don't know if that decision will hold. I'm sure the union will argue that Ed shouldn't have a job over someone who's been there longer. And I don't know what we'll do if that happens. I mean, this house. How will we pay for the house if only one of us is working?"

Sofia carried two cups of tea to the table and handed one to Bea.

"You don't know for sure that Ed will lose his job as well," Sofia said. "And it's not as if the chili factory is the only place to work. There are a lot of jobs at that mall in Silver Lake."

"Those jobs don't pay anything," Bea protested. "And they don't have health benefits."

"As long as Ed is working at the factory you don't have to worry about health benefits," Alex said.

"I can't believe this is happening," Bea said. "We just moved here! Everything about this town seemed so perfect—low crime, good jobs, friendly neighbors. But now everything is going wrong. First those dead girls. Now I've lost my job. And that old bitch across the street has been trying to kill us with her eyes ever since we moved in."

"Don't get yourself worked up about Mrs. Schneider," Alex said. "Maybe the stress of having two girls murdered in her backyard will cause her to drop dead of a heart attack."

"Alejandro!" Sofia said, crossing herself. "That's a terrible thing to say."

"No, it's terrible for her to say that everyone in this household is part of some murderous cult that killed those girls," Alex said without thinking.

Bea looked horrified. "Did she really say that? My God, what if people believe her? We could all be arrested!"

"We're not going to be arrested," Alex said in his best soothing voice. "I'm one of five members of the police force. I assure you that if they think we're murderers I'll have advance notice and we can sneak out of town in the middle of the night."

Bea choked out a half laugh, half cry. "Yes, advance notice will be such a comfort when we're all on the run from a capital murder charge."

Sofia glared at Alex, and he knew she was angry because

he'd mentioned Mrs. Schneider's accusations when Bea was already in distress.

"There's not going to be a murder charge," Sofia said, patting Bea's hand. "Because Alex is going to find out who really did it. Aren't you, Alex?"

Alex thought of the reports he'd hidden in his backpack, and Riley's remark about a murder from 1959. Could he find out who did this? Could anybody?

"Sure," he lied.

11

Lauren found herself walking very slowly to her own house. Normally she would rush to Officer Hendricks's side (*God, you really did do that. What a stupid little puppy he must think you are*), but she didn't want to talk to him today.

It had something to do with Jake and his declaration, she realized. She felt guilty about accepting his invitation to the fair and then talking to Officer Hendricks, even though she shouldn't. It wasn't as if Hendricks was planning on asking her out himself.

And you know that you really do like Jake.

She liked what she knew of him, she amended. He had been kind to her when they were young, and kind to her when she'd been sick. He was smart—she knew that because he'd graduated from high school early, and he would have had to take extra classes to do that.

He listened to music she'd never heard of. On the way

back through the woods he'd told her about the Clash and the Smiths and Iggy Pop. He promised to make her a mix tape of all his favorite songs.

He didn't seem like the other boys. But it was possible that he would be like the other boys—only interested in his own hobbies and not hers, always wanting his own way, constantly turning the conversation back to himself and his experiences, only trying to get into her pants.

That's what boys really are like.

That, she realized, was why she hadn't joined in when Miranda made lists of all the hot guys in their eighth-grade class. "Hot" being a relative term—gawky thirteen- and fourteen-year-old boys with bad celebrity copycat haircuts could hardly be called hot.

Jake wasn't like them. Or he didn't seem to be.

He might be a terrible disappointment, in the long run.

You're not getting married, Lauren. You're going to the fair with him. You don't have to stay with him forever.

This thought made her feel more comfortable. She could always say no if he asked her out again.

She wondered what Officer Lopez would think about her discovery. She liked Alex a lot—not least because he told her to call him Alex instead of Officer Lopez, which made her feel like a grown-up—and she knew he was from Chicago, where they probably had crimes like this all the time. He would know what to do, she was sure of it.

If only he'd been here last year. Maybe then we'd know who killed Dad.

Chief Christie was nice and all, but Lauren didn't think he did a very good job with actual investigations. She was pretty certain he'd never done anything for her father.

It was almost as if there were some kind of spell over him, something keeping him from finding out.

Right, the curse of the three witches and the monster in the woods.

She was still reluctant to believe Nana's story. It was too fantastic, so many girls dying and nobody even knowing that it ever happened.

Even if there was a curse, Lauren reasoned, people had to notice that their daughters disappeared. There would be an awful lot of grieving parents in Smiths Hollow.

No, Lauren didn't believe Nana's story. There was no proof.

But maybe she believed the part about being from a family of witches.

There was the floating book, after all. And the way she found the trail of blood in the woods—Jake could hardly see it while it was bright as sunshine to Lauren.

What else can I do if I'm a witch?

She felt a little clutch of excitement at the thought of secret powers.

Somehow, despite dragging her feet from the Lopez house, she'd managed to arrive at her own. Her mom and

Officer Hendricks stood halfway up the drive, facing one another. Hendricks's back was to Lauren, but she could see her mother's face.

She looked radiant.

There was no other word for it. She was smiling and laughing. The skin of her face seemed smoother, brighter, younger. Her eyes actually sparkled.

Lauren realized with a pang that she'd never seen her mother look at her father like that.

They must have loved each other once, though Lauren didn't really remember that. She remembered her mother always frustrated, always angry, and her father always dismissive.

Yes, he dismissed her. It seemed a little bit like a betrayal to admit that, because she'd held firm to the idea that her mother was a monster who made her father miserable for so long.

But maybe it was the other way around. Maybe her father hadn't taken her mother seriously, had ignored her wants and needs. And the more he did that the more angry and frustrated and nagging her mother became.

It was strange that this prism of insight should occur to her now. Maybe it never would have happened if her father were still alive. Lauren had always loved him best. It was hard to see a person's flaws when your heart was so full of love for him.

Poor Mom—and there was a lot of regret in that thought. She would be a better kid. She would love her mom just as much as she'd loved her dad.

"Lauren!"

Lauren had paused at the end of the driveway, not wanting to be the one who took that look off her mother's face. But at the sound of Miranda's voice Officer Hendricks and her mother stopped talking to look and the spell was broken.

Miranda was coming down the road from the cul-de-sac, the same way Lauren had walked. She was carrying a little backpack. Had Miranda been in the woods, too? What was she doing out there if she was? Had she been looking for Lauren? Whatever she'd been up to hadn't been very strenuous. Her hair appeared to be freshly brushed and her lip gloss had that just-applied look. Miranda was scowling at Lauren as she approached.

Lauren felt another spurt of guilt. She hadn't been a very good friend to Miranda, especially these last few days. Even if they were drifting apart, she should have at least called when she missed their meeting the day before.

"Miranda," Lauren said awkwardly as her friend marched up. Lauren noticed that Miranda's normally pristine white sneakers had fresh dirt on them. "Hi."

"Can we talk somewhere private?" Miranda asked.

Oh, damn. They were going to have a fight. Lauren felt it. It had been coming down to this for a long time, but she'd still hoped to avoid it.

"Sure," she said, although she really wanted to say, *No, I really don't want to talk to you right now.*

Her mother and Officer Hendricks waved to Lauren and
Miranda as they walked up the drive.

"Hello, Miranda," her mom said. "Going upstairs, Lauren?"

"Yeah," Lauren said. It was hard to work up enthusiasm
for the coming confrontation.

"Hi, Mrs. diMucci," Miranda said. Her voice was bright
and cheerful. Miranda was much better at pretending than
Lauren was.

"Hello, you two," Officer Hendricks said, and smiled.

Lauren felt a little pang in her chest at that smile. She'd
always loved the way his eyes crinkled up when he smiled.

I guess it's harder to let go of puppy love than I thought. It
didn't hurt, though. It was more like a memory, a kind of
bittersweet echo of a feeling she used to have.

*I acted so silly in front of him yesterday, and he was so nice
when I fell off my bike.*

Lauren gave him a shy little wave, but Miranda frowned
at him.

"Come on, Lauren," Miranda said, grabbing her arm.

Lauren caught a glimpse of the startled faces of the adults as
Miranda dragged her up the drive and around to the backyard.

"Hey, what was that all about? That was rude."

"I want to talk to you and every time you're around
Officer Hendricks you never want to leave," Miranda said.

She headed right up the back porch like it was her house
and yanked off her dirty shoes before entering the kitchen.

The soles were coated with thick black dirt, the kind that was only deep in the woods.

The kind that was also on the soles of Lauren's shoes.

Miranda opened the screen door and said impatiently, "Don't just stand there, come on."

She went into the kitchen and Lauren ran up the porch steps after her. She paused long enough to unlace her sneakers and heard David's little voice say, "Hello, Miranda."

Miranda didn't say anything in reply. Lauren peered through the screen door while struggling to get her second sneaker off and saw Miranda rush straight past David and down the hall to the stairs.

Now Lauren was really irritated. There was no need to be rude to David. He was only four years old, after all, and didn't deserve to be the recipient of Miranda's bad mood.

David was on the kitchen floor drawing on a large sheet of paper. Their mom had gotten a big roll of butcher paper from Frank at the deli, and David liked to roll out a long sheet and make cartoons.

"Hi, Lauren," David said as she entered the kitchen.

"Whatcha drawing, bud?" she asked, crouching next to him.

"A story," he said, not looking up at her. He seemed very intent on his work. "Like a comic book."

Miranda could wait a minute. Lauren wasn't going to rush upstairs just because she was having a fit. And Lauren felt bad that David was alone in the kitchen, even though it never really bothered him to be by himself.

Usually he drew scenes from *He-Man*, which was his favorite cartoon, and Lauren expected to see several childish renditions of He-Man battling Skeletor. But that wasn't what he was drawing today.

There was a picture of two girls—rendered crudely in crayon, but still identifiable as girls. One of them had short blond hair and the other had long brown braids. Their hands were on their faces and their mouths open in screams. David had drawn these as big black circles.

A huge black shadow hovered before them, a shapeless body with red eyes and clearly defined hands. The hands looked like long silver knives.

There were many drawings before this one. Lauren wondered how long David had been at it.

Mom must have been outside with Officer Hendricks for a long time. She would flip if she saw these.

Lauren scooted around David on the floor so that she was at the beginning of the scroll. David had started from the cut end of the paper and was rolling out more as he progressed.

The very first picture was a tree—the ghost tree, Lauren realized. It couldn't be any other tree because it was the only one in the woods with the split from the lightning bolt. David had never been in the woods, though. He'd never seen the tree.

The next picture was of three women—an old one, a

middle-aged one, and one with red hair—standing on the porch of a house on a hill.

This was followed by a drawing of the red-haired woman walking arm-in-arm with a man. Then one of the red-haired woman with a rounded belly, holding hands with the man. The woman had a silver ring on her finger, a ring made up of woven braids. They were both smiling.

The man went into the woods, and in this drawing the ghost tree had red eyes. It watched the man go.

It watched the red-haired woman follow him, and then the man with the knife follow her.

Then the red-haired woman lay in a pool of blood.

It was Nana's story, exactly. The story about the three witches on the hill. Every detail was there, down to the rich man's house burning and the witches' ritual.

Lauren didn't wonder at all how David knew all these things anymore. He knew them because he was a witch. And Lauren was a witch, too.

David was drawing another picture now. Lauren saw a Ferris wheel, small and out of proportion to the figures in front of it. One of those figures was clearly herself—the hair was dark and curly and David had written *prpel ran* on the T-shirt. She held a box of popcorn in one hand.

One of the figures, she thought, was Jake Hanson. He had dark hair and blue eyes and was a lot taller than the Lauren figure.

She didn't wonder how he knew that Jake had asked her out, either.

He'd started on a third person, in the foreground. So far there was just a round head with no expression.

"Lauren! *What* are you *doing* down there?" Miranda yelled.

Lauren started. She'd completely forgotten about Miranda. Again.

She patted David's shoulder and stood up, wondering if she should tell him to put the drawing away before their mother saw it. He appeared so focused that she decided it was better not to interrupt. Their mother didn't notice what David did, generally, as long as he was quiet.

Is he going to be messed up because he keeps seeing these weird scary things? Lauren thought of the dead redhead in the pool of blood.

"But it's almost like he forgets them right after he learns them," Lauren murmured as she walked slowly down the hall. "So maybe he'll be okay."

Lauren reached the bottom of the stairs. Miranda stood at the top with her arms crossed, glaring.

"I'm coming, I'm coming," Lauren said. Her stomach did a little backflip. She hated yelling, and Miranda was definitely going to yell.

Miranda marched into Lauren's room ahead of her. Lauren followed, her feet dragging. She didn't want this.

"Shut the door," Miranda said. She'd gone to the window

and pulled it shut. The lack of fresh air made the room immediately stuffy.

"It's my room, not yours," Lauren said, but she shut the door anyway. She didn't want her mom to hear them if she came back in the house.

Miranda whirled around. "Just *what* do you think you were doing out in the woods with Jake Hanson?"

This wasn't what Lauren had expected. She thought Miranda would be angry about their missed meeting, or Lauren leaving her at the arcade two days before without a word.

"How did you know?" Lauren asked.

"I *saw* you," Miranda said. "I saw the two of you together."

Miranda had seen them? She'd seen the place where the girls were killed and she hadn't said anything?

"What did you see us doing?" Lauren asked carefully.

"Walking together. And you seemed like you were feeling *very* close."

Miranda put a lewd emphasis on the *very*. It was clear what she thought Lauren and Jake had been up to in the woods. Lauren felt her cheeks heat and wished for the millionth time that she didn't blush so easily. Miranda was going to think her suppositions were true.

"Why didn't you say anything? Why didn't you say hello, or walk with us?" Lauren said, feeling a tiny seed of irritation sprouting inside her. She didn't have to defend her behavior to Miranda. "What were you doing in the woods anyway?"

Miranda's face immediately closed off, her eyes brimming with some sly secret. "None of your business."

Oh, I think I can guess, Lauren thought, and she remembered what Jake had said about Miranda being easy. Well, it was her business if she wanted to give it up to a loser like Tad. Lauren wasn't going to give her the satisfaction of asking about it.

"Well, what I was doing was none of your business, either," Lauren said. She was relieved that Miranda hadn't seen Lauren and Jake getting the backpacks—and she was glad, too, that Miranda hadn't had to see the terrible remains of the girls in the woods.

Nobody should have to see that.

"So you're too good for me now?" Miranda said. "You've got a college boyfriend and you don't need to return my calls or meet me when you say you're going to?"

"He's not—"

"You know he's only interested in one thing. A college guy hanging around a high school freshman? He wants to get in your pants and he knows you're too young and stupid to say no."

"Hey," Lauren said. "I'm not stupid. And Jake's not like that."

Lauren didn't think he was like that, anyway. He might be. But she wasn't going to sleep with him just because he was older. Even if he tried to pressure her—but she didn't think he would, really.

"You're *very naïve* about men, Lauren," Miranda said. "I'm trying to give you good advice here."

"What do you know about men?" Lauren snapped. "Just because you let Tad put his hands down your pants doesn't mean you know everything. He's not a man, anyway, just a boy."

"How do you know Tad put his hands in my pants?" Miranda said coolly. "How do you know it wasn't someone else?"

Miranda had an air of barely suppressed excitement, like she was full to bursting with a secret she wanted to tell.

Lauren didn't care about her secrets, she realized. She didn't have to stand here and listen to Miranda anymore. She didn't have to do what Miranda said or come when Miranda called. It had been a long time since they were really friends, and she wasn't mousy little Lauren following Miranda around like a tail anymore.

"Who cares who you were with?" Lauren said. "If you want to have sex with everyone in Smiths Hollow, I don't care."

Miranda narrowed her eyes. "Oh, I think you would care if you knew."

"I don't," Lauren said. "And I don't want you to call me anymore. We're not friends and you need to stop pretending we are."

It was out now, out in the open. Lauren's words seemed to lie on the carpet between them, red and bleeding.

Miranda's face whitened. When she spoke her voice was shaky. "Really? We're not friends?"

The look on Miranda's face made Lauren feel terrible, but she soldiered on.

"No, we're not," Lauren said. "You just want me to walk next to you and do what you want and tell you how great you are. You don't want to do things together. You don't want me to be a person, just Miranda's appendage."

"Is this about the arcade the other day?" Some of the color had returned to Miranda's face as Lauren spoke. She tossed her hair over her shoulder and glared.

Lauren gritted her teeth. "It's about the arcade, yes. It's about a lot of things. It's about all the times you decided what we were going to do and how to do it. It's about the fact that you're more interested in getting in the back seat of someone's car than anything else."

"Hasn't Jake gotten you in the back seat of his car yet?" Miranda said snidely. "Or does he only grope you in the woods?"

"He hasn't groped me at all!" Lauren yelled. "I'm not a slut like you."

She clapped her hands over her mouth. She hadn't meant to say that. She didn't mean it. And she didn't really believe it, either.

"A slut?" Miranda said, her voice very quiet as she looked

at the floor. "That's what you think I am, huh?"

"No," Lauren said, tears filling her eyes as she sank to her knees. "No, I don't really."

And she didn't really. She'd just been angry and hurt and she'd said something she didn't mean.

Miranda picked her head up and looked Lauren in the eyes. "I don't care what you think of me, you stupid little bitch. Why would I want to hang around with a loser like you?"

She swept past Lauren and out the bedroom door. Lauren reached out as she passed, but her former friend ignored her.

"Miranda, I—"

But it was too late. Miranda was already on the stairs, disappearing from sight.

Lauren wanted to follow her, wanted to fix it. But her legs wouldn't listen. They felt like they were made of water, water that wouldn't press into the ground but kept flowing away beneath her. Her chest felt huge and aching, her face hot and swollen.

It was over now. It was really over. They'd said things that couldn't be mended.

She should be happy. They hadn't been real friends for a long time.

Lauren bent over her legs and sobbed until her eyes ran dry.

12

Karen waved good-bye to Officer Hendricks—*Aaron, he told me to call him Aaron*—as he climbed into his patrol car and drove away. She'd been out front watering the flowers when he pulled up at the end of the driveway.

It had been a surprise when he stopped, and even more of a surprise when she realized he didn't have Luke Pantaleo with him. The two of them were always together.

At first she thought he might deliver more information about Joe's death—a witness that had come forward, a suspect in custody. But he said he'd just come by to see "how all of you are doing."

Somehow a simple check-in had turned into almost an hour of conversation. They'd started chatting about books and movies and travel. Karen had never realized before how much they had in common.

She'd also not realized how long it had been since she'd

talked to an adult like that. Or how long it had been since she'd laughed.

A little ember of warmth burned inside her as she watched him drive away. She hoped he'd stop by again sometime.

He's a little young for you, isn't he?

Aaron had to be in his late twenties, at least. And Karen wasn't that old for a woman who had two kids, one of them a teenager. She was only thirty-five.

Their life experiences were very different, to be sure. He was a freewheeling bachelor and she was a single, struggling widow with two children.

But he said you were pretty, and she blushed when she remembered it.

She'd laughed at an anecdote he'd told about dealing with drunks on the weekend, and he'd reached out to tuck a strand of her hair behind her ear and said, "You should laugh more often. You're pretty when you smile."

That was what Joe had said, too, so long ago.

You're pretty when you smile. And she'd fallen in love with him and gotten pregnant, and she'd never gone away to study art in Italy like she always thought she would.

Of course she loved Lauren and David. She would never give them up for anything in the world. But sometimes it was hard not to look at the life she'd had and the life she'd wanted and wish she could go back and undo some of her choices.

Karen started around the side of the house so she could

re-enter through the kitchen. She felt a little spasm of guilt about leaving David there alone for so long.

David knew where I was. He would have come to get me if he needed anything.

No doubt she would find him in the exact same place and in the exact same position—on the floor drawing pictures. He might not have even noticed that she was gone. Sometimes he got like that—concentrating so intensely on his project that if you spoke to him it was as if he were waking up from a dream, or returning from a place very far away.

She heard the back door slam and then Miranda rounded the corner of the house. The girl didn't even appear to see Karen. Her face was red and her teeth were bared.

"Miranda?" Karen asked, but Miranda rushed past her without a word.

She and Lauren must have had an argument, Karen thought with an inward sigh. They hardly ever argued when they were young, but Karen thought she'd detected more friction between them as they got older. Well, it was inevitable, she supposed. They were growing into two very different people.

I wonder if Lauren is upset, Karen thought. Not that Lauren would tell her mother if she was. But her first period plus an argument with her best friend was bound to result in a moody teenager.

I should make spaghetti for dinner. It's her favorite.

She'd had lots of arguments with her best childhood

friend once they reached high school, Karen remembered as she climbed the back porch stairs.

Nancy Butler, Karen thought. Nancy with her long blond hair and fair skin, so fair that she looked like she was imported from Norway. Nancy had loved all the Motown bands, the Supremes and the Four Tops and the Temptations, and unlike every other girl in the country she had been deeply unimpressed by the Beatles—who were, of course, Karen's favorite band.

She remembered watching them on *The Ed Sullivan Show*, playing "I Want to Hold Your Hand." She fell in love with John Lennon right then and there but Nancy thought they were "just a bunch of weird longhairs."

They had argued about the Beatles and about some boy Nancy had a crush on—*what was his name? Jack something?* He was a senior and was dating Sonya Wojcek, Karen recalled. And Nancy would just sigh every time he walked by in the hallway no matter how often Karen told her she didn't have a chance.

What had happened to Nancy Butler? Her family had moved away or something like that, and they lost touch. It was strange, the way Karen could just forget a girl she was friends with for nine years. But she supposed that happened. You grew up and you lost touch and you moved on.

Best friends since the first day of first grade, just like Lauren and Miranda. Karen smiled to herself, remembering both of them in white blouses and colored jumpers. Karen's jumper was pink and Nancy's yellow.

She realized she was standing on the back porch, woolgathering, and went inside.

David was exactly where she'd left him, drawing with his crayons. The roll of butcher paper had been pushed all the way across the floor and was covered in a series of drawings. He didn't even look up when the screen door slammed shut behind her.

"Wow, you really did a lot," Karen said, leaning over to see what he was drawing.

There was a crayon girl lying flat on the ground, a girl in a yellow dress with long yellow hair all around her head like a halo, and around the yellow halo was a blooming sunrise of red.

The girl's eyes were two black X marks and her mouth was a black circle.

"Nancy," Karen gasped. And she remembered.

I went to school that day. It was the thirteenth of November and Nancy wasn't in homeroom. After homeroom we had biology together with Mr. Parsons, but she wasn't in biology either, so I thought maybe she was sick.

We'd had an argument the day before, a stupid argument about the Harvest Dance.

And it had been stupid, a stupid thing about how they'd both bought the same dress and who was going to wear it and who was going to get stuck wearing an old one instead because—

"We can't show up in the gym wearing the same thing like the Bobbsey Twins," said Nancy.

"So what?" Karen said. "I'm not going to the dance in my same old dress."

And Karen definitely was not going to, because it had taken ages to convince her father that she needed the new one in the first place. If she wore an older one he would be furious about the wasted expense.

Anyway, she wanted to wear the new dress. It was deep red velvet, the color of wine, and it set off Karen's dark hair and eyes. Nancy would just look washed out in a color like that with her pale hair and skin, and Karen told her so.

"For your information, my mother said I looked beautiful in that dress," Nancy snapped.

"Your mother has to say you look beautiful. She's your mother," Karen said. "Why don't you just return it for a different one?"

"Because I want to wear that one!"

"So do I," Karen said, and privately thought that if they both wore the same dress, everyone would agree she looked better in it and Nancy would suffer by comparison.

And Nancy had pressed her lips together and stormed off, leaving Karen to walk home alone.

The next morning Nancy wasn't in school and Karen was relieved, because if Nancy was home sick then maybe she would be too sick to go to the Harvest Dance and the *argument about the dress would be moot.*

But when she got home that afternoon Karen's mother was sitting in the kitchen with Nancy's mother and Nancy's mother was crying like she would never stop.

Nancy had gone missing the night before and no one knew where she could be.

The mothers had looked at Karen and asked if Karen knew where Nancy might be, if she had a boyfriend, if she'd said anything about running off.

And Karen had flushed and said no to all the questions and felt guilty because of the stupid argument about the stupid dress. That couldn't have been the reason Nancy ran away, could it?

Later Chief Christie had come to talk to her about Nancy's disappearance, too. His son Van was a little older than Karen and Nancy. The chief had been very nice to Karen, not scary at all, but she had the same answers for the same questions.

No, she hadn't heard from Nancy.

No, Nancy didn't have a boyfriend.

No, Nancy had never said anything about running away.

All around the school the next day there were whispers every time Karen walked by, and Jack—

"Bingley," Karen said to herself. "Bingley, that was it."

—Jack Bingley had even come up to her while she was at her locker getting her period four math book and told her that he was sorry about Nancy. Karen hadn't even realized he knew who Nancy was, although she supposed he had to have

noticed the way her friend stared at him.

Two days later they found Nancy's body in the woods. Or rather, what was left of her body. She'd been ripped apart, as if by an animal, and all that was really left of her was her head.

"Just like those girls," Karen said. "Exactly the same."

There was a day of mourning at school—they'd all had off—and then the next day everyone came back and it was all normal and regular again, except Nancy wasn't there.

And then Karen forgot about her.

Nancy didn't just gradually fade away. There was no period of time where Karen grieved, or looked at the empty seat next to her in biology. Her best friend was gone and Karen forgot her.

She hadn't even remembered Nancy Butler had ever existed until just that moment.

How could she have forgotten such a terrible event? If she hadn't seen that picture of David's she would never have remembered it at all.

And something about that memory twigged another memory, this one much hazier and hard to grasp. It was something about Joe, the night that Joe went missing.

Lauren at the back door in the middle of the night.

Why would Lauren be at the back door in the middle of the night? Karen reached for the memory. It was like a balloon floating away into an empty sky and she couldn't reach the string.

A rustle of paper made her look down. David was almost done rolling up the scroll of pictures he'd made. He'd already carefully replaced all of his crayons inside the old cigar box he used for storage.

"David," Karen said. She wanted to see his drawing before he put it away. Had he really drawn a dead girl?

(It couldn't be Nancy Butler, though; he never would have heard of her or what happened so long ago)

"What, Mommy?" he asked, rolling the last bit of paper up. His eyes still had some of that faraway quality that he got when he was intensely focused.

He might not remember what he did. I'll look at the picture later, when he isn't around.

"Nothing, sweetie," she said, because he was waiting patiently for her reply.

He might have heard about the murdered girls in Mrs. Schneider's yard, though, even if he didn't know about Nancy.

(You know he heard about them, don't you remember? He stopped dead on the sidewalk and said she was screaming and that there was so much blood.)

Should she be worried about what he was watching on TV or heard about from his sister? Sometimes Lauren and Miranda watched videos at Miranda's house and Lauren talked about them where David could hear, movies where girls got shredded by crazy killers.

(He doesn't need to hear about a movie for that. That

happens right here in Smiths Hollow, every year)

Karen started. Where had that thought come from? Girls didn't die in Smiths Hollow every year.

Lauren came into the kitchen then. She had that hollow-eyed look that came from too much crying.

"How about an ice cream sundae?" Karen asked impulsively.

They didn't really have the money for such a treat, but David was acting so strange and Lauren was so sad and she herself was so bewildered and only ice cream could fix everything.

Joe used to say that.

It was the first time since he died that she could think of him without bitterness.

"Ice cream? Before dinner?" Lauren asked.

David's eyes lit up. "Really?"

"Really," Karen said.

13

SATURDAY

Touhy stared at the headline in the *Chicago Tribune*. His breakfast eggs and bacon lay untouched on his plate and his coffee grew cold as he read the six words over and over.

SHOCKING MURDERS STUN SMALL-TOWN POLICE

"I'll have somebody's head for this," Touhy said and then read the byline:

George Riley, special correspondent

It was that reporter from Chicago stirring up trouble. And a story like this would make more trouble, would bring more reporters from other places asking questions about things they shouldn't even know about.

Crystal gave him a mildly inquiring glance from across the table. She was eating a bowl of cottage cheese with pineapple on top. Lately she always seemed to be on a diet even though she was thin as a rail.

Too thin, actually, he thought. Her breasts were visible through the white lawn nightgown she wore. They were starting to look small and saggy. The more weight she lost, the smaller they were.

Her afternoon lover must like them that way, he thought, but he couldn't work up the energy to be angry about it.

All his anger was directed at the interloper who'd come to his town.

The girls had finally been identified. It appeared that Alex Lopez—*another meddler*, Touhy thought—had come upon the dead girls' backpacks in the woods. Touhy wanted to know what he'd been doing poking around out there in the first place but knew if he asked too many questions then Lopez would get suspicious. He'd only lived in Smiths Hollow for a couple of months. Touhy didn't know if he'd fallen completely under the town's spell yet.

If the spell is even still working, he thought. The news of the previous afternoon's layoffs at the factory had reached him that morning. When he'd heard he'd been unable to squelch the panic that rose up inside him.

His job, his entire existence, was built on preserving the prosperity of the town. That was what the girls died for—so everyone else in Smiths Hollow could stay safe and happy. If people were losing their jobs, then what was the point of the sacrifices?

If out-of-town girls were dying in the summer, did that

mean there weren't going to be any more sacrifices?

His father had never told him what to do in the case of such an eventuality. It had always been assumed that things would go on smoothly as long as a girl's name was drawn from the lottery.

But those two girls didn't come from the lottery. And now people were out of work.

The cracks are starting to show, he thought, not for the first time. *But I can still fix it. I can mend them.*

He'd have a word with the factory owners. He was sure this was some temporary lull in business and that the union would call all the workers back soon. Didn't everyone have a can of chili in their kitchen? Perhaps it was some kind of distribution problem. If so, he could probably call around until the issue was resolved.

All of his attention yesterday had been focused on the Friday night opening of the fair. He'd felt blindsided by the factory layoffs but could deal with them once the fair was up and running. The fair was everything.

The fair was going to draw people to the town. He didn't want any bumps in its smooth operation. He'd ordered Van Christie to have two police officers patrolling the grounds at all times. Touhy hoped that the presence of uniformed officers would discourage juvenile delinquents from thievery and vandalism. He didn't want any Smiths Hollow kids giving the town a bad reputation.

The first night had been a huge success. The fair was filled with people and the town had been hopping with the overflow from the fairgrounds. He'd strolled Main Street in twilight, smiling at all of the folks packed into the pizzeria and the sweet shop. Everything had been perfect.

He hadn't thought about the situation with the girls because he'd thought the situation had been handled. Christie hunted down the next of kin and made arrangements for the remains to be shipped back to Joliet. Christie had told him the girls were runaways, and that the families involved didn't seem too interested in the girls' fates.

Touhy supposed they were troublemakers, and that the families were glad to be shot of them.

That was all well and good, to his mind. No family interest meant no demand for an investigation, and once the bodies were gone it was someone else's problem. Everyone could just settle down and forget the murders ever happened.

Then he saw the newspaper.

"What's the matter, Rich?" Crystal asked.

"Nothing," he said, scowling.

She wouldn't understand even if he tried to explain. She was really very dumb. Why had he married such a bimbo in the first place?

Because she had big tits and a tight ass and you wanted every man in town to be jealous that you got to bang that body every night.

It was easy to ignore her lack of brainpower when he actually was banging her every night. But now that she was getting it elsewhere during the day she wasn't much interested at night, and as her body shrank down to a toothpick he'd become less interested, too.

Why don't I just get a divorce? There were no children to worry about. They'd somehow never managed to have any, even though both of them had subjected themselves to a battery of tests to establish fertility. Everything had come back normal, but the seed had never sprouted.

For a long time Touhy had been relieved by this. If he never had a daughter, then his daughter could never be taken by the monster in the woods. But he needed a son. A son had to take over as mayor for him when he retired. There had always been a Mayor Touhy in Smiths Hollow.

Who would draw the names if he was gone and he had no son to replace him? How could he possibly explain the curse to an outsider?

The Touhys had always been born with the knowledge of the curse, had known and seen it the way no one else did. Did his lack of children mean the curse was coming to an end? Would it all stop when he, the last Touhy of Smiths Hollow, died?

He didn't think so. Those two dead girls in Mrs. Schneider's yard were proof of that.

There weren't supposed to be two dead girls in June. That he knew. So perhaps he just needed to . . . what? Realign the spell?

He didn't know anything about magic. But that old crone who lived alone at the top of the hill did. She was the only one who'd ever known about the girls, besides him.

Touhy remembered the day, about ten years earlier, when she'd stormed into his office and demanded to know what he was going to do about the dead girls.

He'd been so wrong-footed by the accusation that he'd stuttered and stammered and generally acted like he was guilty of something. Which he was.

But it's not my fault, he thought. *I'm not the one who kills them. It's that thing in the woods. And if I don't do my job then it will just go crazy and start killing everyone.*

He'd fended off Joanne Gehlinger by telling her that she was imagining things. It hadn't seemed, at the time, that she knew for certain that he was involved in the process, although she certainly had suspected something.

He knew that she was descended from the relatives of the witches who lived there, though. That was part of the knowledge that was passed down, although he was never certain why.

Perhaps for just this very reason? Perhaps so the curse can be refreshed by someone of the same bloodline?

Touhy wasn't certain Jo Gehlinger would be willing to assist, however. She'd seemed very angry about the dead girls the last time the subject came up.

He was angry about the deaths too, of course. He'd rather not have to deal with such a thing happening at all.

He didn't want to be known as the mayor of Monster Town.

But this was his lot, and the lot of all of Smiths Hollow. This was the price they paid for their prosperity.

So there had to be a way to reset everything. Then the girls would die at their appointed time and the factory would keep running and more people would move to the town and no one would ever know what kept the gears of Smiths Hollow turning except him. The old woman at the top of the hill would know how to fix it. She was a descendant of one of the original witches' relatives. She even lived in their house.

We all have our part to play, Touhy thought.

And the only way the play would keep running was if the curse was fixed.

Jo Gehlinger would know. And she would tell him.

Whether she wanted to or not, she would tell him.

14

Janice was out cold in bed and it was only ten in the morning.

So what if she lost her job, Miranda thought as she passed by her parents' bedroom on the way to shower. *She was only up long enough to drink a bottle of gin for breakfast and now she's back in bed.*

Miranda had returned home on Friday after the argument with Lauren with a credible explanation for her all-day absence. The last thing she wanted was for her parents to suspect she'd lost her virginity that very morning. Though she was certain her expression gave nothing away. She'd been working hard on her poker face.

But it turned out she needn't have bothered. There had been a ton of layoffs at the factory and Janice had been one of them.

Miranda had not been surprised by this, since Janice seemed to come home early to drink pretty much every day. Even before the layoffs she didn't think her mother's job situation was very secure. How long could the owners overlook Janice's constant absences?

But the news of her firing had come as a shock to Miranda's parents. Her father hadn't lost his job, and he seemed to think that since they were both managers, they should have been exempt from these kinds of cold-blooded economic decisions.

"We've both worked there for over fifteen years," he said at dinner that night. "You'd think that would count for something."

Miranda refrained from saying that she was sure lots of people at the factory had worked there a long time and were probably just as outraged that evening. She didn't say it because she didn't want her father looking too closely at her or deciding to take out his anger on her by grounding her for talking back.

So she just murmured, "I know, Daddy," and picked at the pot roast her mother had overcooked.

It didn't taste good and she didn't want to eat too much, anyway. She didn't want Him to think she was a fatass. Now that someone was going to see her naked on a regular basis, it was even more important not to eat like a little piggy.

When she was little if she wanted extra dessert her mother would make a pig-snorting sound and say, "No, Miranda. You're a little lady, not a little piggy."

Well, I'm not really a little lady, either, she smirked to herself as she climbed into the shower.

She hadn't heard from Him since the previous morning,

but she wasn't worried. He'd told her He would find a way to be in touch.

In the meantime she'd agreed to allow Tad to take her to the fair that night.

He'll probably try to feel me up on the Ferris wheel. She rolled her eyes as she lathered the shampoo through her hair. Well, it was a price she had to pay, she supposed.

She knew that He couldn't take her around the fair, because their relationship was a secret. And Miranda still wanted to ride to school next year in Tad's Camaro.

So if Tad wanted to cop a feel or two in the dark, she'd let him.

But what if Lauren is there?

Miranda scrubbed the shampoo out of her hair with more force than necessary. So what if Lauren was at the fair? It was a public place. And Smiths Hollow wasn't that big. They were going to run into one another sooner or later.

It doesn't matter if you run into her. She made it clear what she thinks of you.

Miranda felt a lump in her throat, and she determinedly swallowed it. She was not going to cry. She hadn't cried after they argued and she hadn't cried all day Friday when Lauren didn't call to apologize and she wasn't about to cry now.

Lauren was not going to make her cry. Lauren was just a teeny tiny pathetic loser who still went around on her bike like a baby. She didn't even have breasts yet. She was still a child. But Miranda was a woman, and she had a lover to prove it.

Miranda carefully shaved her legs and underarms—she'd started doing so at the first hint of fuzz about a year ago, and she shaved every single day without fail. The idea of someone catching her with stubble on her legs was too embarrassing to contemplate.

She didn't even want to think what He would say if He touched her and found bristles on her skin.

Miranda was just rinsing the last of the soap off when she heard her father's voice through the door.

"How much longer are you going to be in that shower? You're using up all the hot water!"

It's not like Janice needs to take a shower, Miranda thought. *She's going to be in bed for the rest of the day, probably.*

But she said, "Getting out now, Daddy," and shut the water off. She was finished anyway.

"Don't spend the next two hours in there curling your hair, either," he said.

"Okay, Daddy," Miranda said.

She didn't curl her hair in the bathroom. Her curling iron was in her bedroom and so was her hair spray and he knew that. He was just angry about Janice and wanted to complain about something.

Miranda wasn't going to give him an excuse to get angry with her. She was going to be the sweetest angel there ever was, because she was going to the fair that night and nobody would stop her.

She pulled on her bathrobe, wrapped a towel around her wet hair, and went down the hall to her own bedroom. As she passed her parents' room she saw her father standing at the foot of their bed, looking at Janice. His shoulders were hunched in a defeated way.

Miranda hurried quickly past. She didn't want to see the look on her father's face. Miranda did not want to know if he was sad or mad or anything else that had to do with Janice. Janice was his responsibility. If he wanted to stop her from drinking all day he could have done that years ago. Instead he just pretended that it wasn't happening, and Janice had gone from one too many glasses of wine with dinner to passed-out drunk on Saturday morning.

It wasn't any concern of Miranda's. She had her own life. She closed and locked her bedroom door, then went to the closet to survey her summer dresses. It was too hot out to wear anything heavy, and anyway she wanted something that showed off her body without looking too slutty.

I'm not a slut like you.

Lauren had said that.

You're not going to think about Lauren or worry about her opinion, either. Who cares if she thinks you're a slut? Just because you're getting some and she isn't. She's just jealous.

(But you are a slut aren't you Miranda everyone knows

you're easy and whenever you walk by they talk behind their hands in whispers)

"I don't care what anyone thinks of me," Miranda said firmly, pulling off her bathrobe and putting on her best underwear—a white lace bra and matching underpants that she'd bought at the mall when her mother was not with her. Her mother only bought cotton underwear for Miranda. She looked at herself in the mirror, turning sideways to check that her stomach still looked flat.

And you better not eat fried dough and cotton candy tonight either or else you'll swell up like a balloon.

(little piggy little slut pig)

She shook her head, trying to dislodge the words that wouldn't go away. She shook hard enough that the towel flew off her damp hair.

Miranda ignored the towel and pulled out her three best summer dresses, laying them on the bed side by side so she could choose the most flattering one.

"I'm going to look spectacular tonight," she told herself. "And everyone who sees me is going to say so."

She didn't feel sick when she thought of what else they might say about her. She really didn't.

15

Around midday on Saturday Mom dropped Lauren and David off at the fairgrounds. She handed Lauren two twenty-dollar bills with a worried smile.

"I won't lose it. And I won't spend it all, either," Lauren promised.

"It's okay," Mom said. "You two haven't had that many treats this past year."

Lauren could tell that Mom was trying really hard not to stress out about the expense, and she privately vowed to bring home at least half the money later.

"Have fun," Mom said as she waved to them from the car.

"Okeh," David said, and waved back.

He immediately took Lauren's free hand. She knew she wouldn't have to worry about David darting away in a crowd. He always stayed close and listened, unlike pretty much every other kid in the world.

Lauren stuffed the money in the pocket of her shorts and joined the line of people paying the $1.00 admission fee. She didn't want to wave the money around and have it snatched out of her hand.

The fair was already very crowded with families and large groups of teenagers. From the entrance gate Lauren could see the top of the Ferris wheel halfway down the field, painted white with brightly colored designs on the gondolas. The scent of frying things wafted in the air—corn dogs and funnel cakes and freshly made doughnuts. Screams of delight emitted from the Tilt-A-Whirl just beyond the gate. Bells rang as someone won a prize from the shooting gallery booth.

Lauren bought two orange *Admit One* tickets from the bored woman at the booth and put them in the opposite pocket from her money. She definitely did not want to accidentally drop the tickets when she was digging around looking for her cash.

"Okay, David, what first? Should we eat a lot so that we feel sick on the rides, or ride first?"

Neither of them had had lunch before going, as a cold sandwich hardly appealed in the face of fair food, so she thought she knew what David would choose first.

"Food," he said. "But not too much. I don't want to get sick."

His little face was so serious that Lauren laughed and kissed his forehead.

"Food, but not too much," Lauren agreed. "Not yet,

anyway. What do you want? Cotton candy? Popcorn?"

"Popcorn for lunch?" he said with wide eyes.

"Whatever you want, bud," she said, and winked. "Mom's not here to tell us no."

David took a moment, seeming to think this over carefully. Then he looked up at her and winked back, one side of his face screwed up with the effort.

"Funnel cake first," he said. "With ice cream on top."

They ate the funnel cake quickly because they were hungry and also because several bees kept flying around the plate. Lauren batted them away from David's face with an irritated wave.

"I don't like bees," David said.

"Me neither," Lauren said, dumping the plate—clean except for a few streaks of confectioner's sugar—into the nearby trash can. "Now what?"

David gave the Tilt-A-Whirl a long, thoughtful glance.

"Not yet," Lauren said. "Let's wait a little bit. We just ate that funnel cake."

They went on the merry-go-round instead. David didn't have the best sense of balance so Lauren decided to forgo riding on an animal and instead stood next to him, keeping her hand on his back as the tiger he'd chosen went up and down and he laughed wildly.

She almost never heard David laugh like that, and it made her laugh, too. He was such a serious little kid.

And maybe some kind of seer, too, she thought, remembering the half-finished drawing on his scroll yesterday. She'd meant to go back and look at it, to see what else he'd drawn besides her and Jake at the fair, but then the whole thing happened with Miranda and she forgot about it.

Anyway, you're not going to think about all that stuff today. Dead girls and witch powers and old stories. You're not even going to think about Miranda. Today is just a day to have fun.

She'd been trying very hard not to think about the date with Jake later. Whenever she did all her insides seemed to squish around and make her feel off-kilter.

Besides, she was there to have fun with David, not think about Jake.

After the merry-go-round David wanted to play games. Lauren looked doubtfully at the price of the games and said, "Pick three, that's it."

"Okeh," David said. She didn't even need to explain why.

He pointed to the Whac-A-Mole first, and they enjoyed trying to hit the robotic animals popping out of the holes.

Then they lined up with a bunch of other players to shoot water guns at targets. The pressure of the water made a teddy bear attached to a pole rise up to the top of the booth. The first teddy bear to reach the top won. David had a lot of trouble keeping the water from his gun on the target, but to Lauren's utter shock her bear reached the top first and she won a very small stuffed frog of lurid green.

"Ribbit," she said, putting the frog on David's head.

"For me?" he said, his eyes lighting up.

"Yes," she said, and kissed his cheek.

He tucked the frog in the crook of his arm and hugged it to him.

"Which game next?" Lauren asked. "You can pick one more."

They walked past a game where you had to throw pennies onto a moving platform and one where you had to make three baskets in a row to win a prize. Lauren pointed at that one.

"I'm pretty good at making baskets," she said, and she was, even though she was short. "Maybe we could win another prize there."

David shook his head. "Uh-uh. They make it so you can't get the ball in. Dad told me."

"Dad told you that?" Lauren asked, wondering when such a topic could have come up. She didn't think David had ever seen a game like that before. "When?"

"Just now," he said, and pointed at the Skee-Ball corrals. "Those."

Lauren stopped walking then. She heard Phil Collins's "In the Air Tonight" blasting over the speaker at the top of the Himalaya ride, drowning out the screams of the riders. The scent of cotton candy filled her nose, sickly sweet. Her body felt stiff, clutched with some unidentifiable emotion.

She crouched down to look David in the eye. "David. Are

you telling me that Dad is . . . is . . ."

She couldn't get the words out. The inside of her lungs felt like they were frozen over. *A ghost? A ghost walking around next to David, talking to him?*

"Is what, Lauren?" David asked, frowning a little. "Can we play Skee-Ball now? If you get even one ticket you can win a prize. If we get lots of tickets and put them together we can get a big prize."

"Just wait a second," Lauren said, taking a deep breath. It definitely felt like the air wasn't going all the way through her lungs. The bottom of her ribs was seizing up. "David, does Dad talk to you?"

"Sometimes," he said.

Why do you talk to David and not me? Even in her mind she sounded like a little girl, plaintive and all alone.

"Can you *see* him?"

David shook his head. "No. It's not like he's a ghost, silly."

"Then how does he talk to you?"

He shrugged. "Sometimes I just hear him."

"In your ears?" She felt that this was important, to understand that it was something exterior and not some wishful-thinking voice he heard in his head.

David nodded. "Like a little whisper in my ear."

"But why you and not me?" She hadn't meant to say that, hadn't meant to show that open vein that pulsed and bled inside her.

"Maybe you're not listening right," David said.

He put his hand on her cheek. He still had chubby little baby hands, not boy hands, but his expression was a thousand years old and just as wise.

"It doesn't mean he didn't love you, Lauren," he said.

She choked then, hot tears in the back of her throat, and David put his arms around her neck. She felt the fuzz of his prize frog rubbing against her hair.

"I love you, too," David said. "I think you're the best sister."

She stroked his fine smooth hair. He was still a baby really, only four years old. How could he be so knowing? Her stomach lurched again, this time in worry. What would happen if other people found out about David? He would go to kindergarten next year. What if he made predictions about the other kids and freaked them out, or mentioned talking to his dead father?

Don't borrow trouble from another day. Today is for fun.

"Right," Lauren said. "No ghost and no ghoulies and no beasties today. Only fun. Let's play Skee-Ball."

David immediately unwrapped his arms from her neck and tugged at her arm. "Come on then, come on."

She laughed. "It will still be there in five minutes. It's not going to disappear into a black hole."

"It might," David said. "You never know in Smiths Hollow."

Lauren knew he meant it as a joke, but it felt more like a warning.

No magic, no ghosts, no stories today, remember?

But she thought that she finally, finally might be ready to talk to Nana again. Somehow, hearing that Dad was conversing with David from beyond the afterlife convinced her in a way that nothing else had so far.

There *was* something different about their family, and Nana knew what it was.

I'll go and see her tomorrow, Lauren promised herself.

David managed to earn just one ticket from his Skee-Ball machine—he had trouble rolling the balls high enough to score points toward the center of the target—but Lauren got eight tickets off hers, so they pooled the tickets together to get bigger prizes.

David wanted a jacks set, which was four tickets, and that left five for Lauren. She surveyed the remaining choices with little interest.

"Why don't you pick something else, bud?"

His mouth flattened as he looked inside the case that displayed the prizes. The teenager working the booth appeared amused at David's seriousness. He was a gangly-looking redhead with acne on his neck.

"Hey, you're Lauren diMucci, right?" he said.

She gave him a startled look. "Yes."

"You're friends with that hot blonde, right? Miranda Kowalczyk?"

"Yes," she repeated cautiously. No need to report to this

stranger that she and Miranda weren't friends anymore.

"Do you think you could give her my number?" he asked, scribbling something on a piece of paper and handing it to her.

Lauren didn't take the scrap of paper. "Who *are* you?"

"Oh, sorry. My name's Owen Dahlgren. I'm going to be a senior next year."

"Do you know Miranda?" Lauren asked.

"Well, no," he admitted. "But I thought maybe I could take her out sometime."

"Why do you want to take her out if you don't even know her?" Lauren asked, bewildered by this line of conversation.

"Are you kidding?" he said, and drew the outline of a curvy body in the air with his hands. "Besides, and I'm not trying to be rude or anything, but everyone knows she'll put out."

Lauren was saved from replying as David finally made his choice. Which was a good thing, because she had absolutely no idea what she would say in response to that.

"That ring," he said, pointing at a silver-plate ring. He handed over the remaining tickets while Owen Dahlgren scooped it out of the case and put it in David's hand.

"Let's go," she said, steering David away from the booth.

"Hey, what about my number?" Owen called after her, but she pretended she didn't hear.

"What's that ring you got, bud? Is it for Mom?"

"Nope," David said. "It's for you."

She took the ring from him and examined it. It looked like

a cheap plate ring that would turn her skin green, but it had an unexpected heft when she held it, like it was made of real silver. It had a basket-weave design, two strands woven together.

"Thanks," she said, and slid it onto her right-hand ring finger. It fit perfectly, like it was made for her, and it didn't feel like something cheap and throwaway, either. How could this be a prize for a few tickets at the fair?

"Don't lose it," David said. "It's the same ring that Charlie gave to Elizabeth. It will protect you."

"Charlie?" Lauren asked, tilting her head to one side. Where had she heard that name before?

"Charlie," David said. "You know. Charlie. He married Elizabeth, and Elizabeth was killed in the woods, and then the witches got angry and the monster came."

Lauren stared down at her hand. "The ring didn't protect Elizabeth, though. She died anyway."

And so did all the other girls, too. All the other girls in the woods, ring-around-the-rosy, we all fall down.

Her voice sounded hollow, like it was coming from a faraway place. She felt like she might just untether from the earth and float away.

David squeezed her hand. "But it will keep *you* safe. So don't take it off, okeh?"

He'd never sounded so serious, and that was saying something.

"Okay," Lauren said.

"Promise," David said.

"I promise."

"Pinky," he said, holding out his hand.

Lauren hooked her pinky around his.

"Stamp it," he ordered, and they touched their thumbs together.

As they did Lauren felt a little spark of heat, like a charm that was just sealed.

16

"Jane, Jane, Janey," Mrs. Schneider muttered to herself as she stared out the window. "Jane, Jane, Janey."

She'd forgotten all about Janey, but now she remembered. Ever since that nosy reporter came poking his nosy nose around.

The Mexicans across the street were all home today except for the police officer. The two women were out front, weeding the flower beds together and laughing. The other man was watering the front lawn with the hose. As Mrs. Schneider watched she saw him turn and spray the women briefly with the hose and laugh. His teeth were very white against his brown face and she thought he looked handsome for a moment.

"Like that Ricky Ricardo that Lucy married," she said. Except he wasn't Mexican, she recalled. He was Cuban.

"Not that it matters," she said. "They all look the same and they all jabber at each other in Spanish, what's the difference?"

Her fingers kept rubbing against each other, like she was

washing her hands without any water or soap. She couldn't seem to stop doing it.

"Janey," she said again.

And it wasn't only Janey that she remembered. She remembered other girls too, girls that Janey went to school with or who were a little younger. Girls that ended up in the woods with their bodies all ripped to pieces, nothing left but their heads.

It was like something had peeled away in her brain, a tightly wrapped bandage that was coming undone.

And underneath the bandage was something red and black and pulsing, a wound that had never healed but suppurated.

But now that it was open again she didn't know what to do. Those Mexicans couldn't have killed Janey or the other girls. It had to be somebody else.

"But those girls were always killed in November," she said. "Remember, remember November."

No, that's not how that rhyme goes. It's "remember, remember the fifth of November," and it's nothing to do with America. It's all about some plot in England. But all those girls were killed in November, and my Janey too.

"These girls were killed in June, though, and that's wrong. They're not at the right time. They're not even from Smiths Hollow, either. They're outsiders, just like those Mexicans."

That's why it happened. Because those Mexicans came in and they were outsiders and so outsiders were killed at the wrong time and that means it is their fault after all.

Her hands stopped chafing one another as she realized this. A strong sense of relief washed over her. All was in order again. She'd been right in the first place.

"But what to do about it?"

She didn't think Chief Christie would be any help. He'd hired one of them, after all. And his father had never seemed to care much about Janey.

Poor little Janey. Dead little Janey.

Janey wasn't the only dead girl, though. There had been other girls, other parents who wept. Mrs. Schneider wondered if they remembered now, too.

If they did, then perhaps they could do something about these outsiders that had upset the apple cart.

"But do you really want to go back to the way it was before?" she asked herself. "One girl every year?"

Yes. That was the way of things here. It was sad, but once the outsiders were removed, then everything would return to normal.

And she would forget about Janey again, forget about the years of happiness and the pain that followed.

She would forget, as she should.

Mrs. Schneider went into the kitchen and took out her address book. She thought she knew who might be able to help her.

17

Alex swiped sweat off his forehead with his handkerchief. The fair was on an open field and the sun beat straight down onto the grounds. There was hardly any relief to be found— the one place with guaranteed shade was the performance tent. Alex supposed he could justify spending some time in there since many of the attendees were no doubt having their pockets picked while they watched the circuslike spectacle. The presence of police officers might deter that behavior, even if it was just for fifteen minutes or so.

He and Miller had separated so that they could cover more ground, but Alex was pretty certain that Miller had found a bench near a fried-food booth and was "patrolling" from there.

Alex glanced at his watch. His shift had begun at two and would run until the fair closed at ten. It was only three thirty, which meant many more hours of walking in the heat.

Many of the townspeople who saw him as he walked

along waved and called his name, but Alex saw a good number of people he didn't recognize. The fair was a big success, then—it had done what Touhy wanted and drawn out-of-towners to Smiths Hollow. The previous night Alex had seen the evidence of this as he'd hauled several drunk and disorderly types into the two cells that they had at the station. Almost all of them were not Smiths Hollow natives, and Alex was counting down the days until the fair ended and everything went back to being quiet and normal.

Or as quiet and normal as it could be with one girl being murdered every year.

The day before he'd had some time in the evening to continue his search of the archives. What he'd found had made his blood run cold even as it bewildered him.

There had been one death every year in the woods going all the way back to the beginning of paper records—1937. And Alex felt sure that the deaths went back even further, even if there was no written evidence of it. That meant fifty-plus years of dead girls, always taken on the same day, always found in the same place.

Yet no one mentioned it. No one seemed to think anything was wrong. There had to be generations of grieving families in Smiths Hollow, but it was never, ever discussed.

There's something very wrong in this town, he thought. And he didn't even know how to begin to get to the bottom of it. At first he had an idea that it was somehow related to

Van Christie and the mayor, but the line of deaths going back so far put them out of the picture. The history of the murders went back before they were born.

He had a vague thought that it could be some very old serial killer, one who'd started young and would be ancient now. But that didn't explain why Christie was so intent on pretending the murders never happened. Could this person be a relative of his? Christie's father had been the chief of police before him. Maybe two generations of cover-ups had all been in service of keeping some cousin or uncle or brother out of jail.

Alex shook his head. It didn't make sense. No matter how many ways he tried to fit the jigsaw puzzle together he never got the full picture.

Maybe it's Christie himself? That thought gave him pause. *And, what? His father was a killer before him, and his father before him?*

It would explain why every chief of police (and they were all named Christie, every single one) had so determinedly ignored the murders. But it seemed crazier than any other theory he'd come up with yet—the idea of an annual murder being passed down like some kind of demented family legacy.

He detoured to a food booth where burgers were being charred on a grill and ordered a cold Coke with extra ice. A man with a large black mustache and heavy Greek accent waved away Alex's dollar bill.

"Thanks for being out here, Officer," he said.

"No problem," Alex said. "Thank you."

He popped the top off the cup and pulled out the straw, drinking half the contents in one gulp. He continued patrolling even though he really wanted to sit for a few moments. He felt that he shouldn't sit down unless he was on a meal break. When he finished the pop he fished out the few unmelted ice cubes and chewed on them.

Alex saw Lauren diMucci and her little brother standing in line to play at the half-size miniature golf course. He wanted to talk to Lauren about her discovery of the backpacks in the woods, but he didn't think it was appropriate to talk about it in front of her four-year-old brother, so he decided to leave it until later.

The heat, the smell of cooking grease, and the constant chorus of screams were making Alex feel a little sick to his stomach. He decided to sit for a few minutes, even if it wasn't an official break time.

He found a nearby bench and closed his eyes, breathing deeply in and out through his nose. It wasn't just the atmosphere of the fair that was bothering him. It was a sense that the town had taken an indrawn breath, waiting for a blow to fall.

But that's idiotic, he thought, opening his eyes and looking at all of the people smiling and laughing and stuffing popcorn in their mouths. None of them seemed like they were braced for impact.

His eyes roamed around. As he looked it was like an ugly

seam opened up under the cheerful exterior. There was a stressed-looking mother dragging her teenage daughter by the wrist away from a smirking long-haired boy. There were twin boys fighting over who got to hold the stuffed monkey their father had just won at the shooting gallery. There was a twenty-something man wearing a gray *ARMY* T-shirt arguing with a bottled blonde in the tiniest denim shorts Alex had ever seen this side of Daisy Duke.

Something about the man's face and body language had Alex up and running toward the couple. He was still a few feet away when the man swung a roundhouse fist toward the blonde's pink-glossed mouth.

She stumbled backward, clutching her jaw. "Son of a bitch!"

"And there's more if you keep talking back to me like that, you dumb little cunt," he shouted.

Several people stopped walking to stare at the altercation. They immediately created roadblocks for Alex, who was already pulling his cuffs off his belt.

"Excuse me! Police!" he shouted, pushing his way through the crowd.

A young mother holding the hand of a fat-faced toddler shouted at him as he shouldered past her. "Hey, watch it, you fucking spic."

It had been a long time since anyone had called Alex a spic while he was wearing his uniform. He'd heard it plenty in Chicago when he was out of uniform, and of course Mrs.

Schneider regularly insulted his entire family, but somehow he hadn't expected it in Smiths Hollow.

He thought about stopping, about telling her to watch her language (she'd popped off the F-word without any concern for who might be listening), but the blonde had just been assaulted and his duty was to the victim, not his own feelings.

Before he could clear the crowd, however, a second man wearing a navy blue Hawaiian shirt shot out of the group of onlookers and tackled the man wearing the Army shirt. Hawaiian Shirt held Army Shirt down with his left hand and delivered several punches to Army Shirt's face with his right.

"Dammit," Alex swore, taking two quick steps and dragging Hawaiian Shirt off the first man.

Hawaiian Shirt automatically back-fisted Alex's nose. It didn't crunch, but it made Alex see stars for a second.

"Police!" he shouted in Hawaiian Shirt's ear. "You will cease and desist that shit immediately."

Hawaiian Shirt immediately went limp in Alex's grip. "Sorry, Officer. I didn't realize."

Army Shirt was lying on the ground, not moving, and the bottled blonde he'd punched crawled over to him and began to wail.

"Vinnie! Vinnie, speak to me!" she screamed, shaking his immobile form.

What a fucking pain in the ass, Alex thought. Where the hell was Miller? How was he supposed to deal with the injured man, his hysterical girlfriend, and this third party all on his own?

"If I let go of you, will you stand still and not make any more trouble?" Alex said to Hawaiian Shirt.

The man nodded. "Yes."

"What's your name?"

"Larry Franco."

"You live in Smiths Hollow, Larry Franco?"

"Yeah," he said.

Alex let the man go, confident that if he ran off, Alex would be able to find him again.

"What are you doing arresting him?" someone shouted from the crowd. "He was just trying to help that girl."

Several people murmured in agreement. "Yeah, don't harass that guy. What's wrong with you?"

Alex ignored them. He needed to get the girl off the guy, check his medical condition, and call the EMTs. The girl's jaw was swelling, too—she'd need an ice pack at the very least.

"Ma'am, I'm going to need you to move away from the victim," Alex said. He clicked on his radio.

"Miller?"

No response.

"Miller," he said again, trying not to let his frustration creep into his tone. He felt like he was performing on a stage with all the people watching him, but he didn't have time to shoo them away and deal with the couple at the same time.

He had used his cop voice on the woman, the one that expected cooperation, but he should have expected the woman wouldn't cooperate. After all, she was on the ground hugging the man who'd punched her in the face.

"You arrest that asshole!" she screeched, pointing at Larry Franco. "Look what he did to Vinnie's face!"

"He was just trying to help you, you dumb bitch!" someone shouted. The crowd was growing larger by the second, and Alex felt a current of ugliness running underneath.

"Fuck off!" she shouted at the crowd.

"Ma'am, I need to check your friend's medical condition," Alex said, ignoring the interaction.

Army Shirt's face was far too pale. Alex was going to have to pull the girl off him. She had thrown her body over his torso, making it impossible to so much as check the man's pulse.

"Just drag her off by her hair," someone said.

"That's police brutality," someone else said, and laughed.

Oh yeah, there's something wrong here. And it was getting more wrong by the second.

"Miller!" he shouted into the radio.

Finally, there was a lazy, half-asleep "Wha?"

Christ, he fell asleep somewhere. "Get your ass up and over by the Zipper ride. And call the EMTs while you're at it. We've got two assault victims here."

"Okay, boss," Miller said.

Alex hoped like hell that Miller was awake enough to

follow his instructions. There was nothing for it. He was going to have to pull the crying woman off Vinnie.

He bent over and touched her shoulder, hoping that would be enough to prompt her. It was, but not in the way he expected.

She jerked backward, spinning around in the dirt and screaming in his face.

"Don't fucking touch me, you fucking dirty spic!"

That's it. I have had enough.

He wrapped his hand around her upper arm and pulled her away from Vinnie. She screamed like his fingers were emitting acid.

"Don't touch me, don't touch me, don't you dare touch me!"

A ripple of energy seemed to roll over the crowd, something mean and dangerous.

"Hey, get your hands off her!" an onlooker said.

"It's not right for him to touch a white woman like that," another said.

What is going on? Is there a meeting of the local chapter of racist assholes at the fair today?

He felt a sudden very strong urge to take his gun out of its holster and demonstrate to the shitty crowd of shitty racists just who was in charge. His fingers were on the grip before he even knew what he was doing.

Alex never drew his gun unless he felt he absolutely had to do it. He knew too many officers in Chicago who shot first and asked questions later, and he'd always sworn to himself that he wouldn't be one of them.

He didn't know what was happening now, why he was taking his gun out and pointing it in the direction of the crowd—the crowd that seemed to be swelling like a wound, the crowd that seemed strangely nonplussed by the presence of the gun. They moved toward him in a kind of slow-motion creep, like the inexorable movement of the tide.

"Back away!" he shouted.

But they didn't back away. They pushed toward him, their eyes fixed only on him. The bottled blonde pointed her finger at him.

"You're an outsider," she intoned. "You don't belong here."

The term was repeated over and over by every voice. It rolled through like dominoes falling.

"Outsider, outsider, outsider."

Alex couldn't see over the crowd. Anyone who came within its orbit seemed to be pulled into its gravity, and nobody was protesting. Nobody was going to help him.

Whatever is happening is only happening right here, he thought as his sweaty hand struggled to keep the gun from slipping to the ground. He could hear the sounds of the rides running, bells ringing from the game booths, shouts and screams and laughter. The Zipper was only a few feet away, but it continued to load and run normally. Nobody seemed to *notice* that there was something wrong here.

Alex didn't know what would happen when the crowd

reached him, but he had a horrible sense that they would rend and tear, that there would be nothing left of him but his head.

Just like those girls in the woods.

Was this what happened to them? Were they set upon by a mad crowd of people who forgot what they'd done afterward?

Now is not the time to try to solve the mystery, Alejandro. They're going to eat you in a minute.

Yes, that was what would happen. They would tear him and eat him just like that black-and-white movie with the living dead. He'd seen it on the *Svengoolie* show once, and Sofia had buried her head in his shoulder whenever the screen showed the living dead people eating body parts.

And in that movie the only way to defeat the living dead was to shoot them in the head. Could he do that? Could he shoot people he'd thought were his friends and neighbors? Could he kill someone who didn't appear to be in his right mind?

Why not? I bet some of them are in their right mind. Some of them probably think I'm a dirty wetback, think my kind shouldn't mix with their kind. They're just too polite to say it where I can hear.

In that way, he supposed, Mrs. Schneider was at least honest. You knew where you stood with her.

His finger flexed on the trigger. Directly in front of him was Sam Carpenter, a teenager who worked at the Sweet Shoppe. He also played football for the high school and his hands were the size of dinner plates. Those hands were curled now into gigantic fists, fists that would pound Alex into ground beef in a minute.

But he also snuck bubble gum to Val whenever the Lopez family went into the shop to buy ice cream because, he said, "You might need it for your experiments." And Camila and Daniel never left without their pockets loaded with lollipops.

How could that boy, that sweet-natured boy who bought Alex's kids lollipops with his own money, be standing in front of Alex with murder in his eyes?

And how could Alex live with himself if he shot that boy?

"Hey, what's going on here?"

It was not, as Alex had hoped and expected, Miller's voice. It was a girl's voice, high and angry.

A ripple went through the crowd again, and all of them turned, their heads moving in eerie synchronicity.

"Get out of the way!" the girl said.

Alex felt a strange reverberation in his chest when she shouted, a sense that if she spoke he would have to listen.

The crowd parted. Alex saw, as if at the end of a long tunnel, Lauren diMucci standing there with her brother, David.

For a moment he thought, too, that he saw something else. Something like electricity arcing away from the two of them.

Lauren hurried toward him, her face twisted up. David appeared very calm.

"Are you all right?" she said breathlessly.

Alex realized he still had the gun raised, though Lauren

didn't appear to notice it at all. He hurriedly put it in his holster.

"Yes," he said, then pointed at Vinnie lying very still on the ground behind him. "But he's not."

"Don't worry, we saw Officer Miller and he's waiting for the EMTs at the front of the fair." Lauren said this all in a rush, like she was embarrassed that she had this information.

Then she turned on the crowd, who were now standing like idling cars, their engines ready to rev again at a moment's notice.

"Get out of here," Lauren said. "Go back to what you were doing before."

Alex watched in amazement as the crowd dissolved. None of them appeared to realize what they'd been doing before Lauren told them to leave.

The bottled blonde ran to Vinnie's side again, her floods of tears washing over his face. Alex heard, very faintly, the sweet music of the ambulance siren.

Thank Christ, he thought.

Larry Franco stood off to the side, exactly where Alex had left him before everyone else went crazy.

David tugged on Lauren's shorts. "Can we have cotton candy now? We haven't had cotton candy yet."

"Sure, bud," Lauren said.

She took his hand and they started to move away.

"Wait!" Alex shouted.

They both turned back, identical quizzical expressions on their faces.

"How did you know I was in trouble?" he asked. This seemed the least of the things he wanted to know. He wanted to know why the crowd acted that way and why Lauren had been immune to it and why they had all listened when she told them to leave.

"Oh, David knew," Lauren said, and David grinned at him.

David knew? How did David know? The same way you knew where the girls' packs were in the woods? What else do the two of you know?

"Wait, I want to—" Alex started, but just then Miller and the two EMTs came running up.

Alex directed the EMTs toward the man on the ground, quickly explaining the circumstances. They got to work on the man while Alex directed Miller to call Hendricks and Pantaleo to pick up Larry Franco. They would have to process him at the station so that there would be a record in the event Vinnie pressed charges.

By the time all of this was finished, the diMucci siblings were long gone, of course. He'd expected they would be. Lauren had a guilty look on her face, like she'd done something wrong when she ordered the crowd away from him.

"But I wanted to say thank you," Alex murmured.

The only reason he could go home and hug his children that night was because of those two strange kids.

He wanted to thank them. And he wanted to know a few other things, too.

He looked at his watch and sighed. Whatever he wanted to know was going to have to wait until his shift was over.

A few minutes later Miller jogged up—or at least, what passed for jogging with Miller, who never seemed to exert very much energy.

"All taken care of," he said. "I'm starving."

Alex laughed. He couldn't help it. It was so *normal* to hear Miller say he was hungry.

"Let's get French fries," Alex said, and Miller grinned.

18

Miranda stood on her front porch at seven p.m., tapping her foot impatiently as she waited for Tad to pull up. She didn't want Tad to come to the door. There was the smallest possibility that Janice might decide to stumble into the hallway and pretend to be a mother. Miranda thought she would die of shame if Tad saw Janice in her bathrobe.

The sun still shone, though it wasn't as hot as it had been earlier in the day. It wouldn't get dark for another hour or so, which meant Tad had plenty of time to admire how pretty she was in the slanting sunlight.

She heard the roar of the Camaro a minute before she saw it pull down her street. Miranda hastily reapplied her lip gloss and smoothed down her yellow dress. She thought she looked exceptionally good, and that was saying something. Her hair was curled and sprayed into place so it would stay put if they went on the Tilt-A-Whirl or the Ferris wheel.

The sundress had string ties to hold it up at the shoulders, and that meant that she couldn't wear a bra underneath without showing the straps. She was sure that Tad would notice. It had been a job getting out without her father seeing her, though. He certainly would have noticed and sent her back upstairs to put something else on.

The dress wasn't that short when she was standing, but she knew that when she sat down it would roll back to just above her knee. She had on white leather sandals that showed off pink polished toenails. Tad might not appreciate those as much as her lack of bra, but at least *she* knew she'd put in the correct amount of effort. Her white leather purse even matched her shoes.

She ran down the path toward the car as it pulled up. Tad didn't get out to open the door for her, which irritated her, and then she got even more annoyed when the passenger-side door opened and Billy climbed out, grinning. He pushed the front seat out of the way so he could climb in the back.

What is Billy doing here? I thought this was a date. She wouldn't have put in half the amount of effort she had if she'd known the Third Wheel was going to tag along.

"Hey, babe," Tad said, leering at her legs when she climbed in the front seat.

"Hello," she said primly, arranging her skirt so that it would be as modest as possible. He wasn't getting so much as a glimpse of her underwear tonight. What kind of jerk asked a girl out and then brought his friend along?

Well, what did you expect? Tad is a child.

Not like Him.

She felt a warm flush of pleasure at the thought of Him. Maybe she would see Him at the fair.

Maybe she could sneak away with Him in the dark.

Tad immediately turned up the car radio, blasting Iron Maiden. Miranda hated heavy metal. Def Leppard was one thing—they weren't super heavy. But Iron Maiden, Black Sabbath, that kind of thing was a definite no in her book. She stared out the window as Tad and Billy banged their heads and sang along. She didn't think Tad even noticed that she wasn't paying attention to him.

I might have to find someone else to give me a ride to school next year. Miranda suddenly realized she was sick of Tad, sick of the way he never really paid attention to her unless she was sitting in his lap.

She did not want to spend every morning of freshman year being forced to listen to Iron Maiden. But who else in the junior or senior classes had a really good car and no girlfriend? Miranda would have to think on it.

In the meantime she just needed to get through the next couple of hours. Let Tad pay for her ticket and take her on a couple of rides. If she saw someone else more interesting she could catch a ride home with that person.

And if I don't see someone more interesting I'm calling Dad to come and get me, she decided as they arrived at the fairgrounds parking area. It was just an open part of the field next to the fair itself and there were no actual lines for the cars. Tad parked the Camaro diagonally so it took up as much space as possible.

Obnoxious jerk, Miranda thought, and then *No wonder Lauren ditched all of us the other day.*

No, she wasn't going to think about Lauren at all. That would put her in a really bad mood.

She let Tad sling his arm around her shoulders and they walked toward the bright lights of the fair.

19

Lauren smiled at Jake as they entered the fairgrounds together. He was wearing clean jeans and another one of what Lauren thought of as his Interesting Band shirts. This time there was a woman with dark eyeliner and wild hair staring out from a white background. Underneath her face it read *Siouxsie and the Banshees*. Lauren wanted to know what all of these bands sounded like. She wondered when Jake would make her the promised mix tape with the Clash and the Smiths and Siouxsie and the Banshees and all the other cool things he liked.

She wanted to know about the music he listened to, and the books he read, and how he felt about college. All she really knew about Jake Hanson was that he'd helped her play baseball when they were younger and that he had beautiful blue eyes.

That was not, she decided, the proper basis for any kind of relationship. Even if this date turned out to be a mistake they could still be friends, and friends knew things about each other, and shared those things that they enjoyed.

The way you and Miranda used to do.

No, she was not going to think about Miranda now. She was going to enjoy her first date.

Lauren had dressed carefully in her best jeans and her turquoise high tops and her favorite Prince T-shirt. It felt like good luck to wear it, because David had drawn the picture of her standing next to Jake and her shirt had said *prpel ran*.

"What do you want to do first?" Jake asked. "Get something to eat?"

Lauren laughed and shook her head. "Me and David ate half the fair today. I'm pretty sure I can go the rest of my life without ever having another thing fried in oil. But I'll get a Coke if you're hungry."

"I am," he admitted. "I didn't have a big lunch at work today."

"What do you want? Pizza? A corn dog? A burger? I know where everything is," Lauren said. "I could lead a tour of food booths."

"Burger and fries," he said. He didn't even take a minute to think about it.

"That's over by the Zipper," Lauren said, pointing in the direction they needed to walk.

Over by the Zipper. Officer Lopez needs your help. He's over by the Zipper.

No, she wasn't going to think about that right now,

either—that strange moment when David had seemed to go into a trance. And what happened after—how they'd come upon a crowd of people who were acting . . . well, she didn't know how to think about it except that they were acting *wrong*. As she and David approached the group she'd felt something, something like an aura or a miasma, something that bound all of those present together.

Something a lot like magic.

And the thing she'd done—Lauren hadn't even considered what she would do or how she would do it. She'd simply known that if she spoke, the people caught in the grip of the (*spell? curse?*) would stop.

David had quickly tugged her away when Officer Lopez was distracted, and she'd been relieved. She didn't want to answer any difficult questions.

She sighed, because all of a sudden there seemed to be a lot of weird stuff going on.

According to Nana weird stuff had been a part of the fabric of Smiths Hollow since the beginning. But it seemed that all the weirdness was bubbling to the surface now, that there was an open seam of weird and it was spreading like lava all around the town.

"You went away somewhere again," Jake said.

Lauren started. "Sorry."

"Where do you go when you're thinking those really deep thoughts?"

There was no way she could possibly explain about the dead girls, about the floating book, about seeing the blood on her bike seat and the vision in her head, about how she'd made a whole crowd of murderous adults go away just by telling them to do so.

There was no way she could explain the strange feeling she got from David before she left the house for her date, either.

"Be careful, Lauren."

That was all he'd said. "Be careful, Lauren." But it had seemed like he knew something she didn't when he said it.

It felt like a lot of weight all of a sudden—the burden of strangeness, of knowledge that nobody else seemed to have.

Well, except David and Nana. And David wasn't the ideal person to discuss it with. He *was* only four.

She'd like to tell Jake about it—Jake with his very sympathetic eyes and his sincere interest.

No, I can't tell him about all of this insanity. But maybe I can tell him about the legend.

"I was just thinking about a story my nana told me," Lauren said. "A kind of legend about Smiths Hollow."

"What, the legend of the man who saved the town by opening a meat-processing plant?" Jake said.

They'd reached the hamburger booth by then, and Jake ordered two cheeseburgers, a large fry, and two Cokes.

"Are you going to eat both of those burgers? They're really big," Lauren said. "Me and David split one earlier. Of course, we'd already had a funnel cake and cotton candy by then."

"I'm really hungry," he said. "Anyway, I usually eat two burgers."

Lauren inwardly marveled at the way teenage boys stayed so skinny even though they ate everything under the sun. She wasn't as self-conscious about eating as Miranda was—Miranda wouldn't eat more than a lettuce leaf in front of another person, lest they accuse her of being fat—but she could never eat as much as Jake seemed prepared to do in one sitting.

They got Jake's food and managed to find an unoccupied picnic table nearby. The sun was going down and the fair lights were slowly coming on, the bright colors spinning as the rides whirled in every direction.

Jake took a huge bite out of one of the burgers and then nudged the tray of fries in Lauren's direction. "Feel free."

"Nah, I'm good," she said, sipping her Coke.

She was surprised by how relaxed she felt, how natural. There was a little butterfly in her stomach—no, not even a butterfly, really. More like a moth, one of those tiny ones that occasionally flew out of her sweater drawer. And that smidge of nervousness was natural and normal. It was her first date, after all. But she didn't feel the way she thought she would—awkward, full of worries about possibly saying or doing the wrong thing.

Part of it was that Jake seemed so sincerely interested in her—in who she was *inside*. He wasn't only interested in groping her, whatever Miranda might think. And part of it was, well, whatever it was that had awakened inside her—this power, this *witchy-ness*.

"So tell me about this legend," Jake said. "Before you go away somewhere again. I can see that look in your eye."

"What look?" Lauren asked.

"The one that says you're retreating inside your own mind. The one that says you don't think I'm the most fascinating guy you've ever met." He gave her a crooked smile at this, so she knew he was kidding.

"Okay," Lauren said. "You know that tree in the woods, the one that looks like it was struck by lightning?"

"Yeah, I know the one you mean. It always gave me the creeps."

"Why?" she asked, genuinely curious.

She'd never felt that way about the tree. She still didn't, even after Nana told her the story and she found her bloodstained bike underneath its branches.

"Something about it. It always seems like the tree is watching."

"Well, maybe it is," Lauren said, and then she realized *It definitely is. There's something that lives inside the tree, something that's trapped there. And the witches cursed us so that whatever it is can come out once a year.*

Why had this only occurred to her now? Even after everything that had happened since she heard the story? It was as if her knowledge of the Thing that lived in the tree kept shifting away, hiding behind other thoughts so she wouldn't see it clearly.

"Anyway," she said, before Jake accused her of going away someplace without him again. "This is the story I heard."

She took a deep breath, and began, "There was a hill just off the center of town, a lonely and inexplicable hill, a hill that should not be for it blighted an otherwise perfectly flat and reasonable landscape . . ."

It felt like she was talking for a very long time. As she told the story it was like she went away from the fair, went away from the noise and the colors and the cotton-candy-scented air. She was there with the three witches who lived on the hill, and was there when the red-haired one fell in love with a princeling. She was there when they married and loved and dreamed of the future.

She was there in the woods when Elizabeth was torn to pieces by the man with the knife.

Lauren didn't stop telling the story, but a part of her gasped in realization. That place where Elizabeth died—it was the exact same place where she and Jake had found what was left of the two dead girls.

And that's where all the girls have died. Every single one.

The sun was down by the time she finished. Jake hadn't spoken a word the entire time, and after a while Lauren was only half-aware of his presence. She thought that even if he'd gotten up and walked away she would have finished the story. It was like a compulsion was laid on her to tell it all once she started.

She picked up her Coke and took a sip. Most of the bubbles were gone and all of the ice was melted, so instead of refreshing her, the syrup just stuck in the back of her throat. She glanced at Jake, wondering what he'd made of all this.

He was crying.

"Jake?" she said tentatively, reaching across the table to touch his hand.

"I had an older sister," he said. His voice was dreamy and his eyes faraway. "Seven years older than me, kind of like you and David. Her name was Jennifer. My parents liked names that start with *J*. Jennifer and Jacob. Jenny and Jake. She had really beautiful long dark hair, you know. It went all the way down her back. She used to steal cookies from the kitchen and take them into her room and make a tent out of her comforter between her bed and the desk. Then she'd call me and I'd come in her room and we'd eat cookies in the fort and tell ghost stories. I didn't know a lot of ghost stories, though, because I was little. But she made up really good ones and knew how to tell them, too. I think she would have been a writer, or maybe an actress. She was definitely pretty enough to be an actress.

"One day I woke up and my mom and dad were in a panic. Jenny wasn't in her bed, wasn't anywhere in the house, and nobody knew where she'd gone. Chief Christie came to the house and asked all of us—even me—a lot of questions about Jenny's friends and her moods and whether she'd ever talked about running away. But she would never run away. There was no reason why she would do that. She was only fifteen years old. Where would she run away to, or how? She wasn't old enough to drive and she didn't have a boyfriend.

"I remember my mom crying, just sitting at the kitchen table with tears running down her face, but my dad didn't cry at all. His fists were clenched and his face was made of stone but he never cried. He never cried, even when Chief Christie came to the house two days later and said they'd found Jenny in the woods. I cried, though. I cried like I would never stop for three days after that. My mom started to get worried, thought maybe I'd need to go to a doctor.

"And then all of a sudden I did stop crying. Just *click*, like a switch that had been thrown. And it was weird, you know, what happened after that. We forgot her.

"Slowly at first. There were times when I thought of her, even thought I could see her—standing in the kitchen with a stack of cookies in one hand and her finger over her mouth, or combing out her hair in front of the bathroom mirror. But after a while her pictures were put away, and nobody told funny stories of things Jenny used to do. She was just gone. We never talked about her. It was as if she never existed, like I'd only dreamed I had an older sister."

As Jake spoke, a memory bubbled up inside Lauren—a memory of a girl with very long black hair and pretty blue eyes building Play-Doh sculptures in Lauren's living room.

"She was my babysitter," Lauren said. "I remember her."

Jake's eyes came back from the place where he'd gone, and he gripped Lauren's hand hard. "It's a true story, isn't it? The one that you told me. It's all true. The town is under a curse."

His grip was hurting her hand, but she didn't try to pull it away. "I think so. Yes. It's true."

"How can that be?" His tone was pleading, begging her to say it was all a scary story for a summer's night. "How can there really be witches and curses and monsters that live in the woods? It's the twentieth century, for God's sake."

"I don't know," she said slowly. "But I think it's coming undone. I think that if it weren't, you wouldn't have remembered your sister. And there have been . . . other weird things."

"What kind of other weird things?"

Lauren hesitated, wondering if she should tell him. It seemed he would believe her if she talked about magic. But then again—how would he feel about her if he knew that she was related to the original three witches? Would he turn away from her in horror? Would he blame her for his sister's death? That wouldn't be logical, but then grief wasn't always a logical thing, and Jake's grief was all fresh and new again. She could see it on his face like a bruise.

"Listen, this isn't really the best place to talk about this. I shouldn't have told that story," she said.

His grip softened, but he didn't let go of her hand. He scrubbed at his face with his other arm. "You're right. This isn't a good place to talk about this."

"Do you want to go home?" she asked. "It's okay if you do."

He seemed to come to a decision then. "No, let's stick with the original plan. I wanted to take you out and have fun, and we should do that."

Lauren surveyed him doubtfully. "I don't want to feel like I'm forcing you."

Jake smiled, a smile that made her heart go loop-the-loop.

"I've wanted to go out with you for so long. I'm not going to blow it now just because the town is cursed."

She laughed, and he squeezed her hand gently.

"Want to go on the merry-go-round with me?" he said.

"Definitely."

They got up and headed in the direction of the merry-go-round. He didn't let go of her hand, either.

20

Miranda saw Lauren and Jake Hanson sitting at the picnic table holding hands. They seemed to be having a very intense conversation, looking soulfully into each other's eyes.

He's probably telling her some bullshit about how he adores her and later he'll have his hands underneath her undershirt grabbing at her tiny breasts.

Tad had already grabbed at Miranda's much more substantial breasts while they rode the Himalaya. She hadn't cared so much about that, but his breath had been sour when he put his face close to hers and she turned her head away so he could suck at her neck instead. What she really wanted was to go home. She was tired of pretending that Tad was interesting.

After they rode the Himalaya Tad and Billy decided they wanted to try their hand at the shooting gallery booth. Miranda murmured that she needed to powder her nose and slipped off in the direction of the bathrooms.

On the way she saw Lauren standing alone. Jake must have gone to the bathroom himself, or went off to fetch her some food so she wouldn't have to stand in the increasingly long lines. Miranda thought about detouring over to make a snide remark about Lauren's date but decided against it. They might end up screaming at each other in the middle of the fair and Miranda didn't want to make a scene.

The fair was pretty wall-to-wall then and it was difficult to walk even a few feet without bumping into someone. She'd spotted Officers Lopez and Miller handing off to Officer Pantaleo a man who appeared so drunk that it looked like he was made of rubber. Everywhere she looked people were screaming, running, laughing, stuffing greasy food in their faces. Why had she wanted to come here at all? Tad hadn't even noticed her dress.

A hard hand clamped under her elbow. She started to jerk away, then looked up and realized it was Him.

She relaxed as He steered her away from the crowd. "I'm so glad it's you. I want to get out of here. Let's go somewhere quiet."

He nodded, but there was a strange look on His face. She noticed that He was pushing her toward the deep pool of darkness between the haunted house and the tent where the acrobats were performing. Miranda heard the gasps and cries coming from the audience inside the tent.

She thought she knew what this was about. He wanted a little something from her. Well, she didn't mind. He wasn't Tad, after all.

21

He had to get rid of the little slut. He realized that now. The only way that Lauren would know she was the only one for him was if Miranda went away. He had to show Lauren. Show her that she was his one and only love. Show her what he was willing to sacrifice for her.

Besides, the Thing inside him was hungry again. He could feel its mouth opening wide, feel the curve of its claws longing to sink into soft flesh. The slut smiled up at him and pressed her chest against him as he pushed her into the shadows.

He put his hand over her mouth. There was just enough light for him to see the glint of her eyes, the welcome that shifted into fear.

The crowd in the tent next door clapped and shouted. No one would hear her scream.

22

Miranda looked into the face of her lover, or what she'd thought was her lover. His mouth wasn't right. It was huge and black and seeping across his face in a way that no human mouth should. The hand across her mouth didn't feel like a hand anymore. The sharp tips of his fingers dug into her cheek and tore the skin.

I want to go home. I want my mommy.

23

Lauren fiddled with the hem of her shirt. It seemed like Jake had been gone a very long time, though looking at the lines for every booth it was probably to be expected. She'd lost sight of him in the crowd—*an easy thing to do when you're such a shortie*, she thought.

Lauren had seen a few people she knew—Mr. and Mrs. Arakawa climbing into a gondola on the Ferris wheel, some girls from junior high walking in a large pack and giggling, Tad and Miranda choosing a seat on the Himalaya.

Lauren had made sure not to make eye contact with Miranda. She didn't know what would happen if their eyes met. Probably nothing, or maybe Miranda would flip her the bird. Lauren didn't want to take any chances, though. This day had already been strange and upsetting. She and Jake were still getting their equilibrium back after the story and Jake's fresh memories.

Mayor Touhy was walking around greeting everyone he met like he was at a voters' rally. She'd waved at Officer Hendricks as she and Jake exited the merry-go-round. All of the town police officers seemed to be at the fair that night, and Lauren bet they had their hands full with so many people around. She hoped that Officer Lopez wouldn't try to corner her and ask questions about what happened earlier.

"Hey," Jake said from behind her.

"I thought you would come from that direction." She pointed at the lines of people that were now behind her.

"I thought it would be faster to go a little farther away and hopefully find a shorter line. There was a popcorn booth by the haunted house that wasn't too bad, but then I had to fight the crowds to get back to you," he said, handing her a cardboard container of popcorn. "Want to go in the haunted house?"

"No," Lauren said. "I don't like them."

"Scared?" Jake asked, but it wasn't the way Miranda would have said it, as a taunt. He just seemed curious.

"Not exactly scared," Lauren said. "But I don't like people jumping out at me."

"How about the acrobats, then?" he said. "The tent is right next to the haunted house and we can sit down for a while."

"Sure," Lauren said. She wouldn't mind sitting for a while. David had wanted to walk all over the whole fair earlier. She was pretty active but it was mostly bike riding—

she wasn't used to so much walking in one day.

They strolled at a leisurely pace, eating popcorn and talking about nothing in particular—movies they liked, books they had read. Even though the date hadn't been perfectly ideal so far, Lauren still felt warm and content and happy. He liked her. He wanted to be with her, with no strings and no expectations. And he made her feel like she could be herself. It had been a very long time since she'd felt that way.

Before Dad died. Before Miranda changed.

You changed, too, you know.

Yes, she had changed, although she hadn't realized it when it was happening. They'd grown apart. They wanted different things. And it was okay for that to happen.

She resolved then that she would call Miranda the next day. Even if they weren't best friends forever anymore Lauren should at least say she was sorry. She shouldn't have called Miranda names. And it would be nice if they could at least be friendly to one another, not turn away as if the other were made of poison.

The haunted house and the acrobat tent were on the outermost loop of the fairgrounds, with nothing behind them except the last bit of empty field. They followed the curve of the pathway around to the left, walking in front of the haunted house. A lot of loud screaming and laughter was coming from inside, but there was nobody else around on the path. Everyone in this part of the fair was inside the haunted house or the tent.

Past the acrobat tent was a large barn, a temporary structure built to hold a petting zoo. The ripe scent of animals drifted toward them and Jake wrinkled his nose.

"Don't you like animals?" Lauren asked.

"It's not that," he said, turning his face away and covering his nose and mouth with his hand as he sneezed. "I'm allergic to animal hair."

"Aww, no cute little sheep and pigs for you," Lauren said.

"Pigs aren't cute."

"Baby pigs are really cute," she said.

"I respectfully disagree. The only way I like a pig is when it's been cured into bacon."

"Aww, no," Lauren said, laughing. "Don't say the cute little piggies get turned into bacon."

"Bacon and ham and Sunday pork roast," Jake said, making a snuffling noise like a pig.

She was going to say something else, something about Wilbur from *Charlotte's Web*, but then she noticed that her sneakers were sticking in something. They were just in front of the space between the haunted house and the acrobat tent.

"Hey, what the—" she said, crossing her right ankle over her left knee so she could see the sole. There was something dark and sticky like thick syrup all over the rubber bottom.

A pool of the dark stuff was seeping out of the shadows between the tent and the haunted house. Jake crouched down to try to get a closer look and Lauren joined him. She got a whiff of it then and stood up quickly, backing away.

"Hey, what's the matter?" he said.

"It's blood," she said. "Can't you smell it?"

"No, my nose is stuffed up from the animals," he said, standing up just as fast.

"Something wrong?"

Lauren spun around and saw Officers Lopez and Miller approaching from the direction she and Jake had just come from.

"There's blood," Lauren said, pointing. "A great big pool of blood."

Officer Miller looked indulgent. "Nah, it's probably not blood. I bet it's some trick to do with the haunted house."

"Let's have a look," Officer Lopez said, taking his flashlight off his belt.

He clicked it on and all four of them peered into the little alleyway between the tent and the haunted house.

At first Lauren wasn't really sure what she was looking at, because it was all in bits and pieces and her brain did not want to make sense of it. She thought maybe someone had slaughtered an animal for a sick joke.

Then she saw the yellow dress, or what was left of it. And the yellow hair, stained in red.

And Miranda's head, not attached to the rest of her, her eyes wide and her mouth open in a scream.

"Miranda," she said, and felt her legs turn to water underneath her.

Jake grabbed her before she fell down into the pool of Miranda's blood, and she clutched at his shirt, unable to support herself.

"Oh, Jesus, Mary, and Joseph," Miller said. He made a choking sound.

"Don't puke in the crime scene," Officer Lopez said. "You two, back away but don't go anywhere, all right? I'm going to need a statement from you."

Lauren was amazed at how calm he sounded. He got on his radio and called Chief Christie, and his voice didn't waver for an instant. He lowered the flashlight and Lauren was relieved not to see Miranda's eyes.

Why you? I was going to call you tomorrow. I was going to tell you I was sorry.

Miranda, I'm so sorry.

Miller ran in front of the haunted house and began to retch.

"It's the same as my sister," Jake said. "The same as those girls in Mrs. Schneider's yard."

Officer Lopez gave Jake a sharp look. "What do you know about that?"

"The same as all the girls," Lauren said. Blood was roaring in her ears. She spoke without really noticing what she said. "Except not. This isn't how it's supposed to happen."

"How what's supposed to happen? Lauren, do you know

something? Do you know who's doing this?" Officer Lopez came closer to them, his voice an undertone like he didn't want Miller to hear.

"There's something wrong in this town," Lauren said. "Something very wrong."

"What's all the fuss over here?" Mayor Touhy's voice—too hearty, completely unwelcome—came from the entrance of the acrobat tent. He had just exited and walked over to join them.

Touhy glanced sharply from Miller's bent form to Lopez's somber face to Lauren and Jake, who were holding on to each other for dear life. "Has something happened?"

"Hey, what's that?" Jake asked, pointing at a shadow on the side of the tent just above Miranda.

Officer Lopez raised his flashlight. It swept past Miranda's head and Touhy sucked in a breath. "Not another one," he said, so low that Lauren barely heard him. "It's not time."

The beam of the flashlight touched the tent wall where Jake pointed. Something was written there—something in large, streaky red letters.

ONLY YOU LAUREN

Lauren felt her blood rush to her head and her chest turn ice-cold. The last thing she heard was Jake saying, "Lauren? Lauren?" and then there was nothing else.

24

Karen wasn't surprised that David wanted to go to bed early that night. It sounded like he and Lauren had done every single thing at the fair—"'cept the haunted house," he'd said in his most serious voice. "Because Lauren doesn't like them."

He was a good sleeper anyway—had been since he was a baby. David had never been one of those children who fussed and fought at bedtime. He didn't mind taking a bath, either—the exact opposite of Lauren as a toddler, who would scream if her hair got wet and have to be wrestled down to rinse out the shampoo.

He'd nodded off at the dinner table, just in the middle of telling her about Lauren winning the stuffed frog from the water-gun game. His voice drifted away and his eyes closed and his head lolled forward.

She'd gently shaken him awake. "Do you want to go to bed now?"

"Okeh," he said.

She'd picked him up, thinking *He's so big now, I can hardly carry him at all*. He snuggled his head onto her shoulder.

"Do you think you can take a bath?" she asked. She hated to put him into bed all covered in dust and funnel cake sugar from the fair.

"Okeh," he said sleepily.

He stood, swaying gently, while she ran a warm bath. She quickly washed him and got him into his pajamas and led him to his bedroom. He climbed in and pulled his top sheet up to his chin. The sheets were white with scenes from the *Peanuts* cartoon all over them.

"Good night, David," she said, kissing his forehead.

"Good night, Mommy," he murmured. His eyes were already closed.

It was still light out so she went to the window and closed the blinds and pulled the curtains shut. She tiptoed toward the door, though she thought he was probably out cold already.

He turned onto his side just as she reached the door and said, "Good-bye, Miranda."

Karen glanced back at him. He'd sounded so sad.

He must be having a dream, she thought, and went downstairs.

She cleaned up the dinner things, glancing at the clock. She hoped that Lauren was having a good time at the fair with Jake Hanson. That had been a surprise, and the age difference had given Karen pause, but in the end she decided to let Lauren go. Her daughter had been a little melancholy since the argument with Miranda.

It was too hot to make tea or coffee, so Karen took a can of Tab out to the back porch and opened it there. She wouldn't mind a glass of wine, she realized, but she didn't have any in the house. It had become a very rare indulgence since Joe died.

Lauren standing at the back door, tugging on the knob.

There was that memory again. Karen sat in one of the lawn chairs and put her feet up on the porch railing, thinking. One of her neighbors was grilling. She smelled the smoke and the scent of cooking meat lingering in the heavy summer air. It was such a hot summer already. It made her feel languid and drifting. She closed her eyes against the glow of the setting sun.

Lauren standing at the back door, tugging on the doorknob.

"Lauren!" Joe was standing next to her, shaking their daughter's shoulder, but she didn't respond to his voice or his touch. "Lauren!"

Her eyes were wide open, like she was sleepwalking, but she'd never sleepwalked before.

Karen watched her daughter try to open the locked door and her husband try to stop Lauren from leaving. Karen had a sudden flash then, a kind of terrible knowledge that made her stagger and clutch the counter for support so she could stay upright.

Joe ceased trying to stop Lauren and stared at his wife, and she saw the same terrible knowledge in his eyes.

"We're supposed to let her go," Karen said. "Open the door for her, and lock it behind her."

"And tomorrow she'll be dead, found in the woods. But it's all for the greater good," Joe intoned, like he was reciting something he'd memorized. "And in time we'll forget."

Forget, *Karen thought, and shuddered.* Forget *her smart and beautiful and oh-so-difficult daughter.* Forget *Lauren had ever existed.*

(just like Nancy)

But that memory was only a flash, a nearly subliminal image that flew past as she stared at Lauren and Joe standing by the door. Her husband's mouth was twisted in disgust.

"Does everybody do this? They open the door for their daughters to be murdered?"

"They must," Karen said. "They must, because it happens every year. But then we all forget about it, so that it can happen again."

"It's not happening this time," Joe said. "I'm not sending my child out into the night to die."

"But what will happen if we don't?" Karen whispered. "Will we all die?"

"No," Joe said. "I'm going to stop it, whatever it is."

She thought she couldn't possibly be more afraid than she was, but the idea of Joe going out to confront . . . well, she wasn't certain what he would confront but she remembered at that very moment that all the girls had died in the woods, their heads torn from their bodies.

"It will kill you," she said, going to him then and grasping his arm. "It will tear you to pieces."

"No, it won't," he said. "I'm not some teenage girl blindly walking into its nest. The only way to stop this is if we resist."

"You don't know that!" She was panicking, felt it rising in her throat and choking her. "I won't send Lauren out, but I'm not letting you go, either."

"Listen, you take Lauren upstairs and lock her in her bedroom. Don't let her out until morning, no matter what she says or does."

"Joe, no, I won't let you—"

"You can't stop me," he said, and he gave her that crooked smile, the one that had made her heart flutter on the day they first met.

They hadn't always been happy. Their marriage hadn't been perfect. But she loved him, deep down in her bones. And she didn't want him to die.

"Promise me that you'll keep Lauren safe," he said. "Promise."

"Yes, I promise," she said. She couldn't stop him. Nothing she said or did had ever been able to move him once he'd decided on a thing. He and Lauren were the same that way.

He pushed at Lauren's shoulders, tried to steer her back to Karen. It's like trying to move a mechanical soldier that only wants to march in one direction, *Karen thought.*

Lauren's feet kept moving toward the door, her upper body angled toward it like it was tugging on her. Her face was blank and her eyes were lifeless.

Karen got in front of Lauren and tried to turn her around, but it was impossible. It wasn't that Lauren was stronger than Karen, only that she could not be moved. The compulsion was forcing her in one direction only—toward her death.

It was terrible to realize that her daughter would march willingly to the slaughter, and worse that she and Joe were expected to be complicit in Lauren's death. And this happened all over town, every year. Every year some girl's family let her out of the house in the middle of the night, knowing what would happen to her, and the next morning they would wake up with no memory of their actions, their daughter seemingly spirited away by fairies in the night.

Karen pushed at Lauren's shoulders and was able to shift her a few feet away from the door. As soon as there was clearance she heard Joe unlock the door behind her.

"Wait!" she cried. They hadn't really had a chance to say good-bye. Karen kept a firm grip on Lauren's shoulders and glanced back at the door.

"I'll come back," he said.

All she saw of him was his face framed in the closing door for a moment before he pulled it shut. She heard him locking it from the outside and noticed that he'd had the foresight to grab his keys from the hook by the door. Which was a very good thing, because her grip had slackened when she saw him leave, and as soon as it did Lauren pushed forward again.

Karen dug her heels in, tried to stop her, but all she succeeded in doing was arresting the forward motion. Lauren still marched in place, her eyes locked on the door. Karen thought, almost hysterically, of a Dr. Seuss story that David thought was funny—one about creatures called Zax who only walked in one direction and would never step to one side for an obstacle.

They stood there all night, Lauren pushing toward the door, Karen pushing back and growing increasingly exhausted. Then suddenly Lauren stopped, her legs buckling beneath her like her batteries had abruptly died.

"Lauren!" Karen cried, catching her as she fell. Lauren's head lolled backward, her eyes closed, her breath deep and even. She was asleep.

Karen carefully lowered her to the ground, where Lauren turned onto her left side and tucked her hands underneath her face, like she always had since she was very small.

Her mother sat beside her, stroking her hair, and let the tears she'd been suppressing fall. She knew that Joe was never coming home.

Karen opened her eyes and was startled to discover that it was night. She'd fallen asleep on the porch. Her neck hurt from resting against the hard metal and nylon of the lawn chair.

Strange dream, she thought, then, *No, it wasn't a dream. It was a memory.*

The truth of this and of everything else she now realized made her hunch forward in pain, clutching her middle. Joe had not been cheating on her. He hadn't gone out that night to meet his mistress. He'd run out into the night to save their daughter, and he'd been killed by the monster instead.

Joe hadn't stopped paying the money on his life insurance. The insurance money had disappeared when they'd broken the rules, when they hadn't let Lauren die as they were supposed to.

But the charm or spell or curse had made Karen think things that weren't true, had made her forget that Lauren had nearly died.

"What is wrong with this town?" she gasped.

Why did this happen here? And why did she remember all of a sudden? Why were things rushing back to her now, her childhood best friend and the truth about Joe? Why did she feel as if she could name every girl that had gone missing in the last twenty years?

What was different now?

The phone inside rang, startling her. She got up and rubbed her head, which was aching now. Just as she opened the screen door, David began to wail, crying like she'd never heard him cry before.

Karen ran past the insistently trilling phone without stopping.

25

Mrs. Schneider looked around at the circle of expectant faces in her living room. Many people had come when she called—more than she'd thought. There were twenty of them squashed together on her sofa or perched on the armrests of the chairs

(Mr. Schneider would not have liked that, no he would not, he would have thought it rude)

and some of the younger ones sitting cross-legged on the floor like they were in kindergarten again.

No one was talking. A sense of hushed resolve hung around the room, a feeling that they all knew their purpose and were willing to fulfill it.

For the first time in a very long time her mind felt clear. No fog obscured her memories of Janey or of the other girls. If she tried she thought she could name off every one that had died in her lifetime.

Not died. Murdered.

No. Not murdered either. Sacrificed.

A few of them were her own neighbors, and she saw the knowledge that they, too, had suppressed for so long on their faces.

No, suppressed *isn't the right word.* Hidden. *It was hidden from us, hidden behind other things in our heads.*

And now all the hidden things had come into the light, and Mrs. Schneider knew why. It was because of the outsiders. If the outsiders went away, then everything would go back to the way it was before.

That means girls will die again, one every year.

Well, it was better if it was one girl a year. Better than whatever was happening now. And before it had always been safely in the woods, not in her backyard.

All she wanted was for everything to go back to the way it was. She didn't want to think about Janey, didn't want to hurt inside when she remembered her bright and beautiful daughter.

"Thank you all for coming," she began.

She stopped, clearing her throat. Everyone had turned to look at her expectantly. There was an odd look in their eyes. A look that was almost like they were waiting to be told what to do.

I don't have to convince them, she realized. *They already know.*

"I think it's time we purged our town of these outsiders," she said. "Once they're gone everything will go back to the way it was before."

Heads were nodding all around, no voice of dissent.

"I don't think we should, eh, hurt them, though," Mrs. Schneider said carefully. She did remember how that woman had been kind to her when they found the girls in her yard. And the outsiders had children

(filthy Mexican children that would have more filthy Mexican children, but children nonetheless)

and Mrs. Schneider did not want to be responsible for the death of children.

"I think, perhaps, that we should just frighten them. Frighten them into leaving town forever."

Again, everyone in the room nodded. It was so strange. She felt a flutter of nervousness, a momentary hesitation. It was very much like they were under some kind of spell. But she, Mrs. Schneider, was not a witch. There was something in the air, something that had drawn all of them to her house and made them listen and obey.

"The sooner we take care of this problem, the sooner our lives can return to normal. We will be able to forget again."

"Yes. Forget."

"Forget."

"Forget."

The word went all around the room from person to person like falling dominoes.

Yes, forget this pain. Forget that Mr. Schneider and I opened the door and let Janey out that night and locked it up tight behind her so the monster would get her instead of us.

"I have some things outside that will help us," she said.

They all rose in an obedient line and followed her through the house and out the back door.

26

That's it, Touhy thought as he peeled out of the parking area of the fair. The old bitch was going to talk to him whether she wanted to or not.

He'd tried calling Jo after he'd seen the morning paper. But she hadn't picked up the phone and he'd been forced to leave a message on her answering machine.

She hadn't picked up the other two times he called, either.

The bitch (*witch*) was ignoring him. Well, she wouldn't be able to ignore him when he was standing on her front porch.

And if she did he'd break the door down.

This whole business had gotten completely out of control. Bad enough that girls from out of town had been murdered at the wrong time of the year. Now girls from Smiths Hollow were being left in pieces any old place.

The fair! The fair, of all places.

If word got out that a girl was cut up into little pieces at the fair, he would be finished. Nobody was going to come from out of town to spend money in Smiths Hollow if they thought their children would be chopped up into dog meat when they got here.

And that message on the wall. What did that mean? Did it mean the monster was going to take Lauren diMucci next?

And there were all those layoffs. What was the point of the girls' deaths if everyone was going to lose their jobs anyway?

He barely noticed the streetlights, the pedestrians crossing the road, the other cars. All he knew was that he needed to get to the old house on the hill as soon as possible.

Before some girl is killed right in the middle of Main Street with half the town and that damned Chicago reporter watching.

Touhy had seen Riley sniffing around the fair and knew it was impossible to hope that the man wouldn't discover what had happened there. He should have told Christie to have Riley shown out on some pretense.

Though Christie seemed a little more awake than usual the last time they talked. Normally if Touhy told him to do something, Christie did it, no questions asked. That was all part of keeping the curse in place and out of sight of the townspeople. But Christie had started asking questions, wondering why they weren't doing more to find out what happened to the two dead girls.

It was all unraveling. He could feel it. But instead of relief that his lifetime of servitude to the town and its terrible lottery were over, he only felt panic.

Panic that the unraveling meant not that the curse was over but that it had grown exponentially worse.

And the only person he could think of that might be able to make it right was Jo Gehlinger. So she was going to talk to him and help him put it right.

He slammed on the accelerator as his car climbed the steep hill. The house loomed above him, the lights in the upper story turning the windows into glaring eyes.

He pulled the car to a stop just short of the mailbox. It didn't matter if he left it in the street. There were no other houses up here and no other cars.

Touhy stomped up the porch steps, not caring how much noise he made. He hammered on the door with his fist.

"I know you're in there!" he shouted. "You can't ignore me forever."

He heard the lock on the other side of the door unclick and Jo Gehlinger stood there, her long gray hair unbound and her eyes narrowed.

"What do you want?" she asked.

"You know what I want," he said, pushing his way inside.

He'd never been in her house, though as a young boy he'd run up onto the porch on a dare with some of his friends. There was a moment of surprise when he realized the place looked perfectly normal. He'd half expected a cauldron or bunches of herbs hanging from the ceiling.

Maybe she's not a witch after all, he thought, then shook his head to rid himself of doubt. *No, she's a witch. She's the only one who ever knew those girls were dying.*

She's the only one who ever looked at me like she knew what I was doing.

(But that wasn't my fault. I had to pick the girls. I had to.)

"You need to make it right," Touhy said, turning to face her.

Jo stood by the door, which was still ajar. "What is it that I need to make right?"

"Don't play dumb," he said, his face flushing with anger. "Don't stand there so smug and superior and tell me that you don't know what's been going on in this town. Girls are dying."

"I tried to tell you that many years ago," she said. "But you didn't seem to mind so much when they died on schedule. Even pretended you didn't know what I was talking about."

"It's not supposed to be like this! You know what they did—what your relatives did. It's only supposed to be one girl, once a year."

"And the town will stay prosperous," Jo said.

The way she said it made Touhy feel like a bug under her shoe, as if wanting people to have jobs and food on the table was a selfish thing.

"Yes! And now the town isn't prospering anymore. Things are going wrong. And another girl died tonight. *At the fair.*"

He emphasized the last three words so she would understand how important this was.

She didn't move from her place by the open door. It was fairly obvious that she was waiting for him to go away and stop bothering her. Well, he wasn't going to go away. He wasn't going anywhere until she agreed to fix it all.

"Don't you understand? She was killed at the fair in the middle of summer. Not in the woods. Not in November. The thing out there is just rampaging freely. And," he said, sudden inspiration occurring, "your granddaughter is next. It left a message for her."

"Lauren? It left a message for Lauren?" Jo said, giving him a sharp look.

"Yes, written in the other girl's blood," he said. She was interested now, he could tell. No more dismissive stop-wasting-my-time face.

"What did it say?"

"'Only You Lauren,'" he said. "I think that means she's next."

"No," Jo murmured. "It means it wants to take her away. I've been afraid of something like this, ever since her father died."

Jo didn't really seem to be talking to him—rather, she was thinking through something out loud and he just happened to be present. He was wise enough to keep still and silent, because as long as she talked he might learn something. Anything might help save his town before it crumbled into ruin.

"He was the wrong sacrifice."

Touhy went more still than before. He felt that his insides had frozen into place.

The wrong sacrifice. Everything went wrong when her father died in Lauren's place.

Touhy didn't know how that might have happened, how the father had ended up out in the woods instead of the daughter. But that was definitely when things changed. And it all made complete sense. The monster hadn't gotten what it wanted and nothing would be set right until it did.

Jo went on muttering to herself. "And of course it wants what it didn't get. But more than that—it can feel her power. I've felt it myself, these last few days, for all that she wants to pretend she doesn't have any. If it gets hold of her now . . ."

She trailed off, looking up. Her expression said she'd forgotten that he stood there.

"Lauren is like you?" he asked carefully. "A . . . witch?"

"Yes," she said. "But don't ask me to have her come up here and perform a spell to undo the curse. I don't know how to do that. The first curse was sealed in the blood of a witch. I think that would be very difficult to undo."

"But we don't need to undo it," he said. He understood now what had to be done. He should have seen it from the first. "We just need to make it right. Put the spell back on course, as it were."

He started toward the door but Jo's eyes widened and she slammed it shut, putting her body in front of it.

"You're not going to feed my Lauren to the beast," she said, her face fierce.

"But that's what has to be done, don't you see?" he said. His voice was very calm, but his heart was pounding fast and his head felt like it was filling up with blood. "Someone has to set this right. If Lauren had died when she was supposed to, then Smiths Hollow would have gone on as it always has. But she didn't, and the monster broke free and now it wants Lauren. So if we give it what it wants, then everything will be fixed."

"You can't," she said, holding up her hands and pushing against his chest. "You don't know what will happen if it takes her now, when she's come into her power."

Touhy wasn't really listening to her words. Her hands were small and fragile against his chest. It would be nothing at all to grasp those frail wrists and break them. Why had he been afraid of this woman?

For he had been afraid, he realized now. Afraid of her knowledge, afraid she would expose him to the town, afraid that if she spoke, the dark magic that bound all of them together would unwind.

But he didn't need to be afraid anymore. He knew what he had to do.

Touhy grabbed her wrists—*yes, they were like dry kindling, nothing to it*—and bent them back. He heard a terrible popping noise and then her face twisted up into a grimace and she screamed, staggering away from him.

"No, don't scream," he said, scanning the room. "We can't have the neighbors thinking there's something wrong. Oh, that's right. There are no neighbors."

She held her strangely flopping wrists to her body, back away from him. "Please," she said in a hoarse whisper. "Please, no. Don't hurt her."

He picked up a sculpture that was perched on an end table—some pagan-looking thing, black and made of metal, that had a pleasant heft in his hand.

"The first curse was sealed by the blood of a witch," he said, striding toward her. She was on her knees now, a crumpled and pathetic thing. "You told me so yourself."

"Not Lauren, please not Lauren," she pleaded.

He raised the sculpture. "It's not Lauren you should be worried about."

27

Karen flipped on the light in David's room, her heart hammering. Her first thought was that he'd been hurt, or that someone had managed to get into the house.

Or maybe that he was trying to get out like Lauren had that night.

But he was still in bed, even if he wasn't resting peacefully there.

He thrashed around in the sheets, arms punching, legs kicking. His head shook from side to side and his face gleamed with sweat. Karen couldn't tell if he was asleep or awake but now that she was in his room his screams were more coherent.

"Nana, Nana, Nana!"

She rushed to his side and tried to untangle the sheets from his little body. He hit her in the eye with one of his flailing arms and she staggered back, covering that eye with her hand.

I've got to get him out of there before he hurts himself. She set to work again, mindful of his hard little fists. The sheet was wound around his body and she finally managed to work him free. She scooped him out of bed and into her arms, holding him tight to her.

"Shh, shh, it's all right, it's only a dream, shh," she said, rubbing his back while he cried for his grandmother.

He stopped screaming. His head jerked back and his eyes flew open. For a moment his gaze was far away. Then he seemed to realize where he was and who he was with.

"Mommy," he said, his eyes welling up with tears. "Nana's dead. He killed her."

Karen shivered. He sounded so serious.

"No, honey, it was just a dream. Just a bad dream."

David shook his head and started to wriggle so that she would put him down. She was so surprised by this that she did just that. David was not a wriggler. He always stayed contented in her arms until she was too tired to hold him.

"He killed her, Mommy. He did."

"Who killed her?"

"Mayor Touhy. And he wants to kill Lauren, too."

Lauren standing at the back door, trying to get out. Lauren with that blank and terrifying face, a lamb walking quietly to the butcher.

Karen didn't understand how David knew these things but she thought, finally, that she believed.

And that meant her mother was dead. Something wrenched inside her. Her mother—her difficult, beautiful mother who'd loved her so much even when they didn't always agree. Just like Karen loved Lauren so much even when they didn't get along. Her mother was gone.

She covered her mouth with her hand. "Mom!"

David tugged on her. "We have to go now."

"Go?" Should they go to her mother's house?

"Yes, we have to go now."

"Yes, we have to get Lauren," Karen said, standing up and trying not to panic. The second half of what David said had finally sunk in. The mayor wanted to kill Lauren, too. She couldn't lose her mother and her daughter in the same night. She'd promised Joe that she would keep Lauren safe.

David shook his head. "No. Not Lauren. We have to go to the Lopez house now."

28

Lauren and Jake sat side by side on a bench in the police station. They'd been taken in because they needed to give statements, but because Lauren was a minor they didn't want her to give it without her mother present.

Chief Christie had tried to call her mom, but she hadn't picked up the phone. He'd also tried to call Jake's parents even though he was eighteen. He seemed to think it was the right thing to do even though Jake was technically an adult. But Jake's parents hadn't picked up either, so the two of them just sat there waiting.

Jake had his arm around her shoulders and her head rested on his chest but her eyes were very determinedly open. She did not want to close her eyes again and see Miranda there in the dark.

That was what David was drawing the other day, she thought dully. *You and Jake finding Miranda's body. You just didn't see him finish it.*

If she had asked David what he was drawing, could he have told her exactly what it was? She wasn't sure. It had seemed almost like he was in a trance, like when he told her that Officer Lopez needed her help at the fair. If he'd told her, she could have warned Miranda, told her to stay away from the fair.

Miranda. I'm so sorry.

There was a big aching place in her chest where Miranda used to be, the place where they used to build forts out of mud and race their bikes side by side. The place where the phone would ring and Miranda would say, *Meet me by the old ghost tree.*

Lauren sat up then, pulling away from Jake.

"What's wrong?" he asked. His eyelids were at half-mast. He looked like he might fall asleep any second.

"The ghost tree," she said. "Whatever it is that did this to Miranda is in the ghost tree."

"Like that story you told me," he said.

She nodded. "I have to go there."

"Are you crazy?" he said, his voice low and urgent. "*If* the monster in the woods is real—"

"You know it is," Lauren said, stung. "Your sister. You told me yourself."

His eyes flickered, an emotion she couldn't read moving there.

"Yeah, well, the more you think about it the harder it is

to believe there could be something like that out in the world," he said.

"No person could have done that to Miranda," Lauren said.

"A person with an axe, maybe," he said.

"Did you see anyone walking around the fair with an axe?"

"The field is just behind the place where we found her body," he said. "Anybody could have walked up through there and then disappeared behind the fair without being seen. And the woods are just behind that bit of field."

"I can't believe you," she said. "You *know* there's something wrong here. You *know* and now you're trying to pretend it isn't true."

Their argument was pitched in low whispers, both of them silently agreeing that their discussion wasn't the business of Officers Lopez or Miller or Chief Christie. Those three were on the other side of the room, having a whispered conference of their own.

"That's what we do here," Jake said. "Terrible things happen and we just pretend everything is fine. We forget about them."

Lauren shook her head. "I don't think we can forget about them anymore. Something's changed."

He opened his mouth, ready to argue again, and then closed it. Resignation crossed his face, and something else—pain.

"I don't want to remember," he said. "I don't want to remember Jenny that way."

"I don't want to remember Miranda that way, either," she said.

Her eyes were dry. She would cry later, when she could pour out her grief without an audience. She'd just keep pretending the lump in her throat and the ache in her chest weren't there.

"Anyway, I was saying, if there's something in the woods—okay, there is," he said, holding up his hands in surrender, "the last place you want to be is the ghost tree. For chrissakes, Lauren—it left you a message."

She closed her eyes, and there was Miranda's head with its wide blank eyes and open mouth and just above it the words written in blood on the side of the tent.

"I know," she said.

"If a monster or a killer or whatever had left me a personal message, I would not go chasing after it into the woods," Jake said. "I'd leave town immediately."

"I don't think I can," Lauren said. "I don't think anybody can. It's part of the curse. Even if you leave you always have to return."

Jake looked scared then, his face pinched and white. "So, what are you saying? You're inevitably going to die and there's nothing we can do about it?"

"There might be something I can do about it," she said. The silver ring David gave her felt heavy on her finger. She twisted it around and around in a nervous circle.

"What, you're going to go out there with a machete and fight it? Don't be ridiculous. Whatever's happening in this town is not going to be fixed by one lone girl."

"Why not?" she said, her temper flaring. "One lone girl always saves the day in those movies that Miranda likes—"

Her breath broke on the name, unable to finish.

"Lauren," he said.

"No. I can't explain it to you. You wouldn't understand."

Jake had a lot of good qualities, but she supposed it was too much to expect him to believe she was a witch. She'd hardly believed it herself, and she'd managed to do some strange things already. Not that she knew how to use her power or magic or whatever it was, really. She didn't think the monster in the woods would respond to a direct order from her like the crowd at the fair.

Something shot through her then, something that was like electricity arcing through her. She cried out and everyone in the station turned to look at her.

Nana.

"No!" she shouted. "No, no!"

And she was on her feet and running out of the station before anyone had a chance to stop her.

29

The crowd filed out to the backyard. Her lovely, neat backyard that had been sullied by those murdered girls.

We're going to put things right now.

No one talked. No one even whispered. There was a sense of understanding all around, a resolve to do what was necessary.

Nobody seemed surprised to find the pile of torches stacked neatly beside the porch. She herself was not surprised, though she didn't remember putting them there.

They weren't the kind everyone had in films—jagged sticks of wood with their ends lit. These were the sort that people used around their patio in the summer so they could feel like they lived in Hawaii or some such place. And next to the torches was a large box of matches.

Mrs. Schneider picked up the box and struck the first one.

30

Alex saw Lauren sprint out the door, followed by Jake.

"Goddammit!" he shouted, running after them.

Alex and Miller and Christie had just been having a quiet conversation about how they might keep Lauren safe, for it was clear that whatever was happening, Lauren was a target.

And then the target ran out of the police station and into the night without a care for her own well-being.

Alex ran out onto the sidewalk and looked in both directions, but Lauren and Jake were gone. It was like they'd been beamed away like in that sci-fi show Val watched sometimes in reruns—the one with the spaceship and all the different people traveling around meeting aliens on a goodwill mission or something.

"Shit!" he said. He could run in either direction in the hope that he might spot them, or he could get the car and drive around.

Miller and Christie pushed through the station door as Alex was coming back.

"Where did they go?" Christie asked.

"No idea," Alex said. "I'm going to take the squad car and see if I can find them."

"I'll go with you," Miller said.

"You'd better not," Alex said, with a glance at Christie. "Between the fair, the murder, and all the regular nonsense that happens on Saturday night we're stretched pretty thin as it is."

Christie nodded. "I might need to call you back."

Alex looked at his watch. "How about a half hour? I'll try her house, her grandmother's house, maybe a couple of other places."

"Let's just hope that whoever killed Miranda doesn't find Lauren in the meantime," Christie said grimly.

What does it matter? You're only going to pretend it didn't happen again, just like you did all the others, Alex thought.

Though he wasn't certain that would work anymore. After the article about the murders had come out in the *Tribune* that morning, Alex had heard several people discussing it. He'd even overheard a couple at the fair talking about the "other girls." And Christie had seemed, for lack of a better word, more *awake* than he normally did. So maybe whatever hold Touhy had over him was gone.

There's something going on besides the murders, anyway, he thought as he headed around the station to get the car out of the small lot. *Because it was not normal for people to act the way they had at the fair.*

Whatever was happening, Lauren diMucci seemed to be in the middle of it. He would never forget the way that crowd had just turned away and gone about their business because she said so. And his heart had gone cold when he saw the message the killer left for her.

Alex felt that if he could just talk to her, all the disparate pieces of the puzzle would come together in a way that made sense. Right now he felt like he only had half the answer.

He thought it most likely that Lauren had gone home. He pulled out of the lot and headed in the direction of his own street.

31

Lauren heard Jake's footsteps falter behind her, heard hi ragged breathing.

"Lauren, wait," he said, his voice fading as he fell farthe behind.

She didn't wait. She couldn't wait. She had to get to the top of the hill because something had happened to Nana. She didn't know exactly what

(though David probably knows, David sees everything tha happens in this town)

but it was something terrible. In that moment when she'd cried out her grandmother's name she'd felt a surge of power followed by a sharp pain. The pain had receded almos immediately and that was what terrified her, because i meant that Nana was fading away.

Not again, I never said I was sorry to Miranda and never said I was sorry to you, either, Nana, so don't die pleas don't die hold on until I can get there.

The police station was less than a mile from the top of the hill, and Lauren climbed the steep ascent like it was nothing. Her legs were on fire and her lungs were scorched with fear and the silver ring felt like it was branding her hand.

She saw a car in front of her nana's house, an unfamiliar car that was parked in the middle of the street, but she didn't stop to examine it or wonder about it. She ran up the porch steps and saw that the door wasn't closed quite all the way.

Lauren pushed the door open and called, "Nana! Nana!"

Then she stopped, because Nana was on the floor and there was blood all around.

She screamed then, because Nana's face was gone and the only way that Lauren knew it was her grandmother at all was because her long gray hair floated in the pool of blood like Ophelia's in the river.

"No, Nana," she moaned. "No, no."

Call the police, she thought, but she couldn't make her feet move, couldn't stop staring at the horror before her.

Somebody grabbed her shoulders, squeezed tight. Lauren cried out and looked up into the face of the mayor.

"Mr. Touhy!" she said. "My nana . . ."

There was a strange expression in his eyes. He didn't seem to notice that Nana was dead at all. He stared down at Lauren and he looked—

Hungry, she thought. *He looks hungry.*

"I'm so glad that you're here," he said. "It makes things so much easier if I don't have to hunt around looking for you."

She tried to pull away from him, but his fingers dug into her shoulders.

"Let me go!" she shouted, trying to twist out of his grip. "Let me go!"

"Oh, no," he said, pushing her toward the open door. "There's something waiting for you in the woods."

She struggled and fought and yelled, but his grip didn't slacken.

They were down the porch before she knew what was happening.

If I get in that car I'm never going home again, she thought.

Lauren stomped down hard on his right foot at the same time that she pushed her elbow into his stomach.

She didn't think she'd hurt him at all, only surprised him, but it didn't matter because it was just enough to make him release her shoulders. Lauren didn't hesitate.

She ran.

"Fucking *little bitch*!" he shouted.

She heard his leather soles slapping the pavement behind her, and a second later he tackled her to the ground. Her forehead bounced off the road and blood poured into her right eye.

He grabbed her by her wrists and yanked her up with a surprising amount of strength. Her feet twisted under her as he dragged her toward his car. The blood from the cut on her head made her eye sting and she couldn't see and it felt like her limbs were made of soft wax. She couldn't seem to get her body to struggle or fight or run.

"Hey!"

Jake's voice, she thought, and tried to call his name.

Jake, don't come here. He'll kill you.

Touhy opened the passenger door and shoved her inside. She tried to lift her hand up, tried to reach for the handle so she could get out. But she couldn't see, couldn't make her hand do what she wanted it to do. Her head rolled forward to her chest.

There was noise outside, the thudding of flesh against flesh, grunts and cries. Someone slammed into the car and the whole vehicle shook.

I hope that was Touhy. I hope that Jake is kicking the shit out of him. But it was hard to keep her head up, hard to focus on what was happening outside.

Lauren slumped against the door, her eyes closed.

A moment later she heard the driver's-side door open. Someone got in the car, someone breathing hard and angry. She felt the engine start, heard him mutter.

"That's enough," Touhy said. "It all ends tonight."

The car backed up, turned around, rolled over something that made the wheels rise up and fall again.

Jake. Did Touhy just run over . . . ?

Please don't let him be dead. Don't let him be like Miranda and Nana and Dad. Let him be all right.

Lauren tried to open her eyes but they felt glued shut. She didn't need to see to know where they were going, anyway.

There was only one possible place.

The ghost tree.

32

Alex turned onto his street, his eyes straining in the darkness for a glimpse of Lauren. Either she had run very fast or he'd guessed wrong about her final destination.

Or the killer got her already.

No, he wouldn't think like that. He would find her, and he would keep her safe.

Ever since the two dead girls had been found, Alex had felt like he was three steps behind, struggling to catch up in a game where everyone but him knew the rules.

But this time the killer had actually warned them. He'd told them the name of his target. Alex wasn't about to let Lauren become the next victim if he could do anything about it.

He pulled up in front of Lauren's house. Before he could turn off the car, though, he noticed something strange at the end of the street.

It looked like a line of people filing out of Mrs. Schneider's house carrying lit torches.

And they were walking directly toward his house.

Alex didn't stop to think about what their intentions were. He slammed his foot on the gas, turned on the lights and sirens, and sped down to the cul-de-sac.

He thought that the sight and sound of a police car would make them stop. At the very least it ought to have made them pause. But he screeched to a halt just before his own driveway and found that the crowd didn't seem to notice his presence at all.

Alex pushed the door open and ran across his front lawn. His weapon was drawn for the second time that day, and for the second time that day he had the unnerving feeling that nothing he said or did would affect these people.

They were walking slowly, deliberately, and their faces in the light of the torches had the same dead eyes and blank malice as the crowd at the fair.

He heard the front door open behind him.

"Alejandro!" Sofia called. "Get away from them!"

"Sof, take the kids and go out the back," he said. "Go down to Karen's."

"I will not," she said, coming out to stand next to him.

He didn't shift his gaze from the steady movement of the oncoming crowd, but out of the corner of his eye he noticed Sofia held a large gardening spade in her hands.

Mrs. Schneider, he noted, was at the front of the group.

Of course she is. The Old Bigot has been dying for the chance to burn us out since the day we came here.

Then he thought, with a grim smile, *She'd better not get in range of Sofia's spade or else her head's going to be caved in.*

"Stop now or I *will* shoot," Alex said, and aimed for the Old Bigot's foot. She was the ringleader, he was sure. If she stopped moving, maybe the rest of them would too.

Although I don't know about that, he thought. He'd never felt so helpless before, so certain that his authority was meaningless. Even if he shot them all, he had a strange notion that they would just get up again and keep trying.

To these people he wasn't a police officer. He was a "dirty Mexican," an outsider. And it wasn't only about him. His family was in the house they wanted to burn down, his brother and his sister-in-law and his daughters and his nephew. They didn't think he and his family were human.

He heard something clanging on the side of the house and risked a glance away from the crowd. His brother was unrolling the garden hose.

"Genius," he muttered, then said more loudly, "This is your last warning."

He only had a revolver, so he couldn't shoot all of them even if he wanted to.

But I want to shoot Mrs. Schneider, he thought. *I really do.*

She was only a few feet away from him now.

"Alejandro!" Sofia shouted.

He pulled the trigger.

The bullet hit Mrs. Schneider just at the place where her ankle met her foot. Alex had been careful not to aim for an organ or a major artery, although it was likely that with her brittle old bones the bullet would break something.

She staggered, cried out, but she didn't stop even though she was now limping. Her eyes blazed with hate and her torch blazed with a killing light.

Then Alex felt cold water dripping on his head as Ed turned the hose on. His brother arced the water over Alex and Sofia, aiming the stream at the nearest torch-bearers.

Some of the torches flickered and went out, but their owners kept moving inexorably forward.

Sofia took a better grip on the spade, turning her body like a batter getting ready for a pitch. Water dripped on them as Ed tried to douse all the torches.

Something moved to Alex's left, a small shadow followed by a larger one.

Then David diMucci stepped in front of him. He heard Karen say, "David!" and Alex hastily reholstered his weapon. He was not about to accidentally shoot the little boy. Alex reached for David, ready to grab him and move him away before he got hurt.

"Stop," David said to the crowd.

They stopped. Many of them swayed in place, side to side

like dandelions in a summer breeze. Alex noticed that unlike the crowd at the fair there was no realization of where they were and what they were doing. Their faces remained terrifyingly blank.

"No more fire," David said.

The flames disappeared as if a giant had blown out his birthday candles.

"What the—?" said Ed behind them. The shower of water abruptly shut off.

Mrs. Schneider stared at David like she'd never seen him before.

"You're *one of them*," she spat. "One of the witches."

"Go home," David said.

Alex noticed then there seemed to be a kind of halo all around David's body, like he was giving off a faint bioluminescent glow.

Everyone turned around and went away, shuffling along in the dark, some of them dragging their doused torches behind them. They looked, Alex thought, like children who'd been called home for dinner when they wanted to stay out and play.

But Mrs. Schneider didn't go. Her anger had only been redirected—from the Lopez family to the very small boy staring up at her with no fear in his eyes.

"It's your fault," she said. She was leaning on her torch now like a cane, unable to support herself on the foot that Alex had shot.

Nobody moved. Nobody seemed to be able to move.

"You, and your family, and the curse that you put on this town," she continued. Saliva ran out of her mouth and over her chin, the poison inside her showing for everyone to see.

Curse? Was this why all the girls kept dying? Is this why all of this crazy shit keeps happening? Alex thought, then *I should do something. I should arrest this nutty old bitch before she hurts David.*

But his feet felt chained in place. The air pulsed with a kind of energy, like the smell of lightning that came before a storm.

"It will all end if I get rid of these outsiders!" she shouted, gesturing with her free hand at Alex and Sofia. "If they go away, then we can all forget, the way it used to be."

"No," David said. His voice seemed deeper, more resonant. "You'll never forget again. You, and everyone else, will remember."

Her hand curved into claws. She screamed, raised it to strike him.

Karen diMucci shot out of the darkness and punched Mrs. Schneider in the face.

The old woman did fall down then, flat backward like a tree felled by a lumberjack. She lay on the ground, writhing, her face twisted up with weeping.

"I only wanted it all to stop," she cried. "I only wanted it all to go back to the way it was."

"It won't," David said, and held up his arms for his mother.

Karen lifted him up, and Alex saw that her face was filled with the same bewilderment he felt.

Sofia dropped the spade to the earth and began to cry loud, noisy tears.

Bea and Daniel and Val and Camila rushed out of the house. Alex heard Bea and Daniel exclaiming over Ed while Camila ran to her mother and Val threw her arms around his waist.

They were safe. Whatever David had done, whatever he had wrought, they were safe.

David whispered something in his mother's ear and Karen gave him a startled look. The little boy looked at Alex.

"I'm sorry," he said.

"Don't be sorry," Alex said. His voice felt like it had never been used before. "I think you just saved us all."

David shook his head. "No. That's not why I'm sorry. I'm sorry because you have to go now."

"Go where?"

"You have to go to the ghost tree," he said. "You have to help Lauren before he eats her."

33

Lauren felt the car stop, felt the air rush in as Touhy climbed out.

I have to do something.

It was really hard to do anything when her brain felt like it had been mashed in. The cut on her head had stopped running, but her eyes were stuck together by dried blood. She tried to rub at her eyelashes but her hand wouldn't do what she wanted it to do.

The passenger door opened and she rolled out onto the ground, her body made of water instead of bone and muscle.

Touhy hoisted her over his shoulder as easily as if she were nothing but air. Her head and arms hung down over his back and slammed against him as he walked, but he didn't seem to notice.

He killed Nana. He killed my grandmother. She wanted to wriggle away, to force him to put her down. She didn't want him to touch her with the same hands that had killed her nana.

"Whhhh—" she said.

"What was that?" He sounded very alert, almost cheerful.

Her mouth didn't want to make the shapes she wanted it to make. She focused all her energy on the words that were stopped up in her throat.

"W-w-why k-kill . . . ?"

"Why kill your grandmother? Well, in retrospect I do regret that. She certainly didn't have to die, although she was being very unhelpful to me. All I wanted was to restart the curse and she wouldn't do anything about it, and that did make me lose my temper. Though I suppose in the end she told me what I needed to know."

They were nearing the ghost tree. Lauren knew, not because she could see it, but because she could feel it. The tree loomed in her mind, a thing made of darkness and eyes, in a way that it never had before. She could sense the Thing that lived inside it, sense it waiting for her.

It killed Miranda and now it's going to kill me.

(Maybe I ought to let it. Maybe then all of this will end, all of this pain.)

No, you can't do that. You can't just give up. You can't do that to Mom and David.

The ring that David had given her from the fair pulsed on her finger. But she didn't think it was a fair prize anymore. She thought—no, she *knew*, that it really was the ring

Charlie had given Elizabeth. She didn't know how it was or why it was but somehow it had come to her.

It can feel the tree, too, and the Thing there.

Her mouth was dry but her head seemed less muzzy than it had a moment ago. Her body didn't feel quite as heavy or helpless.

And then she felt something, a kind of energy that felt like a memory, and knew that everyone in Smiths Hollow remembered their dead girls.

It burst across her like starlight, all of their shock and sorrow, and it was a terrible burden. But who else had the responsibility to bear that burden? She was one of the last of the witches, after all. It was her people that had done this, had loosed the monster because their grief had been too huge for them to carry.

Lauren let it wash over her. She didn't want to dismiss it, but it wasn't the time for it to weigh on her, either. She needed to get away. She needed to survive.

Mayor Touhy, though, didn't seem to experience the surge of memory. *And that is because Mayor Touhy has known all along.*

He'd known, and done nothing about it.

Or rather, he'd facilitated it. That came to her, too, the knowledge that every November he drew the name of a girl from Smiths Hollow, and let her go out into the night to be sacrificed.

And for what? The town's prosperity? No amount of safety and comfort was worth all those lives.

Her head was getting clearer every moment, and she thought it might have something to do with the ring, and maybe the tree, and maybe the magic that pulsed deep in her blood. But it didn't matter anymore. There was no time to escape.

They were at the tree.

He threw her to the ground and though she felt achy all over she was able to move again. She scrambled to her feet and he narrowed his eyes at her.

"Don't even think of trying to run away," he said. "If I have to chase you it won't be pleasant."

Lauren wasn't thinking about running away. The Thing in the tree would never let her get that far.

Touhy's eyes shifted over her shoulder and she saw them widen in surprise. "What are *you* doing here?"

She turned, expecting to see the monster she'd seen in her vision. A figure was leaning against the ghost tree, arms crossed, body relaxed like he hadn't a care in the world.

"Officer Hendricks?" she said.

He smiled, and his eyes crinkled up the way she liked.

Then she saw that his smile was not his smile at all. It was like a split opened in his face and inside there was shadow and screams.

She stumbled back and away. "*You?* You killed Miranda? You killed those girls?"

How could it be him? How could it be the man who'd so gently cleaned her scraped elbow, who asked after her every time he passed? Part of her knew, knew deep down that it wasn't him. The Thing was inside him, was working through him, was making him do this.

But another part of her knew with just as much certainty that the Thing could only enter where there was an opening. There had to be darkness inside to begin with or else the Thing would never have found him in the first place.

"I had to," he said.

His arms uncoiled and his hands reached out for her but they weren't his hands. They weren't the knives she'd thought they were, either. They were claws, long and silver and spiked.

She backed into Touhy, who grabbed her shoulders and held her in place.

"Why did you have to?" she asked. Her brain was screaming at her to *Do something, do something now!* but she couldn't think. Where was all the magic power she was supposed to have? Couldn't she shoot laser beams at him or something? Make a tree branch fall on his head? Lift rocks with her mind? What the hell good was it to be a witch if she didn't know what to do with her power?

His smile widened, and it was such a terrible parody of Officer Hendricks's smile that she felt sick to her stomach.

"So you would know you're the only one for me, Lauren," he said. "I was only playing with Miranda for a while. She was my mistress, but you'll be my bride."

Bride? Bride of the monster? No. No no no no no. She struggled in Touhy's grasp, but he held her tight, so close she felt his breath against her hair.

"I've brought her to you," Touhy said then. "And once you have her you'll stop terrorizing the town, won't you? The lottery will return and you'll only come out once a year."

Hendricks—or the Thing inside Hendricks—turned its gaze from Lauren to Touhy.

"What makes you think you can dictate to me?"

Touhy shook Lauren, thrusting her in front of him like a gift.

"Those were the terms," Touhy said. "The terms set down from the beginning. Once a year, on the anniversary of the first one's death. You didn't get Lauren last year but I'm bringing her to you now."

You didn't get Lauren last year. She remembered then, remembered standing by her back door trying to get out— her mother standing in front of her, her father disappearing out the door.

Dad, she thought, and it was like he'd died all over again, the wound just as fresh as it had been the first time.

He'd gone out in her place, just as Nana said he had.

"The terms no longer apply," Hendricks said.

It happened so fast she barely saw it. Hendricks's arm—*no, not* his *arm, the Thing's arm*—shot out from his body, silver claws outstretched. She shrieked but the claws didn't touch her. They swiped past her, then behind her in a casual, almost lazy way, and Touhy's hands were no longer on her shoulders.

Lauren half turned in time to see Touhy's head roll from his body.

"Now, Lauren," the Thing said. "We can be alone."

It walked toward her with Hendricks's body and Hendricks's face and she stepped back. Her heels ground into Touhy's arm.

"Don't be afraid," he said. "I would never hurt you. You're my one and only love. I've watched you ever since you were a child in these woods. I've seen you grow from a tiny girl into a lovely young woman. And I can feel your magic."

That's why you were never scared when everyone else was, she thought bitterly. *Because the monster was looking on you with love—its idea of love—while it wanted to devour everyone else.*

"Your magic will join with mine and we will be one. We will live together forever," he said.

"That doesn't sound like love," Lauren said. *Do something, do something!* But she couldn't think because it kept looking at her with those familiar eyes, the eyes that she'd sighed about in silly daydreams. She knew it wasn't Officer Hendricks, but her brain wouldn't let go. "That sounds like you want to . . . I don't know. Consume me."

The Thing's eyes lit with a dark fire. "Yes. It is something like that. But don't worry, my precious one. It will be painless."

His hands—his terrible clawed hands—reached for her and she closed her fingers into fists and thought, *I must do something. Magic, do something!*

Four shots rang out.

Hendricks's face froze. His mouth opened and blood spilled over his chin and then he crumpled to the ground.

"Lauren!"

Officer Lopez ran to her side.

"Lauren, are you all right?" he asked, putting his gun away.

"How did you know I was here?" she said. She stared at the body of Officer Hendricks on the ground with four bullet wounds.

I guess I didn't need my magic. Because no matter what was inside him he was only a human monster, after all.

She touched his body with the toe of her sneaker, wondering if he would jump up and try to drag her inside the tree again. That was what always happened in Miranda's horror movies. The killer was never really dead. He always came back in the last reel, knife raised. But there was nothing. Hendricks was just a shell, an empty husk that used to smile at her.

And one that had killed her best friend, and tried to kill her, too.

"David told me," he said, looking from Hendricks to Touhy.

Lauren let out a short, slightly crazy-sounding laugh. "Of course David told you. David knows every damned thing that happens in this town."

Lopez looked at Lauren, then frowned down at the body of his fellow officer.

"And now maybe you'll tell me just what's been going on."

She shook her head slowly. She couldn't take her eyes off Hendricks. He wasn't moving. He was definitely dead. But there was something . . .

"No, I can't do that. Not yet."

"Why not?"

The Thing burst from Hendricks's body then, a great shadow that emerged in a rush of wind and swirled into the ghost tree.

"Lauren!" it said. Its voice promised, demanded, threatened all in one word.

Its eyes glowed within the tree and its mouth was a giant hole made of starless night. The branches of the tree cracked, unfurling like fingers. They seemed fluid in a way that tree branches should not be, flowing down toward her. The trunk seemed to twist and bend so that those glowing eyes—*red eyes, red eyes like a vampire in a movie, red eyes like the monster under your bed*—drew closer and closer to her face. It seemed to fill up the whole world.

"Lauren!" That wasn't the tree. That was Officer Lopez, tugging at her arm, trying to pull her away. But she was mesmerized, held in place like a cobra to a charmer.

But the cobra can kill the snake charmer if it wants. It's not helpless.

I'm not helpless.

I won't become the bride of the monster that lives in the ghost tree. I want to live. I want to kiss Jake. I want to grow up. I want to do all the things that Elizabeth never had a chance to do.

Elizabeth!

She knew then what she had to do, and it was so simple that she almost laughed. She didn't need to spin a spell or cast a curse. She only needed to undo what had been done, and Elizabeth had sent her the way.

Lauren twisted the silver ring from her finger. In fairy tales, magic beings could never abide the touch of silver. And this silver ring had tasted the last drop of Elizabeth's life.

Elizabeth's death had sparked the curse, and Elizabeth's death was the only thing that could end it.

Lauren threw the ring into the gaping mouth of the ghost tree.

If Officer Lopez hadn't been there she surely would have died, she realized later. There was a howl of rage and pain and betrayal as the ring was swallowed up by the Thing in the tree.

Then the tree split fully down the middle, starting from the place where the lightning had struck it at the top. One half fell forward and the other backward. Lauren was still staring at the place where the mouth had been when Officer Lopez pushed her out of the path of the falling tree.

The ground opened up, starting at the base of the tree.

Loose soil rolled into empty space and fell away. Rocks and grass and flowers dropped into the widening hole. Lauren saw the roots of the tree extending down, down, down, farther into the earth than she could have thought possible. Officer Lopez and Lauren stumbled backward, their heels barely clinging to solid footing.

The stump of the tree was sucked into the ground, its protruding roots rolling up like the coil of a party horn. The broken halves of the trunk were pulled inside, and the branches that clawed at the sky grabbed Hendricks's and Touhy's bodies as they disappeared beneath the dirt.

After a few moments the hole sealed up, smooth and neat and even, and Lauren saw with amazement that green shoots were sprouting in the place where it had been.

Officer Lopez blew out a breath next to her.

"Now will you tell me just what's been going on in this town?"

Lauren couldn't help it. She laughed.

34

Van Christie stood in Jo Gehlinger's living room, listening to the sound of Miller getting sick outside on the front porch.

Miller always gets sick at murder scenes.

The day before, Christie would have said there were hardly ever murder scenes in Smiths Hollow, and that was why Miller had so much trouble dealing with them. But last night he'd remembered.

He'd remembered all the bodies. He'd remembered all the girls.

And he'd remembered that he had covered it up, pretended it didn't happen, taken their families' sorrow and stuffed it in a file in the basement, never to be seen again.

It didn't matter that it wasn't his fault. It didn't matter that he wasn't the only one who'd forgotten those girls.

He'd been responsible. He was the chief of police.

It was, he thought, time for somebody else to become chief of police.

But before that could happen he still had a job to do.

He sighed, and went out to fetch Miller to help him with Jo Gehlinger's body.

35

SUNDAY

The fair was supposed to open at ten a.m., just like the last two days. But Alejandro Lopez had no intention of patrolling the fairgrounds. Mayor Touhy was dead and therefore so was his directive to protect the fair, as far as Alex was concerned. He didn't know if there would be very much business today, anyway. Sofia had sent him out for eggs and milk. ("I know it's absurd," she said, "especially after what happened last night. But we're out and no matter what's happened the kids will still be hungry.")

He'd run over to the grocery store early, his eyes gritty from lack of sleep but his body wired. Alex drove the squad car, even though he was only supposed to use it for official business. He'd put his uniform on, too. It felt like armor, protecting him from the people who'd tried to kill him and his family the night before.

As he walked the aisles of the grocery store he saw a lot of people looking dazed, like they'd been knocked on the head and were partially concussed. Several of them would stop in front of a display of soup or diapers or oranges and just stand there, holding an item in their hand and staring at it like they weren't certain how they got there.

It was pretty clear that whatever spell the town had been under was broken now.

Could the Lopez family stay in Smiths Hollow after what had happened? Alex wasn't sure. Lauren had tried to explain some of what had happened last night, but a lot of it had come out garbled. There was something about a curse and some witches and a monster that lived in the woods. But she'd been tired and a little hysterical, and then she'd said that Jake Hanson was run over by Mayor Touhy and that he needed to call the chief on his radio and send someone to get Jake to the hospital—if he was still alive.

So Alex had done that, and then insisted that Lauren go there, too, because Touhy had beaten her pretty badly. Somehow David and Karen were already waiting in front of the hospital when Alex pulled up with Lauren.

Well, there was really no somehow about it, was there? Lauren had said David knew everything that happened in this town.

Even if there was nothing else he could accept, Alex knew for certain that there was something different about David.

Different. Ha. Yeah, that's the word for it. And Lauren, too. Just a couple of very different kids.

(different kids who saved you twice)

Alex knew he'd seen a lot of strange and unexplainable things. He also knew that his mind wanted to force those unexplainable things away, to return to a safe and comfortable place where there were no monsters, no magic, no trees that tried to grab people and pull them into the ground, no mobs of people under supernatural control.

But maybe now it wouldn't be like that. Maybe now Smiths Hollow wouldn't be the perfect town. Maybe it would be a regular town, with regular people who fought and lived and loved and prospered and lost and made mistakes.

Maybe it would be a town without shadows.

Alex thought he could live in a town like that.

36

TUESDAY

Lauren hated hospitals, hated the way they smelled like sickness and pain no matter how much disinfectant they used.

But nobody could make her leave Jake's room, not even the doctors and nurses who told her repeatedly that visiting hours were over. She just looked at them and told them she wasn't leaving, and they suddenly decided they needed to do something elsewhere.

She held his hand, which sat still and lifeless in her own. His eyes were closed and his face was covered in bruises. His right arm and leg were in casts. Touhy had run him over with the car at the top of the hill. Lauren was thankful that Jake's head hadn't been crushed beneath the wheels.

But he wouldn't wake up.

Still, she sat next to him, and held his hand, and told him everything that had happened from beginning to end.

"Nana's house burned down," she said. "That happened

yesterday. David says it was because the tree disappeared, because the hill and the tree kept the same time. I don't really know what that means, but David does. He knows an awful lot for a little kid. I don't think Mom knows what to do with him anymore. I don't think she's sure what to do with me, either, but she's a lot nicer than she used to be. Or maybe I'm nicer than I used to be. Maybe we're meeting each other halfway. I think that's what we're supposed to do, anyhow, and we're trying.

"Anyway, it was probably a good thing that the house burned. I don't think it was a place where there was ever very much happiness. And I don't think any of us could have lived there, not after what happened to Nana.

"Everybody in town has been kind of milling around for a couple of days, trying to avoid everyone else's eyes. It's really weird, because you can tell that they all remembered but none of them wanted to admit remembering. They can't forget but they don't want to talk about it either. I think they'll have to, though. Because they want to bury their girls properly.

"I don't mean bury them in the ground. I mean remember and be sad, the way you're supposed to, and then later remember the things that you loved about that person. Like your sister. I remember Jennifer now, really clearly. I remember that she loved Stevie Nicks. Do you remember that? She liked to wear all those scarves around her neck and those gauzy tops like Stevie Nicks, and when she came over to babysit me she would bring her Fleetwood Mac and Stevie Nicks records and play them really loud and we'd dance all over the living room."

Lauren looked at Jake's face expectantly. She was sure he'd heard what she'd said about Jennifer. She thought maybe his eyes moved under the closed lids, just a twitch. She thought he must remember how much his sister loved Stevie Nicks.

"Miranda loved Def Leppard. That made me crazy, you know that? We did not have the same taste in music. But when I slept over at her house we would never actually sleep, because we would just stay up all night talking, and whenever one of her parents would come and tell us to be quiet and go to bed we would pretend to be asleep until they left, and then we would whisper and giggle some more. We never seemed to be able to stop giggling when we were together."

Lauren let out a soft little sigh. She'd never had a chance to tell Miranda she was sorry. But she could remember what had made them best friends, once upon a time.

"You have to wake up now," she said, leaning close to his ear. "You have to wake up because we never ended our date properly. You have to kiss me at the end. I'm sure that's how dates are supposed to go."

He didn't move, didn't speak. His breath rose and fell but so softly that if it weren't for the continual beeping of the monitors she wouldn't have been certain he was still alive.

"If I were any kind of real witch I could fix you," she said.

"I think there's some kind of power in me. I can feel it, like a little ember in my stomach, though I don't know what to do with it. I suppose Nana could have taught me, if I'd listened. I'm going to be a better listener from now on. I think that's just what David does, you know? He listens more carefully than the rest of us."

She sighed again, and looked out the window. Outside the sky was blue and the sun shone. If it had been a different day, a day like so many before, she would have been on her bike, pedaling away under the sunshine.

Meet me by the old ghost tree, Miranda whispered in her ear.

Lauren started. "Miranda?"

Jake opened his eyes.

Christina Henry is the author of the Chronicles of Alice duology, *Alice* and *Red Queen*, a dark and twisted take on *Alice's Adventures in Wonderland*, as well as *Lost Boy*, an origin story about Captain Hook, and *The Mermaid*, a historical fairy tale about P.T. Barnum's Fiji mermaid. Her dark fantasy novel *Alice* was one of Amazon's Best Books of 2015 in Science Fiction and Fantasy, and came second in the Goodreads Choice awards for Best Horror. Christina enjoys running long distances, reading anything she can get her hands on and watching movies with samurai, zombies and/or subtitles in her spare time. She lives in Chicago with her husband and son.

For more fantastic fiction, author events,
exclusive excerpts, competitions, limited editions and more

VISIT OUR WEBSITE
titanbooks.com

LIKE US ON FACEBOOK
facebook.com/titanbooks

FOLLOW US ON TWITTER AND INSTAGRAM
@TitanBooks

EMAIL US
readerfeedback@titanemail.com